A YOUNG GIRL WITH A DEVASTATING
SECRET, TWO BRILLIANT MEN, AND
AN ADVENTURE THAT CHANGED
HISTORY FOREVER.

"A wonderfully entertaining and convincing mixture of truth and speculation."—*Dallas Morning News*

"Flat out engrossing."—*Chronogram*

"Thrilling fast pace and intrigue." —*Booklist*

"Elaborately plotted...If this reminds you of AS Byatt's *Possession* you're not far wrong."—*The New York Times*

"Pages turn quickly and the ending is a neat surprise."
—*The Christian Science Monitor*

Also by John Darnton

Neanderthal

The Experiment

Mind Catcher

John Darnton

THE DARWIN CONSPIRACY

John Darnton has worked for thirty-nine years as a reporter, editor, and foreign correspondent for *The New York Times*. He was awarded two George Polk Awards for his coverage of Africa and Eastern Europe, and the Pulitzer Prize for his stories smuggled out of Poland during the period of martial law. He lives in New York.

THE DARWIN CONSPIRACY

A Novel

JOHN DARNTON

ANCHOR BOOKS
A Division of Random House, Inc.
New York

FIRST ANCHOR BOOKS EDITION, SEPTEMBER 2006

Copyright © 2005 by Talespin, Inc.

The Library of Congress has cataloged the Knopf edition as follows:
Darnton, John.
The Darwin conspiracy : by John Darnton.—1st ed.
p. cm.
1. Darwin, Charles, 1809–1882–Fiction. 2. Evolution (Biology)–Fiction.
3. Naturalists–Fiction. I. Title.
PS3554.A727D368 2005
813'.54–dc22
2005010875

Anchor ISBN-10: 1-4000-3483-3
Anchor ISBN-13: 978-1-4000-3483-3

Book design by Anthea Lingeman

www.anchorbooks.com

Printed in the United States of America
10 9 8 7 6 5 4 3 2

For Bob, with love

History has many cunning passages, contrived corridors
And issues, deceives with whispering ambitions,
Guides us by vanities.

—T. S. Eliot

THE DARWIN CONSPIRACY

Hugh spotted the boat while it was still a dot on the horizon and watched it approach the island, making a wide, white arc. He shaded his eyes but still he had to squint against the shards of reflected light. Already the morning sun had cut through the haze to lay a shimmering sword on the water.

All around him the birds swooped and darted in the cacophonous morning feeding—hundreds of them, screaming swallow-tailed gulls, brown noddies, boobies homing in with fish dangling in their beaks. A frigate circled behind a gull, yanked its tail feathers to open the gullet, then made a corkscrew dive to grab the catch—a flash of acrobatic violence that had long since ceased to amaze him.

The boat appeared to be a panga, but that was odd: supplies weren't due for days. Hugh fixed his stare on the dark silhouette of the driver. He looked like Raoul, the way he leaned into the wind, one arm trailing back on the throttle.

Hugh dropped his canvas tool bag near the mist net and started down. The black rocks were streaked white and gray with guano, which stank in the windless air and made the lava slippery, but he knew the footholds perfectly. The heat pressed down on him.

When he reached the bottom of the cliffside, Raoul was already there. He idled the swaying panga a few feet from the landing rock, a narrow ledge that was washed by an ankle-deep wave every few seconds.

"*Amigo,*" shouted Raoul, grinning behind dark glasses.

"Hey, Cowboy," said Hugh. He coughed to clear his throat—it had been a long time since he had talked to anybody.

Raoul was wearing pressed khaki shorts, a Yankees cap over his thick black hair at a jaunty angle, and a dark blue jersey with the insignia of the Galapagos National Park on the left breast pocket.

"Just stopping by," he said. "What's new?"

"Not much."

"I thought you will be totally crazy by now." His English was almost perfect but sometimes an odd phrasing gave him away.

"No, not totally. But I'm working on it."

"So, how's the *ermitano*?"

"The what?"

"Ermitano," Raoul repeated. "How do you say that?"

"Hermit."

Raoul nodded and regarded him closely. "So, how're you doing?"

"Fine," lied Hugh.

Raoul looked away.

"I brought two *chimbuzos*." He gestured with his chin to two water barrels strapped to the mid-seat. "Help me to deliver them."

Hugh leapt into the boat, unstrapped a barrel, and hoisted it over his right shoulder. The weight threw off his balance and he tottered like a drunken sailor and almost fell into the water.

"Not like that," said Raoul. "Put them overboard and shove them to the mat. Then you climb up and pick them up."

The mat, short for "welcome mat," was the nickname the researchers called the rocky ledge. Raoul had hung around them so long, helping out now and then because he admired what they were doing, that he was picking up their lingo.

Hugh finally got both barrels ashore and lugged them up to the beginning of the path. He was dripping with sweat by the time he returned.

"Want to come on shore, stay a while?" he asked. The offer was disingenuous. The water was too deep to anchor—more than eighty feet straight down—and if the panga docked, the waves would smash it against the rocks.

"I can't stay. I just wanted to say hello. How're your crazy birds— getting thirsty, no?"

"The heat's rough on them. Some are dying."

Raoul shook his head. "How many days without rain?" he asked.

"Today is two hundred something, two hundred twenty-five, I think."

Raoul whistled and shook his head again, a fatalistic gesture, and lit a cigarette.

They talked for a while about the study. Raoul was always eager to hear how it was going. He had once said that if he came back to earth a second time that was what he wanted to do—camp out and study birds. Hugh thought that Raoul had no idea what it was really like—the solitude, the fatigue and boredom and endless repetition of extremes, boiling during the day and then at night when the temperature dropped forty degrees, lying in your sleeping bag and shivering so violently you can't go to sleep even though you're exhausted. Anything can sound glamorous until you do it.

"Say," Raoul said lightly, "I hear you're getting company. Two more guys coming out."

"Yeah—so I'm told."

Raoul looked quizzical.

"Sat phone," explained Hugh. "Satellite. I got a call day before yesterday. The thing scared the shit out of me when it rang."

"Do you know them?"

"No, I don't think so. I don't know anybody in the project, really."

"What are their names?"

"I don't know."

"You didn't ask?"

"No."

Raoul paused a moment, then looked at him closely. "*Hombre,* you okay? You don't look so good."

"No, I'm fine." Pause. "Thanks."

"All that pink skin."

That was a joke. Hugh had been burned and tanned so many times that his skin had turned a leathery brown. His lips were swollen and cracked, despite the Chap Stick, and his eyebrows were bleached blond.

"You think you ready to share this paradise with other people?"

"Sure thing," said Hugh, but his voice sounded uncertain.

Raoul turned and looked out to sea. Far away the dark profile of a ship could be seen moving quickly with a funnel of gulls circling it.

"The *Neptune,*" he said. "More tourists for the Enchanted Isles."

"Whoever thought that one up deserves a medal," said Hugh. He could see by the shadow that crossed Raoul's face that the remark was hurtful. The depth of Equadorean nationalism always amazed him. He smiled, pretending he was joking.

"More work for me." Raoul shrugged. "Well, *tengo que trabajar*." He flicked his cigarette way off into the water and gave a little wave from the hip. *"Ciao."*

"*Ciao*. Thanks for the water."

"Don't drink it all right now." Raoul grinned as he turned the panga, gunned the motor, and pulled out so fast the bow rose up like a surfboard. Hugh stared after him until the boat disappeared behind the island.

He carried the *chimbuzos* one at a time up the long path that wound up the south face of the volcano and then down past the campsite into the bottom of the crater, where in theory it was a degree or two cooler—but only in theory. On hot days, even here, he had seen the green-footed boobies shifting from one webbed foot to the other on the scorching rocks.

He looked at his watch. *Shit*. Almost seven o'clock. He had forgotten about the mist net—he was sure he had seen a bird trapped there, maybe two. He had to hurry and free them before they died in the quickening morning heat. Once, months ago, before he got the routine down, he had lost a bird that way. They were surprisingly resilient if you handled them right, but if you made a mistake, like leaving them trapped in the mist net too long, they were as fragile as twigs. That time, he had recorded the death dutifully in the log, without explanation, in a single concocted word: "ornithocide."

At the top of the island it was even hotter. He grabbed his bag and looked at the net. Sure enough, there were two birds, small dark cocoons that rippled as he touched them. He reached in and held one to his chest while he deftly lifted off the black threads so thin they caught the birds in flight. As he untangled the mesh from the feathers he suddenly had a memory: playing badminton as a young boy during long summer evenings, those moments when the plastic bird hurled into the net and had to be carefully extracted.

He now saw the finch's color, black mottled with gray and dusty white. A cactus finch—*Geospiza scandens*—very common, no surprise there. He held it tightly in his left fist and raised it to look at it. The eyes, deep brown, looked back, and he could feel the tiny heart tickling his palm. He checked the bands—a green and black one on the left leg and a blue one on the right—and identified him in the register. Number ACU-906. A previous researcher had jotted down a nickname, *Smooches,* in a rounded, girlish American script.

After all this time Hugh still had trouble identifying more than a dozen finches by their nicknames, the ones that hung around the campsite. Spotting them was a point of pride with the researchers, he gathered; they told stories of sitting around the rocks and rattling off the names of thirty or forty at a shot. "You'll get to know them in no time," he had been told at the farewell pep talk by Peter Simons, a legend in the field. "Just stretch out your arm and they'll land on it." That part was true at least. He was pleasantly surprised the first week when he was measuring a small finch and another came to perch on his bare knee and peer at him, its head cocking from one side to the other. At times like that they seemed curious and intelligent. But at other times— like when he forgot to cover the coffeepot and a bird almost dove in and drowned—it was hard not to think of them as stupid.

That was back before Victor left. At first it was a relief to be alone— solitude was what he had been looking for, part of his penitence—but as weeks stretched into months, the loneliness he had sought became almost too much to bear. Then when the rainy season didn't come and the lava island turned into a black frying pan stuck way out in the ocean, at times he actually wondered if he could keep going. But of course he did. He had known he would—in that way at least, in brute staying power, he was strong. It was his psyche that was brittle.

He pulled out a pair of calipers and measured the bird's wing and wrote it in the notebook, tattered over the years and swollen from the rain despite its waterproof cover. The bird froze as he measured its beak—the all-important beak—its length, width, and depth. Since 1973, when Simons and his wife, Agatha, first came here, generations of graduate students had braved the miserable conditions to measure thousands upon thousands of beaks and search for meaning among the minute variations.

Hugh freed the bird and it flew off a few yards and landed on a cactus, shaking its feathers. He recorded the second bird and walked around to the north rim to check the traps. He could tell by looking that none had sprung shut. He went back to the campsite and fixed breakfast, watery scrambled eggs made from powder and weak coffee from used grinds. Then he went to the top of the island again to rest and look out over the blue-green water, choppy with waves from the treacherous currents. He sat in his familiar place—the smooth rocks, already hot, formed a throne that fit his rear. He could see for miles.

Darwin was no fool. He didn't like it here either.

Hugh sometimes talked to himself. Or—even stranger—sometimes he couldn't tell whether he had been thinking the words or saying them aloud. Lately, his interior monologues were becoming oddly disjointed, especially during the long hours when he worked hard under the hot sun. Half thoughts flashed through his mind, phrases repeating themselves over and over, admonitions and observations from himself to himself, sometimes addressed in the second person, such as: *If it was Hell you're looking for, buddy, you've come to the right place.*

And it had been Hell that he'd looked for, no doubt about that. Even the name of the island—Sin Nombre—had exerted an attraction the moment he heard it.

So how about it? Was he willing to share this place—this paradise, he scoffed to himself, maybe out loud—with other people?

Ten days later, they came on the supply boat. It was so loaded down with food and equipment that it rode low in the water, and in the glare Hugh could see only that there were three figures on board. He felt his pulse quickening, a churning in his gut—*Christ,* why was he anxious? He scrutinized the campsite with a new eye—his tent, plastic dishes, bags of charcoal, supplies under a tarp. Everything appeared small and bleached out in the hot sun. There was nothing to be done about it, he thought, as he made his way down the path to the welcome mat and waited.

As the panga drew near, a man cupped his hands around his mouth and shouted out: "Ahoy—if it isn't Robinson Crusoe." He had an English accent, upper class. Hugh flashed a grin by way of reply; it was hardly genuine but the best he could do.

He then saw a woman, sitting in the bow, holding a coil of rope. He was shocked; he hadn't expected this. She smiled as she tossed him the line and he fastened it to the iron ring drilled into the rock. The driver draped two tires over the side as fenders and Hugh, extending his arm as far as he could, helped her out.

"Elizabeth Dulcimer," she said, and added: "Beth."

Hugh shook her hand.

"I'm Hugh," he said.

"I know," she replied. "Hugh Kellem."

She turned around to help with the unloading. She was trim, with long tanned legs under khaki shorts, sneakers and a white T-shirt. Her hair, dark and silky, fell across her back as she moved with unstudied grace. A cap shaded her face; the logo on the crest read *Peligro,* and on the back in small letters was written NEW ORLEANS.

The Englishman leapt off the boat, setting it rocking.

"Nigel," he pronounced loudly, smiling. He was tall and heavyset, with long blond hair that fell on either side of his ruddy face. He wore a safari jacket with four front pockets and a neck chain with a plastic slip-out magnifying glass. He gripped Hugh's hand and pumped it, hard, and Hugh had a momentary vision of little finches disappearing inside those thick round fingers.

Nigel looked up at the cliffside, a flicker of doubt on his face.

"I expect we should carry this gear up," he said.

Not a good sign, thought Hugh—he's been here all of two minutes and already he's issuing orders. He looked at Beth, who smiled again.

It took a long time to bring their equipment up. They made three trips each and placed the supplies in three piles—one for him, one for her, and one for the kitchen. When they finished, they were sweating profusely and sat down around the campsite to catch their breath.

"So, this is it," Nigel finally said, surveying the campsite with obvious disappointment. "Somehow I expected more. All those generations of students, you know. You'd think they'd build the place up a bit. I suppose they had nothing on their minds but birds—birds and sex, of course. You can probably get a whiff of that." He inhaled. "Crikey, it does smell, doesn't it?"

"That's guano."

"No shit." Nigel chuckled at his own joke.

"You get used to it," said Hugh. "I don't even smell it anymore."

Nigel looked at him and then turned to gaze out to sea. "At least you've got a world-class view here," he said. "Now, what island is that?"

"Santiago. One of the biggest." Hugh pointed out the other islands, giving a brief description of each. "You'll get to know them in no time."

"I expect so." Nigel paused a moment. "So, what exactly happened to that chap who was here with you—Victor? He came down ill?"

"Yes. He was evacuated. Some kind of stomach ailment."

"I see. And you've been alone ever since?"

"Yes. Six, eight months, something like that."

"Hmm. Well, not to worry. We're here to rescue you. The cavalry." He held a fist to his mouth, imitated the sound of a bugle, and clapped Hugh on the back, startling him. Then, moving uncertainly among the rocks, Nigel chose the best place to pitch his tent and put it up quickly. It had side vents and a canopy, much fancier than Hugh's. Beth pitched her tent, a snug two-sleeper, off to one side.

Nigel emerged carrying a knapsack. "By the by," he said. "Almost forgot. I've got some post for you."

Hugh recognized the envelope—a corporate return address, his name printed in large confident letters. He felt his cheeks redden as if he had been slapped: it was from his father.

"Thanks."

He folded the envelope and shoved it in his back pocket.

After dinner they sat around the fire on the sawed-off tree stumps imported from San Isabel. Hugh was tired after a day of showing them around the island; it had felt odd pointing out the fixed points in his shrunken world—the crater's bottom, the dry, cracked bushes, the mostly vacant nests, the traps baited with bits of banana. "How many finches are not yet banded?" Nigel had demanded. "Six," Hugh had replied. "And they're smart as thieves. I don't think you'll catch them."

"We'll see about that."

Hugh's stomach churned—he wasn't accustomed to meat and Nigel had unpacked two thick steaks and fried them in oil, flipping them in the air like pancakes. Afterward Beth produced a quart of Johnnie Walker Black and poured each of them a strong one. Hugh felt it burn his throat as he leaned back to watch the smoke and embers shooting up into the darkness.

"As I calculate it," said Nigel, after knocking back half his scotch, "this drought is well on its way to becoming one for the record books. Isn't that right? When was the other one again?"

"Nineteen seventy-seven," said Hugh.

"And how long was that? Something like a year?"

"Four hundred and fifty-two days," said Beth. She was seated on the rock, leaning back upon the stump, her brown legs curled to one side. The fire lit up her high cheekbones and her eyes, framed by her black hair, gleamed.

Nigel whistled. "And how long has this been?" He looked at Hugh.

"Two hundred thirty-five days."

"That's good for the study."

"Good for the study, bad for the birds."

"What's been the effect so far?"

"Seeds are in short supply. Not much mating. Some chicks have died in their nests. They're listless. Some are desperate."

"Which ones? What are the variations? The beak sizes?"

"God's sake," put in Beth. "He's not your graduate student."

"That's all right," Hugh said. The truth was he liked having someone to talk about it with. "The *fortis* are hurting, especially the smallest ones. Their beaks are too tiny. They can't handle *Tribulus*. You see them trying—they pick it up and turn it around and then drop it. Some of them get into this herb—it's called *Chamaesyce*—and the leaves coat their feathers with this white sticky latex. It bothers them and they rub their crowns against the rocks until they go bald. Then they get sunstroke. You see them lying around dead, these little bald finches."

"And the next generation?"

"It's too soon to tell, but it'll be like the last drought. The ones who survive will be the ones with the deepest beaks. And they'll go on until one year there'll be heavy rainfall and then you'll suddenly see a multitude with narrow beaks."

Nigel mimicked the tone of an announcer: "Darwin's living laboratory. Step up and watch as natural selection works its daily miracles. How does it go? How did the great man put it?"—he tilted his head back slightly, as if trying to remember, but the words came so easily he clearly knew them by heart—*"daily and hourly scrutinising, throughout the world, the slightest variations; rejecting those that are bad, preserving and adding up all that are good; silently and insensibly working, whenever and wherever opportunity offers."*

Hugh didn't mind the showing off. The scotch was warming his system and rendered him charitable. He looked across the fire at Beth but couldn't read her reaction.

"But of course Darwin didn't quite get it, not when he was here, did he?" Nigel continued. "I mean, he mixed up all his specimens, took finches from the various islands and put them all in the same bag. He had to go begging to FitzRoy to look at his finches."

"That's right," said Beth.

"And there's only one single sentence in *The Voyage of the Beagle* that even hints at the theory."

"So they say."

"Ah, well. You've got to hand it to him. He got there eventually, though he took his sweet time about it." Nigel looked over at Hugh. "Tell me," he asked, "exactly what is it about Darwin that engaged your interest?"

The question had been thrown down like a gauntlet. Hugh was startled.

How to answer? How could he even begin to put what he felt into words? He admired so many things about Darwin—his methodical exactitude, his boyish enthusiasm for experiments (imagine, playing the bassoon to see if earthworms could hear!), his demand for facts, nothing but facts, and his willingness to follow them wherever they led, wading knee-deep into lakes of hellfire if need be. But one thing he admired above all else was Darwin's ability to think in eons—not centuries or millennia but entire epochs. He elongated time, stretched it out, examined cataclysmic events as if in slow motion. He could look at mountain ranges and imagine the earth's crust rising up ever so slowly. Or come upon marine fossils high up in the Andes and envision the antediluvian seabed that buried them there. How extraordinary to possess sight that could stretch so far backward that the infinitesimal wheels of change and chance became apparent in their movement, like Galileo examining heavenly revolutions through the telescope. And how brave to measure yourself against the eons of all that time and recognize you live in a

Godless universe and admit your nothingness. Hugh found that oddly comforting—the nothingness.

"I like that he took the long view," he finally replied.

Nigel turned to Beth. "And you?"

Hugh leaned forward to listen. Beth took a swig of scotch and spoke matter-of-factly.

"I like that when he came to these islands and went inland, he took a single book with him."

"Which was . . . ?"

"*Paradise Lost.* He read it here and then he thought about what he saw here and somehow he put the two together."

"Meaning what, exactly?" asked Nigel.

"He found Eden, he ate from the tree of knowledge, and the world hasn't been the same since."

"I see. 'And they realized they were naked and they covered themselves.' I see what you mean, though—it is like paradise here."

"I'm not so sure," she said. A few minutes later she got up and stretched, reaching her arms above her like a dancer, and then walked off toward her tent, her body disappearing into the darkness.

The two men were silent for a while, and Hugh felt the weight of the other man's presence now that he had finally stopped talking. But Nigel wasn't quiet for long.

"You know," he said, tilting his head toward the spot where Beth had been sitting, "it's interesting to hear her talk about Darwin like that. There're these rumors that she's related to him somehow, somewhere way back there, a great-great something or other."

"But she's American," Hugh said.

"Yes, it's unlikely, I know. Just a rumor. Some people collect these kinds of legends around themselves. And she's certainly a legend, all right."

"In what way?"

"Part of a fast crowd, Cambridge, London, the States. Stunningly beautiful—well, that you can see for yourself. Read everything, done everything. She was married for a while to a brilliant chap, Martin Wilkinson. He had everything going for him—read history at St. John's Oxford, took firsts in every subject under the sun, good family, world at his feet. But he has problems, a depressive actually, an incredible writer and conversationalist but mentally unstable. He went into a downward spiral. They're divorced. It was quite the talk there for a while."

"And you've known each other for . . . how long?"

"Oh, ages. But things have picked up since the divorce."

"Ah. So you're . . . what? Going out together?"

"Not to put too fine a point on it, but yes."

"I see. Well, you'll be hard up for places to go to here."

They fell quiet and in the silence, Hugh felt the scotch thickening his tongue. He excused himself and rose.

"Don't worry about the fire," he said. "You can let it go—there's nothing to burn." As he walked toward his tent, he found that he enjoyed the sensation of moving with difficulty. Liquor had a lot to recommend it. He turned back and looked at Nigel, a thick, dark shape sitting on the stump.

"By the way, you might want to hang your boots on the tent pole. Not to put too fine a point on it, but you'll find a lot of scorpions here— in *paradise*."

The moment he crawled into his sleeping bag, he felt the letter in his pocket. What the hell. He turned on a flashlight and opened the envelope. The familiar script looked back at him, but he felt sufficiently numbed to read it through, to deal with the knowledge that he had, once again, let his father down. His father wouldn't write that in so many words. But Hugh had become adept at reading between the lines.

CHAPTER 2

Charles Darwin saddled his favorite horse and rode him hard to Josiah Wedgwood's estate in Staffordshire. He skirted the villages of cobbled streets and black-and-white Tudor houses and instead took the back lanes, trotting beside hedgerows and through fields pink with sorrel and white with dog-daisies. When he reached the forest and entered the path through the tall ash and beech, he urged the animal into a full gallop, feeling the wind, full in his face, blur his eyes with tears.

Never in his twenty-two years had he felt more wretched. And to think that only a week ago he had been serenely contented, basking in compliments from Adam Sedgwick, the renowned geologist of Trinity College Cambridge. They were exploring the ravines and riverbeds of North Wales, just the two of them, and it had been a glorious expedition. And then he had returned home to find the offer waiting for him, a bolt from the blue that could change his life forever, provide it with meaning. And to be denied it! To have his hopes elevated so high and then dashed the very next moment! How could he endure it? He looked down at the ground's blur, the black earth spewing onto the weeds—how simple it would be to slide down Herodotus' flank and slip headlong under those pounding hooves.

From a distance, young Darwin did not cut a bad figure. He was a bit plump but he was an accomplished and graceful rider, moving in rhythm with the horse's long strides. His upbringing at The Mount, the family estate in Shrewsbury, had been assiduously arranged around the holy trinity of the country gentry: riding, hunting, and fishing. Up close, dressed in soft provincial browns and knee-high boots, he was more compact and disarming than classically handsome. He had a noble forehead, auburn hair giving way to trimmed muttonchops, gentle brown eyes, a slightly prissy mouth, and a nose that he felt was too large. His wit was not as sharp or irreverent as that of his older brother, Erasmus. His speech was marred by a slight stammer, inherited from the patriarchal side; it had so far resisted the lure of a sixpenny reward on the day he could successfully pronounce "white wine." Yet all in all, he was considered a presentable fellow, open and amiable, if not remarkable, and someday he would make someone a fine husband.

But appearances could be deceiving. No one knew the depth of the ambitions lodged within him. And few, aside from his friends at college and university, knew of his passion for natural history. It had been with him as long as he could remember, from the time his father, Robert Waring Darwin, had given him two dog-eared books that had once belonged to his father's older brother, Charles, his namesake, who had died tragically young in medical school; one was on insects, the other on "the natural history of waters, earth, stones, fossils and minerals, with their virtues, properties and medical uses." The passion was rooted in the heart, growing into the very ventricles. It led him to skip anatomy lessons at Edinburgh so that he might go hunting for shells along the Firth of Forth and to spend long afternoons outside the walls of Christ's College Cambridge, patrolling the countryside, ripping the bark off trees and hammering fenceposts, looking for insects.

A parade of mentors filled his eager brain with lore and theory about nature and something more—with *feeling*. That was what was so inspiring about Sedgwick. He was a Romantic—in point of fact, he told tales of traipsing across the hills of the Lake District with his friend William Wordsworth—and he made the prospect of unlocking nature's secrets impassioning. In Wales, hot on the pursuit of geological beds, he had collected rocks of unusual interest, pouring them into the bulging pockets of his long black coat, and then, raising his arms toward the canopy of trees far above, he joked that he required the weight "to keep me grounded in the face of such boundless beauty." Charles remembered another moment: the night the two were dining at the Colwyn Inn and there, seated before a plate of mutton and a mug of ale, the great man had told Charles that their journey was going to lead to critical amendments to the national geological map and that he, Charles, had performed brilliantly. The acolyte felt a flush of pride and confidence so strong that it made him realize how rare the feeling was, one that he'd never experienced in the presence of his father.

And now, racing to Maer Hall for a day of partridge-shooting that he hoped would blunt his burning disappointment, he carried a sealed letter from his father to Uncle Jos. It contained a prescription for "turpentine pills" for a digestive complaint and a note that rebuked his son for his latest folly, a proposed "voyage of discovery" on a ship called the *Beagle* that the Admiralty was sending on a two-year surveying trip around the world. The captain, a temperamental aristocrat by the name of Robert FitzRoy, required a gentleman companion to lift his spirits at sea with convivial conversation, and the old boy network at Cambridge had put forth young Darwin as the perfect candidate. John Henslow, the eminent botany professor who had adopted him during long walks along the Cam and had brought him into his celebrated Friday evening salon, had recommended him to George Peacock, a Cambridge mathematician with connections to Francis Beaufort, the powerful Hydrographer of the Admiralty.

That was how the invitation came to be waiting for him in the letter rack of the grand foyer at The Mount. As he read it, his hands shook, his breath quickened, and instantly he vowed to go. But he hadn't reckoned on his father, who raised objection after objection. What kind of useless and wild scheme was this? Surely others had turned it down before him. Wouldn't it hurt his career if he decided to become a man of the cloth? After changing professions so often, wasn't it finally time to settle down?

Charles could not bring himself to oppose his father. To him the doctor was a giant of a man in more ways than one and yet that one alone, physical stature, was sufficiently imposing. He weighed twenty stone and stood at six feet two inches, so immense that when young Charles had accompanied him on his rounds in the carriage he'd found himself crushed so tightly against the seat's iron railing that he could barely breathe. Charles had no memory of his mother, Susanna, who died when he was eight, other than the dark room where she lay as an invalid for so many weeks and the black velvet gown she was dressed in upon her death. His father raised him—or rather, his two older sisters

raised him while Dr. Darwin presided over the household, a distant figure who harangued them with two-hour-long monologues at dinner.
Charles was packed off to boarding school at the age of nine. Still, he
loved his father and knew he was loved in return, and that was part
of the never-ending conundrum: he was continually disappointing his
father, yet he craved nothing so much as the old man's approval. Two
years before, when he had abandoned medical school in Edinburgh,
horrified by operations conducted without anesthetic, sick at the sight
of blood, and disgusted by the scandal of grave-robbers supplying
corpses for dismemberment, the look of disappointment in his father's
eyes had pierced his soul. And he would never forget his father's words:
"You care for nothing but shooting, dogs, and rat-catching, and you will
be a disgrace to yourself and all your family."

With a heavy heart, Charles had written to Henslow that he could
not accept the post on the *Beagle*. Still, he thought, as he urged on his
horse, whose neck and flanks were now dank with sweat, perhaps all
was not lost. His father had not totally closed the door. After listing his
objections, he had left it open a crack by saying: "If you can find any
man of common sense who advises you to go, I will give my consent."
And what man of common sense was better than Uncle Jos, the doctor's brother-in-law and first cousin? A man of easygoing grace and
quiet humor, he presided over the Wedgwood china-making empire
founded by his father. His advice carried the authority of the modern
entrepreneurial world of the ironworks and steam-driven engines of the
Midlands. Charles adored his companionship. And he loved Maer
Hall, filled with books, resounding with the laughter of his cousins, and
warmed by its benign patriarch, so unlike his own home that he dubbed
it "bliss castle."

He left Herodotus in the hands of the stable boy and entered the grand
hall, the hounds baying at his heels. The girls, Fanny and Emma,
squealed with delight, and his cousin, Hensleigh, six years his junior,
clapped him on the back. Uncle Jos was delighted to see him but at once
read the distress in his face. Charles told them about the proposed voyage and handed his father's letter to his uncle, who repaired to his study
to read it in private. He emerged shortly to propose a hunt. The two of

them meandered on the heath largely in silence, their guns resting comfortably in the crooks of their arms. Charles missed seven out of nine partridges. Even his shooting was off, he thought, as he knotted the cord on his jacket only two times, once for each downed bird. By late afternoon when they returned, the whole of Maer Hall was buzzing about his offer and even the houseguests were unanimous in the conviction that he must not let it pass.

"Come with me and list your father's objections," suggested Uncle Jos, leading him to the study. Charles duly wrote down eight items and passed them over to his uncle, who frowned in feigned seriousness and then dealt with them one by one, knocking each down as skillfully as a barrister at the Old Bailey.

"What do you say—shall we write your father?" he said. Seated at a huge desk of New World mahogany, he composed a skillful rebuttal, turning every objection on its head so that it was somehow transformed into a positive consideration. From time to time he winked at Charles, who was stymied in his own composition. Finally, the young man dipped his pen in the inkwell and began in a hesitant scrawl:

My dear Father—

I am afraid I am going to make you again very uncomfortable. . . . The danger appears to me and all the Wedgwoods not great. The expense cannot be serious and the time I do not think, anyhow, would be more thrown away than if I stayed at home. But pray do not consider that I am so bent on going that I would for one single *moment hesitate, if you thought that after a short period you should continue uncomfortable. . . .*

The letters were posted. They discussed the matter late into the evening and over snuff after dinner. That night, in the second-floor bedroom, Charles could not sleep; his mind wandered as he gazed out the window onto the garden of irises, lobelias, and dahlias and a lake illuminated by moonlight. Was there still a chance for the trip? It would be such an opportunity to further his knowledge of geology and zoology, to view uncharted rock formations and collect specimens in parts of the world never before visited by specialists. He was seized by wanderlust—hadn't he and Henslow been indulging in fantasies about a trip to the Canary Islands? How tame that would be compared to this! It would be a last adventure before settling down somewhere to a life of comfort and family, undoubtedly as a provincial vicar.

But there was more to it, he knew. The world of natural science was expanding rapidly, new discoveries were pouring in to the museums all the time, and a voyage like this could make a young man's name. He had seen how the explorers were welcomed back as heroes, fêted in the marble and wood-paneled clubs, and how at dinner parties in the best homes in Kensington and Knightsbridge the bankers and industrialists hung on their every word, their own lives seeming suddenly humdrum, while the women cast admiring glances over the cut-crystal goblets. His heart longed for fame the way a plant in drought longs for rain.

Some words that night from Uncle Jos popped into his brain. "Do you remember," his uncle had asked abruptly, standing in the glow of the Gothic fireplace, "when you were young, about ten or eleven, you told all those fibs? You told the most elaborate lies—you talked of seeing rare birds during your perambulations in the countryside. You would come running home to claim you had just spotted the most exotic starling imaginable. We were all quite perplexed. Something very curious— I noticed they began at the same time you perceived that your father was interested in ornithology. I told him to cease paying any attention and gradually, by Jove, if you did not drop the habit. I think the reason behind your little fictions was that you were trying to please him."

The remark had struck home. He had changed since then, surely, and his burgeoning love of science had filled him to the brim with admiration for fact. But he viewed truth in much the way a home county parson views God—as a higher abstract that on occasion can be reshaped to bring a wayward parishioner back to the bosom of the Church. His mind drifted to his father—how stern and unyielding he was. If Charles could take this trip and send back specimens and return to lecture the Royal Society of London, how vindicated he would be—all those years of shooting birds and hunting insects would have come to something. How proud his father would be.

The next morning, Charles was up early and out on a hunt when a servant brought a message from his uncle. They should at once proceed together to The Mount for a discussion with his father. This whole business was too important and too urgent to let another moment pass without resolving it. They took a gig, bouncing over the bumps in record time, and shortly after noon they pulled up to the house on a hill overlooking a bend in the River Severn. They found Dr. Darwin alone in the drawing room, drinking tea and seemingly deep in reflection. "I've received your letters" was all he said, lowering his eyebrows. Uncle Jos signaled for Charles to leave them alone and the young man went to the garden and could do nothing but pace up and down the paths through the banks of flowers. Fifty minutes later he was called back in, and with a ceremonial air, as Uncle Jos chortled in the background, his father told him that he had changed his mind. Charles was now free to go on the voyage, "provided that is still your wish."

Charles could barely contain himself. He stammered his gratitude, less graciously than he would have liked, then bounded upstairs to his roll-top desk and dashed off a letter to Beaufort, saying he would be "very happy to have the honour of accepting" the proposal. Later, hugging his uncle goodbye in the courtyard, he asked him how he had "worked the miracle."

"Not at all difficult," replied Jos, clearly pleased. "I merely mentioned that given your interests, this particular voyage was bound to enhance your career. Of all the means for a young man to pull ahead of the pack, it is by far the surest."

Charles dined that night with his father and Erasmus, who was on a rare trip home. In the foyer, his brother grabbed his hand and patted him on both shoulders, congratulating him on "milking the cow"—the favorite of his many expressions for extracting money from the parsimonious master of the house. At dinner, conversation was strained and light, for all the world as if nothing momentous had occurred. Their father was unusually taciturn. Charles made only one reference to the impending voyage.

"I shall be deuced clever to spend more than my allowance whilst on the *Beagle,*" he ventured.

His father relinquished a half smile.

"But they tell me you are very clever," he replied.

Afterward, Charles threw some belongings in a bag, shook his father's hand gravely, hugged Erasmus, and after several hours' sleep set off at 3 a.m. on the express stage to Cambridge, where he took a room at the Red Lion Hotel.

The next morning Henslow was surprised to see him but also, he admitted, not a little envious. Staring at the carpet, his mentor confessed that he himself had considered taking up the offer, but was quickly dissuaded by the look of horror on his wife's face. He could not subject her, as he put it, to "premature widowhood."

Mrs. Henslow served them crumpets and the two men chatted animatedly. Charles's enthusiasm was contagious and Henslow went to the study to fetch a book of maps. Just then a messenger rang the porter's bell and handed him a note.

Henslow tore it open, read it, and blanched. He sat down, theatrically, with one hand across his forehead.

"Come, come," said Charles. "What is it?"

"It's from Captain FitzRoy. He says that he is most grateful for my efforts to assist him in his search for a companion on the *Beagle* and he hopes that I have not gone to great trouble, for he no longer requires one. It seems he has given away the position to a friend."

Charles could not bring himself to speak.

CHAPTER 3

Over the ensuing days on the island, they fell into a routine, dividing up the chores and the fieldwork. Hugh had to admit sharing the burden made things easier. They took turns cooking—Nigel, it turned out, was good at it, inventive with sauces—and doing the communal laundry. When it fell to Hugh on the second day, he carted the small bundle of clothes down to the mat, drenching them in salt water without detergent and rinsing them out in a plastic basin of fresh water. To his amusement he found himself washing two pairs of white panties, thin and small with a narrow cotton isthmus for a crotch, and when he spread the clothes out to dry, he put them on the highest rock. Their whiteness gleamed in the sun.

The project went faster, too. They rotated in teams of two—one to capture and measure the birds, the other to record the entries. Beth was good at handling the finches; her calmness seemed to attract them. They stayed unruffled in her hand and some remained there even when she opened her fingers, standing on her palm and shifting their weight back and forth to keep their balance. Nigel began calling her "Saint Francesca."

On the fourth day they went swimming, diving off the welcome mat. Beth draped her halter over the rocks. Hugh tried not to stare at her breasts, but she seemed totally unself-conscious. She ignored Nigel's ribald comments.

Most of the time Hugh wore only shorts and hiking boots, and his body was lithe and golden. Nigel wore Bermuda shorts and a thin white

T-shirt that rapidly soaked in his sweat and showed a paunch of pink flesh. He moved about the rocks with the graceless tread of a heavyset man. In the evening he liked nothing better than sitting around the fire after dinner, talking. Hugh, looking at Beth, wondered what she was thinking. At night, alone in his tent, he began masturbating again and took it as a sign of returning strength. Once, getting up in the dark to take a piss, he looked over and saw that she was in Nigel's tent. A kerosene lantern threw their shadows onto the canvas; he saw an outline of their movements, an arm raising up, and heard a murmur of voices, and he quickly turned away.

Nigel was getting on his nerves, but when it got to be too much Hugh would drift away and head for the north rim. There was refuge and solitude—the end of the earth, as he imagined it. He had discovered the spot four months before while trying to catch one of the elusive finches; it had led him on a chase between scraggy bushes and withered cacti that ended, between two large boulders, at the head of a natural trail down the cliff. By carefully negotiating footholds and handholds, he had found it possible to descend, and after some thirty feet, he had reached a rocky ledge about two yards wide. It overlooked a sheer drop; far below the ocean threw itself against the rocks, sending up fountains of sea spray.

Beth had brought a stash of books and she chose one for him—a novel by W. G. Sebald. He took it with him to the ledge during the long afternoon hours when it was too hot to do any work. If there was a breeze, he could catch it there. At times he felt almost peaceful, reading and thinking, looking up every so often at the expanse of water and the way the clouds threw their shadows down on it, immense shifting pools of gray-green, deep blue, and black.

On the morning of the first day of the third week, Beth asked Hugh if he would take her to his "hideaway."

Yes, he replied—a little too quickly, he thought a moment later. He was not sure he wanted to share it.

"But—how did you find out about it?" he asked.

"It's a small island," she responded. "No secrets here."

"Don't be so sure."

For the remainder of the morning they worked side by side, taking a census of seeds. She had marked out a square yard of dirt with string

stretched around pegs and was sifting through it with a strainer, identifying the seeds by holding them up to a manual and then laying them
out on a white cloth. Hugh worked on a plot nearby. For the most part
they were silent—like an old married couple, he mused, puttering
around in the backyard garden. The sun was pressing down, a piston of
heat that slicked his torso with sweat. When he scratched his side with
his thumb, it left a smudge of wet dirt. Beth stood up and stretched,
then crouched down again, squatting with her back to him. The top lip
of her shorts hung away and he could see sweat running toward the
cleavage of her backside. He heard the blood ticking in his head under
the hot sun.

After lunch, they set out. Nigel remained in his tent, cleaning it. He
had rigged up a small fan that ran on batteries and had the radio tuned
to the BBC, which blared out news—about terrorism, politics, AIDS in
Africa—that seemed from another world.

Gulls flew overhead, cruising the thermals, but otherwise nothing
moved in the stillness of the afternoon. They passed the boulders and
came to the cliff, and as he started down, hugging the rock face, she
stood above with her hands on her hips and watched him closely to see
where he was putting his feet and hands. Then she came down, five feet
directly above him, using the same footholds and handholds. It took a
good five minutes to reach the ledge—he hadn't realized before how
arduous the climb was.

Once there, she sat beside him against the rock, brushed her hair off
her forehead, and smiled.

"I was beginning to have second thoughts up there," she said. He
knew she didn't mean it.

She leaned forward to peer down at the sheer drop to the water far
below, then sat back with her eyebrows raised in fake alarm. It was high
tide so the surf rode over the rocks and plunged out of sight into the
hollow underside of the cliff, then a second later shot straight back, as if
the island were pumping bilge. Off in the distance where the currents
were rough the waves churned and exploded in tiny whitecaps.

"So this is where you come to get away from it all," she said.

"Yes."

"I can understand that—the noise, the filth, the crowds."

"Nigel."

She threw him a quick look, a slight frown.

They discussed the island and the study and then began, for the first time, to talk personally. He asked her about herself—and what brought her to the island. She sat cross-legged, resting her elbows on the insides of her thighs.

"Me . . . ," she said, making it sound like a riddle. "Let's see. Where to start?" And she told him about growing up in the American Midwest and how at first she loved it but then began to feel out of place there, almost like a pariah as she went up through the ranks of public school. Finally she escaped to Harvard, the only kid from her high school class to go there. She graduated and went to Cambridge, got her graduate degree in evolutionary biology and worked for a bit in London, then got fed up with life there and signed up for the project. And now here she was, before she knew it, about to hit thirty.

"I felt I was at a bit of a dead end," she said. "That's why I'm here, really, to get away for a while, think things over."

"And your parents?"

"They're still in Minneapolis. They're both teachers. We're in touch often—or we were until I came here."

They were silent for a spell.

"I heard you were married," he said.

She gave a start and looked him in the eye. "Nigel told you."

"Yes."

"Well, I was. In England. It was a mistake. I knew it pretty much from the beginning. I tried sticking it out, but it just didn't work. We couldn't make a go of it, as they say. There were some good times but always some bad mixed in, and then the bad got worse and more and more frequent."

"Nigel said your husband was a depressive."

"He certainly talks a lot, doesn't he?" She shook her head. "My husband did suffer from depression but it wasn't his fault that we split up. We were both at fault."

She gazed out toward the ocean. Hugh looked at her hand resting on the ledge, close to his own. Her presence was so strong—it seemed to make the air shimmer.

"I shouldn't be talking so much about myself," she said finally. "I'm sorry Nigel told you."

"Well, as you say, he talks a lot."

"He does. But he's a good man."

She asked Hugh about his childhood and what he had done in his twenty-eight years.

"Not a lot, I'm afraid. I grew up in Connecticut, a little town in Fairfield County. I actually liked the suburbs when I was young–camping out in the woods, Little League, hitchhiking to the beach, the whole deal. Then I went away to prep school, to Andover. I did all right at first but then I fell off the rails. In my senior year, about a month before graduation, I was expelled. . . ."

"What did you do?"

"Nothing all that dramatic. They have what they call four major rules and one weekend, to celebrate getting into Harvard, I broke them all–went off campus, had a drink. I'd signed in to my dormitory so they got me on lying. The fourth rule–conduct unbecoming a gentleman–they threw that in too, which I objected to but without success."

"So what happened?"

"I took a train home–the longest trip of my life–and when I arrived, I was in disgrace. My father could barely look at me."

"And Harvard?"

"They dropped me. I applied later but I didn't get in the second time around. I ended up going to the University of Michigan."

He talked about his parents–his father, a successful New York lawyer, and his mother, who fell in love with another man and left when Hugh was fourteen.

"That's why you went off to prep school," she said.

"Yes."

"It must have been rough."

"It was, I guess. And then, two years after she left, she died. She was living with another man and they were going to get married, and then she suddenly died, just like that–from an aneurysm. She was sitting in bed combing her hair one minute, and the next she was dead."

"How did you feel?"

"Confused. I told myself at the time it was divine retribution."

"But you don't really believe that."

"No."

"So you were raised by your father?"

"Basically, yes."

"Did he ever remarry?"

"Yes. Three years ago."

"So as a teenager you had no woman in your life."

It was a statement, not a question. Odd—he had never thought of it in those terms. "No."

"Are you close to your father?"

He considered the question. It was the hardest one of all. "He's loving enough, I guess, in a distant sort of way. He used to drink a lot. He's stopped now, but . . . I don't know, he went off into his own private world so much—nights, he would just drift away on a sea of alcohol. I could never talk to him, not openly and honestly. I could never tell him what I felt. Which was that I always felt I disappointed him. That I let him down."

That wasn't the half of it, he thought to himself.

"It sounds like he let you down. Strange how children have a way of blaming themselves, as if they were the ones responsible for it all."

He grunted by way of an answer.

"Any brothers? Sisters?" she asked.

He gave an involuntary start. "No." *Not anymore.*

He thought of changing the subject but decided not to. He took a deep breath.

"I used to have a brother, an older brother. But he died—in an accident."

"My God, I'm sorry. What happened?"

"A swimming accident. It's a long story." He paused. "I'll tell you sometime, not just now."

"Of course."

They were silent again, for a beat. Then she took his hand.

"I think you've packed a lot of suffering into your life so far," she said.

"I didn't mean to trot out this catalogue of woe."

"No, I wanted to know. And it explains a lot."

"Like what?"

"Why you're here, on an island in the middle of nowhere, all alone—at least until we came."

"I'm glad you did."

"So am I."

He had the sudden desire to put his arm around her and kiss her; looking at her, he knew she had the same idea. But she stopped him.

"We can't," she said, resting her hand on his arm. "Nigel."

They decided to return. At the top of the cliff, he extended his arm to help her up and said: "Welcome back to reality."

That night, in his sleeping bag, he thought about all he had left out of his story. He had ignored the most important parts—that his brother had been everything to him, the center of his solar system. More than just looking up to him, he had counted on him for *survival*. Those long-ago nights after their mother left: lifting the old man out of his chair—*you take his legs, I'll get his back*—and heaving him into bed. Sometimes father and son would set out to pick his brother up from evening basketball practice, the car weaving all over the road, and he would duck down in the backseat and pray they wouldn't crash. When they got there, the relief when his brother took the wheel, peering over the dash, just learning to drive, going home at fifteen miles an hour, the sudden warmth of safety.

And that his brother was not just older by three years but bigger and faster and better in everything. He could always run faster, jump farther, reach longer. He was the perfect son, always got high marks in school, became president of the junior high school class, actually wrote a weekly column for the town newspaper. For Hugh, he was the impossible standard—tall, good-looking, athletic. On the baseball diamond he was a natural, captain of the team, and when he hit a line drive to the outfield and streaked around the bases, Hugh would turn his head slightly to watch his father's hungry eyes.

"C'mon Hugh, let's play catch." The smell of cut grass in their backyard, the shadows darkening in the late summer afternoon, the cicadas humming. They threw the ball back and forth, grounders, pop flies, line drives. "Give me a hard one, over my head." He'd run, circling back, and look over his shoulder and make a diving catch. The throws straight into the small leather pouch stung his hand. "Bottom of the ninth, bases loaded, here's the pitch. . . . It's a long fly ball. . . . Can he get it? . . . Back . . . back . . . He's got it! That's all for the Yankees. Side retired."

Hugh finally made it onto the team but he spent most of his time on the bench. Once in a while, he'd play right field, lonely in that huge blanket of grass, touching his rabbit foot between each pitch: "God, please don't let it come to me. But if it does, if it has to, please make me catch it." Once he promised to take over his brother's newspaper route, but the papers were so heavy in the sack he couldn't ride the bike without tipping over. He tried stuffing them under the seat and around the spokes but nothing worked and it was soon time for the game so he panicked and left his bike in the bushes and totally forgot about it. "How'd it go?" his brother asked. And Hugh gasped. Later they found the bike in the dark and his father drove them on the route, shaking his head; he had had a few too many and was in a foul mood.

The sat phone sprang to life, an insistent, annoying ring. It took a moment for him to surface from his memories and answer it. The voice on the other end sounded thin, with a long time delay.

"Beth Dulcimer, please? I apologize for calling so late. It's an emergency."

He had an American accent and sounded young.

Hugh pulled his shorts on and carried the phone across the campsite, feeling his way across the rocks with his bare feet. The embers from the fire were still glowing. He opened the flap of her tent and bent down and walked in. She awoke quickly and sat up in her sleeping bag and looked at him, at first in alarm and then, misunderstanding, with a slight smile. Her eyes were puffy with sleep. He explained and handed her the phone and walked back outside. He could hear her talking—her tone was warm but nervous—and then he heard her gasp and cry out. Nigel rushed past out of the darkness and entered the tent, saying, "What? What is it?"

Hugh lit a kerosene lantern and started the fire again and brewed some coffee. When he carried it to her, she looked up at him with tears in her eyes and said that her mother had died—a heart attack. She drank the coffee, dazed, her cheeks flushed.

"I have to leave," she said. "Right away. Tomorrow."

. . .

The next morning she prepared to leave on a panga that had been called to pick her up. Nigel was going too. He explained that he could hardly leave her at a time like this; if she wanted, he would accompany her to Minneapolis for the funeral. From inside her tent, she called her father. Hugh and Nigel could hear her crying softly as she talked and they looked at each other, feeling helpless.

"Hate to leave you in the lurch like this," said Nigel. "Mind you, I'm sure the project will send replacements right away—not to worry about that."

"I'm sure," replied Hugh. But that was the last thing he was concerned about.

At breakfast, she didn't eat much of anything, though Nigel, busily industrious, cooked biscuits. She looked drawn and pale but Hugh thought, with a stab of guilt, that her grief made her look even more beautiful.

By 10 a.m., the panga arrived. She leaned over to kiss Hugh on the cheek and gave a sad little smile. He hugged her, then helped her down the path with her gear. He shook hands with Nigel at the welcome mat. In a matter of minutes, it seemed, they were gone, without even a backward look, and the gulls that had followed the boat returned and began once again circling the island looking for fish.

It felt odd to be alone—odd and yet so familiar. But he didn't resume his normal routine—he didn't even erect the mist net. Instead, he sat on his rock and looked out at the ocean. It was all different now. The equilibrium of his long solitude had been disturbed and he knew that it was gone forever; it was impossible to carry on as if nothing had happened.

An hour later he used the sat phone to call the project headquarters and asked for Peter Simons.

"I'm pulling the emergency cord," he said, using the researchers' slang. Instant evacuation—no questions asked, or at least very few questions—was part of the deal. But Simons did ask a question: "What are you going to do?"

In the welter of emotions, how could he say what he really hoped for? That maybe he could salvage something out of this whole trying experience, recoup his losses and shake that overwhelming sense of failure? He was surprised to hear himself answer.

"I'm thinking of going for my degree," he said. "Not fieldwork but some kind of research, maybe on Darwin. With your help, of course—that is, if you'll give it?"

Simons said he would.

They were as good as their word. A student couple came out, a man and a woman in their early twenties, eager to learn. Hugh showed them everything he thought they needed to know. On the morning of his departure, he walked to the north rim and sat quietly on the rocky ledge for an hour or so. Then he packed hurriedly, taking only a single duffel bag filled mostly with his books. The students walked him down the path and handed him the bag from the mat, then waved, happy to be left alone.

"Finally had enough, heh?" said Raoul, yelling above the whine of the engine.

"Something like that."

"You glad to be leaving?"

"I'm glad to be going somewhere."

"Where you going?"

"England."

"You gonna shave your beard when you get back to civilization?"

"Probably."

"*Hombre,* you looking good."

He was surprised to hear that. He was also surprised to feel a bit of hope rising up. His stay on the island had not all been for nothing and he had nothing to be ashamed of—after all, when others had abandoned the project, he at least had persevered; he had kept it going.

As the panga roared off, he looked back at Sin Nombre. The birds circling above it caught the light on their wings and reflected it back, flecks of silver and ash turning in the sunlight. He realized that all this time living on the island and learning the shape of every rock and every crevice, he had forgotten what it actually looked like. Now he saw with surprise that it was symmetrical—its sides sloped down evenly, like an anthill, he thought.

From a distance it appeared small and dark, a burnt-out volcano sitting all by itself way out in the ocean.

CHAPTER 4

Life, Charles reflected, is a game of *vingt-et-un*. Three days after the disappointment that dashed his hopes, he found himself at the Admiralty in Whitehall in a wood-paneled office with ships' clocks and chronometers, sitting across a felt-topped desk from none other than Captain Robert FitzRoy. He was not quite sure why he had been summoned, but the excitement churning in his stomach told him there was still a possibility he was being considered for the voyage. He began to suspect that "the friend" was something of a smoke screen and that this strange and alluring man across from him was leaving himself an escape hatch if Charles proved unsuitable. Indeed, he felt as though he were sitting for an examination. He was at pains to appear relaxed, for the Captain was clearly assessing him—the dark eyes stared openly at him from time to time and in particular, it seemed, at his nose.

FitzRoy, at twenty-six only four years older than Charles, was worldly wise and self-assured. Thin, with dark hair, long sideburns, an aquiline nose, and a voice accustomed to barking orders, he exuded authority well beyond his age. But he was also spirited and imaginative and, best of all from Charles's point of view, he was a devotee of the natural sciences. Charles had been well briefed by Henslow. FitzRoy had had a meteoric career in the Navy, aided no doubt by his aristocratic connections—he traced his lineage to the illicit relationship between Charles II and Barbara Villiers. Then, too, his rise had been assisted by what the Admiralty delicately termed a "death vacancy," a reference to the fact that the previous captain of HMS *Beagle* had blown his brains out with a pearl-handled pistol off the God-forsaken coast of Tierra del Fuego after scrawling in the ship's log the message: "the soul of man dies in him."

"FitzRoy was given command of the ship for its return voyage," Henslow had related. "He did a good job of it by all accounts, especially considering that the crew refused to relinquish the belief that the ghost of the dead captain was on board the ship." Henslow had paused before completing the thought. "And speaking of suicide, you will remember that Lord Castlereagh's career came to an inglorious end a little more than a decade ago when he slit his throat. He was FitzRoy's uncle. The poor lad was only fifteen at the time. It seems that self-destruction is a motif in his life. I wouldn't be surprised if that doesn't account for his need for some companionship at sea. He can hardly talk to the lower officers, can he?"

But melancholia did not seem to sit on the man's shoulders. His long-lashed, almost feminine eyes sparkled and his voice was light as he described the trim beauty of the *Beagle,* currently being refitted at Plymouth, and the hard freedom of the open seas. The trip was to last two years, but—who could say?—it might extend to three or even four. He said the primary purpose was to chart the coast of South America, and the secondary was to refine the measurements of longitude by taking chronological readings around the world.

"Why South America?" put in Charles, almost breathless with excitement.

"The sailing is treacherous, rough currents, uncertain winds. The Admiralty wants up-to-date charts, the finest we can deliver, every cove and shoreline in detail." His voice dropped conspiratorially. "Trade is increasing, you see, especially with Brazil. The days of Spain are over and we must show the flag, keep the ports open for our vessels. We have the Falklands. Argentina's in a perennial uproar. The Americans are poking around. We already have a squadron of men-of-war outside Rio."

Charles read the turn in conversation as a good sign. But he was taken aback a moment later when FitzRoy abruptly leaned forward and demanded, in a non sequitur, whether it was true that he was the grandson of Erasmus Darwin, the famed physician, philosopher, and "freethinker." FitzRoy emphasized the word "free." Charles admitted that he was.

"I do not care for his philosophy," the Captain said in a tone that brooked little argument. "I could not finish *Zoonomia*. All that emphasis on natural law and the transmutation of species—it's Jacobin, if you ask me, and it comes perilously close to heresy. Do you not find that it detracts from the received and unquestionable wisdom that every bug, leaf, and cloud is the work of the Original Creator?"

"I am certainly not an atheist, if that is your question, sir," replied Charles firmly. "I do not think that one species can transmute into another, despite the obvious similarities. I believe in the Divine Authority. And I think that a trip such as the one you describe might well serve to give substance to the teachings of the Bible. Though I must add that lately I am tending towards the view that the world we have inherited has traveled through successive stages, each with its own distinctive flora and fauna."

"Ha!" yelled FitzRoy, clapping the table with an open palm. "As I suspected, you do not subscribe to the belief in Mr. Paley's Watch-maker."

"To the contrary, my good sir. I've read *Natural Theology* on three occasions. I do believe in the Watch-maker. It's merely the newness of the watch that I find open to question. You see, I do have a fondness for the longitudinal effects of age."

FitzRoy leapt up and paced around the office.

"Old the world is, indeed," he said. "Seeing that it was created on twenty-fourth October 4004 B.C. And we shall find ample evidence of the Great Deluge."

"No doubt."

"Well," FitzRoy blurted, "you're a man after my own heart. Stand up for what you believe but remain true to the Holy Word—heh. We'll have lots to talk about in our tiny cabin, Whig and Tory, locked in intellectual combat on the high seas. Ha!"

And that's how the offer was made.

On the way to the door, FitzRoy asked Charles if it was true, as he had heard from Henslow, that he had once put a beetle in his mouth. It was. Charles recounted the story of how, as a student, he'd lifted a rock and found two exotic beetles and scooped them up, one in each hand. Then a third appeared, and he put one in his mouth so that he could grab that one also, only to have his mouth seize up from pain—the poor insect had secreted an acrid fluid.

"By Jove, I could not eat for days," he said, as FitzRoy's laughter echoed from the walls.

"Ha!" said the Captain. "You can't try that with bugs in the tropics. They'll put you in *their* mouths."

The joviality prompted Charles to ask a question in turn.

"Tell me, good sir. I had the impression—or perhaps it was my imagination—that you were inordinately taken by my nose. Was that the case?"

"It certainly was," came the reply. "I'm a phrenologist, you know, and I abide by physiognomy, which explains my interest in your proboscis. And I must say, it does not speak well for you. It took me a while to realize that it was misleading me—you are indeed trustworthy."

The next day they met again, for lunch at FitzRoy's club on Pall Mall, and again the Captain made a powerful impression on Charles. At times, it seemed, their roles had switched—now it was FitzRoy who was fearful he would back out. At one point, sipping brandy before the fire, he leaned over to touch Charles on the arm and said: "Now your friends will tell you a sea captain is the greatest brute on the face of creation. I do not know how to help you in this case, except by hoping you will give me a trial."

"A trial! By Jove, a thousand trials," said Charles enthusiastically.

"Let us hope that necessity does not materialize."

FitzRoy drifted for a moment on some dark thought and then added: "Shall you bear being told during some dinner or other that I want the cabin for myself, when I want to be alone?"

Charles hastened to reassure him.

"Most certainly," he said.

"If we treat each other this way, I hope we shall suit. If not, probably we should wish each other at the Devil."

FitzRoy did not hold back in describing the rigors of the voyage—the cramped quarters, the tasteless food, the rough seas, the perilous storms around Cape Horn, and the dangers of overland exploration in South America. But with each new peril, as FitzRoy seemed to intuit, Charles felt more and more convinced that the *Beagle* was his destiny.

At one point, the Captain dropped his voice and confided that he had a personal stake in the expedition. He had acquired three savages during his previous trip to Tierra del Fuego—he had taken them as hostages for a stolen whaleboat—and now he was going to bring them back to establish a Christian outpost on the storm-wracked coast of their origin.

"Have you not heard of this venture?"

"In truth, sir, I have," replied Charles—and indeed, he could scarcely have been unaware; for months the Indians had been the talk of London and had even been introduced at court. The Queen took a fancy to them.

"And I heartily approve. A Christian settlement is bound to save the lives of shipwrecked seamen."

"And so it shall!" put in FitzRoy with a slap on the thigh.

They settled on Charles's expenses—£30 a year for mess—and drew up the list of items he would need, including twelve cotton shirts, six tough breech trousers, three coats, boots, walking shoes, Spanish books, a guide to taxidermy, two microscopes, a geological compass, nets, jars, alcohol, and all manner of tools for capturing and handling specimens.

Then they went for a stroll to purchase a pair of firearms. London was filling up with crowds for the coronation of William IV and Queen Adelaide on the morrow. Flags hung from the windows, gas illuminations were blazing, and everywhere were plastered decorations of crowns and anchors and "WRs" for the new king. But Charles was more excited by his purchase of a brand-new pair of flintlock pistols and a rifle. He had them sent to his hotel and could not resist informing the clerk that they were to be used in the wilds of South America. Later he wrote to his sister Susan, asking her to send to the Shrewsbury gunsmith for spare hammers, main springs, and plugs.

After FitzRoy left, Charles, on impulse, bought a seat along the coronation route. The following day he took up his position along the Mall across from St. James's Park and was awestruck at the royal procession, an unending ribbon of liveried attendants dressed in crimson red and glittering gold. As the royal coach went by, he saw the King and fancied that the monarch gave him a slight nod. His heart swelled with imperial pride. How fine it was to be an Englishman. But then the crowd across the street became unruly, pushing and shoving one another off the curb for a better view, and tall equestrian Guardsmen rode up to keep order, the horses rearing up and kicking their back hooves violently. One man was injured and lay flat in the gutter until a carriage came to pick him up. Two officers tossed him inside like a sack of potatoes.

That night, Charles strolled among the crowd on the Westminster Embankment. He watched fireworks explode over the Thames, bursts of reds and blues and whites that lit up the Houses of Parliament and streamed down over the majestic bridges and into the cold black water. Fog suddenly appeared, muffling the syncopated clacking of the horses' hooves and engulfing the knots of people who disappeared and reappeared an instant later. Charles had the uncanny sensation that it was all for him, a stage arranged magically on his behalf that would be struck tomorrow when he departed. His step was light. He embraced the exhilarating and wonderfully lonely feeling that he was unlike anyone around him—a feeling derived, he realized with a quickening pulse, from the extraordinary knowledge that very soon his whole life, and maybe he himself, would be forever changed.

The date was 8 September 1831.

CHAPTER 5

The supervisor of the Manuscripts Room of Cambridge University Library kept Hugh waiting while he sorted through papers on his desk. When he finally looked up, Hugh asked, "Do you have a good biography of Darwin?"

The supervisor paused, as if considering whether or not to answer, and then said, his eyelids fluttering, "*All* of our Darwin biographies are what one might call *good*."

"Fine," said Hugh. "Then I'll have them *all*."

A young man standing behind the supervisor raised his hand to his mouth and snickered.

"I see. And how would you like to receive them?"

"Alphabetically."

"By title?"

"By *author*."

Five minutes later a stack four feet high appeared on the retrieval shelf. Hugh filled out the slips and carried the books to a corner table, where he piled them around him like a pilot in a cockpit.

Still jet-lagged, he had slept late that morning but awoke with a start, dressed, and ran downstairs to the parlor of the rooming house he had found on Tenison Road. Before taking his money the landlady had warned him twice about having guests in his room. He found strong tea and a scone on the sideboard, gulped them down, and hurried out to a dank drizzle. It was only his third day in Cambridge but already he had learned to carry a fold-up umbrella in his back pocket.

At the library, a huge brown-brick repository built around a massive central tower, the note from Simons under the Cornell letterhead had done the trick; he had obtained a reader's card, a photo ID, and access to the vast third-floor room.

He picked his way through the books, reading sections here and there, not at all methodical in his search since he had no clear idea what he was looking for. After two hours he asked for more material; he handed in the request slips, and thin brown envelopes or small blue boxes were delivered without ceremony: manuscripts, notes, and sketches in Darwin's scrawl, books and periodicals with jottings and exclamations in the margins. Then he looked through some of Darwin's letters. There were thousands upon thousands of them. Some, written from the *Beagle,* were wrinkled and stained from long sailing voyages; he held them under his nose and imagined the scent of sea breezes and brine. Others, written in later years from his study, humbly begged for specimens, demanded data from pigeon breeders and barnacle fanciers, or spread flattery while seeming to fish for a review of one of his books.

Hugh scoured them for some clue to a larger mystery, some nugget that might shed light on how Darwin worked or the definitive moment when he formulated his theory. But they had yielded no such secrets, only bits and pieces of trivia about natural history, a throwaway line about the facial expressions of a monkey, a snippet of gossip about a rival—the mundane stuff of a naturalist's daily life.

Hugh realized it was hopeless; he was flying blind.

Shortly after one o'clock he was eating in the library lunchroom and looked up to find a young man standing before him with a tray.

"Mind if I join you?"

Hugh recognized him—the assistant who had been snickering. Although he didn't feel like talking to anyone, he closed the book he was reading and nodded. The young man was thin, his features delicate and his head tending to cock to one side, like an attentive hound. He had a disconcerting smudge of a beard in the center of his chin.

"What's that?" he asked, pointing to Hugh's book.

"Voyage of the Beagle."

"Oh, I thought you must have read that by now."

"Yeah, I did. I'm rereading it."

The young man cut into a slab of meat drenched in gravy.

"Mind if I ask you what line of research you're pursuing?"

Hugh decided to keep his cards close to his chest but couldn't come up with anything that sounded sufficiently esoteric.

"That's kind of a sore subject. Something about Darwin. I'm looking around but I'm afraid I haven't really come up with anything exciting, at least not yet. Actually, I'm a little worried about my thesis."

He smiled lamely. There was more truth than he had expected in his words.

"My name's Roland Damon, by the way," the young man said, stretching his hand across the airspace of their two trays, a gesture that was touchingly awkward. Hugh shook it.

"Mine's Hugh. Hugh Kellem."

"American?"

"Yes."

"From . . . ?"

"New York. Around New York. A place called Connecticut, actually."

"Oh, I know it well. I spent a year there as an exchange student. New Canaan. Loved it. Life in an American high school is adolescent paradise. I joined all the clubs and got five pictures in the yearbook. I mention that only because there was a competition to see who got the most—very American, that sort of thing."

Hugh smiled. There was nothing to be said by way of response.

"So," continued Roland, "you've done what . . . looked through some of his letters?"

"Something like that." Not many secrets around here, thought Hugh.

"They're pretty well combed over," said Roland. "Darwin's known to have written fourteen thousand letters and nine thousand of them are here. I'll bet each one has been read a hundred times."

"Now it's a hundred and one."

"Perhaps you should look for something new. There are only thirty pages extant from the original manuscript of the *Origin*. Incidentally, we have nineteen of them. You could see if you could unearth some of the missing ones."

Hugh perked up. "You seem to know this stuff pretty well," he said.

"I should. I've been working here eight years. A man's got to do something to pass the time." He paused, looking at Hugh, then continued. "You could look for the 1858 Darwin and Wallace manuscripts from the Linnean Society. They've never been found. They're not in any of the collections."

"So where would you go?"

"Some other archive. Maybe his publishers. Anywhere but here. This ground has been ploughed over so many times there's nothing left." Roland raised his voice a notch. "There're so many mysteries about the man. Why don't you tackle some of them?"

"Like what?"

"Here's this wanker who goes around the world, has all sorts of adventures, rides with the *gauchos* of South America, for Christ's sake, and then sails home and never stirs again. What do you make of that? And all his illnesses—he came down with everything in the book. He was a walking infirmary. You mean to tell me that's normal? And he has this theory that'll turn the world on its head and make him famous but he can't bring himself to publish for twenty-two years. You don't find that strange?"

Hugh did find it strange, of course, as did most scholars who took Darwin on, but that was part of the man's attraction—he was nothing if not human.

"Everyone's always making excuses for his procrastination. His wife was religious. He knew his work would bring down the walls of Jericho. He needed time to marshal all his data. His own body was in a state of rebellion at what he was doing— Bullshit! I think people let him get away with murder."

Hugh noticed that the more Roland talked, the more flirtatious he became. So he wasn't really surprised when his luncheon companion posed one or two leading questions about his social life and asked what he did for fun. Hugh pushed aside the advance, gently. He had begun to like him.

"Incidentally," said Roland, "I think Darwin had a freaky side."

"What do you mean?"

"Well, for one thing he was obsessed with hermaphrodites. He kept finding barnacles with two penises and it shook him terribly. He abhorred the whole idea. I think he feared it because there was so much intermarriage in his family. And then later, of course, he saw that her-maphrodites are proof that nature can throw off mutants, which was an important concept for his theory."

"How do you know all this?"

"It's an interest of mine. Not Darwin. I mean hermaphrodites."

Hugh could not help but laugh.

"Hugh! My God."

The woman's voice caught him from behind, a mid-Atlantic accent. He identified it at once and stiffened with anticipation and dread. He turned slowly, but a knot of people was passing through the archway of Burlington House, silhouettes backlighted by the sunny courtyard, so that he didn't spot her right away. She spoke again.

"What are you doing here?"

He kissed Bridget lightly on the cheek and there was an awkward moment as he pulled back while she leaned forward to kiss the other.

His first thought was that she looked older. There was a fleshiness to her cheeks that widened her face, and her blond hair looked a little thinner. But the impression lessened as he looked into her eyes and saw there the familiar mixture of friendliness and reserve. She was like an estranged sister. It hadn't really been all that long: six years. He had last seen her at the funeral, when he could barely speak to her—or to anyone else, for that matter. She had written him a letter—she wanted to keep in touch, she said—but he hadn't answered. In those days he hadn't been able to think of anyone else, only of his own pain. That was still true, come to think of it.

She was staring at him, waiting, and he realized he hadn't answered her question.

"Just visiting," he said, gesturing toward the thick wooden door he had just closed.

"I meant here in London."

"Oh, thinking of doing some research. And you?"

"I live here—remember?"

"Yes, of course. My father told me. I meant now."

"The Hogarth Exhibition." She turned and tilted her head toward the Royal Academy. "But what's in there?" she insisted, looking again at the door.

"Not much. The Linnean Society."

"And what conceivable interest do *you* have in the Linnean Society?"

She hadn't changed—she was never one to stop until she got what she wanted.

"Darwin. I've gotten interested in Darwin."

Bridget was staring at him again, with arched eyebrows, and it made him nervous.

"So I thought I'd take a look at the Society. Of course, it's not where it was when he and Wallace delivered their papers. It's moved since then—and, well, actually, he didn't turn up for his paper. Sick, as usual."

Why was he running on like this? He knew, of course; he felt anxious, but he didn't want to dwell on it. "Still, they've got some good portraits. Here, I've got some cards."

He handed her two four- by six-inch reproductions of the paintings he had just seen. There was Darwin, stooped with the weight of a foolish world on his shoulders, gloomy as Jehovah in his long white beard and dark overcoat. And Wallace, relaxing in a chair next to a painting of a tropical forest. A book depicting a brilliant green butterfly rested on his knee and his eyes beamed behind wire-rimmed spectacles.

"Hardly Tweedledum and Tweedledee," she ventured, opening one of the cards. Inside was the reproduction of a centennial brass plaque that read:

CHARLES DARWIN
and ALFRED RUSSEL WALLACE
made the first communication
of their views on
THE ORIGIN OF SPECIES
BY NATURAL SELECTION
At a meeting of the Linnean Society
On 1st July 1858   *1st July 1958*

"Let's go get a drink," she said abruptly. "I suspect you need one." He tried to find an excuse but she had already locked arms and was marching him up Piccadilly, her eyes scanning the street ahead.

"No pub," he said. "They're never around when you need one."

"Which is pretty much all the time with you, as I remember."

He fancied he heard more and more of her native New Jersey punching through the faint English lilt.

They settled for a small restaurant and he headed for a table by the window where the passersby might provide a distraction. A waitress in a white apron ambled over and he asked for a beer and Bridget ordered a sherry in clipped tones.

"So when exactly was it that you became English?" he asked. "I mean, was there one specific moment when you crossed over the line?"

"Very amusing. If it's kissing both cheeks you're referring to, you should know everyone who's lived here long enough does that."

"Yeah, but you did it right away. Wasn't it in the taxi line at Heathrow?"

"It was in the *queue,* if you must know."

"I see you haven't changed—as quick as ever."

"*You're* the one who apparently hasn't changed."

He didn't answer. Change—if she only knew how much he had changed.

"So, when did this Darwin fascination start?"

"Oh, I don't know exactly. I'm still looking around."

"For what? For what you want to do when you grow up?"

"Something like that."

"I heard that you were a bartender. And then you did something out west, didn't you? Picking apples, forest ranger, something dramatically adolescent like that?"

He let it ride and sipped his beer.

"And you went to that strange place—what's it called? One of those islands in Galápagos."

"Sin Nombre."

"That's it. No wonder I can't remember it. And did your man Darwin visit there too?"

"No. It's only a small island. There's a research project there, looking at Darwin's finches, measuring them—the length of their beaks, that sort of thing—to see how they change when conditions change."

"I see. Measuring bird beaks. And you were doing this for a degree?"

"Yes. Well, I was. But I didn't finish my time there. It was actually kind of rough—in the sense of depressing. I left."

"You left? Meaning what—you washed out?"

"You could put it that way."

"So you never got your degree?"

"No, not yet. I talked to my adviser—he's at Cornell—and I told him I wanted to come here, maybe write something about Darwin."

"I see."

"Trouble is, so much has been written about him. It's hard to imagine coming up with something new, not to mention earth-shattering."

"Uh-huh." She was quiet, thinking, but only for a moment. "I bet your dad's glad he spent all that money for you to go to college."

He stared at her, hard. She had always been proud of her insensitivity and she was always presumptuous, insisting she had the right to give him advice like an older sister. Any minute now she would start talking about his brother.

"It didn't cost so much. Not like Harvard." He realized it was a weak comeback and she paid it no mind.

"Listen to me, Hugh," she said, leaning forward. "From what I heard, you're just drifting. You're what—thirty years old?"

"Twenty-eight."

"Twenty-eight. Don't you think it's time—"

"For what? To get over it, you mean?"

"Well, yes. Others have."

"Like you."

"Like me."

"What do you mean, 'from what I heard'? Who are you talking to, anyway?"

"People. The world's not such a big place, you know."

He looked down at her wedding ring. His father had told him about that too.

"Yes, I've married. And I'm reasonably content." She paused. "I wouldn't say I don't think of your brother from time to time—I think of him *often,* as a matter of fact. But one has to get on with one's life. That's not being heartless, it's just realistic. The world really does go on, you know. That may be a cliché, but it's true nonetheless. You have to get on with things."

"I know that, but—you know—it's different with me."

"Because you always thought he was better than you. And because you think you're responsible for his death."

He was too stunned to speak. He'd known it was a mistake to sit down with her.

"I'm sorry to talk like this, Hugh. But somebody has to. You've got to get over this. It's absurd for you to blame yourself. It wasn't your fault, for God's sake. Everyone knows that."

"Everyone wasn't there. I was."

As he spoke, the loop of memory played in his mind again—the rocks, the waterfall, the shadow of the falling body and the pool of bubbles looking odd in the shaft of sunlight.

He willed her to talk again, if only to interrupt his thoughts, and she didn't disappoint him.

"You know, self-pity doesn't get you anywhere. And it's very unattractive, especially on you, Hugh, of all people. You're young. You're handsome. God, half the women I know were in love with you."

He wanted to bring the encounter to an end.

"Where were they when I needed them?" he said, with a half smile. He looked at his watch.

"Someplace to go?" she asked.

"Yes, as a matter of fact. I've only got a few minutes more." He took another sip of beer. He wanted another one, but more than that he wanted to leave.

"Why didn't you answer my letter?" she asked.

For a moment he thought of pretending he hadn't received it. But that kind of lie never worked with her; she would see through it and just go barreling ahead as if it wasn't worth acknowledging.

"I don't know. I didn't want to go over the whole thing. I didn't want to think about it, I guess."

"So you went off to be by yourself and stare out at the ocean. That's a good way to take your mind off things."

"Yes, well, in any case, it didn't work."

"I would think not."

He decided to change the subject. "What's he like—your husband?"

"Erik. And he's very smart. He works in the City and we have a flat in Elgin Crescent."

"I see. Kids?"

"No."

"And you—do you work?"

"Life of leisure," she said, sitting back and rubbing her ring with her thumb. It was a false gesture, pretending at some bourgeois compromise, and she played it that way. A silence set in and he resolved not to break it. After half a minute, she spoke.

"And your father. How is he?"

"He's remarried."

Her eyebrows rose.

"A good woman, or so it seems. Kathy. They've been married about three years now."

"No kidding. That's amazing. He'd been single for years, ever since . . . how long ago did your mother leave?"

"A long time. I was a teenager."

"And how do you get on with Kathy?"

"Okay, not bad. I don't spend much time with them. They seem good together, but I can't say it's really changed him."

"He's not exactly a touchy-feely kind of man."

"No. But he's stayed on the wagon. He seems to be making an effort to get engaged in things now, including with me. I think Kathy's pushing him in that direction. He kept pressing me to go back to school. So I got into this evolutionary biology, partly to get him off my back, and then ended up liking it."

Hugh didn't say what he was thinking—that his father had made some kind of peace with the past and "moved on," as Bridget would put it, but that he still believed his father had never forgiven him and undoubtedly never would. Certain things you just don't get over.

He could see that Bridget had something on her mind. She leaned across the table toward him and spoke in a low, intimate tone.

"Hugh, there are some things that even you don't know about. I don't know if you even *should* know, but it might help. It might make everything a bit easier."

"Bridget, for Christ's sake. Could you be a little less cryptic?"

"No, I can't. But maybe you should just be open to thinking about things in a different way."

"What the hell does that mean? Bridget, if you've got something to say, just say it."

"Maybe sometime. Let me think about it."

"Have it your way." He put down his glass and stood up. "I've really got to go—sorry."

"No, I'm sorry. I didn't mean to be playing games. I'm not—I hope you realize that. All this is too important."

"Sure. I guess. But I have no idea what the hell you're talking about."

He paid the tab and by the time they reached the door, she was a flurry of resolution. She insisted on taking his phone number, and he found it on a piece of paper in his pocket—the rooming house in Cambridge—and read it aloud as she punched it into a PalmPilot. She said she was going to invite him for dinner.

"Promise you'll come."

"Maybe. I'll have to see."

On the sidewalk, she leaned over to kiss him, both cheeks, saying how glad she was that they had bumped into each other, and then she turned abruptly and walked down the street, her heels clicking against the pavement. He thought she looked broader across the hips and wondered fleetingly if she was pregnant.

What would it have been like, he thought, if she was carrying my brother's child? What would their children have been like? All that powerful DNA conjoining, his brilliance and her drive, making little gods in diapers, almost too perfect for this world.

All that time we were talking, he thought, and we didn't even say his name.

So he said it to himself: Cal.

Cal, Cal, Cal.

He spotted the building at once, number 50 Albemarle Street. A discreetly placed brass plaque announced it as home to John Murray, Publishers. He stepped back to examine the eighteenth-century town house. It was five stories tall, cream-colored with a cranberry-painted cast-iron fence leading to the imposing front door. French windows peered down from the first floor. The blank facade of a NatWest bank next door made it doubly quaint.

He tried to imagine the crush of buyers nearly two centuries ago, shouting up at the windows to obtain the early cantos of Byron's *Don Juan*. Or Jane Austen's messenger delivering a carefully wrapped manuscript of *Emma*. Or the frail figure of Darwin in a top hat, prematurely aged, gripping the railing to climb the steps in order to negotiate yet another edition of the *Origin*.

He had called ahead for an appointment. The archivist said she'd be "delighted" to meet him—though her tone belied her words—and she remarked pointedly that she found his request "intriguingly spontaneous." He ignored the sarcasm and said he'd be there "right away," using the American expression, which forced her hand.

Walking there, he was pursued by memories of Cal. Years ago Cal had been a Rhodes Scholar at Oxford, where he first fell in love with science. Hugh, just kicked out of Andover, was spending a year in Paris and he often jumped on the ferry for a quick visit to England. They'd set a time and place to meet—Piccadilly, the Tower, the pub forty paces from 10 Downing—and they'd surprise each other by arriving incognito, back turned, collar up. (Once Cal came disguised in a ridiculous mop wig.) They'd go carousing through London and then take the late train to Oxford and Hugh would crash on a couch in Cal's room.

There was something liberating about being abroad—two New World vagabonds traipsing around Europe's haunts, trading confidences (they could somehow talk more openly, more honestly so far from home). The four-year age difference melted away. Hugh remembered it as a time of confidence and endless possibilities. He did not dare compete for girls, convinced that Cal was irresistible, and he took solace in contrasts: his brother was the serious one and he was the wit, his brother the responsible one and he the rebel. He smoked Gauloises, letting the cigarettes dangle from his lip, spoke fluent French, wore a black turtleneck, and carried a paperback of *War and Peace* in his backpack.

And then Cal had met Bridget, who was backpacking with a friend.

"I want you to meet her. We're coming over to Paris. A whole week— nothing to do but drink wine, hang around museums, and pretend I love French poetry." And what a week it had been! The obligatory baguette and cheese on the Quai Voltaire. Marie Antoinette's peasant cottage at Versailles. Getting lost in the forest at Fontainebleau. Touring the catacombs, even the sewers. For three days he escorted Bridget's friend Ellen, but thankfully she left. Then the three of them were inseparable. On the final day Cal left them alone to get drunk at an Algerian bar but really, as he put it, " 'cause it's time you two get to know each other." No flirting—a novel sensation. He liked her immediately, maybe loved her, because she loved Cal and Cal loved her. How odd—feeling so comfortable, so at ease, so included. A big sister to go along with the big brother. A trinity. There was nothing the three of them couldn't do.

Where had all that piss and vinegar gone? Had it really disappeared in a single summer afternoon?

The receptionist, inside a glass cubicle in the front hall, directed him past a winding banister to the waiting area, a tiny room under a glass cupola. He rose to greet the archivist, a young woman in tweeds.

"Hello," she said brightly.

"Hello, I'm glad you . . ." He broke off—his words were being splintered, odd echoes bounced around the room. Above him was a hanging disk that refracted his voice. She smiled.

"That's our little surprise," she said.

She apologized, said the house was in the throes of moving, and as she led him up a winding staircase, they stepped around stacks of cardboard boxes. They passed a bust of Byron, under an array of portraits in heavy dark colors with thick gold frames. Hugh read the names: Osbert Lancaster, Kenneth Clark, John Betjeman. There were half a dozen John Murrays.

"That was Darwin's," she said, casting her eyes at a portrait of John Murray III looking out from behind a writing desk with a confident gaze.

"He took over in 1843 and prodded the firm towards science, which was his prime interest. He published Darwin, Lyell, David Livingstone, and of course the famous travel handbooks. They were the first of their kind and very popular. They kept the wolf from the door."

They passed through a rear drawing room decorated in thick gold wallpaper—from Japan, 1870, she said—and entered an office that was cluttered with boxes and files. She explained that the publishing house had been purchased by a larger company and was moving to a corporate headquarters.

"I see the wolf was patient," said Hugh.

She didn't smile. Hugh produced the letter from Simons, which she read twice.

"Well," she pronounced finally. "All of our important Darwin papers are locked away in a secret archive, which will remain with us. We have a few boxes of unimportant material in a storeroom here, which you are welcome to peruse, but I doubt you will find anything of interest. It is commercial in nature, bills and accounts and such."

Hugh recalled Darwin's obsessive bookkeeping. One year when he was too ill to jot down the precious sums of money coming in and money spent he permitted his wife, Emma, to take over the ledgers; a £7 discrepancy cured him of that forever.

The archivist informed him that he was not allowed to search directly through the cartons of material. Instead, she led him to the main drawing room where, she explained, he would be observed as he pursued his research. The ornate chamber was lined with glass-encased books and on the higher reaches portraits covered every bit of wall space. He recognized the French windows he had seen from below.

She offered him a seat at a round felt-covered table set upon a Persian carpet. A box was brought to him and placed beside his chair. She cautioned him to use pencil only in taking notes and said an observer would soon be there to sit at the desk near the window. She lingered for a moment and seemed to have something on her mind. Perhaps, he thought, he was not grateful enough.

"I appreciate that you've allowed me to do this."

"Oh, don't mention it. That's what we do. We take care of our authors even after death." She paused a beat, then added: "You realize this room has remained unchanged for nearly two hundred years. And you are in good company. Southey, Crabbe, Moore, Washington Irving, Sir Arthur Conan Doyle, Madame de Staël. Over there"—she gestured to the center window—"Sir Walter Scott was introduced to Lord Byron in 1815. And over here"—she nodded toward a fireplace with a marble mantelpiece—"Lord Byron's memoirs were burned after his death. It was thought best for all concerned. Especially Lady Byron."

That was it: he had not been sufficiently impressed with the surroundings.

She left Hugh alone. He looked around the room, taking it all in, and then another woman entered and sat primly at a desk near the window, glancing over from time to time as he opened the box and went through the material.

The archivist was right: there seemed to be nothing much of interest. There were business files and account books—bills of sale, royalty statements, translation agreements, account ledgers, and the like. Hugh's interest began to flag.

For an hour, he sifted through the material. Then he picked up an account book and was confronted with long columns of numbers, neat and small in black ink—itemized expenses. He skipped ahead, holding the book by the spine and flipping the pages with his thumb. Soon the columns disappeared, blank pages flew by and then—suddenly, to his amazement—they came alive with writing. A fine script moved quickly across the pages. It was as if a movie had burst onto a white screen.

He looked at the pages more closely. The writing was old; it was in a girlish hand but the penmanship was easy to read and elegant. It was an ocean of script. The *a*'s and *o*'s and *e*'s crested forward gracefully, like waves headed for shore, the *b*'s and *l*'s and *t*'s tall and slanting, like sails.

The first entry began with a date.

CHAPTER 6

4 January 1865

Papa gave this book to me for the New Year to keep my accounts, a duty to be faithfully discharged. I shall record my expenditures (which are pitifully meagre) in columns and subtract as I proceed until I attain the magical tally of nought, at which time he will replenish my monthly sum. But this little book shall serve an additional purpose, one that is secret. I shall use it as a journal, setting down my most personal thoughts and observations when I deem them sufficiently interesting, and I shall pray it does not fall into the wrong hands, for that might prove an embarrassment.

For I have many thoughts of a personal nature and no one to relate them to—certainly not to sweet Mamma, who cannot bear to think ill of anyone, nor to Etty, for though my sister is nearly four years older, she is not, to my thinking, four years wiser. I shall consign this personal journal to the rear of this account book and thus disguise it. My expectation is that it will remain at the bottom of my writing-desk unread by anyone other than myself. Deception, says Papa, is Nature's art and we can all learn from it.

Ever since Papa became famous, we have had a veritable flood of visitors to Down House, many of whom come from distant parts. I quite enjoy the company, and not simply because they tend to be people of noteworthy distinction, modern thinkers and various scientists whose nature makes them peculiar specimens in their own right, but also because they provide a distraction, which I sorely need.

On the morning of a visit, everyone leaps into action in order to put his best face forward. We are like the army mobilising for the Crimea. Mamma organises the household with quiet command. Mrs Davies heaves pots hither and yon on the fire with great urgency and much yelling, so that soon aromas of spiced lamb and baking potatoes fill the house all the way to the servants' rooms. Parslow readies the wine in the butler's pantry. The gardener, Comfort, harnesses the horses and drives the waggonette to Orpington to fetch the guest or guests (since there are likely to be more than one).

Now that I am eighteen years of age, I am forced to wear one of my crinolines and endure the torture of tight lacing (twenty-four inches around the waist—not an inch more). I find I can hardly move nor breathe, I who love nothing better than to run unfettered in the fields and hide in the woods and clay-pits. Etty is permitted to forgo the corset owing to her delicate constitution.

In short, all are busily occupied, with the exception of poor Papa who is usually confined to bed with stomach ailments in anticipation of the socialising to which he must needs submit himself.

The bustle provides the impression, if only for the afternoon, that the Darwins are a normal and contented family. In some ways, we most certainly are, though at times I perceive a strangeness beneath the gaiety and manners. What it is that is amiss I do not know. But an astute observer sitting in our midst at the grand table might notice a forced quality to the laughter and, were he as perspicacious as some of our modern novelists from Mudie's Library like Mrs Gatskell or Mr Trollope, he might be able to detect the reasons for it. We are not as we present ourselves to the unknowing outsiders. Indeed, I sometimes feel that our attempts at hospitality and gaiety are mere play-acting.

6 January 1865

Papa, as always, is at the centre of our household. I feel his moods have grown increasingly worse in the six years since the publication of Origin. He now retreats to his study for hours on end, but not in the old way which I recollect so fondly. Then he would immerse himself in his study of barnacles or some such, scooting around contentedly in his wheeled chair, emerging every so often for a pinch of black snuff from the jar in the hall, looking up with curiosity when one of us children burst in upon him to ask for a foot-rule or a *pin and never taking umbrage at the interruption. Now, he hides himself away for hours on end, almost as if he did not want to be in our company, and try as I might, I cannot fathom the reason for his ill humour.*

Three days ago, in search of a sticking-plaster, I chanced to open the door and came upon him sitting in his black leather horse-hair chair, so lost in gloomy thought that when I spoke, he started like a deer. He rose up and demanded to know why I was 'stealthily creeping up' on him so that he could not have 'a moment's peace'. He thundered on in that vein so long that even when I closed the door, his voice could be heard throughout the hall, with the result that Camilla broke off her German lessons with Horace to come to the top of the staircase and peer down with evident concern.

Recently he directed Parslow to attach a small round mirror to the window-casement so that by positioning himself in his chair he could obtain a view of the front step. He told us that in that way he could catch sight of the postman, but I doubt the explanation. I believe that the arrangement enables him to examine unseen any caller, the easier to support the pretence that he is not at home. My concern is that it is not simply the desire to avoid interruption that impels him to this course but rather something more profound and disquieting.

Nor has Papa's health shown any improvement. Quite the contrary, it has worsened noticeably in recent times. He now retches two or three times a day and often complains of stomach problems, including wind, which is so odoriferous he refuses to travel. In addition to dyspepsia, he is subject to dizziness, fainting-spells and headaches. On some days he breaks out in eczema. Poor Mamma has become a veritable Florence Nightingale, sacrificing herself at all hours to bring him tea and rub his back and read aloud to soothe his nerves and distract him from his various ailments. He has had constructed a sort of water-closet in his study, a basin set inside a platform in the floor, hidden behind a half-wall and curtain, no more than ten feet from his corner of precious books and tiny drawers. It is for emergencies; in this way, he is able to lunge up from his chair, thrusting his writing-board to one side, and run to vomit. At the sound, which is truly horrible, the servants gather nervously in the hall, looking at one another, and only Parslow is allowed to enter to offer aid. Sometimes he has to actually lift Papa, limp and pale and dripping with perspiration, and carry him upstairs to his room.

11 January 1865

Papa has been ill as long as I can remember. When he takes to his bed, a pall is cast upon the household and we all scarcely dare to speak above a murmur. Mamma says the attacks are brought on by his work, by the strain of thinking so hard about natural science. To support her speculation she notes that his initial attack, now almost thirty years ago, came as he was first framing his theory on the transmutation of species and natural selection. For twenty-two years he kept his theory a secret in private notebooks, except for discussions with a few friends and colleagues like Sir Charles Lyell, the geologist, and Mr Hooker, the botanist at Kew, and by correspondence with Mr Asa Gray at Harvard.

Can you imagine, she says, the strain from carrying the weight of all that theorising for all those years? No wonder Papa sought the miracle water-cure from Dr Gully. I accompanied him to Malvern once and was shocked at how willingly he submitted himself to freezing baths and the torture of being wrapped in the frigid 'dripping-sheet' that is intended to send the blood from one organ to another.

I have a conjecture of my own to explain Papa's indisposition, for I marked the occasions when it seizes him most dramatically. It occurs not just when the subject of his theory arises but when an event happens that refers to the genesis of the theory. For example, Papa had an unusually severe and prolonged attack of vomiting after receiving that dreadful letter from the Dutch East Indies in 1858, the one in which Mr Alfred Russel Wallace proposed his nearly identical theory, so close in all its particulars that Papa moaned that the very phrases could serve as chapter-headings for his own book. Then Papa rallied to put his own theory of natural selection before the public, acceding to the exhortations of Mr Huxley and others that the two papers, his and that of Mr Wallace, be presented simultaneously at the Linnean Society. He worked in a frenzy to rush Origin *into print and became so exhausted that he could barely finish it. But the true illness came shortly afterwards, not when the theory itself was challenged but when his achievement was called into question because of the coincidence of its having two authors. That nasty Richard Owen, who dreams of heading up a new Museum of Natural Science and is one of Papa's main detractors, was said to have remarked at a dinner on Eaton Place: 'What can be so unimaginable as a child with two fathers?' To which the riposte, to the amusement of everyone present, was: 'Especially if one of them is an ape.'*

I do not see why people should react that way, even if Mr Wallace did arrive at a similar theory. Perhaps the coincidence can be taken as more proof of its genuine validity, not less, because once a compelling idea is in the air, more than one person is bound to seize it. That is especially true for the theory of natural selection, since it is supremely elegant in its simplicity. In any case, Papa is the one who laboured to make it presentable and understandable. He is so sensitive, I know he hates all the controversy, including those cartoons in Punch *and those horrid drawings in* Vanity Fair, *and it upsets him no end to discover that Mr Wallace has received little credit or that people might think that he himself acted in some untoward way to deny Mr Wallace priority.*

I wish my father would travel, for I believe that nothing is as much a remedy to frayed nerves as new horizons. But he scarcely stirs himself to go to London these days and adamantly refuses to consider crossing the Channel, which seems odd for someone who travelled around the world and experienced so many exotic adventures as a young man. Not so long ago three of his old shipmates from the Beagle *came to stay for a week-end and Papa worked himself into such a state that he could barely spend ten minutes with them. Afterwards my brother Leonard came upon Papa in the garden and they strolled together across the lawn. To hear him tell it, Papa suddenly broke off all conversation and turned away with a horrid expression that made a strong impression upon Leonard, who later told me, 'There shot through my mind the conviction that he wishes he were no longer alive.'*

20 January 1865

I had hoped to be able to report that our lives had improved at Down House, but alas, this is not to be. Our home resembles a sanitarium. Papa has resumed the water-treatment on his own, even going so far as to use the outdoor hut that John Lewis made some fifteen years ago. It is an ingenious contraption out by the well, with a little rooftop steeple that holds four or five gallons of water. Papa undresses inside and pulls a little rope to send the water rushing down upon him with great force. Horace and I sometimes station ourselves outside and we hear such gasps and groans that one would think the person inside was dying. We wait five minutes and then Papa rushes out fully dressed again but looking frozen and so miserable that one of us usually consents to accompany him on his rounds along the Sandwalk, his path for thinking, built specially at the end of the garden behind our property.

Two days ago, I had a row with Papa. I happened to be in his study and I picked up his cosh from its usual place on the mantelpiece. It is little more than a foot-long coil of wire with metal knobs on either end, heavy enough to serve as a useful tool or to fend off an animal, should it come to that. He keeps it as a souvenir of his time in South America since he used to carry it in his belt during his excursions there. Suddenly Papa walked in, and seeing me holding the implement, proceeded to berate me, saying he had told me never to touch it, which I am sure is not the case. He then renewed his accusation that I was 'a petty spy', which struck me as very hurtful and totally unwarranted. I replaced the cosh and held my tongue until I brushed past him to the doorway, whereupon I whirled around and said something wicked, namely, that I thought he was unreasonable and spiteful. Etty heard me and told Mamma, who said I must apologise or do without dinner and I chose the latter, remaining in my room and missing the nightly gathering in the drawing-room. I tried to read this new book by the mathematician, Alice's Adventures in Wonderland, but was so upset I could not at first concentrate on the words, although later I found myself succumbing to its magical spell. Sometimes I feel like Alice: I find myself at odds with this world, as if I too had fallen down a rabbit-hole. At certain moments I believe I am twenty-foot tall and can see things that elude everyone else, and at other moments I fear I am no bigger than a mouse and must run about to avoid being stepped upon.

22 January 1865

I once overheard my father assert that 'a good scientist is a detective on the track of Nature'. I may not be a scientist but, laughable as it sounds, I do think I would make a most excellent detective.

Truth be told, I have been spying, although that is not the word I would choose to describe it. I do so because once my curiosity has been pricked, I cannot help myself. I like nothing better when company is present than to slip into a shadow and make myself inconspicuous in order to overhear what is being said. It is the only way to find out what is going on in the world, and is certainly more interesting than the Edmonton Review *or* The Times. *That was how I learnt about the shocking case of Peter Barratt and James Bradley, who murdered poor little Georgie Burgess; they made him get undressed and beat him with sticks in a brook until he stopped moving. One of the men observed that the two boys were so small their heads could barely be seen over the dock and another said he was pleased they were sentenced to a full five years in a reformatory.*

Best of all are the occasions when the men assemble in the billiards-room, for there is a perfect hiding spot in a corner beside the divan and they become so engrossed in the game that they entirely forget me. In the summer they leave the windows open for air and I sit outside beneath the flower-box of primroses and cowslips. That was where I learnt about the Mutiny in India some years back; Mr Huxley said it all began because the Moors were forced to bite into cartridges that had been greased with pig fat or some such thing which I did not fully understand. Only this week I heard Papa say that the war between the Confederacy and the Northern states in America is causing trouble in Jamaica. He said: 'The niggers are ready to rise up against us.' But Mr Thomas Carlyle was confident that Governor Eyre would deal with them.

It appears that Papa favours the Northern states. I know that he finds slavery an abomination—I have heard him describe arguments he had with Captain FitzRoy on that score—and I am certain he would like to see the institution eliminated from the face of the earth. But I have also heard him speak of Southern Americans as a refined and aristocratic people, close to Englishmen in outlook and sophistication, in contrast to the brash and vulgar Northerners. A Southern victory would mean inexpensive cotton for our manufacturers. When I hear him talk like this I cannot help but think that in his heart he tilts towards the South.

25 January 1865

The thought has occurred to me that I am uncommonly adept at ferreting out the secrets of others. It is simply a gift that has come to me unlooked for, in the same manner that Etty is quick with words or George skilled in calculations.

When we were children, our cousins would visit us on holidays and with our augmented numbers we had the run of Down House. We played at roundabouts, a game in which we sought hiding-places in all the nooks and crannies inside and out, and I was always the first to find others and the last to be discovered. Oftentimes I would lie in my temporary nest for an hour or more, my heart beating like a little bird's, listening to the frustrated shouts of my pursuers as the shadows lengthened into evening. Sometimes I would stay hidden long after the game had been abandoned, turning up in the lighted back doorway to great acclaim.

The key, I discovered, was to cast one's mind into those of the other players; once one divines where they themselves might hide, it is no great feat to find some other place they would never consider. Being a mistress of concealment is not a trick. It is a facility, akin to intuition. I find that if I stop and collect myself and ponder deeply, I can project myself into the mind of someone else and then I can anticipate what that person might think and do.

I myself have a number of secrets, which I would not dare to confess to any living soul. One concerns a son (who shall be nameless) of Sir John Lubbock, whose estate at High Oaks we sometimes visited when I was not yet in full maidenhood—or when I had not yet become unwell, *as Mamma would put it. The two of us would steal off together across the fields to an old walnut-tree that had been struck by lightning, an immense stump rising twenty feet in the air and hollowed out by nature's usage. This we pretended was our dwelling and as we played at man and wife, we indulged ourselves in things that make me blush to think upon. I would permit him, in the act of leaving for his work-place, to plant a kiss upon my cheek, and once or twice we progressed beyond that, though not of course to any extent that would give me cause for repentance. Still, when I see him at church, I am embarrassed. Because Mamma does not believe in the Creed, when the congregation recites it, we turn away from the altar and face them; once or twice I have caught his eyes looking at me in a most provocative way and felt my face burning red. He may be highborn, but he is far from a gentleman to subject me to such treatment; although, as long as I am being truthful, I admit that I do not totally disavow the way it makes me feel.*

28 January 1865

Mamma and I took a long walk this morning because the weather is unseasonably warm for the height of winter. Despite the auspicious day I sensed that she had something pressing upon her that she wanted to tell me, and as we approached the wooded area to the south, she began in a soft voice. She said that Papa's health was better but still not as much improved as she had hoped. And then she said she felt I was aggravating his condition by my behaviour, which she described as 'disrespectful'. She suggested that I look to Etty for 'lessons in deportment', noting that my sister never gives cause for concern. Quite the opposite; she said that Etty is a joy to Papa and even supports him in his work by proofreading his manuscripts.

I am afraid my reaction was peevish. I replied that I thought there were any number of areas in which Henrietta could take instruction from me. I pointed in particular to the area of physical well-being, for Etty is just like Papa and falls prey to all manner of illnesses. She is the acorn that falls close to the oak. Papa sent her away to Moor Park for the water-treatment and ever since her relapse at Eastbourne she has been an invalid herself, and that has made her the centre of attention. Papa coddles her and visits her bedroom to enquire about her health with solicitousness written all over his face. As a result, I said, Etty received numerous special privileges. At this my mother grew angry and asked me to cite an example. I replied that we went to Torquay so that she might take the sea air and that she was given a special bed-carriage for the journey, and also that she was permitted to go sea-bathing in the horse-drawn machine like all the ladies of fashion, to which my mother replied: 'You should be grateful that you are sound in body and not begrudge your sister treatments that might cure her or alleviate her suffering.' At that I fell silent.

I know Mamma and Papa prefer Etty to me. They are always telling her how pretty she is and how becoming such and such a dress is on her and what a fine wife she will be one day and they never pay such compliments to me. When I was a child they looked upon me as unladylike because I loved to run fast and ride down the stairs standing up on the sliding-board and because I was able to climb out the nursery-window on to the mulberry-tree. Mamma said that was the way boys behaved. It was true that sometimes when we opened the old trunk to play 'dress-up', Etty would don Mamma's pearls and long dresses and I would favour the costumes of buccaneers and explorers. But I was not any less of a girl for all of that, and in any case I was not offered the advantages that my brothers were, such as going to Clapham School, but instead had to receive my schooling at home. So it is obvious to me that I got the worse of both ways, though I don't confess this to anyone for fear of seeming to think too much about myself.

Close to the end of our walk, as we were nearing the river-bank, I spotted a large beetle scurrying under a log, and for a moment I thought of pursuing it and bringing it home to Papa. When I was young I was better at capturing grubs and insects than Etty or even than any of my five brothers. As I think about it now I could almost weep, recollecting the look in Papa's eyes when I would open my small dirty hand to present him with a special find and how he would hug me and call me his huntress Diana. I think they were the happiest moments of my whole childhood.

CHAPTER 7

On the day the *Beagle* finally set sail, Charles and Captain FitzRoy spent the afternoon at a tavern, gorging themselves on mutton and champagne. Afterward they rowed out past the breakwater to join the ship. As she rose up before them, they got a good view of her moving in stately fashion down the Channel, fully rigged, with her sails billowing in a hearty breeze. Charles was astounded at his feelings: the sight did not stir him. Where was the exhilaration he had expected? Here he was, after months of endless delays and abortive runs out of the harbor, finally launched on his great adventure, and he felt dread. He shivered with a premonition—somehow, he feared, it was all going to take an awful turn and end in catastrophe.

His foreboding soon took a human form. As he stepped from the boat and placed one foot on the rope ladder, he glanced up and saw a familiar face looking down at him with an air of distaste. He stiffened. McCormick! The last person he wanted to see.

What cruel twist of fate had placed Robert McCormick on the very same vessel? He had heard that the *Beagle* was to carry a surgeon by that name but had hoped it was not the McCormick he had known at Edinburgh. The man had been a petty, ambitious little drudge. The two took the same geology course, which everyone in Charles's circle detested for being as dry as the dust that was exhibited to the students in small glass bottles. But McCormick, the kind of man who mistook information for knowledge, actually enjoyed it and took voluminous notes. Charles had blackballed him from joining a learned society and McCormick had taken the rejection badly. The enmity was reciprocal.

By the time Charles clambered on board, McCormick was gone. Charles walked unsteadily toward his cabin on the poop deck. He passed the seventeen-year-old midshipman he was to share it with, Philip Gidley King, whose father had captained the *Beagle*'s companion ship on her previous voyage.

"Finally we're off," said Charles.

"Aye, that we are," replied the young man, doffing his cap. He was a pleasant enough lad—and proclaimed himself an ardent enthusiast of Lord Byron—but hardly scintillating company.

Across the deck Charles spied the second in command, Lieutenant John Wickham.

"That's a damned mountain of gear you've brought aboard," shouted Wickham, but he said it with a smile.

Charles did not feel as yet close to anyone on the ship, though he felt drawn to Augustus Earle, an artist hired by FitzRoy to record the voyage, and another supernumerary, George James Stebbing, whose job was to service the twenty-two chronometers kept in a cabin all their own, each suspended on gimbals inside a wooden box that was in turn embedded in a container of sawdust.

He did not take to the junior officers, a ragged and unruly bunch. During a boisterous party on shore they had gone out of their way to make Charles feel uncomfortable, using seamen's jargon to talk around him and spooking him with tales of the williwaws off Tierra del Fuego. Afterward Wickham took Charles aside, puffing on his pipe, and explained: "They're good lads, really. They're uncertain as to where you fit in the overall scheme of things. You're not an officer, you're not exactly a passenger. And, if you don't mind me saying so, it doesn't help matters that you mess with the Captain three times a day—and then, of course, there's the fact that you do speak a different brand of the King's English."

Charles entered his ten-foot-by-ten-foot cabin and looked around. In the center was the "great table," which would be used by the surveyors once they reached South America. Above it, on either side, were the hooks for his hammock; the cabin was so snug that lying in it, he could touch the table's top by simply dropping an arm. On the starboard side

were cases for the ship's books, hundreds of them. Along the forward
bulkhead were a washstand, an instrument cabinet, and a chest of drawers. Smack before it, piercing the cabin like a giant tree trunk fallen from
the sky, was the thick oak mizzenmast.

There was a knock on the door. He opened it and was surprised to
find McCormick there, a bottle of rum tucked under his arm.

"I say," said McCormick. "I thought I'd extend the traditional welcome at sea."

They shook hands, a touch awkwardly, and Charles brought out
two glasses, which McCormick promptly filled. They sat down and
toasted each other, and McCormick filled them again.

"So, here's to a good voyage," he said. "I see that the crew appears to
be sober—that's an unlooked-for blessing."

"Yes. Capital."

Three times over the previous five weeks the *Beagle* had set out, only
to be forced back by wintry gales. On the one perfect morning for
sailing—the day after Christmas—the crew had been too incapacitated
from their drunkenness of the day before to stir.

Charles finished his rum, set his glass on the table, and looked at the
man. He was about ten years older, bony and wiry, with an elongated
skull. His face was given to a nervous smile that showed his sharp white
teeth, offset by a black goatee. Charles wondered if FitzRoy had applied
his phrenology test.

McCormick seemed to be trying to make conversation.

"I could not decide whether my cabin should be painted French
Grey or a dead white. I eventually chose the white—more soothing,
don't you think?" He glanced around. "I see the Captain has made this
very luxurious," he said with a hint of petulance. "All done up in finest
mahogany. He made a lot of changes in the ship, improved things considerably. He's raised the deck and added skylights and bull's-eyes."

McCormick slapped the mizzenmast. "And this. He added this."

"So I understand," replied Charles, sipping his rum now. "She's
a compact little brig, isn't she? Snug and well fitted."

"Actually, she's not a brig. The mizzenmast changes that. She's a
bark. A brig has two masts; both are square-rigged and the mainmast
has a fore-and-aft sail. A bark has three masts and the mizzenmast carries the fore-and-aft sail."

"I see."

McCormick was as pedantic as ever.

"Yet I did hear one seaman make a certain reference to a 'coffin brig,' " Charles persisted.

"Yes, well, the appellation is incorrect but the reputation is well deserved. They do tend to sink in rough seas. Very deep-waisted, you see, so that the waves swamp her, especially if the gunwales are closed."

"Let's hope that doesn't happen," said Charles. He was beginning to feel queasy from the rum.

"I dare say."

McCormick topped up his glass though Charles tried to wave him off.

"I quite envy you these accommodations," the surgeon said. "I say, you don't look too well."

Charles didn't feel too well. He tasted a splash of digestive acid in the back of his throat, and his stomach seemed to rise and fall with the ship's movement. A nausea took hold of his gut and spread out in waves through his whole system.

Abruptly, he leapt to his feet, overturning the chair and roughly pushing McCormick to one side. He leaned over the washbasin and retched and retched again, watching bits of mutton and other remnants of his last meal swilling in the bowl. Sweating profusely and groaning, he grabbed the mizzenmast for dear life, hugging it like a man adrift in a squall.

"Perhaps I'd better leave," said McCormick. Charles saw him out of the corner of a teary eye, hurrying away, holding the half-empty bottle by the neck.

Somehow, Charles managed to hang his hammock, pulling out the top drawer of the chest to make room for his feet, as FitzRoy had advised. With a sigh, he got in, again following the Captain's instructions—first sitting on the center and then swiveling to one side to swing up his legs. Lying horizontal, he could almost convince himself he felt somewhat better.

Five minutes later, King bounded in, all youthful enthusiasm. He recounted the day's goings-on outside.

"By the by," he said, sniffing the air and zeroing in on the washstand. "Something in here smells horrid."

King spied the two glasses, picked one up, and sniffed it.

"I say, you haven't been drinking rum, have you? That's the worst thing for you—at least until you get broke in. If that doesn't put you under, nothing will. Only a fool or a villain drinks rum the first day out."

King spotted the vomit in the washbasin and, good lad that he was, washed it out with a rag.

That evening, though still ill, Charles ventured out on deck. The air was cold and he felt so poorly he stayed for only a few minutes. The moon was out big and full, lighting the water in yellow ripples. He watched the luminous clouds racing by. Off in the distance he spotted the Eddystone Lighthouse and saw it slip away—the last remnant of his beloved England—before going to bed with a heavy heart.

The next morning, as the *Beagle* pitched and heaved toward the Bay of Biscay, Charles lay in his hammock and tried with brute willpower to quell his queasiness. He feared it was not a passing ailment. It was what had worried him all along—the scourge of seasickness—and now that it had befallen him, he couldn't see how he would be rid of it.

The misery began in his stomach and fanned outward like some malevolent creature—an octopus, perhaps, unfurling its tentacles, or a microscopic organism sending its minute eggs through his bloodstream, invading his organs and needling his brain.

He knew the symptoms well. He had fretted about them endlessly during the wait for the ship to come out of dry-dock at Plymouth, so much so that his mouth had broken out in sores and he had experienced such strong palpitations that he was convinced he was having a heart attack.

It was hardly the glorious departure he had envisioned.

He gave himself a bolstering talk. True, things had gotten off to an inauspicious start, but they would undoubtedly improve. He would have the opportunity to catch some specimens and throw himself into his work—that was what he had come for, after all. Beyond that, the ship would be docking at exotic tropical ports, where he would examine plants and animals the like of which were rarely seen. And come to think of it, Tenerife was to be the first port of call, the very place that he and Henslow had dreamt of exploring as they pored over von Humboldt's book of adventures. Dear old Henslow—he told himself he must be sure to take exacting notes and write him all about it.

Suddenly Charles felt the ship rolling in a new, vertiginous way. The cabin seemed to drop a full ten feet before it was caught in a sling and swung back upward. He felt like a bowler's ball rounding in the arc of delivery. At the top of the arc the ship struck another wave and he felt a body-wracking thud—the ball landing on the green. He vomited again and lay on the floor beneath the washstand for a full ten minutes.

Finally he rose and steadied the hammock with one hand and lay down again. No sooner had he settled back than he heard a commotion from the deck outside, a scuffling and then an ungodly sound. It was a rippling crack the likes of which he had never before heard, followed by a full-throated shriek. Five seconds later came another crack and another yell and then again another, until the yells became sobs trailing off into a miserable childlike whimpering. Then it started all over again.

At that moment the door opened and King walked in. Charles struggled to sit up.

"What in Heaven's name is going on?" he demanded.

"Flogging," said the young man. "Four of the crew, punished for their Christmas revelries. The old cat-o'-nine-tails. Captain's orders."

Charles was aghast. "How many lashes have been ordered?" he asked.

"All different. Most get twenty-five for drunkenness and quarreling. The carpenter's man gets thirty-four for breaking his leave. Davis, he gets thirty-one for neglect of duty. And old Phipps, he's really begging for it—forty-four for breaking leave, drunkenness, and insolence. Better hurry if you want to watch."

Charles sunk back in his hammock, his head reeling and his stomach trembling. Despondency seized him. What kind of a rolling torment was this ship? What kind of world had he signed on for?

Away from his beloved Shropshire, the flower-filled paradise of meadows and birds, he had toppled into a nightmarish realm of blood and violence, like one of Milton's angels who has been cast out of Heaven and, circling ever downward, follows Lucifer in the terrible fall.

That evening Charles left his cabin again. It was early but already dark because of a fog that refused to dissipate. Visibility was poor. Still, walking past the long whaleboat overturned upon skids, he caught sight of a distant figure lurking beside the forecastle. It was McCormick.

Steadying himself against the whaleboat—he had not begun to acquire the rolling gait of a seaman—Charles walked the length of the ship. McCormick had entered the forecastle and was bending over with a furtive air, apparently examining the locker that had been set aside by FitzRoy for Darwin's specimens.

By the lord Harry, Charles thought, the man is spying on me!

He moved closer, cleared his throat loudly, and turned to look out to sea. McCormick gave a start, quickly straightened up, grasping the railing tightly. He was silent for a moment, clearly flustered, and then spoke in a burst.

"I say, it does take a time to learn this ship in all her particulars. I've been touring incessantly and I still don't have it all down."

Charles nodded and looked at him with suspicion.

"Are you feeling better?" McCormick asked.

"Somewhat," lied Darwin.

"Amazing how horrible seasickness can make one feel."

"Yes, isn't it?"

McCormick was quiet for a moment, then asked out of the blue: "Has your family known the FitzRoys long?"

"No, we are unacquainted."

"I see. I thought perhaps there was a connection." His voice took on a wheedling tone.

The two peered out into the fog and didn't speak for a full minute.

McCormick cleared his throat and gave a nervous smile. "I think perhaps it might be best to bring up a matter now, lest it cause some disagreeable misunderstanding later," he said. "As you undoubtedly know, I am present here in the capacity of ship's surgeon. And as such, *I* am the person officially designated to exercise the duties of ship's naturalist. Now, I understand that you have certain interests, proclivities, what have you, that tend to the same direction, that is, in the realm of natural sciences—"

"Yes, most certainly true."

"—and so I think it would be advantageous, in the interests of all concerned, for the sake of harmony, for the higher good of the ship's mission—"

"Come, come, man. Get to the point."

"The point, as you put it, is this: I would like you to recognize that I bear primary responsibility for the collecting, classifying, and shipping of all specimens. The Government pays for me to do so, although naturally I would be more than happy to have you assist me—"

"Assist you! You must be daft! I would no more assist you and give up my right to collecting than I would marry the Devil."

McCormick was taken aback.

"You can hardly expect me to relinquish my claim," he said. "There's been an exchange of letters. As surgeon I am entitled to make a collection at the disposal of the Government."

"Then, sir, we shall simply go our separate ways. We shall each of us collect on our own and do the best we can. And we shall try our utmost to maintain civil discourse in the ship's company."

McCormick drew himself up to his full height—though he was still a full head shorter than Charles—and glanced at his companion.

"Very well. I do hope you realize my overture was well intentioned. It sprang from a sincere desire to avoid conflict. I would not want the sort of unpleasantness that characterized your relationship with Dr. Grant to re-occur on board here. This is a small ship, after all."

Charles, still gripping the railing, was fuming—the nerve of the man, bringing up that mortifying episode. At Edinburgh, as a protégé of the eminent biologist Robert Grant, Charles had made a small but thrilling discovery—the means by which a seaweed-dwelling zoophyte called *Flustra* reproduced itself—only to be silenced by his mentor, who subsequently published a paper on it. Bested by a jealous scientific rival, Charles had vowed never to let it happen again.

McCormick turned on his heel and hurried away.

If he believes for one single moment that I am going to roll over like a whipped dog a second time, he will find that he is sorely mistaken, Charles thought, wending his way back on unsteady legs to his cabin.

. . .

The following day, Charles was invited to dine in the Captain's cabin, and though hardly in any condition to eat, he accepted, for he was conscious of his duty to provide distraction for FitzRoy.

He was surprised to find that the cabin was smaller than his own, though it was furnished more elegantly with a sofa in addition to a real bunk, a small writing desk, and a skylight.

A table was set for two on port side, complete with a bottle of wine chilling in a silver bucket of cold seawater.

FitzRoy was cordial, gesturing to Charles to sit down and pouring him a glass that Charles was loath to drink. As they paused a moment in a silent toast, the Captain examined him with narrowed eyes, and Charles had the unnerving thought that he was mentally measuring him against the trials that lay ahead and wondering if he would be found wanting.

"I ask myself if you fully understand," FitzRoy put in bluntly, "the need for flogging on board a ship. I venture to say you were shocked by yesterday's exhibition."

Charles, again astounded at FitzRoy's ability to peer into his soul, allowed as how he had been.

"Well, I make no apologies for it. Personally, I abhor corporal punishment, but there are too many coarse natures that cannot be restrained without it, especially among the lower sorts. It is, I regret to say, an indispensable tool of leadership if we are to perform our duties smartly."

"But is there no other method of discipline at hand? Could you not find some other means of enforcing your wishes and commanding the respect of your crew?"

"Ha! You will find, my good sir, that indulgence and coddling do not succeed at sea. There are no Whigs on board this ship, other than yourself, and during a storm I dare say you are apt to find your own sensibilities shifting rapidly towards my determined position."

FitzRoy gave a half smile to suggest that the topic was closed, though with no hard feelings on his side.

Charles was continually confounded by FitzRoy's behavior. No question that the Captain gave him special consideration and had taken him under his wing. He was continually looking out for Charles's comfort, pressing books upon him, and telling him not to worry—if the going got too rough, Charles could always put ashore at the next port. *I'd rather die than undergo the humiliation of returning to England,* Charles told himself.

At other times, the Captain appeared to bore in on a softness in Charles, as if to root it out. He made clear that he expected manliness and stoicism in the face of hardship—he did not care to hear complaints about seasickness, for one thing—and he demanded obedience. Charles tried hard to please him; the Captain was so widely read, so worldly, and so confident in all his dealings.

"I say," said Charles, switching the topic, "have you read Lyell's *Principles of Geology*?"

"I most certainly have," boomed FitzRoy. "A capital book. The second volume is due out in some months and I've ordered that it be sent to us in Buenos Aires."

Charles looked across the table at him. Even after all these weeks, FitzRoy remained an enigma. Some moments, he was filled with bonhomie and an intense, boundless energy. At others, he gave in to a violent temper. The outward show of humor could fade in an instant with a cold look that seized his eyes even as his smile lingered.

Just that morning Charles had heard one officer ask another, with a meaningful wink: "Did you have *hot coffee* this morning?" Later King had told him it was a code for the Captain's anger, which was most noticeable in the mornings, when he would prowl the deck looking for a tail of rope out of place or a knot poorly tied.

Charles himself had witnessed FitzRoy's mercurial temper. During a shopping excursion in Plymouth, furious that a shopkeeper refused to exchange a piece of crockery, he had baited the man unmercifully, requesting the price of a full set of china and then abruptly canceling the fictitious purchase out of spite. On the pavement, seized by a pang of conscience whose onset was equally mysterious, he apologized to Charles. More than once, Charles had recalled Henslow's warning that the man was laboring under the curse of suicidal melancholia.

Charles ate slowly and tried artfully to disguise his poor appetite by spreading bits of the overboiled preserved beef around his plate and hiding some under the blade of his resting knife. He left his soup untouched.

He sensed that FitzRoy was feeling contrite over the lecture he had delivered with such pomposity. In a gentle tone the Captain asked: "Putting to one side matters of crime and punishment, are the accommodations to your liking and does the voyage meet with your expectations so far?"

"Most assuredly," replied Charles. "Although . . ." His voice trailed off.

"Yes? Tell me," put in FitzRoy quickly.

"There is one issue that I feel I must reluctantly bring to your attention."

"Please do so at once."

"There is on board a ship's surgeon, a certain Mr. McCormick, with whom in fact I had the privilege—if that's the proper word—of being acquainted some years back."

"Yes, I know the man. Indeed, I chose him for the voyage. What of him?"

"He seems to be under the impression that he alone has the right to collect specimens. Since that—as you well know—is my singular passion, I fear that our pursuits may come to cross purposes."

FitzRoy threw down his serviette and grabbed Charles by the wrist.

"Let me set your mind to rest on that score. As long as I am Captain of this ship, by Jupiter, you shall have absolute priority in the matter. Say the word, and I shall shut the man down entirely."

"No, no, thank you very much. That's not necessary. I'm sure there is some collecting that he might perform that is quite harmless, provided it is clear that I bear the official title of the *Beagle*'s naturalist and that I alone am recognized as responsible for the duties of that office."

"Ha! Say no more! You have my word as a gentleman—it shall be so! And whatever you collect shall be happily sent to whomsoever you designate, at His Majesty's expense." In his exuberance, FitzRoy added: "Quantity shall be no object."

Charles was overwhelmed by the man's generosity. How wrong he had been to question his steadfastness! What a capital fellow he was!

Both men were embarrassed by the emotions engendered by such sudden accord, and FitzRoy changed the subject.

"I suppose I am something of a naturalist in reverse," said FitzRoy. "As you know—for we have discussed the matter—the *Beagle* is carrying specimens of my own, three of them, though it must be acknowledged that far from collecting them, I am returning them to their natural state."

"Most certainly," said Charles, though it made him uncomfortable to hear human beings referred to in this manner. Indeed, he had been thinking of the three savages from Tierra del Fuego since coming aboard. He had glimpsed them only once, in Plymouth, when they arrived by steam packet and were whisked off to Weakley's Hotel. What a strange sight they presented, three dark-skinned figures with broad faces, all done up in English finery complete with black umbrellas. Hustling behind them was the missionary who had volunteered to run the station at the bottom of the world, Richard Matthews, a mere teenager with long hair, aglow with the Lord's work, who kept his Bible under his raincoat lest it get wet.

As Charles excused himself with a bow and made his way back to his cabin, he thought, with a mental shrug, that on balance the Captain's good traits far outweighed the bad. But a voice within told him to remain on guard.

Two days later, Charles had his first encounter with Jemmy Button, the fifteen-year-old Fuegian who was most outgoing and most popular with the crew. Swinging in his sick berth, miserable as ever, Charles had fallen into a deep sleep. He awoke abruptly when he felt a finger tracing a line across his feverish forehead.

He could scarcely believe his eyes. There, no more than a foot away, was a most strange apparition, a face dark as pitch, with a spatulate nose and wide-set eyes, staring down at him. Slowly Jemmy withdrew his finger and stepped back. Charles looked at him. He was wearing a black topcoat, a double-breasted waistcoat, long trousers, polished boots, and a white shirt whose high collar was held in place by a black tie: he was dressed up like a perfect Englishman.

Jemmy's face collapsed in a twisted grin, which Charles soon realized was meant to be a look of pity.

The savage opened his mouth. The stentorian words came out slowly and with feeling: "Poor, poor fellow!" he intoned happily.

CHAPTER 8

Hugh couldn't believe his luck. The journal had fallen into his hands like a gift, a ripe fruit tossed down by the gods. It had taken him a while to realize what it was—rather stupidly, he thought a moment later. He had stared at the writing. For a second the thought struck him that perhaps it belonged to someone at the publishing house, that an editor or a researcher had come along and thoughtlessly scribbled in it. But the neat writing was clearly ancient. He closed the journal to examine the cover. It appeared innocuous, a simple account book. In the lower right-hand corner the same black pen had scrawled the number 1 and circled it.

Opening it again, he read the first paragraph, then a full page—it spoke of "Down House" and "Papa's fame"—and he was struck by a revelation, a *coup de foudre,* like a door suddenly flung open, actually, a series of revelations and opening doors: This was dated 1865 . . . It was authentic! . . . It was a journal kept by one of Darwin's children!

He read on. *Holy shit*—the language, the descriptions, the names, they all appeared genuine. He examined the penmanship: a rounded handwriting, elegant and feminine. The author was a woman—she spoke of wearing a crinoline and of her sister, Etty. He thought for a while and then guessed the author's identity: Elizabeth Darwin, or Lizzie, Darwin's second daughter. It had to be hers. What was known of her? Hugh searched his memory—his recent reading had provided scant information. She was the other daughter, the one no one quite remembered. The phrase "lost to history" popped into his mind. Let's see. Darwin fathered ten children (for someone so sick, Hugh mused, the old man did okay). But three of them died young, including of course the ten-year-old Annie, whose death broke her father's heart.

In his excitement the other names came to him in a jumble—William and George, Francis and Leonard, another boy whose name he could not recall, and Henrietta, the beloved one, everyone's favorite. It was Etty who read her father's manuscripts and edited them and who imitated him in his perpetual illnesses. She was the perfect woman of her time, even going so far as to achieve a Victorian lady's highest aspiration, namely, marriage. But Lizzie—she got lost in the shuffle. What happened to her? Did she ever marry?

Hugh was captivated by Lizzie's voice. He admired the subterfuge of hiding her journal in plain sight, just like *The Purloined Letter*. The ruse had worked its magic for—how long? he did the math quickly, rounding off—some 140 years. And just think, it had been lying there unread all those years, and he was the first person to crack it open!

He read on. From time to time he glanced at his minder sitting primly at the desk beneath the French window. She seemed to be taking pains to ignore him, like a guard in a museum gallery who doesn't mean to suggest that you're capable of actually stealing the Renoir. But he *was* capable; he knew that. He was already joining in Lizzie's spirit of subterfuge, occasionally picking up papers and shuffling them around nonchalantly. He began to rationalize—any publisher that would burn Byron's memoirs was pusillanimous to begin with and didn't deserve this treasure. He debated: Should he steal the damned thing or not? Perhaps he should just borrow it—that was the thing to do. He could always come up with a way to return it, maybe say it got mixed among his papers.

A phone rang, startling him. The woman answered it and spoke in low tones, then turned to Hugh and said: "I'm terribly sorry, but we're closing early today because of the move." He had more entries to read. "You have only five minutes more, I'm afraid."

Five minutes was all he needed. He rearranged his papers, then placed a stack of them on the table and, sitting behind it, raised his shirt and slipped the journal under it, wedging it firmly in place with his belt. He casually jotted down some more notes, gathered up his things, smiled distantly at the woman, thanked her, and walked down the creaking wooden staircase and out the front door. As he stepped into the cool London air, he felt as if he had just walked out of the Tower of London with the Crown Jewels.

With only minutes to spare, Hugh arrived at King's Cross, leapt from the cab, and ran to catch the train to Cambridge. He climbed into a second-class coach and fell into a window seat just as the train departed. Outside, stanchions glided by at a sluggish pace, then wooden sheds and coal piles and the grimy back facades of railroad flats. It was late afternoon but already darkening.

He was too preoccupied to notice much of anything. Other passengers were seated near him, an almost felt presence in his peripheral vision, but he ignored them. He switched his backpack to his lap and patted the canvas—he could feel the journal inside, its distinctive thick cover with rounded edges—and again the thrill washed over him, a tingling of excitement.

Staring into the gathering darkness of the train window, he was vaguely aware of dim objects whizzing by outside and half images reflected from the carriage interior. He paused to take stock. He knew the excitement the journal aroused in him was not entirely pure, that it had a darker side. For the thought kept creeping in that this discovery could launch his career. It might make big waves among Darwin scholars. Clearly, it wouldn't prompt a radically new view—the man's eccentricities and illnesses were legendary—but this was an account from within his own family. He wondered just how accurate it was. Yes, it sketched the familiar outlines of Darwin as a paterfamilias. But this portrait was more complicated, more nuanced—and not altogether flattering. Lizzie seemed to suggest that the old man buried himself in his family as some sort of refuge. His hypochondria could be triggered by the slightest social interaction and it turned the whole household upside down—or rather, settled over it like a depressive fog. And Darwin's temper and his melancholy seemed formidable; what to make of that business with the cosh? Or the mirror to spy on visitors? Or Leonard's remark that Darwin looked so distraught after the visit from his old shipmates? Lizzie certainly put a spin on things. She practically conjured up the vision of Robert Louis Stevenson's lodger awaiting the dreaded tap of Long John Silver's wooden leg.

Well, as the saying goes, no man is a hero to his valet. He recalled the retort—that it is the *valet* who is incapable of recognizing the hero.

He tried to picture Lizzie, young, not yet twenty, sitting in a high-collared dress, composing her journal entries by the cold winter light coming in through a window. Or perhaps leaning back in bed in a long cotton nightgown while a candle flickered shadows upon the wall. He imagined her straining to find the words to express the tumult of her feelings. Her eyes burned bright with intelligence—at that moment, he could actually *see* her and see her eyes staring back at him. He gave a slight gasp, shook off the daydream, but her eyes were still there—*for real*—reflected in the train's dark window. Startled, he began to turn, felt a hand on his arm.

"I was wondering when you'd notice me," Beth said.

He couldn't believe it. She was smiling, Sphinx-like.

"Beth. My God. What are you doing here?"

"On my way to Cambridge. And you?"

"The same." He was dumbfounded. "How long have you been here?"

"A little longer than you. You passed right by me to sit down. I'd say you were in some kind of trance."

"Sorry. Yes. I don't know. I was thinking."

"I could see that. I almost didn't recognize you. What happened to your beard?"

"I shaved it."

"New look for a new life?"

"Yeah." He gave an ironic half smile. "I'm starting with the little things—life—and moving on to the big stuff, like haircuts."

"I see." She examined him closely. "Well, you don't look like a hermit anymore. Much more mainstream. Basically, you look good."

"So do you."

She *was* looking good—blue jeans, black scoop-neck sweater, her hair up. He shook his head.

"It's amazing—to run into you like this," he said.

"I know. Last time I saw you, from the panga, you were just a tiny figure on an island in the middle of nowhere."

"And you—you were disappearing over the horizon." He caught himself. "God, I'm sorry. I forgot about your mother, and the funeral. I hope . . . all that wasn't too hard on you."

"It was hard, actually, more than I would have thought. It was so totally unexpected." She looked past him, out the window. "It turned out she had had heart problems before, but she kept it from us."

"I'm sorry."

She looked back at him. "You never really believe a parent is going to die—that's trite but true. And we were very close."

She said it matter-of-factly, without a trace of self-pity. He didn't know how to reply. Only gradually was he recovering from the shock of seeing her.

"You learn a lot about yourself at a time like that," she continued. "The scales fall off your eyes. All kinds of things come out of the closet."

"Like what?"

"Oh, I don't know. Feelings. Unresolved conflicts. Things you never even knew existed. You must have felt that."

"Yes," he said. Then he switched the subject. "And your father—how is he taking it?"

"Not well. They'd been married thirty-seven years. Met in college, sophomore year. He was stunned at first, but now that the shock is over his pain is even worse—all the little daily reminders that she's no longer there. I think he still can't quite believe it. He can't bring himself to take her message off the answering machine. I'm going to have to figure out how to spend a lot of time near him in the future."

"And was that a relative who called? On the island?"

"Yes. My brother, Ned. He's five years younger. He lives in California, so he's not much help. That's typical." She shrugged. "And you—tell me about you. When did you leave Sin Nombre?"

"Nearly three weeks ago now. I just got fed up. After you two left, it wasn't the same . . ."

"You missed the crowds."

"No, but I missed something."

She smiled, almost sadly, he thought.

"And the project? Who's running it?"

"A couple came, nice enough, I guess. Serious types."

"And you were the odd man out, once again?"

"Sort of. Speaking of which, how is Nigel? What's he doing?"

"I don't really know."

"You don't?"

"We stopped seeing each other."

His heart rose up. "What happened?"

"Hard to say, really. He insisted on coming to the funeral, even though I didn't want him to. My ex-husband came too, so there was a certain amount of . . . strain. I remember just looking at the two of them, so conspicuously ignoring each other, and thinking I wish I were rid of both of them. So when we got back, we went our separate ways. I expect he's got someone new by now. The gift of gab gets them every time."

"I'm glad to hear it. I didn't think he was—up to you."

She laughed, then said: "Unlike you, for example."

"Yes. Unlike me."

She smiled as the train pulled into a station. They had to stand to let an elderly woman pass. Hugh helped her with her suitcase, carrying it outside to the platform, and when he returned, Beth had her feet propped on the seat across from her, resting on an *Evening Standard*.

"So, what are you doing in Cambridge?" he asked.

"Research," she replied. "And you?"

"The same—research."

He was struck by the realization that something had changed: he had found it easy on the island to confide in her, but now a screen went up between them. He felt as if he were playing chess—their pawns just blocked one another.

"What kind of research?" she asked. "Is it about Darwin?"

"Uh-huh. And you?"

"Darwin."

"I see," he said. "Is it—biographical or what?"

"Sort of. I can't really say yet. And you?"

"The same."

They fell silent, pondering the chessboard. Through the backpack, he felt the journal. If she only knew what he had there . . . but obviously he couldn't tell her, or anyone else for that matter. What was she up to?

After a minute or two, he said, "You know, Nigel once told me he thought you were related to Darwin."

She gave him a sharp look.

"Now, why would he say that?"

"I have no idea. But is it true? Are you?"

"Don't believe everything you hear," she said in a tone that ended the matter.

Checkmate.

They talked until the train reached Cambridge. On the platform, he saw that it was starting to drizzle lightly.

"So . . . You want to get a drink?" she asked.

He looked at his watch. The library was still open for another hour and he was also eager to read more of the journal. "I do, but . . ."

She finished his sentence for him: "You've got something to do."

"Yes. I'm really sorry."

"Stop saying you're sorry so much."

"How about tomorrow?" he asked.

"Okay. My schedule is nothing if not flexible—embarrassingly so."

They fixed a time and place—the Prince Regent at seven—and shared a cab. Inside, they exchanged addresses and phone numbers; she wrote his on the back of an envelope. She was staying with a friend on Norfolk Street, not too far from his rooming house, and so she dropped him off, refusing money for the fare. Through the window, she sized up his place. "Not fancy," she said, "but I like the name: Twenty Windows. Did you count them?"

"Of course."

"See you tomorrow."

Hugh dropped the knapsack off in his room, then turned around and left for the library. He followed the narrow side streets with their ungainly brown brick houses and alleyways. It was raining harder now, but it felt pleasantly cool on his face. At Market Square he entered a Gothic world of spires and ancient arches, turning into the passageway behind the walls of Trinity and crossing the slate-covered bridge across the Cam. The river below was an undulating bright green carpet. Three black swans, their heads bowed, swam through weeping-willow boughs that hung on the far bank. Life suddenly seemed filled with possibilities. It was filled with coincidences and happenstance—you never knew when it might bring you to some crossroads or when you had taken some critical turn, even at the moment you were taking it.

He bounded up the library steps, showed his card, pushed through the turnstile, and mounted the stairs to the Manuscripts Room. Roland was there, shuffling through request forms; he waved hello, then checked his watch and wagged his head in make-believe reproach.

"I need something on Darwin's family life," said Hugh. "What can you recommend? I'm interested in particular in Elizabeth—Lizzie."

"Ah, the mystery retard."

"Why do you say that?"

"I'm only repeating what I hear."

Ten minutes later, Hugh was installed at a corner table, plowing through the half dozen books that Roland provided.

There was little to learn about Lizzie. *Born July 8, 1847. Never married. Died June 8, 1926.* Those were the bare bones of her life. Her father noted, once, that she was given to strange shivers as a child. And Henrietta left behind some lines suggesting that Lizzie was "slow." So that's where the calumny comes from, thought Hugh. He discounted it quickly and almost angrily—Lizzie's own journal belied any such notion. Besides, he knew enough about sibling rivalry to understand that it worked both ways.

One book carried a reference to the curious fact that in 1866 (the year following her journal entries, Hugh noted) she refused confirmation; she turned away from the catechism and told her mother, "I do not feel much heart for it." That same year she announced that henceforth she wanted to be known as "Bessie" instead of "Lizzie." That was curious. Was she acting out of a whim? Or was she experiencing some crisis, some emotional storm that made her want to reinvent herself? And then four years later, just before Henrietta married a man named Litchfield, she seemed to drop out of sight; she went abroad alone and afterward was given short shrift in family chronicles.

Hugh wondered: Just how reliable an observer was she? Was she a Victorian maiden with an overheated imagination? Was she fixated on her father? Jealous of Etty? Some things were clear: she was a rebellious tomboy, hungry for life—but also, by her own account, shy, suspicious, wanting to fade into the background. And a sleuth—what a sleuth! Unaccountably, Hugh suddenly felt protective of her, wanting to side with her against her perfect sister, her uncomprehending mother, and her beloved but autocratic Papa.

She was certainly dead-on about the illnesses that plagued Darwin's later life. He checked the indexes and skimmed the relevant passages: there they all were, the pathetic bouts of nervous exhaustion and nausea, dizziness and headaches, fatigue and insomnia, eczema and anxiety. He had so many symptoms that no single illness explained them all.

Some theorized that he came down with Chagas' disease, contracted from the bite of a benchuca bug in South America, an episode that Darwin described in grisly detail (Hugh made a note: March 26, 1835– *Triatoma infestans*). But the symptoms didn't fit; Darwin did have an incapacitating sickness in Argentina, but that happened before, not after, the famous bite. So most scholars leaned to the theory that his illnesses were psychosomatic in origin. They seemed to involve an amalgam of grief, guilt, and fear, suggesting, said one biographer, Janet Browne, "some deep-seated dread of exposure." But what secret was there in his life? What exposure could he possibly have feared?

Hugh's thoughts were interrupted by Roland.

"Only half an hour to closing."

"Roland, do you have any of Lizzie's letters? Can I see them?"

"I'm afraid not."

"There aren't any?"

"No, there are. They're on the reserve shelf. Someone else has them on call."

"Someone else?"

Roland nodded officiously. "Look, I'm not supposed to say anything. Curators are not supposed to blab about other people's research. What do they say in Vegas? What goes on here, stays here. But the coincidence is just too striking."

"What?"

"For the longest time, nobody's interested in Elizabeth Darwin. And then just a few days ago a young woman comes along and, like you, she wants to know everything about her. She's American too."

"Her name . . . would it be Beth Dulcimer?"

"Ah, so you know her. Or do you know *of* her?"

"I know her."

"Then I do hope you're not rivals. She certainly is attractive."

On the way home, Hugh wondered what Beth could be up to. And why was she so secretive about it? On the other hand, he had to admit, he had not been exactly forthcoming himself. But that was precisely the point: he had something to hide. So what was she hiding?

He stopped off at The Hawks Head, muggy and smoky and loud. As he approached the bar, he noticed a young man seated on a stool who looked a lot like Cal during his Harvard days—the thin back, the dark hair curling just over the collar. Hugh felt the familiar rush of confusion and emptiness and then the long numbing ache.

He brought his beer to a table and ignored a young, sallow blond woman who gave him the eye. He finished a pint, then another. With the alcohol, the ache began to ebb a bit. Relaxed, he let his mind drift back to his days at Andover.

The truth of it was, when he got expelled, he had not been devastated. Quite the contrary: he was secretly pleased, excited; the drama brought everything to a head. He had gotten into the school only on his brother's coattails—Cal had been such a success, they hoped for the same from the younger brother—and, as always, he hadn't quite measured up. But this—this was as good as success in its own way; it made as big a mark, merely upside down. Not for him the easy path. He was a rebel. That morning, he spent a good half hour carving his name into the wooden seat of a bench on campus; he had once heard that Wordsworth did this as a young boy in the Lake District.

"Hugh, Jesus Christ. No, it can't be." When Cal called him in the dorm the next morning to make sure he had not gotten caught, Hugh had to tell him what had happened—that the dorm master had gone looking for him, had smelled alcohol on his breath, and had promptly called the Dean of Students. He was finished. Cal groaned into the receiver, for he was bound to feel responsible. He had come up to Andover to celebrate Hugh's Harvard acceptance and together the two had gone off to a bar. Cal came with him on the train to Connecticut; it was hard to know who was consoling whom. They would confront their father together. Their father did not get particularly angry. But that was worse in a way—he seemed to expect Hugh to fail. The one he was angry at was Cal.

When Hugh left the pub, the rain had stopped. He walked to his rooming house and found a note from his landlady pushed under the door. Bridget had telephoned—he was to call back, no matter how late. He went to the phone in the hall.

"Hugh, thank God."

"What's up?"

"Listen, I've been doing some thinking. We have to meet. I won't take no for an answer."

"Okay. But tell me why."

"I'll tell you when I see you. Noon tomorrow, right? St. James's Park? At the entrance closest to the palace . . . Hugh, are you there? Are you listening?"

"Yes, I'm here."

"So what do you say—will you meet me?"

He paused, only a second.

"I'll be there."

CHAPTER 9

7 February 1865

Mr Alfred Russel Wallace came to Down House today for the week-end and as always his visit precipitated an atmosphere of crisis. Even before our guest arrived, Papa began stammering, as he so often does in Mr Wallace's presence. This is to be expected, I suppose, since Papa responds adversely to the strain of any social situation, and in this instance the awkwardness is compounded by Mr Wallace's rightful claim to be co-discoverer of the theory of natural selection.

As I heard Mr Wallace recount it (on his first visit here three years ago), the theory came to him while he was mapping an invisible boundary between two hostile tribes on the island of Gilolo in the Moluccas. He was stricken with malaria and as he lay feverish on a mat in a palm-lined hut, the idea leapt full-blown into his brain. Influenced by the work of Thomas Malthus, as was Papa, he conjectured that disease, war and famine hold a population in check and of necessity improve the race 'because in every generation the inferior would inevitably be killed off and the superior would remain'.

Mr Wallace is a tall man, somewhat aloof. He gives the impression of not having fully adapted to English society after eight years wandering among the savages of the Moluccas and Papua New Guinea. I see something in him that is as strong as steel. He is enigmatic and arouses some suspicion in me, though why that should be I am at a loss to explain since he has acted only with kindness and deference to Papa and our family. Etty finds him lower class and vulgar in his manners and so of little consequence, but I cannot dispel the notion that he is as swift and cunning as one of his emblematic species that would prevail through sheer instinct to survive.

He and Papa are cordial in their dealings and outwardly correct, but I know that their relationship is not without tension. When Papa first replied to Mr Wallace's letter outlining the theory, he did not receive an answer for the longest time. And when finally it came he was upset, reading it in the privacy of his study and promptly throwing it into the fire-place. I can attest to this myself for I entered shortly afterwards and saw it burning there.

To ease this particular week-end, Papa has invited some other guests, including Mr Lyell and Mr Huxley. Mr Lyell is a bit dreary and talks so softly one must strain to hear him. But I enjoy Mr Huxley, a most entertaining and energetic man who has a quick wit and a lively countenance. He has become Papa's most ardent defender, describing himself as 'Mr Darwin's bulldog' (though I think he more resembles a fox-terrier). I sometimes think of him as a revolutionary general, a Napoleon of natural history, pursuing a military campaign against the Church and scientific establishment under the banner of pure reason.

Our guests arrived at differing times in the morning and Comfort exhausted a number of horses in fetching them. For the afternoon, Mamma packed Etty and Horace and Leonard and me off to Great-Aunt Sarah's house to be out from underfoot. We returned barely in time for dinner. The conversation was animated, with Mr Huxley extolling the virtues of the natural sciences. At one point he declared that to a person uninstructed in its glories, a country stroll is 'a walk through a gallery filled with wonderful works of art, nine-tenths of which have their faces turned to the wall'.

He then described the latest attacks upon Papa's theory and his own efforts at confounding the critics which, to hear him tell it, are unerringly successful. He observed that a new word had come into conversations around London clubs, the word Darwinism. As he said this I could not help but steal a glance in Mr Wallace's direction to see how he would take it, since I sometimes wonder if he is subject to jealousy, but his face was a mask of imperturbability. Shortly afterwards, he proffered a recommendation, which he said would ensure that the theory be fully understood in all its particulars.

He began by saying as follows: 'I venture to suggest that the words natural selection, while accurate from a scientific point of view, tend to be misleading as far as the general public is concerned.'

At this Papa sat bolt upright and demanded: 'By Jove, how so?'

'The phrase opens the door to misinterpretation, since it would seem to imply that these natural forces, which you and I both agree are impersonal

and random, operate as if some higher consciousness were involved. The word selection would seem to indicate that there is in fact some entity or other that performs the selecting.'

'And what term, pray tell, would you use in its place?' inquired Mr Huxley.

'I suggest borrowing a term from Herbert Spencer,' Mr Wallace replied. 'It sums up the theory most concisely and it does so without any reference whatsoever to a higher force.'

'And pray, what term is that?'

' "Survival of the fittest." '

At that, Papa reacted so strongly I thought he would have a stroke. He turned ashen and thrust his hand upon his chest as if his heart would give out. Then he rose shakily, excused himself from the table and retreated to his bedroom for the remainder of the evening.

Mr Huxley, who is nothing if not irreverent, made light of the matter. He said to Mr Wallace over coffee: 'I dare say, if it was a strong reaction you were seeking, you were most successful in provoking one.'

The episode stayed with me for some time. What is there about that particular term, I wondered, that gave Papa such nervous offence?

***

8 February 1865

Today an incident occurred that makes me blush to recall. In early afternoon, with Papa still not stirring from his room and Mr Wallace having departed for the train station, Mr Huxley and Mr Lyell convened in Papa's study. As they had a slightly secretive air about them, as if to indicate that what they were about to discuss was confidential, my curiosity was naturally piqued. And so, after a few minutes, I strolled into the hall and waited outside the door. My intuition was soon rewarded, for I overheard snippets of a conversation that was heated and most intriguing.

Mr Huxley remarked at one point that 'he has become very high-handed indeed', a statement with which Mr Lyell agreed. I was not at all certain to whom they were referring—and feared for a moment that it could be dear Papa—until I heard Mr Lyell continue, saying: 'He should not have been told *that he had been left out of the second edition. That clearly upset him and was a mistake.' This made clear that the reference was to Mr Wallace, for in the past I had heard someone observe that Papa had neglected to mention his competitor in this edition of the* Origin *and had been forced to move quickly to rectify the matter. Scientists care a great deal about such things.*

Mr Huxley, speaking as if from deep conviction, then said: 'He is a fox circling our hen-house. He could cause us no end of trouble and hurt our cause.' To which Mr Lyell posed a question: 'What do you suggest we do about it?' A brief silence followed and then came the reply: 'I am not overly concerned for the moment. He has not many friends, nor is he a member of the learned societies—we have seen to that—and he is continually in need of money. That is his great weakness, and if we are crafty, we can play upon it.'

I knew that I was hearing a most interesting conspiracy and scarcely breathed for fear of missing a single word. But just at that moment who should come down the stairs and spy me but Papa. I tried to slip away, although I was certain that he had caught me in the most unladylike posture of eavesdropping. Sure enough, he followed me into the drawing-room and grabbed my wrist, demanding to know what I was about. My protestations of innocence fell upon disbelieving ears—and rightly so, for I had been caught full in the act. Abruptly he turned upon his heels and left the room.

I blushed scarlet and found it impossible to look either gentleman in the eye for the rest of the afternoon, though whether it was for my trespass or their most uncongenial plotting was hard to say. In any case, I was taken aside by Mamma shortly before supper and told that my father was most upset with me and that I would be sent to London for a spell to stay with Uncle Ras so that his anger might cool.

❖

10 February 1865

I must say that my Uncle's London house is one of my favourite places on this earth. All manner of interesting and elegant persons are drawn to his dinner table: Benthamites and Chartists and Catholics, even atheists—in short, free-thinkers of all stripes. The wine flows bounteously, as does the conversation, and unlike Down House, where Papa is given to banishing me from the drawing-room the moment the discussion turns spirited (which is rare enough), here I am permitted to remain as witness to the verbal thrusts and parries.

This evening, Thomas and Jane Carlyle were present, as were Hensleigh and Fanny Wedgwood, and three or four other notables, including Harriet Martineau, whose lively conversation is more diverting than her journalism. Imagine my surprise after the meal was concluded when yet another couple joined the company. It was shocking enough that the two arrived only to partake of coffee and brandy. But I was overcome with embarrassment when I was introduced to Miss Mary Ann Evans and did not at once grasp that I was standing in the presence of a person I most esteem, the author of The Mill on the Floss *and* Silas Marner, *the confusion arising from her adoption of the pseudonym George Eliot. To complete my discomfiture, I next found myself addressing her paramour, George Henry Lewes, who despite the furore surrounding their relationship, struck me as a perfect gentleman. I find Uncle admirable for opening his door to two such personages who so bravely fly in the face of social convention, especially Miss Evans, living openly as she does with a married man.*

No sooner were we all seated than the conversation took a lively turn. Miss Martineau, as is her wont in her writings, attacked slavery as a most 'hideous institution' and avowed that of all peoples, the Americans are the most uncivilised. Uncle Ras—undoubtedly to throw some oil on the fire, since he has rarely evidenced concern for the impoverished—then inquired as to whether her compassion for 'those in shackles' was broad enough to include poor English working men and women. Another gentleman put in that factory workers in the Midlands laboured in conditions of servitude not much removed from those on plantations in the American South.

To this Hensleigh objected in a most unpleasant manner, saying that the depravity of the poor was their own doing and that the problem with Christianity was that it coddled the sinful. Miss Martineau demurred, and quoted from her own research on factory accidents.

All the while, I was formulating a thought on the earlier question and searching for the courage to put it into words. For though I have been privileged to attend Uncle Ras' soirées, I have never before expressed an opinion, following as it were some unspoken etiquette to remain silent, and I wondered whether my Uncle might be displeased at such a breach. Miss Evans noticed my conundrum and kindly leaning over to pat my hand, said to the assembly:

'I venture that Miss Darwin has something to say.' Instantly, all eyes turned upon me. I had no choice but to voice my view, saying that I felt that there was yet another group that found itself 'in the yoke'. 'And what group, pray tell, is that?' said Mr Carlyle. I felt I should hesitate to accept a challenge from such an eminent thinker but found, before I had barely a chance to consider the matter, that I blurted out my answer in a single word: 'Women.'

This met with great merriment around the table, causing me to blush deeply. But Miss Evans came to my rescue and insisted that I had much evidence and reason on my side. The others laughed again, but then she raised her voice most uncharacteristically and declared: 'I have often had the thought—which I am loath to confess and which for that reason weighs heavily upon my bosom—that I would rather have been born a boy than a girl. For no-one can doubt that from every point of view a man's lot is infinitely preferable to a woman's in the England of today.

'Is it not the case,' she said, 'that a woman's property and fortune falls to her husband in the very first minute of marriage? And is it not the case that a woman can be speedily divorced upon the mere accusation of criminal conversation?' (In saying this Miss Evans showed no sign of shame at her own adultery.) 'And once in court, is it not true that she finds herself without legal rights?'

At this point, Harriet Martineau was moved to recall the case of poor Caroline Norton, whose husband beat her for nine years, robbed her income, filed a malicious lawsuit after separation, and refused to allow her to see her three sons.

This led to consideration of the Contagious Diseases Act, which I consider an outrage since it allows for a woman to be apprehended solely for the act of being found close to a military garrison. The men all defended it, saying the only method of putting an end to the horrible epidemic was for women of dubious virtue to undergo mercury treatment.

'Besides,' said Mr Carlyle, 'the measure is not intended for use against ladies such as yourselves. It is aimed solely at those of a lower order.'

His words caused a visible discomfort around the table for his having linked, however obliquely, Miss Evans with fallen women. Mr Lewes, I thought, was going to square off right then and provoke him to fisticuffs (which I would have viewed with a certain relish), but fortunately for our host the moment passed without incident.

Throughout the evening, I felt Miss Evans' grey-blue eyes and soft round *face seeking me out, and I basked in her warm regard. Upon wishing me good-evening, she leant so close I felt a wisp of her hair brush my cheek, and she whispered in my ear that I was a most excellent woman—a credit to my kind, she said—and that I must always hold true to my beliefs.*

I do believe Uncle Ras heard part of this, for after everyone had departed, he fixed me with a curious gaze and said I was a continual mystery to him, a 'veritable Pandora's box'. He followed what I took to be a compliment with harder words, however, though they were not meant harshly, I am sure. He said he wondered why it was that my Papa doted so on Etty when he had another equal treasure close at hand.

❖

13 February 1865

At breakfast this morning Uncle Ras, who is fond of diversions of all sorts, asked me when in my childhood I had been at my happiest. Something about the way he posed the enquiry, seated at the table with a shadow falling across his set face and staring out the window, was saddening, as if he were reflecting upon the loneliness of his bachelor life, but I took the question at its most superficial and tried to give him a proper reply.

I talked warmly of the early years and especially of his visits to Down House, when we children would gather at his heels like a pack of puppies and follow him all the day long. And indeed I do retain fond memories of the amusements he devised, telling us tall tales of outlandish adventures in Africa and India and drawing devils and monkeys and imps with his long, thin fingers. Seeing that my recollections appeared to warm him, I continued in that vein, talking about our trip to London to see the Great Exhibition, though in fact much of that I was told about afterwards, retaining only the dimmest memory of grasping his hand in fear of the towering crowds. I recalled our visits together to the Zoological Gardens, where I was fascinated by the languid hippopotamus, and to Wombwell's Menagerie to see the orang-utan dressed up in a child's clothes.

'Capital,' he replied loudly, though it struck me that his enthusiasm was perhaps over strong and was intended to cover some deeper malaise.

And indeed, something about recollecting my childhood plunged me into a melancholy that I could not shake for the trying. I began thinking of all the bleak times of my now distant youth and found it impossible to reconcile them with other times that I knew to be joyous. What made the recollection so troubling was that I could not for the life of me fathom the reason for any unhappiness, yet I remained convinced that despite all the occasions of joy and even laughter, a blight of some sort lay upon my early years. Upon considering it at length, I drew a connection to Papa's many illnesses and to the pall of sickness and death that seemed to spread over our household like some cauchemar.

14 February 1865

The cause of our distress may have been the death of poor sweet Annie some fourteen years ago. I cannot honestly say that I remember Annie, since I was only four years old at the time of her passing, and yet on occasion I am able to conjure her up—a gentle creature, with ruby lips and golden curls. I am told she never recovered from the scarlet fever, which struck down all of us girls at once, and she suffered terribly, lingering for weeks on end at death's door in Malvern where she was taking the water-treatment. Papa kept vigil by her bedside but did not attend her funeral, which I find odd. All this I know from Aunt Elizabeth, not from my parents, since they never speak of Annie's death, nor indeed of Annie herself.

Indeed, we Darwins have had our fair share of torment from untimely deaths. There was poor Mary, no bigger than a squirrel, who lived not quite one full year, and little Charles Waring, who did not see two years. We pass their tiny headstones every Sunday on the way to church. And then of course there was the passing of Papa's own father, my grandfather Robert, which was so deeply upsetting. To Papa's eternal regret, he arrived too late at Shrewsbury and could not be present at the burial of the man who made him what he is today.

We are like our poor Queen, who lost her beloved Albert four years ago and yet, to hear talk of it, is still unhinged by grief, wearing nothing but black and having his clothes laid out anew each morning.

Though she is not mentioned, Annie is a spectral presence in our house.

Some years back I discovered at the bottom of a large trunk her very own writing-box, and occasionally when I am alone I retrieve it. It is made of a handsome hardwood and inside there is some cream-coloured stationery with crimson borders and matching envelopes, as well as steel pen-nibs with a wooden holder, two goose-quill pens, and a pen-knife with a mother-of-pearl handle; also red sealing-wax and wafers kept in a small box with decorations reading 'Am I Welcome?' and 'Dieu Vous Garde'. The quills still have ink on their tips and I used to hold them and imagine myself as Annie, dipping them pensively as she chose her words in writing to this person or that.

Of all the deaths and illnesses, it was Annie's that rent Papa's heart. For some reason he holds himself to blame, I believe, as if her being called away at the tender age of ten was some kind of retribution. I recall Etty telling me that she observed Papa closely as he was composing his long memorial to Annie, writing his recollections slowly and sobbing quietly every so often. She said the look upon his face was, to her thinking at least, a look of guilt.

It would not be the first time that he has castigated himself unduly. Some years back, Mamma, in the fullness of her religious belief, wrote him a private letter expressing a deep and secret sorrow: unless he turned to God, she feared, they would not have the blessing of eternal life together. I came upon it in the desk in his study where he kept it hidden and where he was wont to read it from time to time. Once, I chanced to be in the same room, and as he was unaware of my presence, I observed him seized by a strong emotion and heard him murmur an expression of his own culpability, 'If she but knew the reason. If she but knew the reason.' His words have long been a puzzlement to me.

Sometime afterwards I asked him when it was and why he had lost his faith and become an atheist. For I wondered to myself if the cause had not been the crisis brought on by Annie's demise. But his answer was of a different order altogether and a surprising one. He held me at arm's length and looking into my eyes replied: 'It was long, long ago, when I was a young man aboard the Beagle. But there's no more to be said about that.'

15 February 1865

I surreptitiously borrowed from my Uncle a book that is the rave of all London and I can see why it has gained such renown. It is but a slender volume containing a single poem, called Goblin Market. *Though it is frightening in parts, especially in its depiction of those horrid little goblin-men, I find it most uplifting in its ultimate moral message. All's well that ends well, I suppose. I found the book on a rosewood table in Uncle Ras' parlour and took it upstairs without his permission. To my knowledge, he has never asked about it and consequently I am sorely tempted to keep it. The volume is so small I keep it in Annie's writing-box.*

16 February 1865

I returned home to Down House today, in the middle of a downpour that soaked my skirts as I ran from the carriage. But once inside, I was relieved to find sunnier news: all is forgiven. Mamma brought me a cup of tea and afterwards Papa broke off playing billiards with Parslow and instead challenged me to a game of Backgammon. I allowed him to win and he was so content I think he failed to see through my trickery.

Still, I find it most difficult to rein in my curiosity. This afternoon, I decided to look through the specimens that Papa sent back from the Beagle. *He has never explicitly forbidden us to examine them and they are scattered all over the estate in the oddest of places. I found an entire cache in two deep drawers in the greenhouse where Papa has been conducting experiments with those horrid-smelling* Drosera *that eat insects (he has taught the plants to devour raw meat and they are only too happy to oblige). I came across something unusual. Many of the specimens are bones and fossils and such, labelled and dated in Papa's hand, but some of them bear another set of initials: 'R.M.' I find that confounding but do not dare to ask Papa what the letters mean.*

CHAPTER 10

Jemmy Button sat next to Charles at the great table, leaning close to look at the pictures of leopards and snakes and other animals in the natural history textbook. Whenever he saw one he recognized, he would squirm with delight and reach out with his small pudgy brown finger to touch it.

"Me know that one. Me see that one in me own contree." He giggled, taking the book in both hands and raising it to hold the painting of the ostrich so close to his face it was but three inches from his nose.

Charles laughed along with him. Was he trying to smell it? At times like this he found himself asking whether Jemmy's love of learning was instinctual, something that he had utilized in a rudimentary way in his previous world (where it would have found scant application), or whether it was nurtured by the many marvels he had seen in the civilized world. Could one take any reasonably endowed savage by the hand and teach him like a child? And how far could he go? Doubtless he would never rise to the level of a twelve-year-old English lad.

Perhaps the scientist in Charles was frustrated by a lack of specimens to study, for the three Yamana Indians fascinated him. Sick as he was, he sought them out often in the week since he had met Jemmy, observing their responses to the shipboard world. They were not new to it—they had spent eight months aboard on the *Beagle*'s homeward trip two years ago—but still they seemed mystified by its workings. They masked their bewilderment in a heavy-lidded lethargy and spent most of their time belowdecks, venturing up only during the calmest seas and at sunset, which appeared to hold some mystical meaning. They presented a bizarre threesome, dressed to the nines in layers of English clothes and staring wide-eyed at the orange disk sinking below the horizon, their black skins ablaze.

Charles could not suppress the thought that they wore the accouterments of civilization lightly and that they might revert to their savage origins at the first opportunity.

Except for Jemmy. He was different from the other two: Fuegia Basket, a merry but dim-witted eleven-year-old girl; and York Minster, a morose, surly man in his mid-twenties. All had been dubbed with Anglicized names when they were kidnapped. Jemmy Button's came from the circumstance of his abduction: FitzRoy had taken him from a canoe piloted by an old man and, in a fit of angry fair-mindedness, had ripped a mother-of-pearl button from his own tunic and tossed it at the man's feet to make it a trade.

Jemmy, as Charles had been informed, came from a different tribe than the other natives. His were upland Indians, smaller-boned and more advanced; they thought of themselves as an enlightened people. To hear FitzRoy tell it, Jemmy's first days on the *Beagle* had been miserable because he was ridiculed and persecuted by the other Fuegians, who called him *Yapoo,* which apparently meant "enemy." FitzRoy, for all his interest in the Yamana, seemed strangely crass about them. He sometimes waggishly referred to them all as "Yahoos," after the filthy primitives of *Gulliver's Travels*.

As Jemmy examined the animal pictures, Charles studied him. He was a dandy, all right, wearing white gloves and a dress coat, even on deck when a sou'wester would be in order. He paraded around and loved gazing at himself in a mirror; he insisted that the collars of his shirts be blindingly white, and if he so much as got a spot on his boots, he ran to his cabin in a tantrum to polish them. Teased about his foppishness, he would stick his nose in the air and answer: "Too much skylark."

Charles did not know what to make of him. The man was smart but guarded, at times proud and at other times sycophantic. He peppered his English with quaint expressions, so that when a sailor asked after his health, he would reply, with a groveling grin, "Hearty, sir, never better." At other times, he pretended not to understand. He had a bullying streak. He treated Fuegia Basket as if she belonged to a lower animal order, which upset York Minster, who regarded her as his wife. Jemmy's sight was far better than an Englishman's—even on deck, he could spot something on the horizon long before the sailors could—and once, angry that the cook would not give him a second helping of pudding, he threatened: "Me see Frenchie ship, me no tell."

Charles used his scientific instruments to reel in Jemmy for study. The Indian never tired of peering through the microscope, looking at bits of hair and lint. Once, when a bug found in the hold was placed under the instrument and moved a leg, he almost jumped out of his skin. He seemed to feel that he shared a special bond with Charles, much to the amusement of the Englishman, who thought it quaint that the savage entertained the notion that science could unite them. *Sigh-eenz,* Jemmy pronounced it, though whether he fully grasped the abstract concept was unclear.

Jemmy abruptly closed the book and looked Charles in the eye— which was unusual. He seemed to have reached some kind of decision, to want to say something important.

"I go take you to my contree. You go meet my people. You talk much with wise man. Much sigh-eenz, much talk, much."

Charles was touched and hid his amusement at the idea of sitting with a council of naked brown-skinned men to discuss higher realms of knowledge.

"Yes, I would enjoy that," he said.

Then Jemmy said they must not allow York Minster or Fuegia Basket to accompany them. He rose from the table and walked to the door.

"York a bad man," he said. "His tribe all bad."

With gestures, he began to mimic an action, grinning wildly and making sawing motions across his joints and opening his mouth wide and touching his fingers to it. It took Charles several moments after his departure to realize what he was trying to communicate: York Minster's tribe practiced cannibalism.

Propped up one afternoon on FitzRoy's sofa, reading Humboldt, Charles overheard FitzRoy and Wickham talking quietly on the other side of the cabin door.

"I am compelled to tell you, sir," said the lieutenant, "that I believe he will not last out the voyage. When we make landfall, we'll see the last of him, I warrant."

Charles strained to catch the Captain's response but heard no more. He knew that they were discussing him, and he had a complicated reaction. At first he vowed to make a liar of Wickham—he would stick out the voyage, for he wanted nothing so much as to secure the respect of FitzRoy. But then, the thought of a bountiful life upon solid land sinking in, he began to weaken, to feel that he might as well abandon the unendurable hardship of the journey, especially as the two already deemed it likely. They couldn't think any worse of him than they already did.

And Charles had continued to harvest nothing but misery. For the last ten days he could keep no food down but raisins and biscuit; even his dinner with the Captain had been lost overboard. He was losing weight fast and felt he would soon be little more than sallow flesh hanging from bone. When the ship had passed within hailing distance of Madeira, the island where so many of his countrymen took vacation, he could not even rouse himself to look.

Just then FitzRoy entered the cabin and looked embarrassed to see him, confirming Charles's suspicions that they had been gossiping about him. The Captain covered it with an announcement intended to lift his morale.

"By Jupiter, do you have any idea where we shall be at daybreak tomorrow? Santa Cruz, that's where! And for my money, there's no finer port city. Its steeples rise up before snow-capped mountains. All in all, it's the doing of the Creator Himself."

That night, swinging in his hammock, listening to King's snoring and looking up through the skylight at the moon and stars turning in revolutions, Charles felt himself aimless and insignificant. He missed the green, gentle sloping hills of Shropshire with a longing he had not thought possible. He made a decision: he would leave the ship in Santa Cruz, let the Devil take the whole lot of them. He was not cut out for a life at sea—strength of will and fortitude had nothing to do with it. It was his damned stomach and there was nothing to be done about it.

The next morning, as the *Beagle* dropped anchor in the harbor, he went on deck and felt promise in the salt-flecked balmy air. Before him lay a grand vista. Volcanic mountains, splotched with green, loomed over the town. The houses were painted in brilliant whites, yellows, and reds. He could make out Spanish flags flying from the tops of civic build-ings and horse-drawn carts trotting along the quay.

A boat pulled up with orders from the consul and there followed a brief conference. FitzRoy turned away looking disappointed—there was no way for him to break the news gently. If they wanted to touch land, he reported, they would have to spend twelve days in quarantine.

"Quarantine!" spluttered Charles without thinking. "But why? What diseases are there here that we should fear them?"

"None here," replied the Captain. "It's England. They fear *we* may be carrying cholera."

Jemmy Button, lurking not far away, heard the exchange and turned away, his face distorted in a grimace of delight. It was not lost on him that Englishmen could not bring themselves to think their country the lesser in anything.

They lifted anchor and set sail.

Life aboard the *Beagle* improved as she headed southward toward the Cape Verde Islands. The pitching motion eased as she entered the warm waters of the tropics. The morning sun seemed to shoot straight across the blue sky like a flaming arrow—and evenings it plunged into the ocean, a fiery red ball. The moon sent shivers upon the water.

Charles began to find a beauty in the ship's rhythm. He admired the sight of the sailors climbing about the rigging, sometimes seen only as shadows through the canvas. At night he enjoyed the sounds of the waves lapping against the bow and the rustle of the sails flapping around the masts. His shipmates invented a nickname for him—"Philos," short for "Philosopher," in recognition of his love for the natural sci-ences. It quickly caught on, for it sidestepped a dilemma that had made for moments of social awkwardness: what honorific to employ for an upper-class civilian with no official rank.

As Charles felt better, he turned hopeful, even doing a little work. He constructed a plankton net, four feet deep and held open with a curving stick, to drag behind the vessel. When he pulled it up after only two hours and emptied it on deck, he had captured all manner of sea life, including a Medusa and a Portuguese Man-of-War, which stung his finger.

"You were foolish to touch it," said McCormick, hovering about. He had wanted to help but Charles had declined the offer. Charles put his finger in his mouth and tried not to react to the pain the slime caused in the roof of his mouth.

He looked up at McCormick and thought: This soulless man can no more understand the glories of collecting than my hunting dog. How could anyone possibly make him understand the allure of natural science?

"But look at all these creatures, so low in the scale of Nature and yet so exquisite in form and rich in color," he said, his voice quivering with emotion. "Does it not create a feeling of wonder that so much beauty should be apparently created for such little purpose?"

McCormick stared open-mouthed, then turned his back and walked away.

In less than a week the *Beagle* reached the west coast of St. Jago and anchored in the bay of Porto Praya. Charles felt his pulse racing as the rowboat approached shore—at last, to plant one's feet on solid ground! But curiously, once there he found that there was little difference in the physical sensation; being on land did not provide the relief he had long dreamed of. Perhaps he had found his sea legs after all.

With FitzRoy he made the social rounds, meeting the Portuguese governor and the American consul. Then he walked through town sightseeing, past black soldiers carrying wooden weapons, shirtless brown children, and corrals of goats and pigs. He came to a deep valley on the outskirts and here finally, at long last, he encountered Humboldt's tropical paradise.

The hot, moist air struck him full in the face. Unknown insects buzzed around unknown flowers that were brilliant in color. The lushness of the vegetation, the chorus of unfamiliar birdcalls, the canopy of fruit trees and palms and the tangle of vines, shot through with shafts of steaming sunlight—the exotic tumult of it all overwhelmed him. This was what he had been longing for, like a blind man longing for sight.

The next morning he rowed with FitzRoy to Quail Island, a barren stretch of volcanic rock. He examined the geological formations and searched tidal pools that yielded a wealth of specimens, including an octopus that, to his intense delight, changed color. Returning to the ship, he handed up a basket of specimens to the first pair of hands he saw, without realizing that they belonged to none other than McCormick. The man took the bundle and tossed it upon the deck, fixing him with a hard look. Charles was too content to pay it much mind and set about dissecting some of his trophies and bottling others in spirits to send back home.

Three days later, in a spirit of magnanimity, Charles put aside his antipathy for McCormick and invited him to accompany him on a trek into the interior. McCormick agreed, which was surprising, for he had barely been able to contain his jealousy as Charles took up more and more of the quarterdeck to air his specimens.

They had hardly set out when McCormick began complaining about the heat. To take his mind off it, Charles described a curious geological formation he had spotted on Quail Island, a horizontal band of white running through the rocky cliffside about thirty feet above ground; on closer inspection, it was revealed to be a compressed bed of shells and corals. Clearly it had once been part of the seabed. But what had happened to leave it in midair? He posed the question to McCormick.

The surgeon removed his hat and wiped his forehead. He said the answer was obvious. "At one time the seabed was there and so, self-evidently, the water has receded."

Charles was skeptical. "The whole ocean?" he declared. "The volcanic islands themselves do not seem old enough to allow that as an explanation."

"What other explanation is there?"

Charles presented his own theory, based on Lyell, that the cliffside had been propelled upward by violent activity beneath its base. The band was relatively stable, which suggested that the crustal movement causing it had been gradual and incremental, he said.

McCormick was horrified.

"The land moving up into the air? What—like a catapult? More claptrap from you Cantabrigian heretics."

He was silent a moment, then added a bitter afterthought: "And I must say it would have been much easier for me to provide an explanation if I had been privileged to view the island in question firsthand."

Both men sulked. They were quiet for a full fifteen minutes, until they came upon a sprawling baobab tree whose trunk, sixteen feet across, was covered in carved initials. They sat under it to rest and drank water from a flagon Charles detached from a band across his shoulder.

"I suppose you know that Captain FitzRoy has taken your side," said McCormick suddenly.

"My side? I beg to know to what you are referring."

"Come, come. You dine with the man. You read in his cabin. You accompany him on expeditions. How can you possibly expect me to compete under such circumstances?"

"I had not realized we were in competition."

"What's more—as I'm certain you know—he's upbraided me. He took me aside five days back and chastised me for upsetting you, for *presuming*—that was his exact word—that we were equals in our claims to exploration." McCormick bit his lower lip, but whether it was from anger or sorrow, Charles could not tell.

"Can you, at the very least, do me some small favor?" he asked after a moment.

"Most assuredly."

"Can you permit me to send out some specimens with your shipments? You are clearly going to be gathering such a multitude, I can hardly imagine you would begrudge me a tiny portion of the space. Before signing on, I had thought this voyage would afford me the opportunity to make my name as a collector."

Charles thought before answering. He did not want to commit himself to a course he might later regret. But McCormick's lugubrious face moved his sense of Christian charity. He clapped the man upon the shoulder and said with a false joviality: "Of course! But mind you, within reason."

"Within reason."

At that, the two relaxed and fell into argument over the dimensions of the baobab tree, with Charles claiming that it was quite tall and McCormick asserting that it simply appeared so because its girth threw off the mind's perception. They placed a bet upon the matter.

Several days later, an incident occurred that unsettled Charles more than anything that had happened so far. He and McCormick, still bound by their recent truce, went hiking. They walked across a plateau as flat as a tabletop and came to Flag Staff Hill, a promontory noted chiefly for the wild area surrounding it. North of the hill they found a narrow ravine that descended about two hundred feet. After searching for quite a while, they discovered a steep rocky path that led to the bottom, and they followed it.

The dell they penetrated was a world apart, filled with a profusion of vegetation. Vines ran the width of the ravine; trees grew from the rocky ledges, heavy with succulent creepers. Hawks and ravens, disturbed by the interlopers, darted unnervingly close to them, cawing and scolding. At one point a bird of paradise flew up from a hidden nest, disappearing in the gap of blue sky now far above.

Charles felt unaccountably nervous as they descended into the gloom, as if they were blundering into the lair of some unknown beast. He was not accustomed to such superstitious thoughts and tried in vain to shake off the feeling. Then he heard McCormick, reaching the bottom of the fissure, give out a yelp. He rushed to the spot and found him staring down at an assortment of bones, some with bits of meat still upon them.

"From goats, I warrant," said McCormick. "There must be a large animal about."

They resolved to explore. Charles, readying his gun, took one end of the ravine and McCormick the other. They were working their way toward the center when Charles heard a sound and turned in time to see McCormick no more than ten feet away, his rifle pointing straight at him. A look of cold calculation played upon his face.

"For God's sake, man!" shouted Charles, looking into the gun barrel.

At that moment, the barrel swerved and Charles heard a rustling behind him and the crack of the gun. Turning, he saw something—a flash of color, the hind leg of an animal bounding into the opening of a cave. He surmised that it was a large cat.

They hurried to climb the path, and when they reached the open air, Charles breathed a sigh of relief. He felt that he had narrowly escaped a brush with death, though from which quarter—man or animal—was hard to say.

The following day, an expedition made its way to the baobab tree. FitzRoy measured the tree twice, using a pocket sextant and then climbing to the top to let down string. Both methods agreed on the conclusion: the tree was nowhere near as tall as it appeared. FitzRoy drew a rough sketch to prove the point, and McCormick, exulting in his victory over Charles, made a show of demanding his money on the spot. As Charles fished in his trousers to hand over a coin, he again spied that cold look upon his antagonist's face.

But he was even more troubled by what happened next. As they were walking back to the launch, McCormick sidled over to him and said, with superficial camaraderie: "By the by, I happened to visit Quail Island yesterday and I spotted that rock formation you mentioned. Curious, isn't it? I do expect your theory as to its formation is correct."

Charles was surprised that he had come around so quickly.

"And did you notice," McCormick continued, "that the shells in the band were the same as those to be found on the beach?"

Charles had not noticed. "What of it?" he replied, a bit defensively.

"To me that indicates that whatever geological activity may have caused it to rise—a quake, say, or some other shifting of the earth—must have occurred relatively recently."

"Now it is my turn to salute you," said Charles, touching his hat. "Undoubtedly, you are correct."

His words were gracious but his thoughts were less so. This man is no fool, he said to himself. He learns his lesson quickly and he expands upon it to an improvement. We must ensure that the student does not surpass the master.

After twenty-three days in Cape Verde, during which time FitzRoy fixed the position of the islands with exactitude, the *Beagle* hoisted sail again. As they moved ever southward, the temperature rose by the day. Charles, still nauseous most of the time, now also felt drugged by the torpor, remarking to King that the sensation was like being "stewed in melted butter."

They stopped briefly at St. Paul's Rocks off the coast of Brazil to stock up on fresh food. FitzRoy and Charles took a whaleboat to the island, where they had a grand time. The birds were so tame, the crewmen could walk right up and club them. They even grabbed some with their bare hands. A second launch, carrying McCormick, went to join in but was waved away. Instead, it plied the harbor for fish; the sailors threw out their lines and pulled in groupers, wielding their oars to fight off pillaging sharks.

Finally, the *Beagle* came to the Equator. As might be expected, Charles had heard various tales of the ancient ceremony, replete with schoolboy pranksterism, called "crossing the line." But none of his shipmates would be specific; quite the contrary, they had delighted in teasing him by keeping their allusions vague yet threatening. Still, he was not prepared on February 16 when he and thirty-two other "griffins"—novices—were confined to the lower deck with the hatchways battened down, leaving their prison dark and stiflingly hot. Charles had caught a glimpse of the forecastle and he was convinced they had all gone mad: FitzRoy, dressed as Father Neptune, complete with toga and trident, presided over a tribe of half-naked, painted men, dancing wildly to flutes and drums.

The hatchway opened and four of Neptune's constables descended. They made directly for Charles and grabbed him by the shoulders and legs. After stripping him to the waist, they blindfolded him and led him to the upper deck. The air resounded with chants and the boards shook with the thud of pounding feet. Buckets of water were tossed over him, so that he could scarcely breathe. He was led to a plank and forced to stand on it.

Then his face and mouth were lathered with pitch and paint, and he was "shaved" with a rusty piece of iron hoop. He felt bits of his beard pulled out. Then at a signal—from FitzRoy, no doubt—he felt himself twirled upside down, landing in a sail filled with seawater. There two men dunked him, one of them handling him roughly. He gasped for air, was dunked again, held under for what seemed like minutes, and just as he felt about to drown, was allowed to surface, sprouting from the water like a breaching whale. The initiation was over. It had been one of the most terrifying experiences of his life.

Charles was tossed a towel and he dried himself. The deck was awash in water, paint, and soapsuds, so slippery he had to grab the rigging. He stayed on to watch the others and thought that most of them were treated even more roughly than he had been, except for the final dunking, which in his case had been far worse. He then noticed that one of the two bullies standing knee-deep in the sail, his forearms glistening with sweat and seawater, was McCormick.

That night Charles felt he himself had crossed a Rubicon. He knew that the crew accepted him, that he was one of them. They had always admired his marksmanship when he brought down a bird with a single shot and now they laughed good-naturedly whenever he rushed on deck to catch sight of dolphins or some other sea creatures.

Standing near the bow and feeling the warm breeze in his face, Charles looked up at the sky and spotted the Southern Cross. Abruptly he realized that he had come to a decision without even realizing it. He had decided not to abandon the voyage but to remain on HMS *Beagle,* come what may. He was in it to the end. There was no place on earth he would rather be than on this ten-gun, ninety-foot vessel crammed with seventy-four souls whose seagoing valor he had come to appreciate and whose fellowship he had come to value—all, that is, save for one.

CHAPTER 11

The more Hugh read Lizzie's journal, the more enigmatic it became. Why did Darwin act so strangely? Why did he hightail it away from the dinner table at the mere mention of that famous phrase "survival of the fittest"? And what to make of that conversation between Huxley and Lyell about Alfred Russel Wallace? This last—if true—was especially intriguing because it flew in the face of history: scholars all agreed that Wallace accepted his position as junior author of the theory of evolution with quiet deference, a tugging of the forelock; that he was "content to be moon to Darwin's sun," as one writer put it. But this new information suggested the opposite. Wallace seemed to be causing trouble, acting "high-handed" and posing some kind of threat. Lyell and Huxley had ganged up to oppose him. But *was* it true? A snippet of gossip overheard by a high-strung young woman was hardly a foundation on which to build a radically new analysis of the key people around Darwin.

That night, Hugh had fallen asleep without finishing the journal. He awoke late, jumped in a cab to the station, caught a train to King's Cross, and took the Underground to South Kensington. He walked to the Cromwell Road, passed through the wrought-iron gate, and strode up the curved walkway toward the Natural History Museum.

The majestic building with its fine, handcrafted bricks rose before him. He savored the irony: Richard Owen, the brilliant comparative anatomist, was so blinded by ambition that he could not open his eyes to the overpowering truth of what Darwin and Huxley were saying; he became their bitter foe, ridiculing their assertions, which after all could not be empirically tested. As superintendent of the Natural History departments of the British Museum, he drew up plans for this spectacular temple to the glory of science and raised money to see it through; yet his name was engraved nowhere on it. And then in 2002, within the facade arose a new seven-floor annex to house zoology specimens: the Darwin Centre.

Amazing how Darwin always got the last laugh, Hugh thought.

Inside the cavernous main hall half a dozen children stared wide-eyed at an animated *Tyrannosaurus rex*. The central staircase swept upward and spread onto the mezzanine like a fan. Arches picked up conversations and threw them fifty feet across the lobby. From the reception desk Hugh called administration, where a public affairs officer eventually put him in touch with an assistant curator who agreed to see him.

Her name was Elizabeth Fallows and she greeted Hugh warmly, rising from her desk of piled papers and cat skeletons to pump his hand. Her head ducked and bobbed with enthusiasm and her black bangs waved across her forehead. Of course, she was more than happy to show him around. She led the way with an athletic lope, declaiming over her shoulder like a tour guide.

"It's called the 'spirit collection' because the specimens are preserved in alcohol to kill the bacteria that cause tissue degradation. There are four hundred and fifty thousand jars, including over twenty-five thousand of plankton."

They entered an airtight chamber; the door behind them locked and a few seconds later the door in front clicked open. He looked at her quizzically.

"For temperature control," she explained. "We keep it at thirteen degrees Celsius, below the flash point of alcohol. That also reduces evaporation. If there's alcohol spillage, sensors pick it up. There's nothing like this collection anywhere in the world. It goes back to Captain Cook in 1768–earlier, actually."

They entered the storage rooms, rows upon rows of metal cabinets stretching in all directions. She continued the tour.

"We have twenty-two million specimens on seven floors–the largest such collection in the world. We're especially proud of our type specimens—they're the definitional archetypes by which a species is first named and described. We have almost eight hundred and seventy-seven thousand of them. They're extremely important—during the war they were secretly transported to underground caves in Surrey for safekeeping. Couldn't let the Jerries bomb them. That's how essential they are."

Hugh nodded to show he was impressed—and he was.

"The whole point of type specimens is lost on us today," she went on. "Of course it was rooted in the nineteenth-century mania for classification—God bless all those amateur scientists for trying to make sense of the natural world: you know, a place for everything and everything in its place.

"But it was also rooted in religion. If the Lord made each and every species, and if they were fixed and never-changing, then it made sense to hunt down the best representative of each one. That was the only means of settling arguments about what belonged where. You found a bird, you opened a drawer, you compared it to the best of the lot, and you knew where you stood. So collectors were actually documenting God's work. Everything fit neatly. There was no contradiction between science and religion."

Her bangs shook with enthusiasm as she talked.

"Until Darwin came along. He upset the apple cart with his idea that every living organism was part of an ever-growing tree of life, with many branches. That's why he called his theory the *transmutation* of species. He didn't use the word 'evolution,' you know, not until *The Descent of Man,* in 1871."

"And do you have many specimens from Darwin himself?" Hugh asked.

"Thousands. He sent back everything—not just pickled stuff for the wet collection. We have birds and reptiles and fish and bones, eggs and shells and pollen, everything you can imagine.

"Here's one"—she pulled a drawer, which slid open quietly, and held up a bottle labeled in black ink—"a baby parrot fish. They munch coral in their beaks. Darwin theorized that's what caused sandy beaches." She gave a snort of a laugh. "No one's right all the time."

"And do you have any of his finches?" He thought of using the proper name, *Geospizinae*—the subfamily for Darwin's finches, named after him in honor of their pivotal role in leading him to understand differentiation among species—but refrained. Name-dropping was discouraged among British scientists.

"Of the thirteen species, twelve are represented here; we have five hundred fifty skins, sixty spirit specimens, and ten skeletons."

"They include the ones he himself collected?"

"Of course. He collected thirty-one specimens, of which twenty-two reached the museum. We retain nineteen."

"How are they labeled? I mean, he mixed up all his specimens, didn't he—took finches from the various islands and put them all in the same bag? Years later he had to implore FitzRoy to show him *his* finches."

"You've hit the sore point, haven't you, you naughty boy." She was smiling. "In terms of location, our labels simply follow his best guess. I suppose in the long run it was fortuitous."

"Why?"

"It proves that he had no inkling of the theory back then, doesn't it? If he had come upon it while he was in the Galápagos, he would hardly have made such a ridiculous mistake, would he?"

"I guess not."

"So we know that the theory dawned on him after he returned to London, just as he said. It took a year or two. There was no *Eureka* moment. He returned to our shores in 1836 and he sketched a thirty-five-page outline in 1842."

"Why did he take twenty-two years to write the damn thing?"

"Well, that's what Americans call the sixty-four-thousand-dollar question, isn't it?"

He followed her into the control chamber—again they were briefly locked in together.

"Personally," she said, "I don't believe the answer is all that complicated."

"What is it, then?"

"Think of it this way: Christianity was around more than eighteen hundred years. It took him two decades to overturn it. A ratio of ninety to one—that's not so bad."

The lock clicked open. She escorted him down to the first floor and the top of the majestic grand staircase leading to the lobby below. They were eye-level with the dinosaurs.

"Tell me," said Hugh. "Do you have any specimens from the *Beagle* marked 'R.M.'?"

"We do," replied Ms. Fallows. "From Robert McCormick. I suppose you've heard of him."

Hugh had, but only that morning. Two days ago he had found the *Beagle*'s crew list on the Internet and printed it out; it began with "Ash Gunroom—*steward*" and ended with "York Minster—*passenger*." On the train he had scanned it and found the name that matched the initials "R.M."—Robert McCormick, *surgeon*.

She continued: "There are just a few dozen. Some were mixed in with Darwin's and sent along by him after the ship's return. There aren't many because of course he abandoned the voyage early on, at Rio, didn't he?"

"Did he?"

"Indeed. Darwin himself wrote that. He even provided a catchy little description: the chap walked off on dockside sporting a parrot on his shoulder. That's how we know it occurred."

"Are the specimens dated?"

"Yes, of course. McCormick was trained as a scientist, even if he wasn't a very good one."

"And the dates are . . . when?"

"All from the first few months, up until the ship docked at Rio. Well, they could hardly be after that, could they?"

"I suppose not."

"You *suppose* not. I should think you're on safe ground there."

Hugh detected a mild reproach. She seemed to think he was doubting the great man's word.

"Yes," he said. "And whatever happened to him?"

"McCormick? Oh, I'm not sure I know. He undoubtedly continued his voyages and stayed abroad for many years. Then, as I seem to recall, he perished somehow, perhaps in a shipwreck."

She seized his hand to say goodbye with the same enthusiasm as when she had met him, her bangs swinging across her forehead.

"Hardly matters," she said quietly. "I mean, he was a marginal character in the whole drama—wasn't he?"

.   .   .

Hugh got caught up in the traffic jam because of the Changing of the Guard at Buckingham Palace and was twenty minutes late meeting Bridget. When he reached the park, threading his way through the crowd, he saw her at the entrance, leaning against an iron railing, her flowerprint dress pinned tight around her thighs. Her hair gleamed in the sun.

Surprisingly, catching sight of her unawares, he was struck by her beauty. He quickly damped down the thought, not because she was married but because she had once been his brother's fiancée. When she saw him, she walked over brusquely.

"Don't worry about it," she said with a tense smile.

"The traffic."

"I figured." Uncharacteristically, she wasn't making a big deal of it. "All the goddamned tourists. Let's go this way." She led him along a path that curved left into the lush foliage of the park. He figured she had plotted their walk in advance. The sun had come out.

"Fine day," he said.

"Cut the small talk." Whatever overlay of English intonation had been there was gone.

"Okay. It's a lousy day."

"What's that called anyway, that literary device, the one when nature mirrors your innermost feelings? Wordsworth and all those other dreary poets?"

"The pathetic fallacy."

"That's it. Well, this is the opposite. Nature is definitely *not* mirroring my feelings. And I definitely feel *pathetic*."

"You sounded upset on the phone."

"I am, a bit. More than a bit. And the way I look at it, you're responsible."

"Me?"

"You suddenly appear out of nowhere. You don't know what you're doing, where you're going. You're still hung up on your brother. It stirs everything up."

"What things?"

"Emotions, dummy. Emotions."

He was quiet.

"If you had answered my letter," she said, "we might have kept up. We could have dealt with some of this back then and maybe laid it to rest."

At the time he had known that that was in the offing. He suddenly realized that was why he hadn't answered.

They passed a bank of flowers in full bloom, their blazing colors turned toward the sun. The air was dizzying, with perfumed scents and honeybees. She must have loved Cal deeply, he thought, and that called up a rush of affection and gratitude that reminded him of the first week he met her, in Paris.

"Maybe you haven't moved on after all," he said gently.

"That's not the problem. The problem is *you* haven't, and if you don't, then I can't either."

"How come? Christ, I haven't even seen you for six years. What does my life have to do with yours?"

"A lot. Don't forget, we were almost brother and sister."

"I know—another three months and you two would have been married."

She paused, looking away. "I'm not so sure about that."

"What? What do you mean?"

"Look, there are certain things you don't know. There are *a lot* of things you don't know."

They came to a crowded bridge over a pond so that they were forced to walk single-file, and his questions were aimed urgently at the back of her shoulder—"Like what? What do you mean?" He caught up and took her elbow in one hand. "Explain what you mean."

"Hey, not so hard."

"Goddamn it, Bridget. Stop being so fucking mysterious. If you know something, just say it."

She shook him off. "That's the problem. I don't *know* anything, I just wonder about things. There's an awful lot to be explained."

"Like what?"

"Things you have no idea about."

They came to a bench; she sat down and he sat facing her. Across from them scum and paper floated on the pond's edge. A handful of ducks waddled along the rocks, lunging at soggy pieces of bread tossed by a little boy in a sailor's suit.

She was quiet for a moment and he waited her out, staring at her.

"Look," she said finally. "This is awkward. I don't know quite where to begin. But you should know that things weren't so good between Cal and me at the end." Hearing her pronounce Cal's name made every-thing suddenly real.

"When he went back to the States—I know that you thought he was just on a visit, but it wasn't clear to me that he was coming back. He didn't know himself. When we said goodbye, we thought there was a chance we might never see each other again."

"But you were going to be married in England. His whole life was here. You mean he was breaking it off?"

"Not really. But he was acting strangely. He wasn't himself."

"How do you mean? In what way wasn't he himself?"

"You always think of him as the older brother, the confident one, the one who knew exactly what he was doing. But he wasn't always like that. He had devils of his own."

"What are you saying? He told you he wasn't sure about getting married?"

"No, not exactly. He found it hard to talk about."

"Talk about what?"

"That he was so troubled."

She gave a half sigh, opened her purse and reached inside, pulling out a postcard, which she handed to Hugh. The edges were worn. It was a photo of the Statue of Liberty, standing radiant in the sun, the water an unnatural bright blue. On the other side, with a start, he recognized his brother's hand. The writing was so small it took a while to decipher it.

> Dearest B,
>
> Sorry I haven't written more, but not much to say. Nothing's resolved. I haven't told Dad about the lab. No idea what I'll do. Please bear with me. Some bad times, especially at night. Churchill's black dog is still baying at my heels. I love you more than I can say. Someday, perhaps, if we're lucky, we'll look back on all this as a dream—rather, a nightmare. Please, please forgive . . .
>
> Love, C.

There was a P.S. Hugh stared at it, unbelieving: *I'm hoping to talk to Hugh.*

It struck him through the heart.

"When he left," she said, "he was in a bad way. He quit his job at the lab. He was in a bad car accident. He wasn't sure of anything. And he was low. He tried hiding it from me—I could almost cry when I think of it . . . I *did* cry—how he tried hiding it. Because he couldn't bring himself to talk about it. I'm not sure he even knew what it was; just that he felt miserable."

"Churchill's black dog . . . ?"

"That was his expression for it—depression."

Hugh couldn't take it in: Cal depressed. Cal needing him. "And the lab—he loved that job. Why would he quit?"

She shrugged. "I don't know. He didn't tell me. He just came home one day and didn't want to work there anymore. He said he didn't believe in the place, that they'd lost track of their *mission*."

"What was their mission?"

"I have no idea. It was a government lab, doing whatever they do. Biology."

They stood up and resumed walking and soon came to the band pavilion.

"This is all so . . . incredible," Hugh said. "I had no idea he was in trouble."

"Didn't you? When he came home, you didn't notice anything . . . different? Anything wrong?"

"No." But he wondered. He was not so sure.

"So you never had that talk?" It was the question he had known was coming and dreaded.

"No. There wasn't much time. He was only there for two or three weeks before, you know, it happened. And I was away part of the time. I was running around, trying to find work."

"I see." She didn't sound convinced. "So we'll never really know."

"You mean—know what was troubling him?"

"That too."

They reached the Mall, traffic moving vigorously in both directions, a line of stately government buildings across the way.

"There must be someone who knows," he protested. "Someone who worked with him, a boss, a friend."

"As a matter of fact, there is someone. If you want to make contact, perhaps that can be arranged. Perhaps I'll make a dinner party and then you could meet together later on."

"Bridge, please do. I'd be deeply grateful."

"I shall."

They kissed goodbye and walked in different directions, Bridget toward Buckingham Palace, Hugh toward Trafalgar Square. He turned to watch her and thought for a moment that she might turn also and wave, the way she did when she and Cal had left Paris. But she didn't, moving away with a steady, sure gait.

Beth was already at the Prince Regent, sitting in a corner, her back to a mirror. She was wearing a clean white shirt, jeans shorts, and sneakers. Her hair was still piled up on her head, strands curling around her face. An empty beer glass sat on the table.

She smiled and Hugh leaned over to kiss her cheek.

"Sorry I'm late," he said.

"You're not."

"I'm not sorry either—just wanted to see if my apologies still piss you off."

He went for beers. The place was crowded and loud and a cloud of smoke hung low in the air. He elbowed his way to the bar and made it back clasping two mugs in one hand—no spilling.

"Something tells me you've had practice at this," she said.

"I have."

She smiled and picked up her drink.

"How's it going?" he asked.

"The research? Fine." She smiled. "And you?"

"Okay, pretty good."

The screen was up again.

She looked around. "Wonder how this place would go over in New York."

"It'd sink in a minute. Too sociable, too well lit."

"I never really got into the whole pub scene."

"Me neither. I like the names, though—The Golden Crown. Elephant and Castle."

"Slug and Lettuce. That's my favorite."

"New York goes in for *bars*. Someplace dark, shot glasses, a suspicious Irish bartender, empty stools on both sides of you. Frank Sinatra on the box singing 'Come Fly with Me.' "

"Stop. You're making me nostalgic."

"If you want nostalgia, I'll show you something. Come."

They drained their beers. She followed him outside. He led her a couple of blocks and stopped in front of Mickey Flynn's American Pool Hall.

"Now you're talking," she said.

They drank two more beers each and played to a one–one tie. They bet five pounds on the third game. She broke like a demon and beat him. He paid up in coins and she scooped them into her shorts' pocket with a grin.

They walked to Parker's Piece and sat on the grass, watching an evening cricket match, men in white moving quickly with each *thwack* of the ball.

"I never got this game," he said.

"It's baseball, only longer and with stupider rules."

They talked some more, then walked around the park and settled on a bench near Regent Terrace. It was getting dark.

"Tell me about your marriage," he said, regretting the way he phrased it—so awkward and predictable in an I-want-to-know-you way. But he did want to know her.

"What about it?"

"I don't know. What went wrong?"

"Does anyone ever know the answer to that?"

"Try."

"Well, at first it was fine, the exciting newness of it. I really cared about Martin. He was witty, charming, more knowledgeable than anyone I knew. He could dazzle you in that subtle, underspoken British way. You never read a book he hadn't already read, but he didn't let you know it right away. He'd drop it in after you already tried to explain what you thought it meant—and his explanation would always be more profound.

"I was the American, the breath of fresh air, the one who said what others were thinking. I was falling in love with England and Martin was part of all that. Good dinners, lots of friends, deep conversations. Rainy Sundays with a fire going and a huge pile of newspapers next to my chair. Country weekends in drafty old houses. Dinners at Oxford with half a dozen different wines. Radical politics filled with rectitude and judgments—judgments about everything and everyone. It was all very . . . secure."

"Sounds good."

"Yes, it was for a while. But then Martin got sick. He began acting strangely, wild mood swings, deep depressions. His friends told me he had been that way off and on for years before I met him. I would have stuck with him—at least I like to think I would have—but we were still too new to each other. I wasn't really in love with him, I mean, not in a head-over-heels sort of way. I thought when we were married that that was okay because my love would grow over time and become stronger. But that didn't happen. It didn't grow. We became just friends. It all came to an end one day at a luggage carousel at Heathrow."

"Explain."

"We were away on a trip. We had been fighting almost nonstop for over a year and we went on one of those desperate, let's-work-it-all-out trips. We went to a little island off the coast of Montenegro, a place called Svedi Stefan, with converted fishermen's cottages. It was beautiful. But we began having rows. The littlest thing would set us off. Martin got violent, then depressed. One day while I was out swimming, he trashed the room. He knocked out every single windowpane. We had to leave. On the plane back he wouldn't sit next to me and then we tried to make up and we did make up and there were more promises—but I knew they wouldn't work. As we got to the airport and were waiting for our suitcases, I looked at him. His jaw was set in a hard, familiar way and I suddenly realized it was hopeless. So we talked and decided to call it quits. We got divorced. That was two years ago. And we're on better terms now, we're almost friendly. I sometimes feel there's no one who knows me inside out the way he does."

The words had come out in a rush, and when she stopped, she looked directly at him.

"Here we go again," she said, running her hand through her hair. "Talking about me. How about you? Tell me something about you."

"Interesting, isn't it, this need to exchange confidences? It's like a script or something."

"No, you don't—you're just trying to escape. Tell me something."

"Like what?"

"Tell me about your brother."

He glanced at her. She was looking at him searchingly, ready to listen. He remained silent for a moment, wondering whether to plunge ahead.

"His name was Cal. He was older than me and I looked up to him. He was everything I wanted to be. In some ways he was more of a father than my real father. And then, six years ago, he died in an accident. Except that he didn't have to—I mean, I think maybe I could have saved him."

There—he had said it. It was out.

"What do you mean?"

"He came home to Connecticut from his job in Oxford—he was working in a lab there. He was a biologist, brilliant, very committed. We had always been close, but this time, for some reason, we were a little awkward together, maybe because it had been several years since we had seen each other. And so this day, we went out to Devil's Den, that's a swimming hole we used to go to when we were kids—rocks, a steep cliff, a big waterfall. Way off in the woods. You have to walk an hour just to get there. I guess we wanted to connect again, the way we did when we were young."

He paused, took a breath, then continued.

"We always knew it was dangerous—to swim at the bottom of the falls. We never did it. We were told by someone . . . I don't remember who . . . all the kids knew it, that you never went in there. Something about the way the water falls, when it hits it becomes aerated. It churns around and just won't support you. Trying to stay afloat is like trying to tread water in thin air. There was this story of some kid who went in and just went down like a stone. So we all knew you didn't go there.

"And this day Cal and I thought for old time's sake we'd go to Devil's Den. It was a hot day. I carried a six-pack. We didn't know if we'd swim or not, up above the falls where it was safe, but we had our suits on under our pants just in case. And we got to the waterfall and we were walking up the trail next to it . . . And he slowed down. I got a bit pissed off, it was so hot and I decided I wanted to swim. I wanted to get there and put the beer in the water and he seemed to be holding back so I went on up ahead—"

He stopped again. The memory loop played.

"—and then I don't really know what happened. I was walking ahead and I heard something behind me, a sound, a sort of cry, and I turned around and I saw Cal going down, he was falling against the rocks, only sort of slowly, like maybe he could catch himself . . . But then he went faster and he actually spun around, tumbled upside down, and went straight into the water. I saw the splash. I saw his head up for a moment and then an arm, I could tell he was struggling, and then suddenly he disappeared below the surface. He just wasn't there anymore. Nothing, nowhere. And I ran down the slope as fast as I could but when I got there, there was nothing I could do.

"I was just looking at the water—it was dark and filled with little bubbles. I thought . . . I thought I should go in, jump in after him. But I was afraid. Because I knew if I went in, I'd never come out. And so, that was it, I just let him drown. I didn't even try to save him. I went looking for a stick, some kind of branch maybe, to shove down in the water, see if he could catch it down there. But there was nothing. And then time seemed to be going by very fast. I remember thinking, How long can he hold his breath? How long can a human being live without breathing? What happens? When does brain damage set in? And then I thought, Not this long. I went downstream to see if maybe he came up down there but he wasn't there. He wasn't anywhere, no one was around and suddenly it just seemed very quiet. I couldn't tell how much time went by, I couldn't hear anything much, even the waterfall sounded far away.

"So . . . I had to hike back. I went to the road and got in my car and drove to a crossroads where there was a phone and I called the cops. They came and we went back in and they looked a while, and called for more reinforcements. And then this one cop comes over and puts his arm around me and gives me a cell phone and asks if I want to call anyone. And so I call my dad—I had to walk off in the woods by myself to do it—I remember looking up at the trees and the leaves and thinking, So how do you do this, what do you say? How do you tell someone that there were two of you and now there's only one, the other one's gone? What words do you use? How do you say, I let him die? And he answered. And I don't remember what words I did use. But he came. He knew right where we were. And by then more police were there and they dredged for his body, and Cal came up. He had the hook caught in one leg, and he looked so pale. His hair was plastered down on his head and he looked water-logged; he weighed so much it took three men to pull him on the rocks. They didn't even try resuscitation.

"So that's it. I had a brother and that's how he died."

By now it was dark. Headlights from Gonville Place swept through the trees. Beth, who had been holding his hand, reached over and pulled his head down to her chest.

He said: "If I hadn't been so . . . childish, if I hadn't gone up ahead, maybe I could have saved him . . . caught him before he fell, stopped him somehow."

"That doesn't sound likely."

He couldn't talk any more without crying.

They sat there for a long time not saying anything.

"You know," he said, "I've never told anyone all this before—not like this."

"Everyone has a secret—that's what my mother used to say. Some are good to talk out, some are not. Yours is one of the good ones."

Hugh sat up and looked at her.

"It wasn't your fault, you know. Anyone can see that."

"I always felt—I don't know how to say this—I always felt my father favored him. Cal was clearly so much better than me, in every way. And so the real thought I had later that day, and the next day, and just about every day ever since, was"—he paused, it was hard to talk—"that *the wrong son died.*"

"Your father never said that, did he?"

"No, not in so many words. But I bet he thought it."

She reflected for a moment, then said softly: "You could be right. Some parents do have favorites. Maybe some even love one child more than another. But what's certain is that many more children believe they're not deeply loved even when they are, especially kids growing up in the shadow of an older brother or sister. So there's the distinct possibility that you're wrong. Then think of all the needless suffering you're causing yourself. And maybe even your father.

"And another thing," she added. "If you had gone into the water after him, then your father would've had no one at all."

"There's something else," he said. "I've been finding out some things recently."

"Like what?"

"That Cal quit his job at the lab. That he was depressed and needed help."

"It sounds like you want to get to the bottom of that."

"Yes."

They started walking down the road toward her place in the darkness. Street lamps poured light on the sidewalk in yellow funnels. He was so preoccupied that he didn't notice that his arm was around her waist and hers was around his, gently resting there with her thumb tucked inside his belt.

In front of her house, he kissed her good night—a short, intimate kiss, not a passionate one. She did not invite him in and he was just as glad. His brain was feverish with thoughts.

CHAPTER 12

At nine o'clock on a steamy February morning, two months out of England, the *Beagle* reached South America. Moving across calm waters along a lush coastline of banana trees and coconut palms, she slipped quietly into the Bay of All Saints beneath the ancient town of Bahia, San Salvador.

For Charles, it was not a day too soon, for he had discovered the wearisome underside to life at sea—namely, that a brig that one day seems huge enough for an army can transform itself the next into the hellish confines of a prison; if one has an enemy, one trips over him at every turn. His relations with McCormick had deteriorated beyond incivility into something approaching barely disguised hostility.

The evening before, he had confided his dislike to his cabin mate, Philip Gidley King, as the two lay swinging gently in their hammocks.

"The man pulls my beard, I can't say why. He's an ass, a plodding martinet who scarcely deserves to be called a natural scientist. No curiosity whatsoever. And he's vulgar. There's no getting around it—much as I dislike saying so—he's simply lower class."

"That much is obvious."

"And I can't for the life of me think why he has taken such a dislike to me."

"That too is obvious. Clearly, you stand in his way. You are an obstacle in the path towards a goal he dearly desires."

"And what might that be?"

"Who knows? Fame perhaps, social advancement, all that vain and worthless sort of human striving."

Charles did not reply. He cast his mind back to naturalists he had known who had used their work to climb up the social ladder. It was certainly possible, if one amassed a fine collection and garnered a reputation as an expert, to achieve a certain status. Even a knighthood was not out of the question.

By happy contrast, Charles was secure in the scheme of things, able to pay his own way and devote himself to science for pure epistemological motives. He told himself he was not a snob—he prided himself on his ability to mix with people from all walks of life—but he found it strange that he should feel so much more comfortable in the presence of a savage like Jemmy Button than in the company of his own countryman.

Young King had ended the conversation, turning to face the wall in a brooding posture befitting a man who had seen much of the world's perniciousness, by saying: "Anyway, I have read all of Byron and I don't give a damn for anyone."

Pacing the deck, Charles could hardly wait to go ashore. He was the first one in the skiff. When he stepped from the boat onto the wharf, his legs wobbly on solid ground, he wandered the narrow streets, walking toward the cathedral on the main square. He felt lost among so many people and studied the crowds. There were priests in cone-shaped hats, beggars, British sailors swaggering about, and beautiful women whose long black hair streamed down their backs.

But soon he came upon sights that made him feel he had blundered into a hell far worse than anything he had experienced on the ship: slaves from Africa, black as boot polish, being worked without mercy. Stripped to the waist on boats servicing the harbor, they threw their upper bodies into oars under the lash of a whip. Ashore they carried huge bundles on their heads and scurried loaded halfway to the ground to keep up with their masters.

Beasts of burden are treated better than this, thought Charles. He noticed in dismay how the slaves scampered to get out of his way and avoided his gaze by looking at the ground. Instantly, all the anti-slavery diatribes he had witnessed at Uncle Jos's dinner table, all the passionate speeches he had heard, all the evangelical sermons came flooding back to fire up his blood. He thought of John Edmonstone, the freed slave who years before had kindly taught him taxidermy at Edinburgh, and his anger reached such proportions he began to lose himself in the righteous feeling of it.

At that very moment, back on the *Beagle,* McCormick was engaged in a conversation on the same topic with Bartholomew James Sulivan. The surgeon had positioned himself on the lower deck to be within earshot of Captain FitzRoy but pretended to be oblivious to his presence.

"Did you not know," remarked McCormick, "our Mr. Darwin's family was in the forefront of the abolition campaign?"

"No, I did not," replied the second lieutenant.

"Indeed, the Wedgwoods, to whom he is related both directly and through his wife, were active in the Anti-Slavery Society. They designed the china piece of the little Negro boy in chains on bended knee under the words: 'Am I Not a Man and a Brother?' "

"I've seen that."

"Undoubtedly. It is quite famous."

"Slavery is a most troubling but complicated issue," said Sulivan. "It's one thing to make trading illegal and quite another to abolish slaveholding in the overseas territories."

"I agree, but I'm afraid Mr. Darwin would not subscribe to that view. He is a zealot on the subject."

"Is he now?"

"Most assuredly. In fact, I've heard him remark that he cannot bear to associate with those who think otherwise. Indeed, he says he can scarcely abide taking his meals with a man whose morality is so different from his own."

Sulivan was taken aback.

"Are you referring to our Captain?"

"Indeed. Mr. Darwin is most put out that Captain FitzRoy does not enlist the *Beagle* in the drive to root out the Spanish and Portuguese slave traders. I would venture to say he is most presumptuous and insolent in speaking of the Captain in this regard."

FitzRoy withdrew into the shadow of the mainmast, his face clouded in anger.

That evening, when Charles returned from his promenade, he found FitzRoy unduly quiet, and throughout a meal in which neither spoke he once again fancied himself the object of the Captain's darkly appraising eye.

As it happened, some days later the two dined with a Captain Paget of HMS *Samarang,* which shared a mooring in the harbor, and the visitor, by coincidence, could talk of little else than the horrors of slavery of which he had been hearing so much. He recounted story after story—of slaves being beaten to within an inch of their lives, of families broken apart and sold to different masters, of men escaping and being hunted down like dogs.

Some owners, Captain Paget conceded, were humane in their treatment, but even then they remained blind to the suffering of the chattel. He recalled one slave who said: "If I could but see my father and my two sisters once again, I should be happy. I can never forget them."

FitzRoy demurred. He recounted a visit to an owner of an *estancia* who, to prove that his slaves were not unhappy, called them up one by one and asked if they would prefer to be free.

"And each and every one said: no, they would not. Ha. They were better off living under him than perishing of hunger on their own," he pronounced.

With that, the Captain finished off his last bit of mutton, drained his wine, and tossed down his napkin, as if to end all discussion on the matter. Shortly afterward, Paget returned to his ship. Charles, burning with indignation, could not let the subject drop. Over cognac he asked the Captain if he did not share his outrage at an institution that reduced human beings to the status of animals.

"Far be it from me to defend slavery," replied the Captain. "But what I do not share is your conviction that slaves are of necessity in misery over their God-given lot. On my family estates I have seen how grateful the peasants are when someone looks after their welfare. A kind master, it strikes me, can be a blessing to a person who has little recourse of his own, a fact that many of them will admit."

Charles, barely containing himself, asked if FitzRoy did not deem it likely that a slave questioned before his owner would give whatever answer he thought the owner would want to hear.

At that FitzRoy flew into a rage.

"The Devil take you," he blurted out. "You can barely hide your conviction that you are morally superior to everyone around you. Your contempt ill suits you."

He stood up and smashed his glass against the wall.

"If you persist in foisting your obstinate Whig views upon everyone around, then I do not see how we can continue to take our meals together."

And with that, he stormed out, leaving Charles sitting there with his mouth agape. He quickly followed, for he could hardly remain in the man's cabin after such a display, and no sooner was he outside than he witnessed FitzRoy berating poor Wickham mercilessly for some imagined infraction or other. The first senior officer could do nothing but hold himself in check, staring at the deck with a reddened face.

Later, Wickham offered to let Charles eat in the messroom with the other officers. But shortly afterward, FitzRoy, again the captive of an unpredictable mood, sent a handsomely worded apology, and Charles decided for the sake of the ship's equilibrium to let the offense pass. Still, he no longer felt the same about FitzRoy. He gave up his almost boyish idolatry and vowed that when the *Beagle* reached Rio de Janeiro, using the city as a base for soundings up and down the coast, he would spend the time on shore.

When the ship docked, Charles, true to his word, rented a cottage on the outskirts of town in Botofogo, at the foot of Corcovado Mountain. He shared it with King and Augustus Earle, the ship's artist, who knew the city well and provided a tour of its sin-encrusted lower depths.

Charles spent a full week packing his specimens, crating them, and shipping the lot off to Henslow in England. Then, eager to investigate the interior, he fell in with a local Irishman, Patrick Lennon, and joined him on horseback for an excursion to Lennon's coffee plantation some one hundred miles to the north.

At last, I'm in my element, he thought, as he came face to face with Nature in myriad new and exotic guises. He encountered butterflies that ran along the ground, spiders that wove webs like sails and rode them in the air, and army ants that reduced lizards and other animals to skeletons in a matter of minutes. He slept on straw mats in *vendas* along the way, lulled by a chorus of cicadas and crickets and awakened by howler monkeys, screeching green parrots, and beady-eyed toucans with gigantic red beaks. He marveled at the hundreds of humming-birds, the armadillos that dug into the earth in the time it took to get off a horse, the mindless ingenuity of moths disguised as scorpions, and the mating signals of fireflies.

He hacked his way through the jungle, past orchids sprouting from decaying tree trunks, Spanish moss and lianas dangling from tree limbs like rope. He walked under a profusion of leaves so thick they blotted out the sun and sheltered him from the short, heavy rains. His muscles were strong, his mind clear, his body taut and tanned.

On his return, he met King, who was relaxing on the porch with his feet on the railing. The midshipman handed him a glass of rum and eyed Charles's specimens, weighing down a pack mule, with merriment.

"You Englishmen," he said, excluding himself from the category, "with your fascination for peering at bugs through microscopes and your love of collecting bones—how piddling are all your preoccupations in the larger scheme of things."

Charles stared at him in amusement. He was accustomed to the young man's diatribes.

"What are you in reality next to the noble Roman, the learned Greek, even—I dare say—the noble savage of this continent?" King continued. "Simply because you have mastered the steam engine—a bit of metal that pushes other metal around—you believe you've earned the right to rule the entire world. You are convinced you are sitting on the top of the bloody pyramid and you have no idea of who built it or why."

"I say, could you give me a hand with some of my acquisitions?"

"Certainly."

King leapt from the porch, lifted a wooden box, and provided a bit of welcome news.

"By the by, I dare you to guess who has invalided," he said, using the seamen's term for aborting the voyage because of irreconcilable disagreements. Charles knew instantly who it was, but did not have a chance to speak before King blurted out the name.

"McCormick."

"McCormick?"

"Yes, he visited the admiralty of the station last week and obtained permission to ship home on the *Tyne*. He walked off early this morning, carrying his bags and sporting a parrot on his shoulder."

Charles could barely suppress his glee.

"And what was the cause?" he asked.

"A row with the Captain over you and your damnable specimens. He charged that the Captain was playing favorites, that you were able to hang all manner of nets and trawls over the side while he, the ship's senior surgeon, was cut off from his duties as a collector. The final straw was two weeks ago when you used the ship's carpenters to send off your bottles and boxes. It got quite heated, I hear."

Charles raised his glass to his good fortune.

"I say," continued King. "There is a bit of truth in his complaint, what?"

"Perhaps," replied Charles. "But Nature smiles upon those She favors."

King looked at him quizzically and said: "Byron himself could not have phrased it better."

That evening, Charles confessed his lightheartedness in his journal. "I feel a great weight has been lifted off my shoulders," he wrote. "The man has some merit to his argument—custom decrees that the surgeon is the ship's collector. But he had set himself up as my competitor and I often felt he tried to undermine my position with the Captain. Besides, he was hardly grateful to me for those specimens of his that I did include in my shipments. Altogether a most unpleasant fellow."

He read over the page, frowned, ripped it from the book, and tossed it into the wastepaper basket. Instead, he composed a letter to his sister Catherine, informing her, among an avalanche of other news, of McCormick's departure, saying simply: "He's no loss."

That same night, McCormick sat in the bar of the Hotel Lapa drinking with Sulivan, the sole shipmate who hadn't deserted him. The ex–ship's surgeon was the worse for wear—four king-sized jugs lay empty before him—and he wasn't sure the innkeeper would honor his demand for a room for the night. The parrot was on a nearby table, pecking at crumbs.

They had been speaking for some time and now McCormick's voice dropped to a conspiratorial purr.

"The trick for you, mind, is to get your own command. Only way to survive in this God-forsaken navy—otherwise the captains grind you up like a millstone and . . . toss you to the wind."

Sulivan nodded through the smoky haze. The words "your own command" had perked up his interest.

"But how is that to be done?" he inquired. "The ranks are filled with lieutenants and the wait is interminable."

"Why, simply follow Captain FitzRoy's example."

"What? So arrange the world that the commanding officer blows his bloody brains out?"

"No, no, no. Prove your worth. Show your mettle."

"Yes, but how?"

"The way Captain FitzRoy did—by impressing his commanding officer. Get hold of a sister ship. Show you can command her. Move into a position of authority and then acquit yourself so well that everyone applauds you. Wear your command like an admiral's jacket."

"All well and good, but we don't have a sister ship."

"Ah, that's where you connive. You're well acquainted with FitzRoy—make him buy one, work on him, tell him how necessary it is for the success of the survey. Tell him we can't begin to finish the soundings without it. He's got the purse for it and he's got the desire to do it. You'll be shouldering against an open door."

Sulivan was silent for a moment. The ploy might work, and in any case it couldn't hurt. Should his pleadings fall upon deaf ears, at least they could be ascribed to enthusiasm for the mission.

"And, of course, there is an additional consideration," McCormick said darkly.

"And what might that be?" asked Sulivan.

"You yourself alluded to it but a moment ago. I'm sure we would all agree that Captain FitzRoy is hardly the finest specimen of mental health. You've seen his moods—he sinks into a slough of despond at the slightest provocation. Should anything happen to him—well, let's just say that would reshuffle all the cards in the deck."

Sulivan stared across the table. "And what's in it for you, pray tell? You're not even on board anymore."

"Ah, but I could be persuaded to return. Especially if there were the prospect of another ship on the horizon. Another ship means another berth for a surgeon."

"You'll still have Philos to contend with."

"But it would be so much easier with some seawater between us."

"Perhaps Wickham would get to command the sister ship—he's number two."

"Then at the very least you ascend to number two on the *Beagle*. Hardly a downward move."

Sulivan conceded: the man had a point.

"Buy me another ale and I'll take your proposition to heart," he said.

"One more consideration," put in McCormick.

"Yes."

"Should you become Captain, I would expect you to extend me all the traditional courtesies befitting a surgeon. That includes sole responsibility for specimen collections, which are to be sent home at Government expense."

They said no more but touched their glasses in a silent toast that spilled not a drop.

It was weeks later when the *Beagle* returned from her local surveying to continue the southward journey. The crew was in mourning because three sailors had perished of illness during a snipe-shooting trip upriver. Charles had his own reason for despair, but it was so petty by comparison that he could scarcely confess it: as he was waiting on the quay, he'd spotted McCormick's luggage, piled for boarding, complete with parrot cage.

Blast it, he said to himself. *I had thought I was done with that infernal man.*

Minutes later the surgeon himself appeared, a congenial smile on his face, acting as if nothing had been amiss.

"I see you brought all your belongings," said Charles. "Were you expecting a long shore leave?"

"Quite," came the reply. "One never knows the duration of these charting expeditions, does one?"

Charles could think of no riposte.

That evening, with the ship underway and his stomach once again in distress, he supped with FitzRoy and raised the subject of McCormick's departure and reappearance. At first the Captain seemed too preoccupied to answer, but then he frowned, waved his hand vaguely, and suddenly brightened, saying: "Ha, yes, he asked to come back, pleaded with me, actually, and I thought: why not, what's the harm in it? And so by Jupiter, you see, here he is."

Charles could not help looking crestfallen, so much so that FitzRoy leaned over to pat him on the arm.

"Don't worry so, Philos—you're still the *Beagle*'s naturalist. Your collections are swamping my decks and are being sent home at His Majesty's expense. Am I not a man of my word—what? Do I not deserve some little mention years hence when you are a famed lecturer?"

Charles had to concede that FitzRoy had a valid point.

Some weeks later they entered the waters of Argentina, and they soon learned firsthand that the land was far more rugged and wild than any they had seen before. As the *Beagle* approached the harbor of Buenos Aires, an Argentinean guard ship fired a shot across her bow, enforcing, in a most unfriendly way, a quarantine. FitzRoy was beside himself with anger; he sailed past the vessel, threatening to blast it to kingdom come, and then moved on up to Montevideo, where he convinced a British man-of-war to head back to Buenos Aires to rectify the insult to the Union Jack.

No sooner had the warship left than the local chief of police, rowing frantically to the ship, clambered aboard to ask FitzRoy for help. Negro soldiers had seized the town's arsenal and were in full rebellion. Charles, standing next to the Captain, felt his blood rise: at long last, a chance for action!

FitzRoy dispatched some fifty crewmen armed to the teeth, and Charles jumped in a boat to join them. Jamming his pistols into his belt, he couldn't wait to reach shore. They marched through the dusty streets as a hoard of merchants rushed to their doorways and leaned out of windows to cheer. Grinning ear to ear, Charles felt a warm camaraderie with his shipmates. Looking behind, he spotted McCormick and was surprised to find the feeling of kinship extended even to him. The two men smiled at each other. Charles raised a pistol in the air and mimicked firing it.

But the rebellion, sadly, quickly fizzled. The insurgents promptly gave up, and when the crew arrived at the arsenal, there was little to do but round up the prisoners and sniff around the fort for holdouts.

Come evening, they were cooking beefsteak over roaring fires in the courtyard. Still, wolfing down the sizzling red meat, Charles appreciated the few moments of exhilaration.

"If only they hadn't given in," he said ruefully to McCormick, who, with a cutlass slung from his belt, looked more dashing than Charles had thought possible. They shared a spot of rum.

For all its comic opera overtones, the adventure stirred Darwin's spirit. As the ship moved four hundred miles south to Bahia Blanc and began to survey the coastline in earnest, he spent his days on land. The pastimes of his youth played to his advantage. On horseback he roamed the windswept plains of the Pampas, shooting ostrich, deer, cavia, and guanaco. He brought fresh meat back to the Captain's table and a grateful crew—no more dried beef and biscuit but instead armadillo roasted in its shell. He took to the outdoor life with passion, even venturing deep into territory where wild Indians were known to torture and kill foreign wayfarers.

He rode with the rugged *gauchos,* who admired his marksmanship, and tried to learn to sling *bolas,* the three rocks connected by strands of rawhide. One day he tripped up his own horse with the infernal weapon; that night, smoking a *cigarrito,* he wrote to his sister: "The *gauchos* roared with laughter; they cried they had seen every sort of animal caught, but had never before seen a man caught by himself."

He hired a cabin boy, Syms Covington, to help with his shooting and skin his specimens. Now that he had a companion to witness his exploits, there was no stopping him. His blood was up and he was filled with a twenty-four-year-old's conviction that great exploits and great discoveries awaited him.

And sure enough, one fine September day, when Charles, FitzRoy, McCormick (still unaccountably amiable), and two others were in a launch exploring the mudbanks of the coast, they made a significant find. They were rounding a headland, Punta Alta, when McCormick, alone facing the shore, yelled out: "I say, what's that over there?" The others rushed to his side. He pointed to a mudbank some twenty feet high, in which curious white objects were embedded, rising up behind a forest of reeds. At first it looked like a quarry of purest marble, collapsing in on itself, gleaming in the sunlight. But when the launch pulled closer, they saw that it was something much more interesting—bones packed firmly inside the solidified silt.

Darwin leapt from the craft and waded to shore, parting the reeds with his cosh and sending crabs scurrying out of his path. By the time the others caught up with him, he was already deep into the embankment, which contained a soft sedimentary deposit of gravel and clay. Forking out handfuls, he dug up to his elbows until finally, with a burst of energy, he pried loose a massive three-foot-long bone and held it up like a prize.

"By the lord Harry, what do you suppose it is?" he cried out. "A massive thigh bone of some sort? Do you think it possible—could it be a fossil?"

They looked around. Gigantic bones surrounded them, tusks and femurs and a rounded carapace, sticking out from the earth as if trapped there by a landslide. They were in a natural ossuary, and the fossilized bones were more than likely from an earlier era—they were much bigger than those of beasts walking the earth today. All afternoon they worked the graveyard, unearthing immense relics, which they left on the narrow beach before returning to the ship.

That evening Charles could talk of nothing else, speculating on what the bones might be, poring through books on zoology, biology, and paleontology, coming up with one theory, abandoning it for another, then circling back to it. Finally, after dinner, FitzRoy, amused at the mania that had seized his friend, pushed him out the cabin door, saying: "You have the look of a man possessed who is likely to pace about ruminating all the night long. I require a respite. Wake me only if the bones come to life."

The next morning, Charles returned with McCormick, who almost matched him in enthusiasm. Covington and a band of crewmen carried pickaxes. They labored through the day, stopping only for a meal of salt beef and biscuit, which Charles would have gladly forgone if the others could have. By dusk the two scientists conferred over an array of twenty bones laid out upon the sand. The two were in agreement: they were prehistoric and extinct. Though some bore a resemblance to living animals, like the common guanaco, they were two and three times their size. Charles thought one, a skull that took hours to dislodge, belonged to a *Megatherium,* which he had once heard described in a lecture. McCormick thought it might be a *Megalonyx* instead. Together, they tried to drum up the snatches of learning they retained from Edinburgh. Sitting there exhausted on the beach, their faces streaked with dirt and their beards caked with mud, they began smiling, then laughing. Charles loped up and down imitating a giant sloth. McCormick picked up a skull and drew it over his head, staggering around under the weight. The crew howled with laughter. On the ride back, Charles looked over at his companion and thought: He's not such a bad bloke.

After a week, the main deck of the *Beagle* was so strewn about with fossils that it was difficult to walk from one end to the other. First Lieutenant Wickham grumbled about "the bedevilment" of his ship—"turned as it is into some sort of museum"—but his consternation was feigned. Much of the crew was swept up by the enterprise. They listened attentively as Charles endlessly theorized as to what had driven the animals to extinction. He talked of changing habitats and mountains rising up and of an emerging landbridge in the isthmus between North and South America. FitzRoy roundly disagreed: they died out, he insisted during one of his on-board Sunday sermons, because they did not make it to Noah's Ark.

Jemmy Button was for some reason especially excited by the bones. He walked around touching them at every opportunity, and was heard to remark that he had seen such things before, close to his home village. Charles marveled at how cleverly the savage succeeded in thrusting himself into the limelight.

After two weeks, FitzRoy put a stop to the excavation. It was time for the *Beagle* to move on. He was eager to resume his surveying and, not incidentally, to get on with his own project—transporting the Yamana Indians back to their native land and planting the seeds of Christianity in that forlorn part of the world.

The departure from Buenos Aires was rushed and complicated. Charles was eager to send the entire consignment of bones on a ship that was to leave for England the same day as the *Beagle* was to travel across the river to pick up supplies, including bottles and preserving spirits and walking boots that he himself had ordered. So he arranged for Edward

Lumb, an Englishman long in residence, to handle the transfer. Charles returned two days later to pay him and was relieved to learn that the shipment had left on schedule.

As Charles handed over a stack of pound notes, Lumb posed a question: "By the by, sir, I should have asked before it went, but I noticed that there were two of you fellows—what do you call yourselves?—*naturalists*. Yourself and that other one—what the devil's his name?"

"Mr. McCormick. What of it?"

"Well, sir, the manifold asked for only a single name, so I put down yours. Is that all right, I'm wondering?"

Charles felt his breath catch. So the fossils went to Henslow under his name alone. He felt a rush of excitement, followed by a pang of guilt. He could not take credit for them alone, it must be shared. After all, McCormick was the one who first spotted the site, though Charles was quite sure he would have seen it himself at some point. Well, there was nothing for it—the questions of ownership and credit would have to be settled later. In the meantime, the fossils were headed to safekeeping in Cambridge—that was the important thing. And undoubtedly there would be many more fossils ahead.

"That's fine," he said to Lumb. "Pray do not exercise yourself about it. We'll sort it all out back in England."

CHAPTER 13

10 April 1865

I have lately come upon something very curious. Papa has long had the habit of leaving a stack of paper in the staircase-cupboard for the younger children to draw on and, since he is exceedingly frugal, these are often the reverse sides of drafts of his writing. Two days ago, when I fetched some paper for Horace and Leonard, I began reading the pages, which were early versions of his book The Voyage of the Beagle. *I could not help but notice that there were discrepancies. For some reason or other he had decided to make various changes.*

In the pages I read, I could see he had excised entire passages describing events that transpired during the voyage. In particular, he eliminated several conversations that occurred between himself and one Robert McCormick, who, if memory serves, was on board in the capacity of ship's surgeon. I compared the manuscript pages to those in the published journals and found that much of what they said to each other, some of it argumentative, had never appeared in print. In particular, I noted the elimination of sections that showed Mr McCormick to be jealous of the many kindnesses proffered to Papa by Captain FitzRoy. There is one episode in which Mr McCormick, who is put out because the Captain brought Papa and not him to visit some island or other, turns his back and walks away while Papa is speaking to him. Why he should have deleted this material I have no idea, especially since he is so thorough in recounting all other aspects of the voyage. Perhaps he did so because the passages cast Mr McCormick in a bad light—indeed, he appears to have been a most unpleasant, spleen-filled man.

Still, the omissions set me to thinking and I resolved to see if there were others. Surreptitiously, as my brothers were occupied drawing, and as Papa was outside taking his constitutional on the Sandwalk, I slipped into his study. There, on a shelf above his wooden desk, I found some of the notebooks he kept on his voyage. They were numbered, so I could tell at a glance that some were missing. There was no indication where they might have been put. I glanced at some of the others, pulling them down carefully so that I might replace them exactly as they were to avoid discovery, and I was surprised in looking through them to find that Papa had changed some of the entries after the fact. I could discern this because the ink was of a noticeably different shade than that of the original entries and was also uniform throughout, whereas the writing done during the trip varied from week to week. In some instances, the jottings were fitted in awkwardly, sometimes scrawled along the margins, making it obvious that they had been added subsequently. In addition, some earlier entries had been crossed out altogether.

I wondered if these changes might be the sort that one might make upon re-reading a draft and wanting to add some further reflection or elaboration. But they did not appear to be of that nature, since it was clear from even a cursory reading that they tended to alter the very narrative itself. Some of the changes dealt with Captain FitzRoy and others were about Jemmy Button, the infamous savage whose treachery knows no bounds. Still others concerned the aforementioned Mr McCormick.

But I did not dare to linger too long to read them and, truth be told, I was feeling sorely guilty, knowing that I was reading something that was not intended for my eyes—or for that matter, the eyes of anyone. As soon as I heard the tapping of Papa's cane on the front step, I quickly replaced the notebooks and closed the study door only seconds before he entered the hall. As I write this, I think I may search for some opportunity tomorrow, perhaps when Papa is once again out on the Sandwalk, to continue my investigation into his writings.

11 April 1865

Somehow I must contrive to meet Captain FitzRoy. I must talk to him and implore him to provide explanations, for all this is simply too much! There are too many mysteries that set my head spinning. I must find out what hap-pened during the journey of the Beagle. *From reading Papa's journals—the* unexpurgated *journals, I hasten to point out—it is clear that certain events transpired in the course of the voyage, events of great importance, which were not properly recorded. I have no inkling of what they were, but that they were crucial to the outcome of the trip, I have no doubt.*

Something happened when the ship was in South America. What it was, I do not know, but Papa writes about it in guarded but tantalising language. He refers to it as a nuit de feu. *What he means by that is not at all clear, but the term suggests some sort of violent upheaval. Perhaps it occurred when the Englishmen met the savage Indians, whose appearance was depicted as most frightening; Papa has described it vividly, how they stood on shore slobbering like wild animals, their long hair matted, their faces streaked in red and white and their bodies greased and naked save for mantles of guanaco skin about the shoulders.*

Perhaps the nuit de feu *was something that happened later in the voyage, some horrible occurrence involving a member of the crew. Or perhaps it had something to do with Jemmy Button, for we now know that, far from being a person who opened his heart to Christian civilisation, he was capable of the most harrowing barbarity.*

Captain FitzRoy may prove to be my Rosetta Stone. But I do not know how to approach him and, truth be told, I am apprehensive about the prospect. I have heard enough about him in the whisperings at Down House to know that many feel he is not right in the head. And of course he bears a deep enmity towards Papa, whom he blames for trying to overturn all the beliefs of Christendom, while no doubt blaming himself for commanding the vessel that allowed him to do it.

I know this at first hand, for I was present at the now famous confronta-tion between Mr Huxley and Soapy Sam Wilberforce at the British Associa-tion for the Advancement of Science in Oxford, where Captain FitzRoy made a spectacle of himself. The scene is still so vivid in my memory—even though I was but twelve years old—I can scarcely believe it happened nearly five years ago. Uncle Ras had sneaked me in and I took pains to make myself incon-spicuous behind his chair as I watched the proceedings.

Some five hundred people were packed into the sweltering lecture-hall of the new museum. The Bishop attacked Papa's theory from every angle and then uttered the famous mocking question: was Mr Huxley related to an ape on his grandfather's side or his grandmother's? Mr Huxley leapt up. He defended Papa's work with characteristic vigour and concluded with the riposte that rapidly made the rounds: that if he had to choose between having an ape for an ancestor or a man endowed by Nature with reason who yet employs the faculty for the purpose of introducing ridicule into a grave scientific discussion, 'then I unhesitatingly affirm my preference for the ape'. It let loose pandemonium. People cheered and booed. Some tossed their programmes into the air. I peered over Uncle Ras' chair. Just in front of us a group of raucous students chanted: 'Mawnkey, mawnkey!' A pregnant woman not two rows away rose and suddenly fainted and fell to the floor.

At that moment I saw FitzRoy, dressed in an old rear admiral's uniform that was so tattered and worn he looked like an Old Testament prophet. He wandered through the crowd like a man possessed, waving aloft a Bible with a trembling hand, a bit of spittle in the corner of his mouth, his hair unkempt. He pronounced Papa a 'blasphemer'. He said he regretted the day he agreed to take 'that man' on board ship and uttered that his ingratitude was 'sharper than a serpent's tooth'. He called him 'the Devil's own Pied Piper, leading the unsuspecting onto the downward path of hellfire and damnation.' At one point, looking wildly at the cheering gallery, he declared: "But this is all wrong—the man's a villain.' He went on in this vein, muttering various oaths and damnations that I could scarce hear—except for one, which he threw over his shoulder in my direction. It was: 'So that's how it is, eh, Mr Darwin?' He repeated this meaningless sentence several times, delivering it in a bitter-sounding singsong that made my blood run cold.

I could not help but notice that Mr Huxley, surveying the entire scene with a certain satisfaction, like a general whose troops have routed the enemy, spotted Captain FitzRoy, and as he did so, his complexion turned white as candle-wax. He immediately said something in an aside to a young man who moved through the crowd and confronted Captain FitzRoy, who by now had slumped back into a seat in exhaustion. The young man quickly got the Captain to his feet and trundled him off the floor and out a side door, whether out of exasperation or kindness I could not say.

For some time the Captain's words echoed through my head—'So that's how it is, eh, Mr Darwin?' What could he have possibly meant? I suppose the phrase could have been meaningless twaddle from a mind worn down by grief and suffering to the point of lunacy. Indeed, with his countenance pale and crazed, he did appear a most pathetic figure—sad but unsettling and, I *must admit, threatening. Nonetheless, I feel I absolutely must talk to him to seek an explanation! One mystery piles up upon another, and I feel desperate to get to the bottom of it all.*

15 April 1865

I'm in luck! We were visited this weekend by the Hookers—Joseph, the botanist at Kew, and his wife, Frances, who is also the daughter of dear old Henslow, Papa's beloved teacher, departed these four years. Frances, who is most clever, suggested a strategy to reach Captain FitzRoy.

We went out for a walk in the garden, it being unseasonably warm, and we opened our hearts to each other. She confessed to me how upset she had been when Papa did not attend her father's funeral, pointing out that the berth on the Beagle had come about through her father's intercession and that he was the one who had received the crates of Papa's famous specimens. I was obliged to make his excuses, which of course revolved around his ill-health, and then suddenly I blurted out that I found it odd that Papa continually avoids funerals, even that of his own father. I remarked that it was a grievous shortcoming and then found myself reciting various other shortcomings in him. It was a great relief to be able to confide in someone.

I did not talk about my investigation or my deepest suspicions but simply said that I needed to talk to Captain FitzRoy. She said that would be difficult because he had lately moved from South Kensington to Upper Norwood, south of London. I most assuredly would not be invited there, she noted. But then she had an idea. She had it on good authority that FitzRoy, now in the Meteorological Office, would shortly meet Matthew Maury, his counterpart in the American navy. My Uncle Ras could surely discover the schedule and arrange for an encounter that would appear accidental.

I thanked her and hugged her. She then cautioned me, saying that she had heard that FitzRoy had become unhinged through grief and misfortune. She recounted his woes, which did indeed seem legion. His ambitions have been frustrated at every turn. His surveying work on the Beagle did not bring him the recognition he expected and he turned to politics. He won a vacant seat in Durham but got embroiled in a vicious rivalry with a fellow Tory candidate that led to a brawl outside his club in the Mall. The scandal dogged him in office and so he accepted the governorship of New Zealand, only to fall prey to a bitter land dispute between settlers and native Maoris. It proved his undoing, leading to his recall, and after a horrible voyage home, his wife Mary died, leaving him with four motherless children. Then his eldest daughter died. Bit by bit, his fortune has dwindled to nothing.

Aware of his destitute state, his colleagues—'including your own papa', said Frances—got him elected to the Royal Society. The Society recommended him to the Board of Trade to be appointed weather statistician, a post that was not glamorous but held interest for a scientific man. He remarried and attempted to make the most of his new position, embracing the use of the barometer, and had tried to collect all sorts of observations not simply to record weather as it occurred but to make predictions for the future. He called it 'weather-forecasting' and thought it could save ships at sea; but despite some initial successes, it had not worked out. His faulty predictions were widely ridiculed—and The Times had recently dropped his 'forecasts'.

'You should know too he is no friend of your dear father's,' Frances said.

'I am aware of that,' I replied. 'Papa says he has been attacking him in reviews under the name of "Senex". He recognises his arguments from the old days.'

'There's little doubt that his religious fervour has increased. He's become a strict literalist of the Bible. My husband has often remarked on the turn of fate that made the Beagle *into a cradle for the faith of one man and a coffin for the faith of another.'*

Frances then said that of all the shocks and jolts FitzRoy had received, the one that cut the deepest was the news of the massacre of the crew of the Allen Gardiner *and the accusation that Jemmy Button himself had led it. We began to discuss the shocking tale, but at that point others joined us in the garden and so we broke off.*

21 April 1865

I am staying with Uncle Ras, who is amused by my interest in Papa's past and has kindly agreed to arrange a meeting with FitzRoy in a week's time, promising to keep the matter 'our own little secret'. He, too, warned me about the Captain, saying that the man was succumbing to what he himself has termed 'the blue evils'.

To pass the time, I decided to learn more about the massacre in Tierra del Fuego, and so I called upon William Parker Snow, the Captain who found Jemmy Button twenty-two years after Captain FitzRoy had returned him to the wild. Mr Snow, then employed by the Patagonian Missionary Society and now its major antagonist, has seized upon Jemmy's vengeful guilt in the massacre as part of his campaign to bring the Society's work to an end.

He received me most graciously in his second-floor office on Harley Street, holding a chair for me to be seated and saying that it was an honour to meet 'Professor Darwin's daughter'. I promptly assured him that my father was not a professor by any means, but simply an amateur naturalist, to which he replied: 'Were all amateurs of his ilk, we would be fortunate indeed.'

After such inconsequential talk, I asked him to recount the story of the massacre. His brow furrowed and he told me the bare bones of what was known. I made notes of what he said.

'When Jemmy was returned to Tierra del Fuego, he disappeared for years. I found him in November 1855 and was astounded at the change in him. We sailed in through the narrows into Yahgashaga and spotted fires burning on a small island. I ran up the ensign and two canoes approached, one carrying a fat, dirty, naked Indian who stood up and shouted "Where's the ladder?" We brought him on board and couldn't believe it was really Jemmy Button: he seemed to have totally reverted to a primitive state. But he hadn't forgotten his English. And another curious thing—he refused to answer to the name Jemmy. He said he wanted to be called Orundellico instead. I have no idea what that was all about.

'It was awkward and Jemmy was none too friendly. He demanded clothes and so I gave him a pair of my own trousers and a shirt, but he was too fat to wear them. He wanted meat, but when we took him belowdecks to feed him, he was too overwhelmed to eat. I asked him if he wanted to go to the new mission station on the Falklands and he resolutely refused. I gave him some gifts, including a music-box, which delighted him, and I told him to come back the next morning for more.

'At daybreak, more canoes surrounded us. Jemmy and his brothers and other men came on board and the mood turned ugly. I gave Jemmy more presents than he could carry. They were shouting "Yammerschooner" over and over. That means "give me" and believe me, once you've heard it you never forget it. Some of the others pushed me, saying "Ingliss come—Ingliss give—

Ingliss plenty." Jemmy would not help us. So I shouted for the sails to be loosened, which made them think we were leaving, and fearful that we would kidnap them, they scrambled over the side. That was my last sight of Jemmy, as we sailed off—he and his wife in a canoe, fighting off the others to keep their pile of gifts.'

Mr Snow explained what happened next. A new missionary leader arrived, the Reverend G. Pakenham Despard, fixed on the idea that Jemmy should become the spearhead of a mass conversion. He hired a new captain, who returned to Tierra del Fuego and somehow brought Jemmy and his family to the mission settlement at Keppel in the Falklands. They learnt little, did little and stayed there only four months. To go home, they had to promise others would take their place, and so an exchange was made on the next trip—Jemmy returned to his island and nine more Indians came. They had appeared to fit in at the settlement, singing hymns and being baptised. But their return voyage began badly. Despard believed they had stolen things from the missionary workers and ordered a search. They threw their bundles down on the deck of the ship, furious at being called thieves, and when articles were indeed discovered and confiscated, they became even more angry.

Their fury did not dissipate during the rough crossing. When the Allen Gardiner dropped anchor, and the other Indians rowed out to the ship, those on board raised a clamour. Jemmy was brought on board to mediate and he took the side of his tribesmen, demanding more gifts as compensation. But there were no more. Then a sailor told the Captain that some of his personal items were missing. Another search was ordered—the items were discovered—and the Indians went into a frenzy, tearing their clothes off, throwing away their Bibles and all trappings of civilisation, and, naked, clambering down into the canoes. Their shrieks resounded from shore until nightfall and fires were lit, billowing smoke into the dark sky.

For days the ship gently rocked in the bay, as the crew constructed a rudimentary mission-house on a quiet spot above the beach and hundreds of canoes bearing Indians arrived from all directions. On Sunday, the missionary decided to hold a service in the house. Dressed in clean shirts, leaving only the cook on board, the crew rowed to the beach and made their way through crowds of Indians. The cook watched from the boat. Once the Captain and crew were inside, the Indians seized the long-boat and pushed it into the water. A hymn struck up from within the house, then an outcry, then shrieks. The white men stumbled out into the sunlight, as the Indians pursued them, beating them with clubs and stones. Others arrived with spears.

One sailor reached the water, waded out to his waist and was felled with a stone to the temple. The beach was soaked in blood. The terrified cook lowered a dinghy, rowed frantically to shore and disappeared into the woods. He was rescued half-crazed, months later, by a ship sent to investigate, naked and covered with boils, his eyebrows and beard plucked out by the Indians. He told a tale of horror. The ship that returned him to the Falklands also brought Jemmy Button.

Mr Snow sighed and said, 'I expect you know the rest from the newspapers.' And indeed, I did. An official enquiry was held. Amid a welter of confusing testimony and political opinion running against the Patagonian Missionary Society, Jemmy was not found guilty, despite the statements of the cook, who said, among other things, that Mr Button had climbed aboard the ship after the massacre and spent the night sleeping in the Captain's quarters.

'All very sad,' opined Mr Snow. 'But I knew in my bones that something like this would happen. It was a chain of events set in motion by the meeting of the first Englishman and the first Indian. It was pre-ordained from the moment that Captain FitzRoy tore that button from his uniform and paid for that young boy.'

I felt myself nodding in agreement.

'And as I expected, it has ended badly for the Indians. At last report, their ranks have been decimated by disease. Here, look at this—'

And so saying, he handed me a copy of the Mission's newsletter, The Voice of Pity. I saw there an article reporting 'a burst of mournful news'— the death of Jemmy Button. Mr Snow waited until I had read it, then spoke again.

'I knew that underneath all the smiles and bowing, Jemmy didn't really respect the glories of Western culture. That very first evening on board, when I found him after his long reversion to his primitive habitation, he said something I have never forgotten. He said: "Inglish sigh-eenz is for the Devil." It took me some time to understand what he was saying—that our science is not all that he expected it to be. He said it with what can only be called contempt.'

Mr Snow looked me in the eye and added: 'It seems strange to be telling that to Darwin's daughter.'

28 April 1865

My interview with Captain FitzRoy did not go at all well. I was totally unnerved by it and I fear that it did little good to the Captain—quite the contrary. I fear I have worsened his condition, which, I can now attest, is quite wretched.

At Uncle Ras' suggestion, I asked for the Captain in the antechamber of the Meteorological Office, where I arrived without an appointment, knowing that he would be there to meet with Lieutenant Maury. An assistant, hearing my request, raised an eyebrow and smirked in a most disconcerting way, as if to say I did not know the half of it, and appeared to be weighing whether or not he should notify the Captain of my arrival. He held a ruler in his left hand, banging it on his opposite palm, and kept me standing there while he thought upon the matter. I doubt I have been treated so rudely in all my life. When finally he did agree, he left the room, making it clear that he would not return, so that the idea of being alone with a person who might not be quite right in the head filled me with apprehension.

The room itself was oppressive and might have been described by our own Mr Dickens. It was heavily curtained and quite dark, with a single gas-lamp in the centre. Old wooden cabinets lined the walls up to midway, above which hung yellowed charts and water-stained prints of ships, the frames tilting at odd angles. Dust was everywhere, covering even the inkwells on the cracked leather desk and the faded green velvet chairs. A threadbare carpet completed the picture. It had the appearance not of a Government office but of a mortuary.

I was musing on the disarray when I heard a step bounding down the hall staircase. In popped Captain FitzRoy, looking most queer. He had lost his military bearing and was oddly stooped, his head hung slightly to one side, his eyes so wide-open as to appear bulging. His hair was unkempt, his beard scraggly. Indeed, it seemed he had travelled a long and arduous road from those days when he proudly commanded a ship in Her Majesty's Navy.

He appeared puzzled by my presence, but thrust out his hand in some vestigial memory of politeness, gave a short awkward bow and proceeded to sputter, thus: 'Captain Robert FitzRoy . . . To what do I owe . . . To whom . . . What is the purpose . . . hmmm.' And so on—unable to complete a thought.

He had a most daunting sense of energy, like a tightly wound spring in a child's toy, and he kept moving his hands up and down and his legs side to side. His constant agitation made it most difficult to concentrate. Gathering my courage, I led him to a chair and forced him to sit down. I sat next to him. There was nothing for it but to start right in.

'Captain FitzRoy,' I began, 'I am sorry to burst in on you, and I pray you will not think me unmannerly, but I would dearly like to ask you some questions pertaining to the Beagle *and her voyage.'*

'By all means . . . by all means . . .'

I then mentioned South America and Tierra del Fugeo, and the very name seemed to derange him further. 'The land of fire . . . land of fire,' he began, and his words poured out so quickly that I could hardly catch them. I realised he was talking about the early explorers who named it for the fact that the natives lighted fires on shore, leading the sailors to believe they were gazing upon Hades itself—which was not, he said in a bitter aside, far from the truth.

Those were the last coherent words I heard from him. I asked him about the nuit de feu *and he gave me a most singular look, started to talk several times, then broke off in mid-sentence. It was a jumble of nonsense. He kept shaking his head, to show disagreement, and saying 'No . . . no . . . not Tierra del Fuego, the Galápagos . . . the enchanted isles—heh! That's where it all happened . . .' and then he fixed me with a frightening look and said, in that singular singsong, those horrible words, 'So that's how it is, eh, Mr Darwin?' After which, he laughed; a low-pitched, hollow, evil sound.*

I was on the point of leaving when he placed his hand upon my arm, holding me down, and said with urgency: 'Seven wounds, that's what they found. Seven wounds . . . like our Saviour Christ's wounds . . . that's what it is to be Captain . . . the loneliness, salt in your lungs . . . all my money gone, spent on the Adventurer *. . . enemies and ingrates in the Admiralty. I was warned . . . beware, they said . . . Sulivan, my very own second lieutenant, knighted, knighted . . . And me—what am I?'*

He said this last fragment with such vehemence that I bolted up. But he did not release my arm and leapt up next to me, leaning close to my face, still babbling. I felt a spray of his saliva on my forehead and my heart was pounding.

'Darwin's a heretic, an infidel . . . the Devil's hand-maiden . . . The stones on the beach do not lie, they're rounded, from the Flood . . . The Flood

happened just as the Bible relates, I tell you . . . the door of the Ark was too small to admit the Mastodon . . . Heresy's a sin and so are violations of the Commandments, eh, Mr Darwin? So that's how it is, eh?'

I resolved to leave at once and tore my arm from his grasp.

'Jemmy Button,' he cried. 'Jemmy Button did not do it! They attempted to crucify him . . . as they are crucifying me!'

'Kindly let me leave,' I cried.

'You English—no lifeless,' he screamed in an accent, as if he himself were the Indian boy.

At that, I grabbed up my skirts in both hands and rushed towards the door without a backward look. I heard a flood of invective follow me and more incomprehensible words and that horrible hoarse laugh.

I rushed out the front door and down the steps. I managed to wave down a phaeton—they almost never stop but I suspect the driver took pity, seeing my dishevelled state—and I went directly to Uncle Ras'. I did not recover easily, even after several cups of hot tea.

That night, as I was trying fruitlessly to sleep, his grotesque words echoed through my head, especially that meaningless final phrase, 'You English—no lifeless.'

※

30 April 1865

Horror upon horrors! I have just heard that Captain FitzRoy took his own life. I can scarcely believe it! And here I saw him not more than two days ago.

Uncle Ras informed me of it, and he did not spare my feelings but in his excitement described it in gruesome detail. The account had been told by FitzRoy's poor wife and was the talk of the Athenaeum. The day before his death, FitzRoy could not sit still; he would spring up, pace around, start to speak, then stop and sit down again. He insisted he needed to go to his office, but having set out turned back, then left for London in the afternoon, returning in the evening extremely upset and rambling incoherently. He insisted he must see Maury again, even though the next day was a Sunday and they had already said good-bye.

He did not sleep well that night. In the morning, when his wife stirred, his eyes were already open. He asked why the maid had not awakened them and she told him it was Sunday. He remained in bed by her side for half an hour, rose quietly, went into an adjoining room and kissed his daughter, Laura. Then he went into the dressing-room and bolted the lock. A minute later, she heard his body strike the floor. She screamed for the servants, who smashed through the door and there he was lying in a pool of blood. He had taken a straight razor from his shaving-kit and, with a single stroke, perhaps even looking into the mirror, ended his misery by pulling it swiftly across his throat.

The horror of it! The poor wretched man. I cannot help but wonder if I contributed in some small way—or even a large way—to his fevered state of mind. If this were true, I could not easily live with myself—and yet I will never know for certain one way or the other. I tremble to think upon it! Enough of this spying and snooping, this childish play at investigating! I will have no more of it. I shall stop it at once and force myself to change. I shall become a new and better person, no longer the suspicious, arrogant Lizzie I've been these many years.

Poor Captain FitzRoy. How can God allow such misery in this world? How can we poor human beings endure it?

CHAPTER 14

Hugh finished his Scottish breakfast—a bowl of steaming oatmeal, bub-bling under a half-inch pool of thick cream, eaten with a wooden spoon. He sipped his coffee, looking at a vista of pointed green pines and the deep blue of Loch Laggan. A road hugged the shore and in the morning sun it looked tranquil and pristine, a necklace beside a mirror. But last night, when he had driven from Inverness across the mountains, follow-ing the road's embedded cat's-eyes through the drifting fog, it had been treacherous.

A long trip for what could turn out to be a wild goose chase, he thought.

He returned to his room, packed his bag, and carried it to the front parlor of the old inn, bowing his head to pass through the low-slung wooden doorways. He paid the bill and asked for directions to walk to the owner's house. The woman seemed surprised that FitzRoy Macleod had agreed to receive him.

"Now don't you be aggravating him," she chided in a brogue. "He's a grand man, he is, but old enough to be your grandfather. And what might you be wanting with him, anyway?"

"Just a wee chat," replied Hugh, smiling.

The woman leaned over and wagged her elbow at him, as if to poke him in the ribs.

"Aw, you Yanks."

Outside, the air was crystal clear and cool enough to bite his lungs. He stashed his bag in the trunk of the rental car, buttoned his coat, and walked up the dirt path beside the inn. A massive, moss-covered stone wall listed away from the house. The path entered a wood, then mounted steeply to the top of a hill and came to a crossroads. He took the path to the right, which after fifteen minutes led him to a bright green meadow dotted with sheep, their coats gray and tangled. They lifted their heads from grazing to stare at him blankly.

He looked forward to seeing Macleod. It had not been difficult to trace him. Nora Barlow, Charles Darwin's granddaughter, wrote of a meeting in London in 1934 with Laura FitzRoy, the very same daughter upon whose cheek the deranged Captain pressed a kiss moments before taking his life. From this, Hugh found Laura's obituary and traced other FitzRoy family members. Macleod, now in his nineties, was one of them. He was famous in the inner circles of Whitehall as a Tory strategist and a war hero who took a German bunker single-handedly.

Hugh arrived at a grove of tall evergreens. They rose up so abruptly they appeared to form a gigantic wall and through it, like a door, was the dark opening of the path. Hugh followed it and emerged at the other end of the grove to find a breathtaking vista—an old manor-house set in rolling hills beside a small lake. He saw that it had once been grand, but now its slate roof was sagging and its windows crooked. The path narrowed and dew on the knee-high grass soaked his trouser legs.

As soon as he walked up the front steps the door opened so quickly, he surmised his approach had been scrutinized. Clutching the knob was a woman in her eighties, thin, small, and birdlike in her quick move-ments. Hugh introduced himself and she did likewise: Mrs. Macleod.

"He's expecting you," she said, gesturing behind her to a wooden staircase that rose in tiers along the squared-off walls, its dark banister as thick as a ship's mast. Hugh thanked her and mounted the faded red runner, held in place by brass stays. At the turn halfway up he stopped in astonishment. He was face to face with a large marble bust that was instantly familiar: the almond eyes, the sensitive mouth and aquiline nose, the broad forehead with hair brushed forward like Napoleon's. It was FitzRoy himself.

Macleod received him upstairs in a huge room, with tall ceilings of ancient plaster and rough-hewn beams. He sat before a window with the sun streaming in behind him so that he was hard to see at first, a man shrunken with age but still sitting erect, a wool blanket across his legs. He motioned to Hugh to join him and Hugh chose a seat to one side so that he could better examine the man. Macleod had long white hair that curled around his ears, red veins tracing tributaries on his nose, and moist pink eyes.

He offered Hugh a Scotch. Hugh declined and saw a glass half full on a small table next to his host. He sneaked a look at his watch: ten o'clock.

After a bit of small talk, Macleod knocked back a healthy swallow, banged the glass down, and asked him to state his business. Hugh explained, as he had over the phone, that he was interested in learning about Captain FitzRoy, that he was thinking of researching a book, that he wondered if perhaps there just might be some letters or other mementos lying about.

"Ah, poor man. He was brilliant, you know. First to try weather forecasting—invented the damn thing. First to use barometers. His survey maps are used to this day."

He spoke with such passion, he might have been talking about his own son.

"They hounded him to death—the bankers, the businessmen, the Whigs. He had enemies everywhere and they brought him down. No loyalty, no appreciation . . . Years he spent, charting the toughest coast of them all, Strait of Magellan, Cape Horn, Tierra del Fuego . . . Spent his own money to hire the *Adventure*. Had to pay for it all but he got the job done. And was the Admiralty grateful? Not a bit of it—not so much as a thank you."

Hugh nodded sympathetically.

"He took to the sea at fourteen. Given his own ship at twenty-three. Aye, what a lonely thing it is, a captain aboard Her Majesty's vessel . . . What's the name of that captain who shot his brains out on the *Beagle*?"

"Pringle Stokes."

"That's it. Holed up in his cabin off the God-forsaken coast, weeks on end, storms lashing the ship, never so much as see the sun. FitzRoy used to go on and on about him . . . talking about 'seven wounds, seven wounds' . . . whatever the blazes that meant. The loneliness of it all. No one to help, no one to turn to."

Hugh changed his mind and said he'd like a drink after all. Macleod, delighted, shouted to his wife, who brought him one instantly.

"And that Darwin didn't help poor FitzRoy much—he and that Huxley fellow . . . Got him into the Royal Society, a small job as a weatherman, no pension, no future. No wonder he was pressed to take his own life. Here was his shipmate, world-famous because of the journey he had made possible—a heretic to boot—and they give the Captain a pittance."

The mention of Darwin brought the conversation around to the fickleness of history and this gave Hugh an opportunity to renew his request for documents.

Macleod drained his glass.

"They're gone, nothing left, picked clean. You should have been here years ago."

Hugh enjoyed Macleod's reminiscences and ended up staying the day. At Mrs. Macleod's urging, he accompanied the old man on a tour of the grounds, pushing him in a wheelchair over rocky walkways. After that came lunch, partridge served with an excellent Merlot, and then cigars in the parlor. Shortly after lighting up, Macleod fixed him with a steady eye and remarked casually: "There is one bit of paper I've saved that you might be interested in."

Hugh raised his eyebrows.

"It wasn't the Captain's. It belonged to Bessie—that was Darwin's daughter, the one who never married. Some called her Lizzie. She said she got it from her father but she always thought it should have been the Captain's, so she gave it to his daughter Laura long after both their fathers had died. It's been in our family ever since."

Macleod instructed his wife, who disappeared for quite some time and reemerged with dust on the underarms of her sleeves, bearing a frayed leather briefcase. She placed it on the blanket across his lap.

"I was thinking of selling this over eBay," Macleod said. "But, what the blazes—I can't bear to part with it. I'll let you look at it but be warned: handle it with care."

So saying, he passed over a single sheet of ancient paper. It was creased from being folded and shredding from multiple readings. Hugh stared at the childish printing in black ink:

I seen your ships. I seen your cities. I seen your churches. I meet your Queen. Yet you Inglish know life less as we poor Yamana.

"I'm betting you don't know who wrote that," said Macleod proudly. But Hugh knew at once. "Bet I do. Jemmy Button."

Macleod was impressed. "That's right. Seems he wrote it for Darwin. He sent it to FitzRoy from the Falklands round about the time of that inquiry over the massacre, and FitzRoy gave it over to Darwin."

Hugh handed it back.

"I'd say it's worth keeping," he said.

"Aye. It's a relic, all right. The last words of a poor Indian, tormented by a voyage between two worlds."

Shortly afterward, with the sun already sinking in the afternoon sky, Hugh said his goodbyes and left.

As he walked back through the woods toward the inn, he felt the satisfaction of a detective who's nailed down a clue. The phrase in Lizzie's diary, the words that FitzRoy had spoken to her in his madness, wasn't: *You Inglish—no lifeless.* It was: *You Inglish know life less . . .*

So that was it—a message representing Jemmy Button's final disillusionment with the English and the civilization they personified. For all their knowledge, for all their accomplishments, the overlords knew less of real life than his own fellow Indians.

Hugh had long been intrigued by the saga of Jemmy, plucked up from a canoe, paraded around London, then dropped back into his natural world. He had wondered about his role in the *Allen Gardiner* massacre, for history had been moot on that particular point: Jemmy had been charged with the heinous act but never positively cleared of it. That detail from the cook's testimony, the description of the plundering savage bedding down in the Captain's cabin while his tribesmen hacked and roasted the white men's flesh on the beach, had a compelling ring of truth. Hugh had sometimes tried to imagine himself as the Indian, what it must have been like to contend with the dueling worlds, the confusion he must have felt, the rage and self-hatred.

This little piece of paper was a cry from the grave. It didn't solve the mystery of Jemmy's schizophrenic existence, but it suggested that he had come to terms with it. Against the power and complexity of nineteenth-century industrialized Britain, he had chosen his own people and his own primitive but vital life in the hellish southernmost spur of South America.

. . .

The following morning, bolstered by a feeling of success, Hugh decided to pay a visit to Cal's laboratory to see what he could find out about his brother's termination. He pulled into the driveway of the Oxford Institute, grateful at least that the facility was situated sixteen miles south of Oxford and not in the town itself. This way he wouldn't have to run the gauntlet of ghosts that would surely be waiting for him in every courtyard and every doorway of the High Street.

The appearance of the lab was disappointing. In his mind's eye, from hearing Cal brag about it, Hugh had pictured a large campus, four or five buildings set among the shire's hills and dells. He had envisioned scientists in white coats—some of them attractive females—bustling about the place, taking breaks on slate-paved terraces, drinking hot coffee from thick china mugs as they worried along their experiments. Instead, there was one ugly, low-slung brick building with an unprepossessing entrance, a thrusting slab above a single revolving door, surrounded by an asphalt parking lot.

A security guard found his name on a list and raised the bar obstructing the entrance. He was to see an administrative assistant, one Henry Jencks, and he had been led to believe on the phone that he would not be able to obtain much information. He had gotten the appointment only through old-fashioned American badgering.

A receptionist gave him a toothy smile and asked him to wait, tilting her heard toward a bank of modern metal and vinyl chairs next to some vending machines offering soft drinks and candy.

He had trouble imagining Cal here, nodding hello to colleagues, walking down the bright laminated hallways. The place seemed lifeless and sterile, not a hothouse of cutting-edge research, but as deadening as an insurance company.

"Hugh, it's time to grow up, boy. Time to get serious. How many times have you driven cross-country now—seven, eight? How many different jobs have you had? Bartending, picking apples, construction, the post office, selling souvenirs at the Empire State Building, for Christ's sake."

"They're summer jobs. I was in college."

"But you're not now and it's time to decide what you're going to do with your life. You want to end up a deadbeat lawyer like Dad? You want to run for the six-fifteen train every night and grab a drink at Grand Central and hardly wait until you're home to grab another one and conk out? When I was your age, I already knew what I wanted to do."

"You sound like you're fifty already. You're only twenty-seven."

"It's never too soon to smarten up."

"You're lucky. You found something you love. I'm still looking."

"Well, hurry up. Sometimes I think you carry this bohemian shit too far. You act like you're trying to accumulate a résumé of shit jobs for the back of a paperback novel."

He had been talking about Cal a lot to Beth. She was a good listener, asking few questions but always the right ones, quick to point out the false notes in his well-constructed, self-taught narrative. Yesterday, when he had recited the story of his expulsion from Andover, she had been surprised to learn that Cal was involved. "You mean he drove up from Cambridge to celebrate your getting in to Harvard and you ended up losing your admission there?" she had exclaimed. "Think about that for a minute."

Later that night he had remembered a visit to London when he and Cal attended a gut-wrenching performance of *Long Day's Journey into Night* at the National Theatre. In the fourth act, the brothers have their climactic moment of truth. Jamie, the elder, his tongue loosened by drink, swears he loves Edmund and then abruptly lashes out and warns him to be wary of him: *"Never wanted you to succeed and make me look bad by comparison. Wanted you to fail. . . . Mama's baby, Papa's pet!"* At that moment, Hugh turned his head slightly in the darkened pit of the theater and saw Cal looking back at him. Their eyes met. Not a word was said. Nor did they ever talk about it afterward.

"Mr. Kellem? May I help you?"

The voice was thin and reedy, already sounding defensive. Hugh followed Henry Jencks down the hall to his office, settled in across the desk from him, and explained that he had come to learn as much as he could about his late brother's work.

"I'm afraid I cannot be of much help. That information is confidential, for reasons you can surely understand."

They fenced for a while.

"Tell me this," Hugh finally said. "Did he actually quit his job or was he on some kind of holiday leave?"

A pause. "I have checked the record. He was in fact no longer working here as of June the tenth six years ago. I'm afraid I cannot say more than that."

"So he did quit?"

"I cannot say."

"What kind of research was he doing?"

The question caused some consternation. "I don't believe I am at liberty to answer that either."

Hugh drove back to Cambridge breaking every speed limit.

That afternoon, sitting at his customary place in the library—the corner table—Hugh felt stymied. He had come to the end of Lizzie's journal and was still none the wiser. There were those intriguing passages about Darwin vetting his own journals and changing his manuscript, but they were short on specifics. He'd not been able to track down the journals themselves; a number of them were indeed missing, but that was hardly proof of misconduct in and of itself. There was that enigmatic reference to a *nuit de feu,* whatever the hell that was. And some dramatic stuff about FitzRoy's suicide, which—aside from Lizzie's encounter with him—was already known (he checked).

Even more, he was beginning to have doubts about Lizzie's veracity. The thought occurred to him that perhaps she was just a young woman hung up on her father, who saw drama and conspiracy where none existed, filtering everything through an overwrought Victorian sensibility teeming with repressed emotion. Or worse, maybe she got her kicks out of laying little clues that would explode in the face of some future historian—such as himself.

Roland came over.

"Things that bad, huh?"

"You know the expression 'two steps forward and one back'? With me, it's the reverse."

"Anything I can do?"

Hugh shook his head. Roland walked away but Hugh called him back.

"Maybe one thing. Have you ever heard of a poem called *Goblin Market?*"

Roland shot him an odd look. "Now you're far afield. Yes. But what of it?"

"Just curious. I heard of it recently. Tell me about it."

"It's by Christina Rossetti. A big hit in its day. It's about two sisters—one pure, one who gives in to the temptations of the flesh. Very Victorian. Spirituality and concupiscence, arm-in-arm . . ."

"Concupiscence?"

"Yes. It was written for the whores of Highgate Prison where Rossetti worked. It's supposed to be about the virtue of abnegation, but personally I think it must have turned all those working girls on. It oozes eroticism."

"I see." Hugh remembered: Highgate—that's where Lizzie ended up doing volunteer work, reading to the female inmates.

"And why are you interested in it?"

"It was important to Lizzie. It held some special meaning for her."

Roland raised his eyebrows. "Ah, light dawns. Stay there—and don't move a muscle. That's an order."

In five minutes he was back, carrying a thin volume, unable to repress a smug smile.

"Not only did I bring you her favorite poem," he said. "I brought you her very own copy."

Hugh was genuinely amazed. "How?"

"Our Darwin collection is huge. Elizabeth—Lizzie—lived out her spinster days in Cambridge, in a small house right here on West Road. When she died, her effects, including her library, came to us."

He handed Hugh the book. "You have no idea what we have back in those stacks. Darwin's papers alone fill sixteen boxes. Acid-proof, you'll be happy to know."

Hugh held the book on his palm. It had a thick, clothbound cover but was remarkably light.

"I thought you said it had all been raked over."

"The Darwin material, yes. Lizzie, no. In fact, you're the first person to request that book—at least since 1978, when we went to computers. I didn't bother to go all the way back in the card catalogue."

Roland left and Hugh began to read. The two sisters in the poem were Laura and Lizzie.

Lizzie, he thought; no wonder she identified with it.

The sisters hide among the brookside rushes in the woods and hear the ugly goblin men hawking their luscious, tempting fare—*"come buy our orchard fruits, come buy, come buy . . ."* Lizzie, the virtuous one, plugs her ears and flees, but Laura is irresistibly drawn to them and succumbs, paying with a lock of her golden hair.

Then:

> *She sucked and sucked and sucked the more*
> *Fruits which that unknown orchard bore,*
> *She sucked until her lips were sore . . .*

Laura returns home, addicted to the fruit, thrashing about in a passionate frenzy when it is denied her. The yearning becomes so strong that she falls ill and is finally at death's door. Lizzie can stand it no longer; she must save her sister. She puts a silver penny in her purse and goes to the goblin men. They want her to feast with them. When she refuses and demands her penny back, they attack her and try to force her to eat their fruit. But she keeps her mouth closed and *"laughed in heart to feel the drip of juice that syruped all her face and lodged in dimples of her chin."*

She runs home and shouts for Laura:

> *Did you miss me?*
> *Come and kiss me.*
> *Never mind my bruises,*
> *Hug me, kiss me, suck my juices*
> *Squeezed from goblin fruits for you.*

Laura does. *She clung about her sister, kissed and kissed and kissed her.* She falls into a swoon that lasts through the night and awakens rejuvenated. Years later, when both are wives and mothers, they gather their children around to tell them of the goblin men and how one sister saved the other.

> *For there is no friend like a sister,*
> *In calm or stormy weather,*
> *To cheer one on the tedious way,*
> *To fetch one if one goes astray.*

Hugh put the book down thinking of Lizzie, Darwin's Lizzie. Of course the poem would hold an almost hypnotic appeal for her. She would be drawn to it the way Laura in the poem was drawn to the fruits of the goblin men. *Come buy my fruits, come buy, come buy.*

A shaft of sunlight fell on the book. Hugh raised it and turned it in the golden stream and as the pages twirled, a piece of paper floated down and dove to the floor. He bent down and picked it up. A letter. It was written on thick stationery with a heavy watermark—actually, half of a letter on half a sheet of paper. The top, with the salutation, was missing, as if it had been torn.

He assumed it was written to Lizzie because it had been secreted in her book and he thought he recognized the thick-stemmed, squat letters of her mother Emma's penmanship. The script was jagged, as if it had been composed in a frenzy.

Even if I did not tell your Papa, your transgression would soon become all too obvious to him. It will break his heart. I do not know what advice to give you except to say that you should pray for his forgiveness and for the Lord's forgiveness. Be prepared for the worst and submit yourself with a repentant heart to whatever punishment you receive for you well deserve it. You will have to be sent away. Daughter, how could you have done this? How could you have been so thoughtless and cruel? Do not you care at all for our family? Do not you think of how your actions will reflect upon us all? Contemplate for one moment the shame you have brought upon our poor household. This is what comes of turning away from God and from our Saviour Jesus Christ. I knew from the moment you refused confirmation that you had set foot on the wrong path, but I never thought it would lead to this. Oh, what shall we do? How shall we go on from here?

I am in full despair.
Your mother who loves you still,
Emma

Hugh put the letter in his pocket, crossed the vast reading room, and entered a sideroom with a Xerox machine. He copied the letter, then placed it back in the book and brought the book to the return counter.

Roland was gone.

He checked his watch. Beth would be waiting for him at the Prince

Regent. He felt like having a drink. As he walked down the front steps, he patted the photocopy in his pocket.

My God, he thought. She's pregnant. This is unbelievable. She's gone and gotten herself pregnant. What's going to happen to her? It's strange, this attempt to put a life back together 150 years after the fact, to make sense of things. Sometimes the pieces fit and sometimes they don't. And sometimes the historian knows more than the actual person living the life.

In this case Hugh knew that at some point in the not-too-distant future, Lizzie would get pregnant by a man she didn't marry. That singular event would bring her world crumbling down. That knowledge, while she was chattering on in her journal, not yet in her twenties, musing about visitors to Down House and playing roundabouts and all the rest, was terrible to have. It was like seeing a speeding car and knowing that it is soon to crash. Possessing that knowledge was like being God.

CHAPTER 15

As the *Beagle* followed the coast of Tierra del Fuego, Charles stood on deck, holding fast to the rigging. The ship lunged and heaved in the choppy swells. He peered through the fog at the shore and gave a small involuntary shudder—he had never seen such God-forsaken terrain. Sharp rocks marched down to the sea. The land was cloaked with a dismal mist, the only vegetation sad-looking Antarctic beeches. Distant mountains rose in jagged peaks like edges of oyster shells, appearing not majestic but menacing. All around swirled a perpetual rain-soaked bog. Everything was desolate and gray.

Jemmy Button walked over and stood beside him. In recent weeks, ever since they had journeyed far enough south to experience the chilly climate and inhale the dank smell of land, the three Fuegians had been acting strangely. Fuegia Basket, whose body was swelling (to Charles's eyes she looked pregnant), remained belowdecks much of the time and rarely spoke. York Minster turned possessive and went into a sulk whenever someone else sat near her. Jemmy himself lost his customary jovial air and seemed anxious, sometimes appearing eager to reach their destination, sometimes seeming to fear it.

Now, holding on to the railing with his white gloves, his face looked blacker in the fog, the color of polished ebony. With his finely cut collar flapping in the wet wind, he cut an almost comical figure except for his forlorn expression.

Charles was moved to chastise him. "Come, come, lad. You're going home soon. A little appreciation is in order. Captain FitzRoy has gone to great lengths to return you to your native land and you ill repay him with your sullenness."

"But dees no be my people. Dees be Oens-men. Very terrible."

"Yes, but remember: You have lived in England. You have even met the King. You are above them. You have the armor of civilization to protect you."

"My peeple very civilized. You come meet my peeple, meet great man. Der be no Devil der. Promise."

"I haven't forgotten. I have given you my word. I shall meet your people and your great leader."

Jemmy turned to stare once more at the forbidding shore. At times like this Charles deemed the young man as petulant and demanding as a six-year-old. In fact, that was the way all three of the Fuegians were acting—like children. He sighed. He had long believed that all human beings were essentially the same on some fundamental level; it was the force of disparate societies that made them different, one higher than another. Humanity was a ladder of progress leading to rationality and morality; primitive tribes occupied the bottom rung, Englishmen and certain Continentals the top. The alacrity with which the savages had adopted the civilized code underscored the correctness of his view. But now he wondered, as they approached their native habitat, if they weren't losing the qualities of civilization as quickly as they had gained them.

Jemmy moved away and Charles became aware of another figure lurking behind him. He sensed who it was before he turned.

"Enjoying the view?" asked McCormick laconically.

"Quite."

"I say, has Jemmy been on to you about visiting his village?"

"Yes, why?"

"He's been pestering me about it relentlessly. Wants us to trek inland and meet his family and his tribal chieftain. Some chap named Okani-cutt or something like that."

"I told him I would do it."

"So did I, though now that I think of it I can't for the life of me say why. It's something like a day's hard going just to get there." He paused a beat, then continued. "Have you ever noticed these people don't seem to have a word for no? Perhaps it's the conception they don't have. I've certainly never known them to give up when they want something."

Charles didn't respond. The truth was he had absolutely no idea what went on in Jemmy's mind. He could not imagine what it was like to inhabit his mental universe. Jemmy's way of reasoning seemed so opaque, so alien, so far removed from normal categories of space and time, cause and effect. It was magical, riddled with superstition and animism. A thing didn't have to be one thing or another, it could be two things at once. Everything seemed to flow out of everything else in some causal way that Charles couldn't grasp. It was organic, like a bud opening into a flower and then becoming a piece of fruit, except that the bud and the flower and the fruit had nothing to do with one another.

"I say," McCormick interrupted his thoughts. "Have you heard that we may be taking on another ship?"

"Another ship? Why in Heaven's name?"

"It seems that Captain FitzRoy believes we need additional support if we're to get the surveying done. There's no time to contact the Admiralty, so he's prepared to pay for it out of his own purse and then seek reimbursement."

"But that's daft. He must not undertake something like that without permission. What if they disapprove?"

"Oh, I dare say they won't. He has excellent contacts, you know."

Charles harbored misgivings but did not have a chance to voice them. For at that moment as the *Beagle* rounded a headland and moved closer to shore, a hole opened up in the fog. What Charles and McCormick saw stole their breath away.

There at eye level, no more than forty feet away, were a dozen savages, naked except for some kind of filthy skins thrown over their shoulders. Their long, matted hair hung to their breasts and their faces were smeared with red and white paint. They jumped from the ground and waved their arms in the air, gesticulating and yelling hideously. As the ship moved, they ran along the shore, lunging from rock to rock. Soon some began frothing at the mouth and bleeding from their noses, so that their brown bodies were smeared with grease and blood and spittle.

"By Jove," said McCormick, "I have never seen the like. Do you think they are dangerous?"

Charles was hard put to answer. To him they were like spirits from another world, like the devils he had seen as a student in the Weber opera *Der Freischütz*.

The ship rounded another promontory and he observed that all around, on rocky islands and small plateaus in the foothills, fires were burning, sending up smoke that mingled with the fog. It was what Magellan had seen, the fires that moved him to call the land Tierra del Fuego. Had they lit the fires to encourage the ship to land or to warn other natives of her arrival?

Some days later the *Beagle* anchored in Good Success Bay and sent down boats to shore. Charles and FitzRoy were in the whaleboat. Jemmy, resplendent in a blue jacket and white breeches, huddled in the stern, clearly afraid. Scores of natives had gathered on the shore, moving up and down and shouting in sonorous whoops, while others looked down from rocky outcroppings.

"These are Ona," said FitzRoy. He explained that unlike Jemmy Button's people, these were Indians of the forest, who did not use canoes and hunted with bows and arrows. They were tall, usually around six feet. Half a dozen fractured words in Spanish—usually for things they wanted, like *cuchillos,* knives—were proof of some contact with foreigners.

The boats reached shore and the Indians crowded around, pointing at objects and yelling. The crewmen handed over all sorts of gifts, which the Indians grabbed and immediately took away. The natives slapped Charles and one or two others full in the chest, somewhat roughly, and they slapped back with equal force. It seemed a friendly enough greeting, though there were no smiles to dissipate a sense of menace in the air. The Indians circled Jemmy Button, poking him and talking among themselves, puzzled. He could not speak their language and his eyes were wide with fear.

"Dees not my peeple," he said, almost tearfully.

The crewmen broke out a fiddle and pipes and began playing tunes, which caused a hilarity among the Indians that grew more and more frenzied. One Indian stood back-to-back with the tallest seaman to compare their respective height; found to be taller by half an inch, he went bounding down the beach, shouting like a madman and swinging a club. A crewman suggested a bout of wrestling matches, but FitzRoy, looking around at the ever-growing number of natives pouring down from the surrounding hills, thought better of it. He ordered the men back into the boats.

The Indians followed them into the water, wading beside the boats and tugging at the sailors' belts and shirts. One midshipman threw some boxes of ribbons overboard—immediately, the Indians released his boat and struggled to retrieve them. An Indian grabbed Charles's boat by the side and pulled it to a stop, but the oarsman smacked his fists with the blade and he let go. They quickly moved into deeper water.

On the way back to the *Beagle* Charles noticed that Jemmy, collapsed back in the stern, kept his legs tightly closed. He soon saw why: a yellow stain had spread down the thighs of his white breeches. Back on board, he hurried down to his cabin to hide his shame and did not emerge for the rest of the day.

That evening, dining alone with FitzRoy, Charles thought the Captain looked crestfallen. He worried about him and tried to buck him up.

"I dare say that business on the beach was a bit disconcerting—but it was only the first contact. I imagine things are bound to improve in the days ahead."

FitzRoy made no reply; indeed, he stared down at the table as if he did not hear the words.

All in all, Charles thought, it was hardly an auspicious beginning to FitzRoy's grand scheme of bringing civilization and Christianity to this benighted part of the world. Weeks ago, when the Captain had talked about it during their dinners, at times getting so excited that he broke off his meal and paced about the cabin in a kind of delirium, holding up the Bible, it had sounded so feasible that Charles had half expected the savages to be awaiting them on shore with open arms.

Captain FitzRoy faced a difficult decision: where to set down his human cargo.

Jemmy Button and young Richard Matthews, he had decided, should be put ashore close to where the young savage had been abducted two years earlier. The spot was roughly halfway through the Beagle Channel, which cut through lower Tierra del Fuego and had been named by the Captain himself on the previous trip. But he took it into his head that York Minster and Fuegia Basket, coming as they did from a different tribe farther to the west, should be dropped off at the channel's Pacific side. This meant sailing around Cape Horn, the most treacherous waterway in the world.

For twenty-four days, the *Beagle* battled horrendous storms, including one that nearly sank her with a wave that Charles, holding on for dear life and sick to the gills, estimated at two hundred feet. But eventually, even though the summer months were supposed to make the passage easier, the weather proved insurmountable.

FitzRoy relented. He turned back north, entered the channel from the east, and, protected on both sides, reached the calm waters of Ponsonby Sound. All along the way, Indians besieged them. They rode out in canoes, gesticulating as they drew alongside, banging on the sides of the ship and screaming *"Yammerschooner"* over and over. These, said FitzRoy, were the Yamana, a vast tribe with many clans. They sheltered in makeshift wigwams, lived off shellfish and seals, and moved to a new site every four or five days. Virtually naked, they were protected from the cold by only a thin layer of grease, mostly seal fat. The three Fuegians were Yamana, he said, but their clans were very different. Jemmy's was the most advanced, as evidenced by the fact that it eschewed consumption of human flesh.

After two days' sail, the *Beagle* came to Woollya, a protected cove off Navarin Island. By chance, it was a sunny afternoon. The land rose gently around a half-moon bay. There was a beach and beyond that a strip of grassy ground that looked fertile and a thick grove of trees at the base of gentle hills. They could see steams that carried clear water. FitzRoy declared it ideal for the settlement.

Immediately, the crew set about building the mission station. They constructed three small wooden huts, one for the missionary Matthews, one for Jemmy, and one for the other two Fuegians. They dug and planted two vegetable gardens and raised a small fence and marked the boundaries of the station with a ditch. Then, when all was completed, came the great unloading from the ship: they carried off crates of goods donated by the London Missionary Society, items that spoke more to the mentality of the donors than to survival in this brutish part of the world: soup tureens, tea-trays, butter-bolts, wineglasses, beaver hats, fine white linen, a mahogany dressing case. The sailors laughed as they handed down china chamberpots.

All this time, the local Yamana stared in bewilderment. More and more of them arrived by canoe and by foot, drawn by the prospect of gifts, as word of the interlopers spread. Soon they numbered about three hundred. They squatted to watch the work and wheedled, endlessly repeating *"Yammerschooner."* As the days wore on, they became bolder. Sometimes they stole—belts and shirts, nails and axes, whatever was left unguarded for the briefest moment. The sailors set up night patrols, but even this did not stop the pilfering.

Charles watched Jemmy closely during his times on shore. Strangely, he had lost his native tongue. He addressed his tribesmen in English, and when that didn't work, he tried his few words of Spanish. Nothing could induce him to speak the guttural grunts of the Yamana and he even seemed to have lost the ability to understand the language. York Minster, by contrast, seemed able to follow bits and pieces of it, though he remained resolutely mute. Fuegia Basket, dressed in an Easter bonnet for the occasion, was equally silent. She appeared appalled by the nakedness of the savages.

The missionary Matthews, too, was acting strangely. He stayed on board most of the time and showed no interest in the construction of his home, an odd aloof smile on his face. It was almost, remarked Charles to King, as if the entire enterprise had nothing to do with him.

On the fifth day, an ugly incident occurred: a sailor pushed an elderly Indian away from the boundary and the old man turned furious; he spat in the sailor's face and then enacted a grisly pantomime: he pretended to strip off the man's skin and to eat it. Charles recalled Jemmy's warning given so many months earlier. FitzRoy ordered up some target practice on the beach to show the Yamana what English muskets could do. The natives flinched at the noise, withdrew in small nervous groups, and then inexplicably disappeared in the hills for the night, returning the next morning as if nothing had happened.

Notwithstanding the tension, FitzRoy carried on with his plan to leave Matthews at the camp. He presented it as something of a trial, saying that the *Beagle* would sail up the channel for a week or so to explore its western arm and then return to see how the missionary was getting on. The teenager was given a hearty last meal on board, which he scarcely touched, and then was rowed ashore in a spirit of forced merriment. He sat in the stern, his head high, that same disconnected smile frozen on his face while the sailors sang lustily. Jemmy and the two other Fuegians were rowed to the beach in a separate boat.

On shore, as the sailors watched from the boats, the young white man and his three companions walked up the beach toward their new homes, moving toward a silent crowd of Yamana. The crowd opened to let them pass and then closed around them and they were lost to view. As soon as the boats rowed back, the *Beagle* set sail.

Exactly nine days later, she came back.

As the ship drew close, the sailors saw something that filled them with foreboding: Indians on the banks were wearing strips of tartan cloth and white linen—adornments that could have come only from the settlement. Charles wondered if they had sent the young man to his doom. When the ship reached Woollya, dozens of canoes were beached and a hundred or so Fuegians milled about, their bodies painted red and white and ornamented with bits of British cloth tied around their necks and their hair and wrists.

FitzRoy launched a whaleboat and stood nervously in the bow. The moment it touched land, the Yamana besieged it, shouting *"Yammer-schooner"* and grabbing for gifts. Then suddenly, to the Captain's infinite relief, Matthews appeared, running down the beach. He sprinted for the launch, jumped in, and made frantic motions to be taken out to the ship.

Onboard, he told a tale of terror. He said that the first few nights had passed peacefully enough but that then a new, more aggressive group of Indians arrived. More and more of them crowded into his hut, importuning, begging, threatening. They stole his belongings, and if he tried to stop them, they flew into a rage. Twice they carried in large stones, threatening to crack open his head. On the last night, they held him down, plucking out the hairs of his beard with mussel shells. He said that if he were forced to return, he would surely be murdered.

FitzRoy, surrounded by his crewmen, walked up the beach to the huts. There he met with the three returning Fuegians. Jemmy had also been robbed and badly treated. He was no longer wearing fancy clothes and his body was covered with bruises. York Minster, a strong man with a commanding presence, had held his ground and beaten off anyone who threatened him or Fuegia Basket. But despite considerable prodding by the Captain, none of the three wanted to leave their homeland and return to England.

FitzRoy distributed a final round of gifts—the last of Matthews's stores—in hopes that they might ease the path for Jemmy or perhaps someday secure humane treatment for a shipwrecked Englishman. Matthews asked to be carried as far as New Zealand, where he had a brother who was also employed as a missionary, and FitzRoy readily agreed.

Leaving Woollya that evening, Charles and FitzRoy dined alone. Rarely had Charles seen the Captain so depressed, and he realized that in the space of a single day the man was relinquishing his obsessive dream, three years in the making, of spreading God's word to the poor, benighted natives.

"I still believe," FitzRoy pronounced gloomily at one point, "that we are all children of Adam and Eve, though some have wandered farther from Eden than we and have simply lost all recollection of Paradise in any form."

A week later, after some more surveying, the ship doubled back to see how the three transplanted Fuegians were doing. This time the scene was much more tranquil. In the bay, women fished from canoes. The few Fuegians on shore seemed peaceful and remarkably uninterested in the Englishmen. The huts had been repaired and even the garden, which had been trampled, showed a few vegetable sprouts.

The three had no complaints—all, that is, but Jemmy. He invited FitzRoy, Charles, and McCormick into his hut and told them he felt badly used because they had not visited his village.

"You say you come to my contree. You no say true. You no meet my famlee. You no meet my great chief."

FitzRoy responded instantaneously. Perhaps it was a rush of relief that the Fuegians were still alive, or the dim hope that the seed of something he had so fervently hoped to plant might still germinate, but he rose and acted like the Captain of old. He held both of Jemmy's hands in his, closed his eyes, and raised his head, almost like a campfire preacher.

"We have much work to do first," he intoned solemnly. "But as God is my witness, I pledge to you that we shall return, and when we do, we shall go with you to visit your village and meet your people and exchange views with your great chief."

As the *Beagle* set sail, moving back east again toward the Atlantic,

Charles thought that FitzRoy regained a modicum of hope for his great experiment, but the Captain rarely spoke of it—as if talking about it might break the spell once and for all.

It took almost a year for FitzRoy to make good on his promise to return. During that time the *Beagle* retraced her route all the way to Montevideo as she charted the eastern seaboard of South America and the Falklands. To accomplish the job, FitzRoy decided to acquire a second ship, as Sulivan had suggested, and so he advanced £1,300 of his own money to purchase an American sealing vessel, which was refitted and renamed the *Adventure*. She was to chart the shoals and shallower inlets under the command of Sulivan, who brought McCormick aboard the vessel.

The work was exacting and arduous and there were continual setbacks. FitzRoy's clerk died on a hunting expedition. Several seamen deserted. Augustus Earle, the artist who was Charles's good friend, became too ill to continue and was replaced by Conrad Martens, a bohemian bird of passage who readily adapted to shipboard life.

Charles's stature on board continued to grow. His character—self-reliant, robust, enthusiastic—was emerging under hardship. On more than one occasion he proved himself a hero. Once, a party exploring deep inside the arid terrain of Patagonia got into serious difficulty; exhausted, weak with thirst, FitzRoy and the others could go no farther, and Charles alone saved them by staggering on to bring help. On another occasion, a group of crewmen on shore was so enthralled by the sight of a calving glacier that they did not realize its danger; with great quickness of mind Charles ran to secure their beached whaleboat so it would not be smashed by the wave it spawned.

In gratitude, FitzRoy named a body of water and then a promontory after Charles—Darwin Sound and Mount Darwin—and this did not sit well at all with McCormick, who could barely contain his jealousy. The surgeon groused to Sulivan that the Captain was naming landmarks after people "on the slightest of pretexts, thereby demeaning the honor for those who truly deserve it."

Yet for the most part, whenever the ships anchored and the crews mingled, McCormick buried his feelings under a mask of indifference.

As one of the few who could ride horseback (most of the sailors were hopeless on land) he sometimes accompanied Charles on forays to hunt for game and for specimens. Though invariably he fell behind, he did unearth a number of his own, which Charles magnanimously included in his shipments.

Charles spent months on land and flourished. He enjoyed toughening up. Down south, on the frozen shore, he undertook excursions tracking and shooting seals. He slept in makeshift tents, lived in a shaggy fur overcoat, and grew a black beard so long he could grasp it with both hands. Up north, where the climate was more hospitable, he took longer and longer expeditions, meeting up with the *Beagle* hundreds of miles up the coast. Finally FitzRoy agreed, reluctantly, to let Charles make a six-hundred-mile journey from the Rio Negro all the way to Buenos Aires, much of it through land where Spaniards were battling indigenous Indians.

Charles loved it. His gun at his side, he rode with a band of hardened *gauchos* as bodyguards. He admired their gallantry and even their bloodthirstiness and began calling himself a *banditti*. He finally learned to throw the *bolas*. He hunted ostriches, amused by the way they raised their wings to sail the wind as they trotted in all directions. At night, he read *Paradise Lost* by campfire light; he had read the book so often that he developed a game: letting it fall open where it would and selecting a passage at random. Then he fell asleep under the stars, his head upon his saddle, listening to the sounds of night creatures he had never before heard.

One day he entered the area controlled by General Juan Manuel de Rosas, the notorious strong-arm leader who ran a private army and whose strategy for dealing with Indians was to surround their villages and kill every man, woman, and child. The General, who was said to be dangerous, especially when he laughed, heard there was an Englishman in the area and invited him to his encampment. He received him graciously. Charles was impressed by the General's skill—the man could mount a high platform, drop upon the back of a wild colt, and ride it to exhaustion. Rosas gave him a laissez-passer and did not laugh once.

These happenings at last sated Charles's appetite for adventure. This was life at its fullest. He felt himself the romantic hero of a novel, wandering the ranges of the Pampas, seeing sights and animals no Englishman had seen before. Shropshire seemed so small compared to this, the lives there so prosaic.

Finally, he came to the outskirts of Buenos Aires, only to find his way blocked by a military rebellion. General Rosas was laying siege to the capital. Charles managed to pass through the blockade—by dropping the General's name and showing his laissez-passer—only to discover once he reached the harbor that the *Beagle* was no longer there. He panicked that he had been left behind.

But the ship, it turned out, was just across the mouth of the Rio de la Plata in Montevideo, and after doling out considerable bribes at roadblocks along the way, he was able to join her there. FitzRoy confided to him, during their reunion dinner in which Charles regaled him with his adventures, that at least one person on board the sister ship had been eager to depart and let Charles find his own way home.

"I'll wager you'll be able to guess the identity of the person advocating this particular course," he said, smiling.

Charles did not have to guess—nor did he smile in return.

That night when he let *Paradise Lost* fall open where it would, the passage he read was unsettling. It applied so personally to him that it could have been penned with him in mind. Satan, filled with envy, is hunting down man to ruin him. To fool the Archangel Uriel into guiding him, he disguises himself as a Cherub:

> *For neither man nor angel can discern*
> *Hypocrisy, the only evil that walks*
> *Invisible, except to God alone . . .*

Two weeks later, the ship entered the Beagle Channel once again and pulled up to Woollya, her crew eager to discover what had happened to the settlement and the three Fuegians. Even from a distance, they could see that the place was a shambles. Two of the huts were destroyed, only the bare wooden frames remaining. The garden had disappeared.

But one hut was still more or less intact and out of it walked Jemmy Button. He rowed out in a canoe with his new wife. It took a moment for them to recognize him. Wearing only a loincloth, he was so thin his ribs showed and his hair was matted and his face painted. He motioned for them to join him on shore. Before sitting down to talk, he dis-

appeared into his hut and emerged a short while later transformed—
dressed in his fine pants with a white shirt and dinner jacket, now
loose upon his frame. His wife stayed in the hut, too shy to meet the
foreigners.

He said that York Minster and Fuegia Basket had long since
departed. Most of his belongings had been taken but he was content
enough.

"Now you promise," he said. "I wait long time. Now you visit my
contree."

"Yes," said Charles. "Now we come."

FitzRoy decided to forgo the trip and remain on the ship to keep
order, for some of the crew, who had by now developed a hatred for
the place, had been heard to mutter mutinous phrases. Charles,
McCormick, and Matthews, his spirits somewhat revived after seeing
the place where he had spent his week of terror now so calm and
deserted, were to travel to the village.

As he led them up the crest of a hill and into the woods, Jemmy fairly
leapt with joy that the encounter he had been dreaming of for so long
was about to take place.

Above them, storm clouds were gathering, large and dark. They saw
occasional bolts of lightning illuminating them inside, so far away that
they could barely hear the distant rumble of thunder.

CHAPTER 16

Hugh, groggy with sleep, heard the landlady shuffling toward his door. She rapped quietly. Telephone. He threw on his shirt and pants, opened the door, and found the receiver dangling from the hall phone. He checked a china clock on a nearby bookshelf: 7:30 a.m. Since when do the English call at this hour?

"Hello."

"Hugh. Bridget here."

"Oh, hi."

"I didn't wake you—did I?"

Her tone said it all: he shouldn't be sleeping so late. She was her old feisty self.

"As a matter of fact, you did."

"Well, it's time to get up anyway." She paused, letting her words sink in. "I want you to come to dinner tonight. Eight o'clock."

"Did you line up someone for me to meet?"

"As a matter of fact, yes. But I trust you'd come anyway."

"Give me the address."

"Take the six-ten train and Erik will meet you at the station. On second thought, I'll come too—I just remembered, he doesn't know what you look like."

"Never mind, just give me the address."

She did, adding: "Incidentally, I'm sorry I woke you. You sound . . . a bit under the weather."

"No, no. I'm talking softly is all. I'm fine."

And he was.

Hugh slipped back into his room and looked over at Beth, still sleeping. Her back was facing him—he could see the smooth curvature of her shoulder. She had bundled the pillow up under her left cheek. Her right leg angled out from under the sheet and he looked at the soft back of her knee and the tiny blue veins leading up to her lower thigh.

He wondered if he should wake her, then thought better of it. He finished dressing, retrieving his socks from the corner where he had tossed them, and separating out her clothes and placing them in a neat pile on a chair. He held up her panties—lace, this time—and put them on top.

He left a note, reminding her that he had said he would be off in the morning. He thought of adding something witty but decided instead to just jot down practical information—how to work the coffeemaker, find the bathroom in the hallway, avoid the dragon landlady. He signed off with three X's.

By the time he reached London, the sun was out and he decided to take the tour boat up the Thames to his destination, the National Maritime Museum in Greenwich. He caught it on the wharf below Parliament and heard Big Ben strike eleven as he boarded. He took a seat in the front where he could catch the breeze. It felt good to be tired, not from a night of insomnia but from staying up almost until dawn making love and talking and making love again. He smiled at the corny spiel of the guide. The river was high, which cut down on the smell, and the water glistened as they passed St. Pauls, the Globe Theatre, Tate Modern, and the forbidding seawall of the Tower.

When the boat docked, Hugh strode up the long hill toward the Observatory and turned off to enter a long, low building with thick walls and marble floors. It was cool inside. The receptionist guided him to the research room and there he introduced himself to the chief archivist, a thin, reedy man with a broad forehead.

He listened patiently to Hugh's request—to see material from the *Beagle,* in particular, the Captain's log and the roster of crewmen and passengers. Hugh wanted to know the names of those who did not complete the voyage for one reason or other, those who left and those who died, and in particular whether FitzRoy had set down any unusual incidents that he hadn't included in his book on the voyage.

The archivist shook his head in friendly discouragement and told Hugh to wait. Minutes later he was back with a sullied photocopy that he placed upon the counter. It contained bits and scraps of writing in FitzRoy's hand that was hard to decipher, but mostly it was blank, a large hole in the center.

"I'm sorry to disappoint," the archivist said, "but it was as I had anticipated. The *Beagle,* you understand . . . so many people have come here over the years, handling the documents, copying them. In those days our efforts at preservation were not up to today's standards. This is all there is, I'm afraid. I have no record of the log whatsoever. Nor does the Admiralty. I realize this is not much help."

Bridget's place on Elgin Crescent was just what he had imagined, quaint and expensive—a four-story brick town house with cream-colored bay windows, a flagstone walk, and a yew tree near the front door.

Before he pushed the bell, he looked through a half-shaded window. He saw a modern coffee table stacked with art books, a woman's fleshy legs, and the darkened back of someone handing down a drink. The muffled chatter of friendly voices reached him. It seemed so cheery it made him feel lonely.

Just then the door flew open so violently he felt a breeze in his hair, and he was facing Bridget, in a cashmere sweater and slinky black skirt, all kisses and bustling enthusiasm.

"Hugh," she said, pulling him across the threshold. "Glad you made it."

He handed her a bottle of wine. She lifted it out of the bag, checked the label skeptically, and set it on a side table. Erik rushed into the hall-way to join them. He was tall and handsome in an aristocratic English sort of way, with a mop of hair swooping nearly to his eyes. He rocked on the balls of his feet with delight as Bridget introduced them, and, as they gripped hands, Hugh's vow to dislike him eroded on the spot.

The introductions in the drawing room were artful, enough snippets of information to make connections and keep a conversation going. Hugh heard himself presented as "an old, old friend from the States and, incidentally, Cal's brother—younger brother, isn't it, Hugh?" Bridget's casual air was a giveaway: they already knew who he was.

One guest—Neville Young, a ruddy-complexioned man in a baggy crimson sweater—looked at Hugh with an appraising eye.

Before dinner Hugh cornered Bridget in the kitchen and she told him that Neville was the one who had worked in the biology lab with Cal.

"But I'm afraid he's not the one I really wanted you to meet. That's Simon. He was Cal's roommate at Oxford. At the last minute he couldn't make it. Bad luck."

She looked at him with moist eyes. "How's your father?" she asked in an abrupt non sequitur.

"I don't really know—okay, I guess." The truth was Hugh's father had written twice and even telephoned, but he hadn't written or called him back.

"I think you're too hard on him. He's not such a bad guy, you know."

Erik hurried in, his eyebrows adither. "Darling, they're all sitting down." He looked at Hugh, smiled awkwardly, and turned to Bridget. "Sweetie, are you pissed?"

Hugh was relieved to sit at the table.

The meal passed amiably enough. Bridget and Erik kept the wine-glasses filled and the conversational ball in the air; it bounced around the usual subjects—the latest outrage from the Tories, Israel's venality in the Middle East, bits of gossip. A fluttery woman on Hugh's left, having learned that he was interested in Darwin, wanted to talk about the rise of creationism in America.

The man on his right said: "I gather from Bridget you're doing some sort of research project on Darwin."

"Yes."

"Amazing man, wasn't he? Brilliant the way he held back his theory until he could nail it down completely, all those years studying barnacles, pigeons, whatnot."

"I suppose."

"Clearly a genius. But not like Newton or Einstein. Much more sympathetic, don't you agree? I mean, they're just so far above the rest of us. He seems more like a regular chap, if you know what I mean. You can almost imagine doing what he did, plodding along—he's like us, only more dogged. 'It's dogged as does it,' as Mr. Trollope wrote."

Hugh nodded. He felt Neville's eyes peering at him through the candlelight.

"And the beauty of the theory he came up with, the simplicity of it. In retrospect, it seemed obvious. What was it Huxley remarked of himself? 'How extremely stupid not to have thought of that.' A brilliant quip, that."

"Yes," said Hugh.

"Did you ever wonder," the man continued, "why Darwin didn't write about the unobservable? I mean, for such a close student of human nature there were some subjects he never wrote about."

"Like what?"

"The mind, for instance. Thought processes, questions of conscience and guilt. They never interested him—perhaps because they weren't tangible. Either that or they were *verboten* to him. He was such a bundle of complexes, you know."

"He was. And guilt-stricken on top of it all," said Hugh. "But despite all that, he carried on." He felt suddenly paternal toward Darwin. "He was the embodiment of courage."

"That he was. That he most certainly was."

Afterward, as they moved back into the drawing room for coffee and cognac, Hugh made up his mind to talk to Neville. He suggested that they "take some air." It was more of an order than an offer, without even the pretense that it might be considered odd for two men who had just met to wander off by themselves.

They walked outside into the garden and through a wooden door in the back fence to the communal green, a hidden patch of rough grass and towering elms behind the twin rows of houses. Neville appeared ill at ease.

Finally Hugh said: "Bridget tells me you knew my brother."

Neville replied quickly, as if he had been expecting the question: "Yes. That's true."

Hugh waited to see if Neville would offer more and finally he did. "We were reasonably close. We did see each other every day in the lab."

"And what sort of work did you do in the lab?"

He was not prepared for the response he got.

"Look here. I know this is awkward for you—it certainly is for me. Bridget told me you'd be interested in discussing Calvin, but quite frankly, it's all a bit dicey."

"What do you mean?"

"I know you must have been upset. Bridget said you two were close. But I hope you know how upsetting it was for me—for all of us—when we heard about his death. And I'm not sure I care to talk about it."

Hugh didn't know what to say.

"Well, I can understand, but surely a few harmless questions wouldn't—"

"There's no such thing as harmless questions in a case like this. A sudden death . . . you know . . . it really makes everyone feel horrible. One goes back over old ground, reassessing everything. I need some time to think."

Hugh was taken aback. Before he could decide what to say next, Neville broke the silence.

"We should be getting back." He turned and started walking toward Bridget's, then stopped. "Look, I don't mean to be rude. I understand you're on . . . something of a quest. I will think seriously about this and give you a call in two or three days' time with my answer." He looked deeply troubled.

"Fair enough."

Hugh put his hand out to shake on it but Neville deterred him. "No need for that." They went back in just as the others were preparing to leave. Hugh lingered behind as the guests said their goodbyes on the doorstep, a cacophony of kisses and exclamations. Bridget closed the door and turned to him.

"Well?"

"He didn't answer any questions at all. Said he wanted to think about it. He acted like he had been bushwhacked."

"Typical. In point of fact, I never liked him."

"Do *you* know what happened at the lab?"

"No. I was counting on you to find out."

On an impulse, he said: "That other man you mentioned—Simon— do you have his number?"

"Yes." She wrote it on a slip of paper, pushed it into his pocket, and walked him to the door.

"Thanks for coming and thanks for the wine. And remember: It's important for you to know your brother better." She looked him in the eye. "So you know he was human."

"I know that. I know he was human."

"Do you?"

"Yes." But even as he said it, he wasn't sure.

She didn't try to kiss him but looked at him searchingly for a moment and then turned, adjusted her skirt with a tug, and walked back inside.

He returned to Twenty Windows just as it was starting to rain. He called Simon's number; there was no answer but he left a message. Then he looked around his room to see if Beth had left him a note. There wasn't one. He smiled when he saw she had made the bed and propped up the pillows. His glance caught the bottom of the bookcase where he kept Lizzie's journal. It was lying on its side in its proper place, but the binding was facing out. That was not how he had left it. He felt a wave of disbelief, then anger. *She read it!*

He went out and flagged down a taxi. It didn't stop. He ran to her house, getting soaked through by the time he arrived. The back door was answered by a young woman who introduced herself as Alice, gave him a searching look, and quickly guessed who he was—which, despite his anger, he took as a good sign. He dripped water on the kitchen floor.

"She's upstairs. First room on the left. And here—" Alice reached into a drawer and threw a dish towel at him. He dried his head quickly and threw it back.

The bedroom door was open. Beth was inside, sitting at a desk, reading. She didn't seem surprised to see him and looked up calmly as he walked in.

"How the hell could you do that?" he demanded.

"Read it, you mean?" A look flashed across her face that he couldn't decipher—not guilt exactly, more like uncertainty.

"Yes, *read it*. Where the fuck do you get off?"

She stood up. She was wearing black jeans and a T-shirt that made her look slim.

"Let me see if I can explain." She began to pace, her fingers jammed in her back pants pockets.

"You better."

"I was looking around. I didn't mean to go snooping but . . . in effect that's what I was doing. I wanted to find out more about you. You know, left behind in a room belonging to somebody *important* to you. Well, I hate to say it, but it's an opportunity. Who would pass that up?"

He looked aghast.

"Okay, maybe you would. I couldn't. I was just looking around and I found the journal. The moment I opened it and read the first page, I was hooked. I mean, *Jesus Christ,* what a find! It's Darwin's daughter—Lizzie, right? Where did you get it?"

"Keep going."

"So I read the whole thing. It's amazing. I'm sorry. I know I shouldn't have. I was just interested in . . . whatever you had in your room. I didn't expect to find anything to do with Lizzie. I thought, you know, that I might find something more about you."

Hugh's anger was subsiding.

"But you just put it back hoping I wouldn't notice?"

"Not really. I turned it around. I figured you'd notice. I thought of writing a note but it was pretty hard to put it all down on paper."

His anger had dissipated, replaced by something else—concern, primarily, that the secret was out and that she might make use of his find. Still, it would be good to have someone to talk it over with.

"You know, you could have asked me," he said.

"Ask you? How could I ask you? I didn't know it existed."

"I mean about the whole thing—my research."

"And you could have asked me."

She had a point there. "You're looking into Lizzie too—right?"

"Right," she replied.

"Why?"

"Because . . . because she was my great-great-grandmother—that is, if I've counted the generations right."

Hugh dropped on the bed, his mouth open. "You mean that? You really mean that?"

"Yes. I've known for a while. My mother always told me that we were distantly related to Darwin. But I never really paid attention. I thought it was just one of those wild family rumors, you know, like somehow being related to royalty."

"How did you finally find out?"

"When she died. The information was part of the estate. Here, take a look."

She opened the desk drawer and pulled out a piece of paper and handed it to him. It was a letter from a London solicitor, the firm of Spenser, Jenkins & Hutchinson, dated May 20, 1982, and addressed to Dorothy Dulcimer of Minneapolis, Minnesota.

"That's my mother," said Beth, anticipating his question.

He read on. The letter stated that certain documents had been placed in trust with the firm in 1882 because it represented Charles Loring Brace, the founder of the Children's Aid Society, with the proviso that they remain "confidential and undisclosed" for a period of one hundred years. These papers, it said, were left with the firm by Elizabeth Darwin, daughter of the famed naturalist, upon his death, and were believed to contain information that she deemed "important for history but too injurious to the reputations of persons still living or their descendants to be revealed in the intervening future."

The letter continued:

Our files and a check of existing records lead us to believe that you are the closest living relative of the person for whom the package was left in trust—namely, one Emma Elizabeth Darwin, born out of wedlock on 1 April 1872, and given over for adoption that same month through the auspices of the Children's Aid Society.

Kindly review the enclosed documents to ascertain your claim upon the papers in question. Should you care to pursue the claim, you are requested to present yourself in person to our offices. . . .

There was an address that Hugh recognized as being near the Old Bailey.

"This is amazing," said Hugh. "Unbelievable." He held it up: " 'important for history but too injurious to the reputations of persons still living . . .' What could that be?"

"Something Lizzie found. Or wrote. From reading the journal, I'd say she was on the trail of her father for some reason."

"So your mother never went to get the papers?"

"No, she left that for me."

Hugh kept shaking his head. "Nigel said you were related—do you remember? I asked you about it on the train and you denied it."

"What I said was: don't believe everything you hear. I stand by that as a general observation."

He smiled. "I knew Lizzie had gotten pregnant but I never connected it to you."

"No reason to."

"And who is Charles Loring Brace?"

"A social reformer of the mid-nineteenth century. He founded the Children's Aid Society to provide for homeless street urchins in New York. It sponsored the 'orphan trains' that sent them out west—some two hundred fifty thousand of them."

"And he knew Darwin?"

"Yes. Darwin admired his book, *The Dangerous Classes*. In the summer of 1872, he invited Brace and his wife to Down House. That's when they became friends."

Beth handed over three other documents. One was an old birth certificate that listed the mother as Elizabeth Darwin and, in the space for the father's name, said simply: "unrecognised." The second were adoption papers, signed, in a shaky hand, by Lizzie. The third was a letter written to Brace by a Society member who accompanied an "orphan train" carrying sixty-eight homeless children from New York City to the Midwest in August 1872.

"You will be pleased to learn that I have successfully handed over baby Emma to the family from Minneapolis, according to the adoption arranged by you, this very day in Detroit. The new parents plan to call her Filipa." The author of the letter went on to describe the "joy of seeing so many of our innocent charges wrapped in the bosom of new families." She wrote:

They were taken in despite their condition, which, after a rough crossing on the steamer across Lake Erie from Buffalo resulting in all of them being seasick, together with the soil of excreta from the animals on deck and the long train ride to Detroit, left something to be desired. Indeed, they did smell something awful. At each stop, families gathered in churches and meeting-houses to take their pick of the youngsters gathered in a circle, some prospective parents moved almost to tears by their plight, others being more practical and hardened, squeezing their muscles or opening their mouths to check their teeth. By now, only a dozen or so of the least presentable children remain to be adopted.

Hugh handed the papers back.

"Any idea who the father was?"

"None. I don't even know if Lizzie's parents ever knew."

"Oh, they knew all right. At least her mother did—I found a note from her chastising Lizzie in no uncertain terms."

Beth was impressed. "Where do you keep finding this stuff?"

"Luck, mostly. The letter was in a book she owned. The journal you saw I found in Darwin's old publishing house. You notice she disguised it."

"Yes. And I think she makes a convincing case about her father. He was acting strange. Of course we have no idea what she suspected him of doing."

Hugh could not help but notice that she had said "we." "So what have you been doing here, at the library?"

"Research—like you. Finding out as much as I could about Lizzie."

"Meanwhile, you've got those papers waiting for you at the solicitors, right? Or did you get them?"

"Not yet. I've been to the office in London but I had to supply all kinds of credentials to prove I am who I say I am. It's taking forever. These British lawyers are real nitpickers. They tell me I can get it soon. You want to see them?"

"Of course."

"So . . . what does this mean?"

"What?"

"About us. Are we working together? Are we partners?"

"How about it? You want to?"

"Yes."

"Okay, then we're partners."

Events were transpiring so quickly that Hugh's feelings barely caught up. He discovered he was relieved that the competition was over, the screen down. It would be good to have someone to share in the adventure—and who better than Beth, Darwin's blood relative? He also acknowledged that the documents from the estate were bound to unlock some of Darwin's secrets.

"I had a thought," Beth said suddenly. "Did you notice Lizzie's journal had the number one on it? It was circled."

"Yes."

"Why would you put a one unless there was a two?"

"You mean there's another journal out there?"

"Yes."

"And if it's not in the publishing house, chances are it's lying around in that vast collection at the library."

"Yes."

He put his arm around her. "You're brilliant."

She picked up the birth certificate with a mischievous smile. "I come by it naturally."

That night, in deference to Alice in the room next door, they made love quietly, but in some ways the restraint only heightened the passion.

The next morning, inside the Manuscripts Room, Roland was yawning as if he were still recovering from a rough night out. They approached him together.

"I see you've joined forces," he said. "I figured it was just a matter of time."

"We need your help," said Hugh. "Let's go get a cup of tea."

In the cafeteria they began by asking questions about the Darwin collection as a whole, and, as usual, Roland was a fount of information.

"His wife, Emma, died late in the nineteenth century. Their son, Francis, was interested in the family heritage and he amassed quite a few papers. Ida Farrer, who married Horace, the youngest and feeblest of Darwin's sons, kept family letters. In 1942, the treasure trove was bequeathed to the library."

Hugh looked him square in the eyes.

"Roland, could you do me a favor?"

"Boy, I've been doing you nothing but favors since the day we met."

"Could I see the papers? Could I go back in the stacks and look at them?"

"You mean look at them as in look *at* them, or look at them as in look *through* them?"

"The second."

"You must be joking."

"I'm not."

"Hmm. Highly illegal, you know. It's a restricted area. I'd probably lose my job. And there's a second curator on duty who might see you."

"Not if Beth distracted him."

She smiled at Roland.

"My, my," he said. "You two do like breaking the rules, don't you?"

Ten minutes later, when the Manuscripts Room was virtually deserted, Beth went over to the other curator with a request. While they remained hunched over a research book, Roland led Hugh behind the counter to a blue door, swiped a card, and they were inside. It was quiet except for the hum of air conditioners. A large metal case faced them, holding several small stacks of manuscripts with slips hanging down from the pages, reserved by readers for continual use. They turned right and walked past row upon row of metal shelves until deep in the bowels of the building they came to Case 20, the area reserved for Western manuscripts. They followed the rows until they came to number 137.

"Here you are," said Roland. "If you have to touch anything, put it back exactly as it was. You have precisely one hour—that's when the superintendent returns. And for God's sake, if you hear the other curator, hide!"

Hugh looked down the aisles: each had ten bays, five shelves to a bay, extending for about 130 feet. Three of the aisles were for Darwin material, most of it kept in brown and blue boxes. Some of it was labeled: "From family," "From Down House," "From botany."

He started with "family," opening one box, then another, moving quickly down the aisle. Most of the material was in small dark brown envelopes, bundles of letters, which he ignored. After twenty minutes, he came to a large box marked "Accounts." He opened it and found stacks of ledgers and bills and account books, some written in Darwin's hand. Toward the bottom, lying upside down, he came upon what he was looking for—a small account book with the numeral "2" on the cover, circled. He opened it, flipped to the back. There it was: Lizzie's handwriting!

He found a small label stuck on the binding with a reference number: DA/acct3566. He wrote it down, replaced the account book in the box, and the box on the shelf. Then he calmly walked back to the blue door, opened it slightly, peered out to see if the coast was clear, and returned to the reading room. No one saw him.

He filled out a request form and handed it to Roland.

"Middle aisle, three quarters of the way down, on the right," he said quietly.

CHAPTER 17

10 June 1871

How strange to resume my journal after all this time, nearly six years since I gave it up (and what unhappy, disillusioning years they have been!). Indeed I would not do so, especially after forswearing it, were it not for the whirlwind of emotions bearing down upon me. I am prey to joy and agony at one and the same time. Sometimes I feel as if my heart is so full and overflowing that it will burst and I shall fall stricken on the floor for all to see and to wonder: what could have befallen the poor maiden that she expired thus in the bloom of her years? I feel an overwhelming desire to confess, to unburden myself, to pour out my innermost thoughts and desires. But alas, there is no-one, absolutely no-one, to serve as my confessor, no-one into whose ear I might discharge my burning secret.

I am in love. Heavens, am I in love. I think of no-one but him. I long to be with no-one but him. I dream of him. Wherever I go, I see his nimble form, his handsome visage, his gentle brown eyes. I hear his soft voice and feel his look upon me, which makes me blush to the roots of my hair. I would spend my life with him. And he has no idea that I am consumed by my adoration of him.

There!—I have admitted it. I have put my secret to paper. That at least is something, but I cannot say that it has brought me great relief. Even in this writing, I must exercise caution and not disclose the name of my beloved or in any way reveal his identity. We have been thrown together by circumstance, like the lovers in one of Mrs Gatskell's novels. I long to put down his name or at the least his initials and to read them and re-read them, but I dare not, lest this fall into someone's hands. I shall call him X. Sweet X. Dearest X. I do love you with all my heart and soul. How trite those words sound now that I look at them—oh, how woefully dumb is language compared to the heart's longing.

I must not ramble. To do so simply makes it all the harder to bear. There, I have confessed my secret and I must have done with it.

But the burden feels no lighter.

❖

12 June 1871

My life, by which I mean my external life, is to all appearances much as it was when last I closed my journal. I am now twenty-three years of age. The startling events in the Meteorological Office and FitzRoy's grotesque death affected me deeply. I could not discard the idea that I myself bore some responsibility for it, having upset him so during our interview. As a consequence, it took a severe toll on my health. I collapsed and fell into convulsions, which occurred off and on for weeks. I lost my appetite and became very pale and thin, so much so that I had no need of a corset (though I had no desire to venture outside and spent most of the time in my bedchamber).

I also turned away from the Church, becoming an unbeliever. This troubled Mamma no end. She pressed me continually to attend services and prayed for me to pursue 'the Lord's light and grace'. She was brought to tears during our first argument on the matter when I refused confirmation; she asked me for my reasoning and I forgot myself and shouted that I believed neither in the Trinity nor in baptism nor, in fact, in God Himself. She was so shocked that she fell silent and then turned on her heel and took to her bed weeping. I expect she was thinking that now our household held two non-believers, the other being of course Papa.

Little could I confide to her that my conversion to atheism was in part due to my feelings about Papa. For my suspicions that something horrible had occurred during the voyage of the Beagle—*perhaps during that* nuit de feu—*had hardened into the conviction that he himself was guilty of some wrong-doing. The feeling became all the more painful since it placed his character so at odds with the world's view of him. My suspicions strengthened when I saw Papa's reaction to FitzRoy's death; far from being saddened, he acted as if a weight had been lifted from his shoulders. Shortly after the funeral, I saw Mr Huxley clap him upon the back and overheard him saying, 'Well, that puts an end to the whole sorry business; the weather-man shall get no more stipend from me.' I thought it a most cruel remark.*

For a period I ceased talking altogether. Out of concern for my behaviour and what Dr Chapman called my 'mental lassitude', I was trundled off to Europe in hopes that a change of habitat might inspire a recovery. For by that time I had indeed fallen grievously ill, though naturally, as I have said, I could tell no-one the true cause of my malady—that I had begun to suspect that Papa is not the man he pretends to be. I visited Germany and then took up residence at Baden-Baden, where the fresh mountain air and curative springs gradually restored my peace of mind. I remained there for almost three months and returned to Down House only after George was dispatched to fetch me. My homecoming was cause for some celebration, at least out-wardly (Parslow was most moved, almost to tears), and I pretended to par-take of the festive air. Abroad I had come to a resolution and I informed my family of it: to make a clean start of things I wanted to relinquish the name Lizzie and to be called Bessie instead. They were puzzled and it took them some time to accommodate my wish. The servants were the first to learn to address me by my new name and then Mamma and my brothers. Etty and Papa took the longest.

---

15 June 1871

Papa's health has not improved. He has been following John Chapman's remedy of applying ice to the spine; he straps cold-water bags to his lower back several times a day, setting his teeth to chattering. He is a sight to behold, moving around the house like a great lumbering bear or lying on his bed groaning. But for all of that it does little good.

Papa's illnesses cannot be laid to the opprobrium of society, for in recent years, far from being treated like a pariah, he has been placed upon a pedestal. His fame has continued to spread beyond all expectation. His theory on natural selection (which some are now calling evolution*) is gaining in acceptance. Most notably, the attacks from the Church seem to be lessening. A* *year ago, Oxford awarded him its highest honorary degree, and every day the postman brings stacks of letters from all corners of the globe. In short, he has attained great status as an innovative thinker, esteemed even by those who disagree with him. Perhaps because he has reached the venerable age of sixty-two or because he and his circle have mounted such an effective campaign to promote his theory, but he has practically become a national institution.*

In disseminating his views, he is deucedly clever; he never confronts an antagonist straight on but works on him indirectly, using allies to persuade while he himself strikes a disarming stance of reasonableness. He is good at proselytising and adept in his use of language. For example, he has a meta-phor he often uses to take the steam out of debate. When an adversary ridicules him for asserting that our forefathers were monkeys, he denies it steadfastly, saying that he contends merely that men and monkeys have a common ancestor. He then describes what he calls 'the tree of life'. In the depic-tion, the simplest creatures are at the bottom and the most complicated animals are at the top; as species vary, they branch off from one another in such a way that those with the greatest difference are farthest apart. In this way the essence of his argument strikes home.

Origin *is soon to reach its sixth printing, much to the delight of John Murray. It has been translated into just about every European language, although Papa is upset with the French version, which he believes ties him too closely to Lamarck. For the past two years, he has been working on his 'man book'.* The Descent of Man, *which finally appeared last month, makes the evolutionary link between men and animals explicit, which he did not dare to do before. Etty helped him, proofreading the manuscript and scrawling her suggestions in the margins; as always, her changes toned down the conclu-sions and eliminated improprieties. She acts and thinks like an old maid.*

I've read the manuscript, although I was not asked to do so. Papa's theory on 'sexual selection' is arresting; it accounts for the persistence of traits that determine how people and animals choose their mates, and it explains the dif-ferences among races and why we here in the West are the most advanced. He states that men are intellectually superior to women. There is one aspect to it that bothers me: the thought that in the most civilised societies it is the men who choose the women, not the other way around. I find that upsetting—it treats women as passive receptacles without a will or mind of their own. I have heard too many women talking below stairs, as it were, to find this assertion convincing, and I have confirmed my view on the matter in conver-

sations with Mary Ann Evans, who has become a friend of mine. If Papa could only read my heart, and see the amorous tempest brewing there whenever X walks into a room where I happen to be (not by chance), he would surely alter his view.

❖

25 June 1871

X called this afternoon at 3:15, riding all the way out from London. As we were already engaged in receiving visitors (Mrs Livington, a dreadful bore to boot!), he left his card. It was on the hall table and my heart skipped a beat when I managed to steal a glance at it. To my great joy, he had turned down one corner, signifying that the visit was intended not just for Mamma but for us daughters as well. I was stricken to have missed him but glad at least that he did not display the bad manners of sitting Mrs Livington out.

❖

27 June 1871

Oh, happy, blessed day! I spent most of this Sunday with X. He organised an excursion for the Working Men's College to take fresh air in the countryside around the village of Kidlington and asked Etty and me to go along. We spent a most delightful morning, walking through the fields and footpaths and took a merry lunch on the grounds of an inn there. Then on the train ride back, we struck up song after song—X has a rumbling baritone— that kept us all rollicking. One man was proficient at making bird-sounds by cupping his hands together and blowing through his thumbs, which amused us considerably.

It is now one month since X entered my life, since Etty met him at the Wedgwoods' and invited him to visit Down House. I have so much in common with him. We hold the same views of human nature and progressive politics. Like him, I support the Reform Act, since I believe that expansion of the electorate is the only way to further democracy and reduce inequities among the classes. I share his vision for a Utopian future and I could listen to him

talk about it for hours. Although I am not acquainted with all the thinkers
he espouses, such as Thomas Hughes and Vernon Lushington, I have read
works by John Ruskin, whom X knows well. X is more radical in his political views than I am, but I am sure I could be elevated to his position with a
little more education. At one point he expressed a certain sympathy for the
current events in France; he admitted that the Paris Commune had raged out
of control and ended sadly in its 'week of blood' but he said that some of
the ideas of a workers' revolt were not misplaced. I think he is absolutely
brilliant.

❖

29 June 1871

I cannot tell if X reciprocates my feelings. Sometimes I dare to think he likes
me. He came to Down House for dinner yesterday evening and afterwards
the family withdrew to the drawing-room where he played the grand piano
and I turned the pages for him. As I did so, I fancied he looked at me out of
the corner of his eye. Later he smiled at me in a way that made me turn red
and feel flushed. My heart was throbbing so, I feared it would give me away,
that he could almost hear it once the music stopped. He played like a man
possessed—I could see the muscles on his strong fingers stand out as they
pressed the keys. Then he played the concertina and sang a madrigal while
Etty accompanied him on the piano.

When the music was done, he and Papa fell into a discussion about Papa's
theories on 'sexual selection'. X said something that caused Papa to become
excited—namely, that he had often thought that animals used song to court
their mates. I could see Papa registering this thought for some possible use
later on. X then said that he thought human beings did much the same thing
and I fancied that as he said this he was looking in my direction.

When he was about to depart, he brushed against me in the entrance-hall.
I could not tell whether this was an accident or intentional, but I felt his
hand touch the inside of my arm and a sensation shot through me like a
charge. I am sure he noticed how flustered I became. My cheeks were burning
scarlet. He said he would return soon as he kissed my hand and Etty's. At
that point I saw Mamma, standing behind him, break into a sly smile.

Afterwards, Etty and I acted giddily. We talked about him and she said *she liked his big brown beard and she laughed, saying that he reminded her of Papa in many ways, not the least of which is his devotion to work and his ideals. I could not bring myself to talk about him at length, because I thought my shaking voice would betray me.*

At night I have difficulty sleeping. I thrash about in bed and awaken often. Sometimes I find myself dripping in perspiration from the warm night air that blows in from the garden, bringing the scent of honeysuckle. I have strange thoughts, which I am loath to confess, and most vivid dreams. Recently I have taken to reading Goblin Market *just before bedtime. It arouses feelings that are difficult to explain. The refrain sung by the horrid little goblin-men—*'come buy our orchard fruits, come buy, come buy'—*echoes through my sleep along with visions of ripening oranges and straw-berries and peaches, all dripping their juices.*

The only person to whom I might confess my love is Mary Ann Evans but, alas, I have not seen her for some months now. And even to her, I would not reveal his identity.

◪

2 July 1871

Despite my vow to do so, I have not totally given up my efforts to shed light on the events on the Beagle *and the underlying cause of Papa's misery. I do not go out of my way to unearth clues, but I pick them up and examine them when they fall into my lap. I think life is like that: it is when one stops exert-ing oneself that one often succeeds in attaining a goal. So it was with my sleuthing.*

Over the years I have heard of a secret dining club established by Mr Huxley called the 'X Club' (lately, whenever I hear of it, I think of my own Mr X). The club contains a handful of eminent scientific thinkers and activists like Messieurs Hooker, Spencer, Lubbock and Busk. As far as I can tell, its main purpose is to infiltrate the Royal Societies and the rest of the sci-entific establishment to form a beach-head for Papa's ideas. Yesterday, some four club members came to Down House for the weekend and, listening in on the after-dinner conversation, I was shocked to learn that one raison d'être *for their visit was to collect money for poor Mr Alfred Wallace, who is per-petually in financial straits. I had heard that the club was pressing the gov-*

ernment to give Mr Wallace a pension of some £200, but it now appears that Mr Wallace was demanding such a pension.

'He made it crystal clear,' Mr Huxley said. 'To put it bluntly: if he doesn't get it he will expose everything.'

I immediately thought back to another conversation concerning Mr Wallace that I overheard years ago. What could he possibly know—and threaten to reveal—that would make it so important to buy his silence?

The club members agreed to do it. Papa himself said he would inform Mr Wallace and, in carefully worded code, tell him in no uncertain terms that he 'must not murder our baby'.

I later looked at his accounting book and saw that he entered the monthly sum under the label 'miscellaneous household expenses', a category he is customarily loath to employ.

6 July 1871

What a coincidence! Here it was only four days ago that I wrote in my journal that clues often come unexpectedly and then this afternoon I discover the single most important clue to date.

I was looking through a stack of Papa's papers in his study—with his permission this time, since he is considering writing an autobiography and had asked for help in its preparation. Papa was seated in his leather chair on the other side of the room. Imagine my surprise when from out of the papers dropped an artist's sketch from the Beagle's voyage. It was done by Conrad Martens, who at one point served as ship's artist. Staring at it, I was immediately struck by something that was not right: in a flash it put the lie to Papa's story about what had happened on that fateful voyage.

My hands started to tremble. I chanced a look at Papa, but he did not notice my agitation—he was busily making notes for his book on facial expressions in men and animals. I looked again at the sketch of Papa and another man standing on either side of a tree. The man was identified as Mr McCormick. Its significance was unavoidable now that I had grasped it. Were it introduced as evidence in a trial, it would instantly undermine the alibi of the accused and lead to a verdict of guilty.

Ever so quietly I put the sketch between two blank sheets of paper, which I slipped inside a book. I then told Papa I needed to rest from my work—a pretext he was always quick to honour—and left the study. I went to my bedroom and hid the book under my bed. That is not a good hiding-place, though, for the housemaid is certain to find it.

I know what I shall do. Relying upon the same theory that I used in disguising my journal—the theory of hiding in plain sight, which proved so useful to me during our childhood games of roundabouts—I shall secrete it in the house's central place. I have a hiding spot there, a loose board that no one else knows about.

◈

8 July 1871

The sketch has pricked my curiosity, causing me to resume my investigation. I have conceived of a bold plan to get to the bottom of the mystery once and for all. Miraculously, things seem to be falling into place. I do believe that Fate is on my side—perhaps the gods are conspiring to finally shed light on the dark doings of four decades ago.

Our family has been planning a retreat in the Lake District, where we have taken a cottage. I have contrived with Hope Wedgwood to go there five days earlier on the pretext of helping to ready the cottage. With just the two of us and some servants in attendance it should be easy for me to slip away one morning and travel north to visit the family of R.M., for I am convinced that he is the key that will unlock the past. I heard his name mentioned in connection with Mr Wallace only last week (it was during that same conversation wherein I learned of Mr Wallace's extortion scheme). I found the family's address in Papa's old papers and have already written ahead to request a quick visit without, of course, revealing anything of my purpose. I asked them to send a reply to me at the cottage in Grasmere rather than here. I remember Papa once berating me for 'spying'. Little does he know how proficient at it I am!

Hope and I leave early tomorrow.

◈

10 July 1871

Success at last! But why do I not savour my triumph, feeling instead a hollowness inside? The answer is not hard to come by: now that I know what occurred during the notorious nuit de feu, *I have learnt that Papa really is something akin to an imposter. His capacity for deceit far outstrips my own. Shame on him! I now understand his feelings of guilt which have taken such a toll on his health all these long years.*

Why do I feel so miserable, having been proven correct in my suspicions? I believe that on some level I wanted my imaginings to be false, that without knowing so I had hoped in some corner of my heart that Papa might turn out to be the great person the world thinks him, instead of this, a trickster who has built his edifice of renown upon a bed of quicksand. Fie! I do not know how I shall be able to look upon him without registering disgust—that is not too strong a word for what I now feel towards him.

The mystery was not so difficult to solve, after all. R.M.'s family wrote that I was welcome to visit, though they confessed curiosity as to my motive. I reached them easily in little over two hours by changing trains at Kendal. They live in a small house in the centre of town. The woman died two years ago, at seventy-five, and as R.M. had never returned from abroad, the house has been taken over by a cousin or two, whose relationship to each other and to R.M. I never got straight, though they share his name. They received me cordially and served tea and cake, and when I stated my purpose—that I had come out of interest in their relative and wondered if he had left them any papers or souvenirs—they warmed to my enterprise. The man searched the attic and after half an hour returned with a sheath of yellowed letters bound together by a blue ribbon. He said that R.M.'s family had saved his letters from abroad, written those many decades ago, and he gladly turned them over to me for my perusal. The cousins appear distinctly uninterested in R.M.'s adventures on the Beagle. *I got the impression that they never read the letters and in fact did not know or care much about him whatsoever. Indeed, they did not seem well informed about my father's work, as they asked me no questions about him, which I've come to discover is unusual in social settings. They certainly did not know that one of the letters contained information of singular importance; nor did I tell them or register any reac-*

tion of surprise upon the reading of it. I handed it back as casually as if it were a blank piece of paper and watched the man replace it in the bundle, which he then tied up again.

During the entire train-ride back, my mind was reeling. What should I now do? Do I dare to confront my father with my new-found knowledge of his treachery?

◈

11 July 1871

How unfathomable life is; how Fate does play with us!

Imagine my surprise this morning when I went out for a walk alone and, crossing a gorgeous sun-lit meadow, saw a man walking by a grove of trees, looking lost in thought. Upon drawing closer, the figure appeared familiar. My heart suddenly leapt up into my mouth when I realised who it was—none other than my X! He saw me at the very moment I spotted him and looked equally surprised and—if I may say so—more than a little pleased. He quickly joined me and as we walked side by side I discovered that his presence here was not a coincidence, for he had learnt that our family was to spend a vacation in Grasmere and had arranged to rent a cottage nearby. At that, I thought I might die of happiness on the spot, but I was careful to disguise my joy. Looking down, he asked when the others would arrive, and I told him they were due the day after tomorrow. At that, he looked up towards the sky, which was a brilliant blue, and breathed deeply, almost as if he were sighing.

I could scarcely believe my good fortune, for chance had truly smiled on me. Under no other circumstances could we have been alone together. To be by his side without others present was what I dearly wanted and yet I was innocent of having brought it about. I had done nothing other than take a morning promenade; luck alone had guided my footsteps and his. My friendly angel had even conspired to leave Hope back in the cottage. Yet even so, I knew that I should not be there. And the knowledge that I should have immediately returned to the cottage after a polite greeting made our meeting somehow more thrilling.

We soon found ourselves headed into the woods. As the trees cast the path

into shadow, he asked if I were chilled, and though I was not, I for some rea-
son replied yes. At that he kindly removed his jacket and placed it upon my
shoulders, touching them as he did so. I felt my blood quicken. We walked
deeper into the woods and although the trees were tall oaks, for some reason I
thought of fruit-trees and the goblins' call: come buy our orchard fruits,
come buy, come buy.

A branch lay across the path. It was hardly an obstacle, but he stepped
across first and reached back to take my hand and help me over. Afterwards
he did not let my hand go but grasped it tight. I felt the strength of his fingers
around mine and a sensation of being overpowered that affected me deeply.
Soon he dropped my hand, only to slip his arm around my waist, drawing me
closer to him. As we walked I could feel his thigh against mine. All this was
done without speaking and so nonchalantly that it seemed the most normal
thing in the world. I did not feel normal, however. My insides were churning
and I found it hard to breathe.

He suggested that we stop and rest for a bit, to which I could only nod my
assent. Much to my surprise, he stepped off the path to one of his own mak-
ing. As we were now holding hands again, I could do naught but follow.
Indeed, I felt I had very little will of mine own to support me and would at
that point have followed him wherever he led. We ducked under the branches
and after only a dozen or so steps we came to a small clearing the size of a
house, entirely surrounded by tall trees. In the centre was a patch of sunlight
on the grass. Here he took his jacket from my shoulders and spread it on the
ground that I might sit upon it. I did so. Quickly he was by my side, and
before I knew what was happening, he turned towards me and took me in
his arms and kissed me hard upon the lips. I thought I would faint. I tried
to push him away, but not very forcefully, and he seemed to discern that my
resistance was feigned. For in truth I did not want him to stop. At that
moment the oddest thought popped into my head—I remembered years ago
kissing the Lubbock boy in our hollow tree-trunk. I felt my blood flowing
hotly as it did then.

X did not pause in his seduction. He kissed me again and this time I
returned his ardour, placing my hand upon the back of his neck and holding
his face close. I felt his hands upon me. I did not know what to do. He kissed
me again. It lasted so long that I became dizzy. I felt his hands again, more
insistent now. Finally, I was able to push him away. He had a strange look
upon his face, almost angry—I would not have recognised him had I chanced

upon him in that state. He suggested that I lay back to rest but I demurred. After some time we began talking, about this and that, inconsequential things—I honestly do not remember, my thoughts were such a jumble—and we both pretended that nothing extraordinary had happened.

But it had. I feel I shall never be the same. I have drunk from some deep well of whose existence I had only dreamt.

We left the clearing and this time his hand upon mine felt natural. He began talking excitedly and used an endearment: 'angel', he called me. I liked the sound of it, though it was a strange term to use. I felt nothing like an angel at that point.

When we parted, he suggested that we meet again tomorrow, at the same place, for another 'walk'. He gave me such a look that there was no doubting his intention. I readily agreed. He then stared me full in the face in such a way that I blushed. I cannot describe the look that followed, except to say that it did not seem to be one of affection; indeed, much as it pains me, it seemed the very opposite.

I am now writing this in bed at night. All day I have been in a state of confusion and excitement. I know I love him and I believe he loves me in return. I do not know for certain what will happen tomorrow, but I am sure of one thing: whatever happens, whatever actions my emotions dictate, I shall do nothing that I will later come to regret.

CHAPTER 18

On the train to Preston, Hugh cradled Beth in his arms while she fell asleep. He stared out at the dreary Midlands moonscape of Birmingham and Manchester and imagined it during Victorian times—the coal mines and slag heaps, the steaming pits and belching smokestacks. Most of it was abandoned now, used up and sucked dry, a burnt-out battlefield. He thought of Josiah Wedgwood's china factory on the Mersey Canal, the fortune it spawned that enabled Darwin to putter about with beetles and ferns and shells. The might of industrial England, conferring leisure, power, and the right to rule, had gone the way of Ozymandias's statue.

Lizzie's second notebook was a godsend. He and Beth had discussed it late into the night, lying next to each other in bed—how the new pieces fit into the puzzle.

At least they now knew why Lizzie had become an atheist and why she had changed her name to Bessie.

"It was the whole trauma of FitzRoy's suicide," Beth said. "She felt guilty for it and so she wanted to reinvent herself. She swore off spying and abandoned her journal."

"So why did she resume it six years later?"

"She fell in love. As she says, a woman in love has to confess it to somebody, even if that somebody is only a blank piece of paper. And love can have a curative effect, even if it's directed at a scoundrel."

The shock was discovering the identity of *X,* which became obvious once they added up the clues: he was a progressive, a friend of Ruskin's, and affiliated with the Working Men's College. In addition, he was someone known to the Darwin family, who visited them at home and accompanied them on outings. Beth was the first to say X's name aloud—she pronounced it under her breath and later she would claim that somehow *Goblin Market* had figured in her deduction. "Litchfield!" she said. "My God, it's Litchfield. Etty's fiancé."

Hugh knew instantly that she was correct. And it filled him with foreboding. In analyzing her correspondence, Beth had noticed that there were two long gaps when Lizzie had written no letters to anyone. She mentioned them to Hugh. One gap came shortly after April 1865, when FitzRoy died and Lizzie fled to Germany and her first journal ended. The second came in mid 1871—and here the second journal also ended. Hugh knew what had occurred then: Etty had married Richard Litchfield and Lizzie had gone abroad again, this time to Switzerland.

"Beth," he said. "You better face something: if Lizzie is your great-great-grandmother, then Litchfield is your great-great-grandfather."

"That bastard!" was all she said.

But now, with some of the missing pieces filled in, the puzzle was even more frustrating.

"She discovered what the *nuit de feu* was," Hugh complained. "Why the hell couldn't she just write it down?"

"I know. It's exasperating."

"She makes it out to be some sort of singular event that affected the whole outcome of the voyage."

"Well, at least we're getting somewhere. We know who R.M. is. And the key to unlocking the mystery is that letter that Robert McCormick sent home. Lizzie tracked down his family, found the letter, and everything fell into place."

"It apparently laid out the whole story of what happened on the *Beagle*—and the story was disturbing enough to turn her against her papa." Hugh got out of bed, retrieved the photocopy of the journal, and searched for the passage. "Here it is: she calls him an *impostor* and says he fills her with *disgust*. Strong words."

"The blackguard is Litchfield, who 'deflowered' her, as they put it so eloquently back then. That last entry—it's heartbreaking. She's about to run off for a rendezvous with him and she has no idea where her passion is taking her."

Again, Hugh thought of the historian as God, the speeding car. The accident was about to happen. He didn't want to dwell on it.

He pondered the sketch by Martens—significantly, it was of Darwin and McCormick together. It was important enough for her to steal it from her father. But what did it show? She called it evidence that could lead to a verdict of guilty. Evidence of what? Guilty of what? And then she had hidden it in a "central place"—no, that wasn't the exact wording. He opened the journal again and found the passage. She hid it in "the house's central place"—wherever the hell that might be. Someplace *in plain sight*. Thanks a lot.

"What do you make of that bit about Wallace demanding a pension?" he asked. "She calls it out-and-out extortion. She says if he doesn't get it, he threatens to expose everything."

"And you know what?" replied Beth. "They *did* arrange for a pension, that X Club. I checked. They pressured the government. Gladstone himself awarded it—two hundred pounds a year. Not enough to make him rich but enough to live on. And when Darwin died, he left money to Hooker and Huxley and a bunch of people, but not to Wallace. Wallace got nothing. It's almost as if Darwin gave him a kick in the teeth."

The pension was something concrete, thought Hugh, a nugget that appeared to bolster Lizzie's credibility. On the other hand, perhaps she had simply heard about it and misinterpreted its meaning—or intentionally misconstrued the motive behind it.

"I know what you're thinking," Beth continued. "You're wondering if she went off the deep end. I don't think so. Her words strike me as genuine. Her anger's authentic. She found out something about her father, and whatever it was, it was enough to disillusion her for the rest of her life."

Hugh wished he could be so certain. It had all suddenly struck him as incredible. Darwin was a great man, one of the greatest in history, and here they were, trying to accuse him of . . . of what exactly? Amateur sleuths, that's all they were—looking for evidence of some misdeed they couldn't even fathom, and, worse, being disappointed when they didn't find it.

The swaying of the train was reassuring. Beth's head, nestled into his shoulder, rocked ever so slightly and her far hand rested on the seat, palm up like a small child.

He thought of another train ride—that long one from Andover to New Haven. Cal boarded the train in Boston so that they would confront the old man together—"a united front," he had said on the phone. And on the way there, for the first time, Cal told Hugh some of the family secrets, fights he had witnessed between their mother and father.

You were too young to know what was going on. I used to sit on the back stairs, where I could hear them in the kitchen—they always had their fights in the kitchen, long, knock-down, drag-out affairs. I'd hear Mom cleaning up, the sound of the pots and pans, then Dad's voice, deep and so sure of itself, smug. And she would be needling him and he'd get back at her—you'd hear the pots banging around—and then she'd come in with a zinger, like, "I saw those charges on your AmEx card," or, "You don't even clean out your pockets. I found her earring." You know, Hugh, don't you, that he had affairs?

Hugh hadn't known. He was shocked—he had never figured that into the calculation of what had gone wrong between them. Before, he had blamed his mother, not his father, for the divorce. It was hard to go back and recalculate things. He admired his brother for keeping it a secret all those years, and he was grateful that he revealed it at that particular moment.

Once, he and Cal and a few teenage friends were hanging around the river and began tossing rocks at a red and white metal buoy out in the water. They cheered every time a rock hit it, sending forth a resounding *twang*. Out of nowhere a man leapt from the bushes behind them, his face flushed red, sliding down the embankment on one side and pivoting on the other, like a second baseman touching the ground, tossing a rock as large as a baseball. It struck Hugh in the thigh, hard, but no one saw, and he held his peace while the man stood over them, berating them for causing damage to his buoy. Then Cal saw his tears. He turned to the man and shouted: *"You hit my brother, you son-of-a-bitch,"* and the man wilted before their eyes, apologized, and slunk away. Hugh had never felt so secure and loved in his whole life.

An hour after arriving, Hugh and Beth stood on the stoop of a semi-detached house on a narrow street in the center of Preston. He glanced up at the knocker, a brass claw holding a ball that was tilted slightly off center.

"Lizzie called it ugly," he said. "I'd say she's not far off."

"Right on the money—as usual."

The building itself was run-down; the roof sagged, the stone facade was grimy, and the windowsills were peeling strips of bright blue paint. The street curved and no cross streets were visible; the identical houses lined it like slats in a barrel, giving it the artificial feel of a stage set.

Hugh tried to imagine what it looked like when McCormick lived there. He had read up on the man, what little about him there was to be found, and knew that he must have been proud to be a house owner. McCormick had grown up poor in Scotland and dragged himself up by his bootstraps, turning to medicine as a profession for advancement. He had taken on various commissions at sea as an assistant surgeon; in 1827–before the *Beagle*–he accompanied Edward Parry on the *Hecla*'s fruitless quest for the North Pole.

It seemed almost certain that he had never returned from the adventure that began with the *Beagle,* though what happened to him after he left the ship at Rio was not clear. Perhaps his peregrinations took him to the Far East. Or perhaps the curator at the Darwin Centre was right and he died in some sort of subsequent shipwreck. His widow, Hugh imagined, would have husbanded whatever money he left her. She seemed, at least judging from Lizzie's account of the letters tied by a blue ribbon, to have treasured his memory before she, too, passed away.

Hugh hadn't found McCormick an engaging personality–he seemed petty, ambitious, and self-important–but standing before his dwelling, which must have been a dreary *petit bourgeois* house even in its heyday 150 years ago, Hugh regarded him with sympathy.

It had not been that difficult to locate the place. From notes kept by Syms Covington, Darwin's assistant, Hugh learned that McCormick lived in Preston, southeast of the Lake District and indeed, as Lizzie had written, about two hours by train from Kendal. He had pinpointed the address using other historical accounts–including one by Bartholomew Sulivan, the *Beagle*'s second lieutenant. Then, cross-referencing the street address with various family records on the Internet, he was able to track down a living descendant. The trail, however, was not all that clear-cut; he had not been able to identify "the cousins" Lizzie had described.

A phone call early in the morning had secured them an invitation to visit, though it had been grudgingly given. The young man who answered the phone was none too friendly and had hinted that, if whatever Hugh was after was all that important, a little money might help grease the wheels.

Lifting the knocker, Hugh said: "Well, here goes nothing." He was curious to see what the young man looked like.

They didn't have to wait long to find out. A man in his mid-thirties opened the door and squinted suspiciously. Hugh and Beth introduced themselves and he opened the door and let them in without a word. He was dressed in black leather pants and a T-shirt; there was a tattoo of the Union Jack on his right arm and his hair ended in a rat's tail. His skin was pallid and he was short in stature—like McCormick, thought Hugh.

"Name's Harry," he said, with a deep smoker's cough, leading the way to a front room darkened with thick draperies and heavy furniture. Hugh and Beth sat on hard wooden chairs while Harry sank into a dilapidated purple easy chair. A TV against the wall blared out a soccer game.

Hugh explained that they were looking for McCormick's letters. He tried to ward off the notion of payment by making their quest sound unimportant. They were researchers, interested in history, and looking at a project that might enhance Mr. McCormick's reputation. All the while their host—if that was the word—looked over Hugh's shoulder at the game.

Then Beth spoke. "So do you have other distinguished relatives in your family?"

"Uncle's a foreman in the pits. But he's been made redundant."

The fans on the television cheered. A chant rose up. Harry pulled himself higher and sat on the edge of his chair.

Beth turned to Hugh. "Manchester United," she explained.

They watched the tail end of the game—a penalty kick with seconds remaining. The ball flew to the upper left-hand corner of the goal and sunk into the net. The stadium exploded in a frenzy of cheers and flag waving: three to two, Manchester.

"I had five quid on the game," said Beth.

Harry brightened. "Had you pegged for Chelsea."

"Not on your life."

"Good," said Harry. "Let's go get a fookin' pint."

They went to a pub around the corner.

After two Guinnesses, Harry warmed up and became downright friendly. He recounted his life, which was remarkably uneventful. He had never been to London. A welder in an auto shop that had gone bust, he was currently on the dole. His father had retired and was spending the summer with his mother in Malaga, Spain. He had one sister who was off in the States—hadn't seen her for years.

He took a long swallow of Guinness and wiped his mouth with the back of his hand.

Yes, he acknowledged, he had been told he was related to McCormick, the adventurer who shipped out with Darwin on the *Beagle*. " 'E was my great-great somethin' or tother," he said.

And he knew nothing at all about any papers left by McCormick. Nor, he was sure, did anyone else in his family. He offered to let them search his attic for ten quid but then, after a third Guinness, succumbed to a rush of generosity, took them back home, and showed them the attic for nothing.

Nothing was what the attic contained. One old box of Venetian blinds, a dusty fan, and not a thing else.

Hugh thanked him and said they had to be getting back.

On the doorstep, Beth shook his hand and Harry gave her a reluctant smile. She said she'd like to ask a question that had been troubling her.

"I thought that Mr. McCormick was childless," she said, smiling. "So I take it you're distantly related, through cousins or something. Is that right?"

But he did have children, came the answer, or at least Harry thought so. "Can't say for sure. I seem to remember two sons. Father'd 'em before that last trip with Darwin. But I could be wrong. Don't know anything about cousins."

On the train ride back, rereading the photocopy of Lizzie's journal, Hugh despaired of ever finding the letter.

"C'mon," said Beth. "We haven't reached a dead end yet."

"I'm just wondering what to do next."

"Well, there's one possibility. When I was looking through Lizzie's letters, I checked out some that she received. And among them I found one from Mary Ann Evans."

Hugh perked up. "Did it say anything?"

"Not in and of itself. But it referred to a letter Lizzie had written her. So it's clear they had a correspondence."

"That's good. We can go to George Eliot's archives—wherever they are."

"They're in Warwickshire. Nuneaton. And guess where Lizzie sent her the letter from. Zurich. Which is where she had the baby."

Hugh reached over and gallantly kissed the back of her hand. "Brilliant. You know," he added, "I never pegged you for a Man-U fan."

"Only in the Midlands."

"By the way, did you notice the name of the pub we went to?"

"No."

"It was called The Wild Goose."

He finally reached Neville on the phone. He had tried twice before, leaving a message each time, but Neville hadn't called back. When Hugh identified himself, the voice on the other end of the line didn't exactly ring with enthusiasm.

"Bridget's friend. We met the other night at dinner at her place."

"Of course. How could I forget?"

"Good," Hugh said, not knowing how else to respond. "I hope we can meet and—you know—carry on the conversation we, ah, started."

A lengthy pause, but when Neville finally spoke, Hugh got the impression he had reached a decision even before the call.

"I don't see why not," he said, adding a slight exhale of resignation. "I hope I can trust you."

"You can," said Hugh, adding, "I want you to know, I'm deeply grateful."

They set the rendezvous: the following afternoon at the entrance to the Royal National Theatre. Good spot, thought Hugh—they could walk along the Thames, maybe cross Waterloo Bridge, a proper setting for an intimate talk. He was surprised at what Neville said next.

"I hope you realize that anything I might tell you—and mind you, I'm not saying that I *will* tell you much—I hope you realize it must be treated as strictly confidential."

"Of course." Hugh's fears rose along with his hopes.

"In point of fact, I must insist upon it. We sign non-disclosure forms here and they are taken very seriously. Infractions are punishable."

"I understand."

Hanging up, Hugh was mystified. He had checked out the lab on the Internet and found a number of references to its various research projects and contracts, including some from the government, but nothing that seemed controversial. And Cal was not someone who would have worked on weapons systems or the like; he was far too idealistic.

Neville was probably just indulging in the British penchant for secrecy. Still, Hugh could not shake a feeling of foreboding.

It was hard to think about Cal, let alone talk about him—and the prospect of doing so with a stranger, and someone who had troubling information to impart, was upsetting. Hugh had achieved a kind of truce with the past; he hadn't put it to rest but he had knocked it back so that it no longer haunted him every day. But things were happening, changing, perhaps because of those intimate conversations with Beth.

He walked over to the desk, opened a drawer, and pulled out the photo that always traveled with him, a black-and-white picture of Cal and him together. He had studied it hundreds of times, the two of them on the Andover campus, him a freshman, Cal a senior about to go off to Harvard. It had been snapped at midday, or perhaps at night, with some phantasmagoric flash that threw their shadows clear across a lawn. Cal, as darkly handsome as a movie star and a full head taller than Hugh, grasped the neck of a tennis racket and a pair of sneakers by the laces. Hugh's mouth was open, as if he were about to speak.

Hugh had carried this photo with him for years and looked at it from time to time. More often than not it called up an anxiety, a vague distress. Only this time, he saw fresh details: how ill-fitting his own jacket was, how he was looking up at his brother while Cal stared straight ahead, his jaw set, ready to take on the world. What he saw now, he realized with a shock—and what caused his distress—was the tension between them. He could see Cal's distance and ambition and his own pitiful need for acceptance and love. The photo seemed to capture the very moment when as brothers they were leaving childhood behind and abandoning each other.

·   ·   ·

On the way to Down House, Hugh stopped off at the church of St. Mary's in the village and wandered through the shaded churchyard. Some of the ancient tombstones were sunk deep in the earth, the epitaphs readable only by worms. Others lunged up at precarious angles, the writing mostly obliterated, spotted with lichens and moss or worn wafer-thin and white as seashells.

The sixteen-mile trip from London had been quick. The station at Orpington was still in service but he decided instead to take the train to Bromley South and then the number 146 bus—half an hour, forty minutes at most. It was hard to imagine the rigors of a train ride and a phaeton in Darwin's day that had made the voyage so insupportable to him.

The village of Downe was much as he had expected—quaint and quiet, constructed of stone, with an apothecary, a grocer's, a petrol station, and various other small shops. When Darwin was alive, the elders had decided to add an *e* to the spelling—even back then the lure of *Ye Olde England* was irresistible, Hugh thought—and he admired his man for standing firm: Down House it was when he had bought it and Down House it would remain.

In a corner of the churchyard, he found what he was looking for. There, under a yew tree, was the tombstone of Erasmus, Darwin's brother. Two tiny stones nearby marked the graves of two of Charles's children, Mary and Charles Waring. He recalled reading Lizzie's diary—how she and Etty and Emma and the others would pass them every Sunday on their way to church.

He left through an iron gate and walked up Luxted Road. Following it, he thought of Beth. He had smelled the scent of her when he awoke and he carried it with him through the day. Out of nowhere, a line from *Paradise Lost,* which he had lately been reading, popped into his head:

> *So hand in hand they passd, the lovliest pair*
> *That ever since in loves imbraces met . . .*

And another line, this one from the Bible: *At her feet he bowed, he fell, he lay down.*

After a long curve in the road, he came to Down House, a square Georgian building painted white, with a slate roof and ivy clinging to the walls. When Darwin first laid eyes on it, he pronounced it "oldish and ugly," but he soon fell in love with the place, and Hugh could see why. It was comfortable and expandable—rooms could be added on like slides in a trombone. It was a world away from London, full of country smells and sounds—the wet hay in the meadow, the rattle of the fly-wheel in the well, the lime trees buzzing with bees. Phloxes, lilies, and larkspur grew in the flowerbeds. The grounds must have carried Charles back to his childhood at The Mount.

Hugh entered through the obligatory gift shop and paid admission. It was a Tuesday, so there were not many visitors. He followed a herd of schoolchildren touring the ground floor; their teacher, warning them to touch nothing, patrolled like a nervous collie. A curator from English Heritage, a gray-haired woman in a tweed suit, provided the commentary.

The tour started in the drawing room. He glanced at Emma's grand piano, the marble mantelpiece, the breakfront bookcase, the special case for the backgammon set that was designed to look like the spine of a book and titled *History of North America*. They passed into the central hall and Hugh noted the long base-clock, a wall table with the jar for Darwin's snuff, and Christian-themed lithographs hung by Emma. They entered the billiard room with its pale brown felt table and three balls ready for a shot. A butler's tray set for two drinks of port (he wondered: was one of them for the butler Parslow himself?) stood in the corner.

They stopped off in the dining room, which was lit by three bay windows facing the garden. The Regency mahogany table was set for twelve, close by the sideboard with Wedgwood "waterlily" tureens ordered by Darwin's mother. Grim portraits stared down from the walls. The schoolchildren were bored and anxious to move on.

At last they came to the famous study. Hugh's eye was drawn immediately to the large dark armchair set on casters. Here Darwin composed the books that changed the world, supporting his paper on a fabric-covered slab of wood that rested upon the arms. With a cane propped against one side, the chair looked as if it were waiting for its owner. Behind it, tucked into a recess as snug as a ship's cubicle, was a small wooden desk filled with cubbyholes and slender sliding drawers, each one carefully labeled. A bookcase mounted to the ceiling. Over the fireplace was a gold-framed mirror, turning dark as a New England lake, and above that were portraits of Joseph Hooker, Charles Lyell, and Josiah Wedgwood.

In the center was a Pembroke table. Various items were placed on it to suggest that Darwin himself might have recently left them there: a bell jar, a pair of scissors, a primitive microscope, three upturned glasses, a wooden box, a monkey's skull, a feather, various papers, a wooden spool of string, and half a dozen books. One was a second edition of *Das Kapital,* inscribed by Marx himself ("To Mr Charles Darwin on the part of his sincere admirer . . .") A young boy reached out to touch it. The teacher quickly smacked his wrist, hard.

"What's this?" asked a dark-skinned girl, pointing to the far left corner. There, behind the half wall, was a thick porcelain basin mounted inside a platform. A dressing gown hung from a wall peg and a wooden stand next to it held white china pitchers and towels.

"That, children, was built especially for Mr. Darwin because he worked so hard he sometimes fell ill. Don't forget, he had traveled around the world and he picked up many diseases."

"But what's it for?" persisted the girl.

"That's enough, Beatrice," said the teacher. "You heard what Mrs. Bingham said. It was used when he was ill."

"But used for what?"

"He was sick in it," said a boy. The others giggled.

Hugh wandered over to the chair and peered out the window. The mirror that Darwin had ordered Parslow to attach was no longer there.

The tour moved back to the central hallway.

"Now let me show you something you'll find captivating," said the curator. "The Darwins were a close, loving family and they played many family games." She stood below the grand wooden staircase, which turned twice as it mounted upward to the floor above. "Here's one the children invented themselves—they used wooden boards as sleds and rode them down the staircase. As you can imagine, it was dangerous sport. But they quite enjoyed it."

The schoolchildren stared at the staircase.

She moved to a cupboard under the stairs. "This is where they kept many of the games they played outside—croquet mallets and tennis rackets and skates. At one point Darwin even kept an outline for his famous book here."

She opened it with a quick pull on the knob.

"One of the children called this cupboard 'the place of all others where the essence of the whole house was concentrated.' "

Hugh caught her eye. "Excuse me, but would you know which child said that? Would it have been Elizabeth?"

"Oh, I don't think so. I'm not sure which one it was, but we know that Lizzie, as she was called, was considered slow. It is unlikely she would have kept a record of the family's activities for posterity."

Hugh broke off from the group, which moved outside to see the garden and the Sandwalk, the boys tearing across the grass. Another group took its place in the central hall. He mounted the staircase to the exhibition on Darwin's life.

The floor was deserted. He peered into glass cases and stared at the pictures. There was a painting of Charles's father, Robert, leaning forward in a chair, huge and stern. Nearby, a quotation was framed and mounted; it was Robert's famous chastisement of his son, which had always struck Hugh as unspeakably cruel: "You care for nothing but shooting, dogs, and rat-catching, and you will be a disgrace to yourself and all your family."

Hugh suddenly thought of his own father and felt a stab of guilt for not answering his letters.

He turned to a portrait of the young FitzRoy, handsome and sensitive-looking, with his dark hair, sideburns, upturned nose, and delicately lined mouth. Various artifacts were on display: a cutaway drawing of the *Beagle,* mahogany fittings, glass collecting bottles, a clinometer, dissecting instruments, a pocket pistol, a sketch of round-faced Jemmy Button, a compass in a wooden box, a sketch of Darwin being "shaved" while crossing the Equator, a Bancks microscope with a swiveling brass eyepiece.

Alone, in a special case, were *bolas* with their leather straps attached to stones. And next to them—Hugh drew his breath—was the cosh, the very one that Darwin had chided Lizzie for removing from the mantelpiece. It was a foot-long metal cable with heavy metal fittings at both ends, dangerous if used as a weapon but hardly lethal to the touch. He stared at it for some time before moving on.

A number of Darwin's quotes were displayed in the cases. Next to a box of bones sent back to Henslow from Tierra del Fuego, Hugh read: "I could not have believed how wide was the difference between savage and civilised man." In a framed letter to Hooker was a note of despair: "What a book a Devil's chaplain might write on the clumsy, wasteful, blundering, low and horridly cruel works of nature!"

Across from this was a depiction of the "tree of life"—branches that ended in drawings of animals inside balloons, hanging like Christmas bulbs, the simpler ones like hydra and fish at the bottom, the complex ones like tigers and monkeys at the top. On the very summit was man.

Hugh went back downstairs. Now the central hall was deserted. He listened—footsteps upstairs, some chatter from the gift shop around the corner, a clattering of dishes in the teashop. He walked over to the cupboard and casually opened the door. He leaned down and poked his head inside; it was empty. In the dim light he examined the interior. It ran deep to the left and rose up about four feet, lined with unfinished planks about three inches wide. Wooden pegs protruded two thirds of the way up. A baseboard ran around the bottom.

He looked at the baseboard. At the far end a section looked as if it had been cut out and replaced, leaving a slight crack on either side. He reached in with his left hand and touched it. It moved. He grabbed it and pulled it toward him. It gave way easily and he saw a dark hole behind it. Inside, he could make out a small packet. He retrieved it, replaced the baseboard, closed the cupboard door, and, with the packet slipped under his coat, walked over to the gift shop. Smiling at the young woman behind the cash register, he passed the shelves of books, postcards, and bric-à-brac without stopping.

On the train ride back, his heart thumping, he untied a ribbon, opened the wrapping, and looked at his prize—the sketch Lizzie had described. It was a bit wrinkled, yellowed and rolling up at the edges, but clear enough. He examined the drawing closely. There were two figures, identified in a caption as Darwin and McCormick, standing on either side of a tree, and at the bottom the artist's initials: C.M. He was puzzled. To Lizzie, its importance was immediately apparent, but he couldn't for the life of him figure it out. There was nothing to identify the place—it could have been anywhere. The tree was certainly not the baobab tree the two had discovered during their outing at St. Jago. It was an ordinary, nondescript tree. Behind it were a few rocks that offered no clue about the location. So where was it? And what was its significance? What had Lizzie seen? Hugh was stumped.

On the ride back, he pulled it out several times and looked at it but still he could not decipher its meaning.

Beth spent the night in the George Eliot Hotel. She had her morning coffee outdoors in the main square, a stone's throw from a statue depicting the author in a flowing Victorian gown, glancing over her shoulder—as if, thought Beth, she couldn't wait to get away. She was amused to find a George Eliot Art Gallery, a George Eliot Pub, even a George Eliot Hospital. How's that for irony? Beth thought. As a woman Mary Ann Evans couldn't even publish under her own name and now the whole damn town is living off the man's name she chose as her pseudonym.

She made her way to the Nuneaton Library. The supervisor was a woman in her thirties with porcelain skin and light blond hair, the prototype of the English rose. She received Beth graciously and ushered her into the workroom, a fifty- by fifty-foot chamber with elegant windows and solid oak desks.

The library housed the largest public collection of George Eliot material in the country, the supervisor boasted, but virtually all the author's letters had already been published in some eight or nine volumes, thanks in part to a Yale English professor who began collecting them in 1920.

Beth explained that she was interested in letters that Eliot had received, not sent, and particularly those whose writers had not yet been identified.

"Ah. That's another matter."

She disappeared and returned some ten minutes later. Behind her a shabbily dressed young man pushed a cart stacked with thick looseleaf binders.

"From the vault," she said. "I'm afraid that William here will have to sit with you as you go through them. Can't be too careful. You don't look like a thief, but one never knows. The other day we caught a little old lady with an engraving rolled up in her umbrella."

"Of course," said Beth. "I understand."

William sat beside her, seemingly glad to have nothing to do, and she began to sort through the binders.

After some two hours, she gave a little cry.

William looked up. Her finger was resting on a plastic cover sheet. Underneath was a letter with crimson borders and printed across the top were the words *Dieu Vous Garde*.

"I'll be damned," she said out loud. "She's using Annie's stationery."

The letter came from Switzerland.

CHAPTER 19

Oddly enough, it was after the *Beagle* reached the tranquil waters of the Pacific that Captain FitzRoy lost his mind.

I suppose, thought Charles, as he looked down at the poor disheveled man, it is when the worst is over that we lower our guard and fall prey to torments of the spirit.

The passage through the Strait of Magellan had been rough. For a month the ship had battled winter gales, her rigging frozen, her decks covered with snow. She maneuvered perilously through canyons of giant blue glaciers, which every so often split, toppling ice into the water with a thunderous crack and unleashing enormous waves.

During this time Charles and most of the crew not needed to man the rigging stayed belowdecks. Happily, he did not see much of McCormick, because the naturalist was still aboard the *Adventure*. When the two did find themselves together on land, each was understandably awkward in the other's company.

Charles had begun viewing the whole world differently. He scribbled excitedly in his journal. Everything opened up to him. Everything now seemed palpable and manifest—the cloud of butterflies that engulfed the ship like snowfall, the phosphorus trailing behind in luminescent silver, the electrical field that crackled around the masts one moonlit night. These were not phantasmagoric phenomena; they were all too real, Nature exposed in all her glory. Charles felt that he could make sense of all the natural events around him, that he possessed insight to illuminate them at a single stroke, like a lightning bolt in a ghostly nighttime landscape.

Before crossing through the strait, the *Beagle* was beached for repairs to the hull at the mouth of the Santa Cruz and the *Adventure* anchored nearby. For the first time since Woollya, Charles and McCormick were thrown together. For the most part they avoided one another. The distance between them had now turned into an unbridgeable gulf. To kill time, the two posed for a sketch by Conrad Martens, one on each side of a tree, barely looking at each other the whole time.

At last the ships reached the Pacific and put in at the quaint port of Valparaiso on the Chilean coast. Charles could not wait to be back on land and explore the Andes. He managed to find lodging in town with an old school chum and then struck out for the high Cordillera. He wandered for six weeks, stepping over ravines that would have sent him hurtling to his death and crossing suspension bridges that swayed in the howling wind. He caught mountain birds, found minerals, uncovered marine deposits. At night he slept huddled for warmth against his two peasant guides. He had returned in triumph, trailing mules loaded with specimens, including whole shell beds from the mountains, more evidence for his theory that the range, once seashore, had been thrust up by geological forces.

Seeing the ship from the dock, he quickly noticed something was wrong. The *Beagle* looked to be in a sorry state, the crew lounging about at loose ends. Lieutenant Wickham, pacing up and down, rushed over when he saw Charles.

"The Captain's gone off his head," he said. "He's resigning his commission and wants to be invalided and returned to England. Go and talk to him, Philos. Maybe you can return him to himself."

"What precipitated the crisis?" asked Charles.

"He received notice from the Admiralty rebuking him for the purchase of the *Adventure* and refusing to pay the cost. He's had to sell it. That's what pushed him over the brink. I partly blame myself."

"Why?"

"Sulivan had been hounding him for weeks to buy the *Adventure*, and once he got command, he told him she was essential to complete the work. I should have put a stop to it."

Charles found FitzRoy in his cabin, lying on his bunk with the curtains drawn. His tunic was open and he rested with one arm thrown across his eyes, the other trailing to the floor. He scarcely looked up.

His face was pallid, his eyes sunk deep in their sockets. Charles helped him to a glass of water.

At first FitzRoy said very little, but then he turned verbose, the words rushing out in such a maniacal torrent that Charles became alarmed. FitzRoy roundly condemned the Admiralty, the Navy, Whigs, the entire government. Wickham heard him ranting and came in. The two stayed with the Captain for hours, gently persuading him that there was no need to return to Tierra del Fuego, that the survey there was essentially finished, and that all that remained was to take the chronometrical readings for the remainder of the voyage.

They did the same the next day and the next. Charles was impressed by Wickham; the man stood to gain if he stepped in as Captain, as FitzRoy had done for Pringle Stokes on the previous voyage, but he seemed more concerned about the Captain's health than his own advancement.

On the third day, their soothing words seemed finally to take effect. FitzRoy was much improved. He got up, shaved, dressed, and decided to venture outside. Charles came to help him. Before leaving the cabin, FitzRoy stood at the door and looked all around, as if waking from a dream.

"Do you have the remotest idea why I spent a fortune refitting this ship in Plymouth?" he asked.

Charles said he did not.

"In order to change the Captain's quarters. I moved the entire cabin. I refused to live in the same one as my predecessor so that I would not be haunted by his ghost—Pringle Stokes, that poor wretch."

"I see," said Charles. Without thinking, he added: "I suppose it was the loneliness of command that unhinged him."

FitzRoy looked Charles directly in the eyes.

"You know," he said, "after his death, they performed an autopsy. They found the ball lodged in his brain, but they also found something else. They opened his shirt and what did they see there? Seven wounds, seven knife wounds, nearly healed. *Nearly healed*. The bloke had been trying to kill himself for weeks. . . . He had no one to help, no one to turn to. He was alone."

With that, FitzRoy went on deck, took a deep breath, and said he would resume command. A good wind had come up.

As they hoisted anchor, Charles looked up and saw McCormick on the quarterdeck with his canvas bag, returning from his berth on the *Adventure,* heading toward his old cabin. He emerged five minutes later and approached Charles, standing resolutely before him.

"I see we're shipmates again, Mr. Darwin," he said.

"That we are," replied Charles.

They would head up the coast and then due west, six hundred miles, toward the famed archipelago named after the shell of the tortoise.

Charles was standing next to FitzRoy when they drew alongside the first island. He could hardly believe his eyes. He had been looking forward to the Galápagos because legend called the place Eden.

But this! There was nothing paradisiacal about this place—a dismal heap of black lava rising up to the sky with scarcely a jot of vegetation and nothing to see but birds.

"And what island, pray tell, is that?" he asked.

"That," replied the Captain, "is a Spaniard's joke. It is so insignificant it has no name—and that's exactly how it is noted on the chart: Sin Nombre."

He sniffed the air and continued: "Do not be misled by Islas Encantadas. The Spanish does not mean 'beautiful' but rather 'bewitched,' an appellation derived from the treacherous currents that make landing difficult. It is true that the animals and birds, having no acquaintance with man, show no fear in proximity but rather a blithe indifference. Still, mark my words, 'tis a shore fit for pandemonium."

The ship dropped anchor at the second island. The men threw their lines in the water and the decks were soon alive with parrot fish and angelfish flapping about in a riot of bright tropical colors. Charles and eight sailors took the whaleboat to shore. They found the black beach so hot they could feel it through the soles of their boots.

They walked along the coast: the place was teeming with life. Marine iguanas littered the lava rocks, their spotted black hides invisible at a distance but hideously distinct close up. With combs of scales along their backs, cold eyes, sagging chin pouches, and long curved tails, they looked like malevolent dragons, but were in reality sluggish and harmless. Charles picked one up by the tail and heaved it into the water.

Rounding a point, they were surrounded by a profusion of birds. Red-footed boobies perched in trees. Below them, on the ground, masked boobies tended their nests and blue-footed boobies covered every ridge, some ponderously raising their pale blue feet one at a time in an awkward two-step mating dance. The birds paid the men no attention whatsoever. Charles raised his gun to a nearby hawk, which didn't move, so he pushed it off the branch with the barrel.

With Covington at his side, he followed a path inland and at last came upon the islands' most famous denizens, giant tortoises—two of them munching prickly pears. The animals hissed and withdrew their heads, but soon poked them out again and resumed eating. Charles measured the circumference of one of their shells: a full seven feet around. They walked on and came to a sight that stopped them in their tracks: a wide path that was a veritable thoroughfare for tortoises, long processions of them mounting and descending.

The two followed the trail to the top of the hill where a spring-fed pool was filled with an entire congregation of the creatures. Some sank up to their eyes in the pure cold water, swallowing it in great, lugubrious gulps. Others wallowed deep in the mud. Charles was overwhelmed—he felt he had blundered upon some clandestine rite, an antediluvian spectacle in which beasts had dropped their savage masks and revealed their innocent natures.

The men turned and pursued the tortoises that were lumbering downhill. On the spur of the moment, Charles climbed up one and sat on it, then so did Covington. They rocked back and forth with the movement and held on to the edges of the shells to keep from falling. Looking at each other, they burst out laughing. They rode down the hill, overcome by waves of merriment until they rounded a corner at the bottom. There, to their astonishment, they came upon a scene that quickly sobered them. Their shipmates were slaughtering the tortoises, turning them over and slitting open their pale undersides. Dozens lay on their backs, their legs flailing in the air, awaiting transport to the ship's hold. The beach was already littered with carapaces.

The sailors were as surprised as they were. "Better jump off and be quick about it," shouted one, "or you'll end up in turtle soup."

Aboard the *Beagle* that evening, Charles was shaken by a tumult of emotions. He had recently begun to see everything in a new, effulgent dimension: the fish, the iguanas, the birds, the tortoises. He was a witness to primordial Nature and her workings—the beauty of it and the savagery too—and he felt he understood it, as if he had observed a moment of creation. Opening his notebook, he wrote: "Here, both in space and time, we seem to be brought somewhat near to that great fact—that mystery of mysteries—the first appearance of new beings on this earth."

The next day the *Beagle* sailed on to Charles Island, the site of a penal colony that held two hundred exiled prisoners. The English acting governor, Nicholas Lawson, entertained a party from the ship for lunch on his verandah set in a plantain grove. Serving chunks of roasted tortoise meat and grog, he regaled them with stories of castaways and pirates.

At one point, discussing the tortoises, he chanced to remark that he could tell which of the twenty or so islands any one of them had come from merely by examining its shell. This was proof, he said, that somehow their differing habitats had bred distinctions. FitzRoy and the others paid little attention to the comment, but Charles took it in and quickly glanced around. There was McCormick, sitting directly across and looking back at Charles, as if he too had noted the observation and perhaps mined its significance.

That afternoon, the group rowed over to James Island. Charles wanted to expand his collection of birds. They too seemed to follow the rule that had caught the eye of the acting governor: on every island they displayed minute differences, as if adapting to their various habitats. On each island he visited, Charles made a point of shooting several birds—especially the finches—tagging them, stuffing them, and keeping a meticulous record. As always, Covington was with him that afternoon, and the two wandered off alone.

The sun was beating down mercilessly and Charles was feeling dizzy from the heat. They came to a lowland thicket and found dozens of finches and mockingbirds flying around the bushes. Guns were not necessary, for they had discovered that by holding up a branch and making a shushing sound they could lure a finch to land on it, then grab it.

Seeing an unusual yellow one, Charles pursued it alone, stumbling through the wood as it flew off. His foot struck something hard and he looked down and gasped. There, sticking out from a bunch of leaves and shining in the sun, was a human skull.

He felt a wave of nausea and held on to a tree to steady himself. Then he reached down and pulled the skull from the earth. He held it up, turning it in his hand; it was both repellent and irresistible—the bleached white dome, the serrated cracks in the temples, the dark triangle of a nose, and the rotted teeth pulled back in a hideous grin, a hive of maggots where the tongue would have been.

He again felt faint. Listening closely, he heard not silence but a steady soft roar, the sound of insects everywhere, a multitude of them, flying, buzzing, rubbing their wings, munching on leaves. He could hear the birds diving into the sea for fish and the iguanas chewing algae. Panic seized him, something he had never felt before. Of a moment, it all was too much—the hot lava rocks, the hideous lizards, the slaughtered tortoises, the skull, the maggots. It was a ghastly cycle of life and death, repeating itself endlessly and without meaning, and he was a prisoner of it. Nature was an omnivorous god—vile and monstrous.

Suddenly, McCormick appeared. He looked at Charles, still holding the skull.

"I say, that must have been the ship's Captain the Governor was talking about," he said. "It seems his crew turned mutinous and slew him on this very island."

Covington joined them. "What shall we do with it?" he demanded. "Add it to the collection?"

Charles was aghast at the suggestion. He ordered Covington to dig a hole and give it a proper Christian burial.

That evening, he penned a letter to Hooker. He did not tell him of the incident, but he signed off with a *cri de coeur:* "What a book a Devil's chaplain might write on the clumsy, wasteful, blundering, low and horridly cruel works of nature!"

Three days later, the ship anchored off Indefatigable Island. The weather was warm, with a slight breeze from the west, perfect for hunting. Charles was eager to collect some underwater specimens, and McCormick, suddenly amiable, said that he would like to do the same.

The two set off in a boat with Second Lieutenant Sulivan and Philip Gidley King.

They found a good spot to anchor and dove for several hours, leaving one person in the boat as a lifeguard since none were accomplished swimmers. By noon, they had brought up all manner of fish, crabs, seaweed, and coral, so they headed to the shore for lunch. The beach was lined with sea lions, lolling in the sun, showing not a whit of interest in the two-legged creatures. Charles pulled out his matches to start a fire, and they grilled some fish, washing it down with wine. Afterward King and Sulivan wanted to rest, but Charles and McCormick returned to the boat to hunt for more specimens.

The two rowed along the shore until they came upon a lagoon encircled by reeds. McCormick, standing watch in the bow, proclaimed it a good spot and offered to remain on board. Charles jumped in and dove half a dozen times, surfacing with shells and other treasures. Each time McCormick, peering down from above, motioned him farther away from the boat.

Charles was floating on the surface, looking down, when he saw a dark shadow beneath him, a rapid movement, the ripple of a tail. Then another and another. The water churned with dark shapes. He raised his head, stole a breath, and plunged his face back in to look again. He could see them clearly now, silvery-gray with white tips on their fins and tails, five and six feet long—sharks, four of them; no, more. A dozen. They glided through the water sleekly, effortlessly, circling in a hunt for food. Quickly but calmly, staying close to the surface, Charles swam back to the boat, fearful of calling attention to himself. He reached up and McCormick grabbed his forearm and helped hoist him aboard.

Charles sat on the stern seat, his heart pumping. He looked at McCormick as his blood continued to race; the man was upset, babbling. "Thank the Lord you've made it to safety," he said. "I warned you, I shouted, but you didn't hear me."

Charles said simply: "Let us leave this place."

McCormick rowed back toward the beach. As Charles, shivering, looked behind to the near-fatal patch of water, he wondered whether he could see small bits of fish, perhaps the remnants of their noonday meal, floating upon the surface—the few that the sharks had not devoured.

CHAPTER 20

Sonnenberg Clinic
Zuriberg
Zürich, die Schweiz
10 April 1872

My dear Mary Ann,

You are kind enough to ask how I am. My answer can be summed up in one simple word—wretched! Alone in the world, despised by my family, betrayed by the man I loved—all this has been heaped upon me, payment enough, I think, for the sin that has blackened my soul. But now to undergo this final punishment, the utmost sorrow for any woman . . . it is insupportable. I speak truly, Mary Ann, when I say that I fear it is more than my mind can bear.

Even now, sitting on the sun-porch of this clinic, I feel nothing but hopeless despondency. Nothing helps me. I recoil at the loveliness of this place, the wildflowers, the blue lake, the snowy Alps. It should be a sight to soothe my soul but it has no power to heal my suffering, for I am sunk too low. And to think that I brought this misery upon myself only makes it the harder to endure.

I hesitate to commit the sad tale to a letter, but for the thought that confession may prove balm for pain. Some of it you know already—namely, my infatuation, nay, my love, for X.

What you do not know is that during our family sojourn in the Lake District, I contrived to meet X secretly in the woods and not just once or twice but five times. They were amorous encounters. I could not help myself. Each time for me was more heated than the previous one. So carried away was I by passion that I put off all consideration of the consequences of my actions. Indeed, I thought of nothing but him and desired nothing except to be with him.

Imagine then my distress when I felt him drawing away from me. Each occasion, it seemed, fed my ardour but acted to lessen his. At first, after intimacy, he was solicitous, holding me in his arms and praising my qualities, which did help somewhat to mitigate my guilt for having given in to his silken entreaties. But soon he seemed to think he had call upon my person, indeed, upon my body, as of right, and he began to show disrespect. I felt that I was prisoner of a drama that sprang full-blown from some penny dreadful—except that what was hanging in the balance was not foolish make-believe but my very life.

At first his visits to our family in the cottage at Grasmere were thrilling. I would wait all morning for the sound of his horse galloping up to the stable-gate and delay meeting him in full company for the pure pleasure of the anticipation. When others were present I took joy in disguising my inner turmoil with a mask of insouciance. I revelled in casting a glance around the room so as to pass over him as if he were no more than an ordinary visitor. And then there were the illicit moments—a secret look, a passing touch under the table after dinner—all this fed the flames of my desire more than I can say.

But then came the time when his visits began to taper off. He would miss a day, then two, then three. I grew so desperate and rash as to send him a note by messenger, which he did not answer. One night, after he had played in a quartet and I could hardly take my eyes off him, I caught him alone in the hall and demanded to know why he was treating me so—the words came out far differently from the casual phrases I had practised—and he pretended not to know of what I was speaking. He tore his arm from my grasp and hurried away.

I fell into a melancholy and feigned illness as an explanation. Yet I was puzzled—why, if he seemed to want no more of me, did he continue to visit our family? Was there still hope? I took walks in the morning along the path we used to take but never saw him there. Once in a moment alone with him I suggested that we fix a rendezvous, and as I said it I abased myself by lowering my eyes to the floor and casting a coquettish look, but he refused the offer, saying he had an appointment to go hunting. He departed, walking quickly away, as if in relief.

Our family returned home and I was so unhappy I did indeed fall ill and missed many gatherings in the drawing-room below. The sounds of music and merriment floated up the stairs, only serving to worsen my misery.

Then, one evening, we were all called together. Papa said he had an announcement. Etty blushed as he took her hand and held it high, smiling all the while. He said he was pleased to declare that she would soon be Mrs Richard Litchfield. Mamma cried, my brothers began making jokes and I almost fainted on the spot. I could not control myself but ran from the room in tears. So great was the commotion that only Mamma noticed my anguish.

The plans were laid hurriedly for a wedding in late August, a bare three months after he walked into our lives. George arranged the settlement—I looked at Papa's books and saw that it amounted to £5,000, with a yearly stipend of £400. The sum would allow the couple to live in comfort, I overheard Papa say, as Litchfield had accepted a post in the Ecclesiastical Commission. Papa told George that he doubted the man was a 'gold-digger'.

I had a single encounter with him. To arrange it I attended St Mary's for the first time in years and we walked home trailing behind the others. I asked for an explanation for his conduct and he had at least the grace to look embarrassed. He said that he had long ago discussed with Papa the idea of courting one of us and that Papa had ruled that he should ask for Etty's hand, she being the elder. He said that when he met me in Grasmere so unexpectedly, he had been carried away by emotion, but that soon he began to feel base and unworthy and decided to bring our meetings to an end. He said he would always regard me fondly as a sister.

I did not attend the marriage, for by mid-August, I had become aware of my condition. I informed Mamma, who could not bring herself to believe what I had done. When she did she became most distraught and angry. She slapped me full hard across the face more than once, but I did not cry out. She said she knew who was responsible but that we must never tell anyone, especially Papa. Instead, she fabricated a story involving the son of an estate owner in the Lake District and made me promise to hold to it.

Papa was devastated. He called me into his study. He was seated in his leather chair where I had seen him hundreds of times before. He did not strike me but instead looked old and feeble as if he himself had been dealt a deathly blow, which made me feel thrice worse. He did not demand to know the name of the father, since, as Mamma had informed him the person was married, that would serve little purpose. He said I should be hard put to regain his respect, no matter how much I repented my actions, and that I was now condemned to life as a spinster. He said that he would never consent to pay a dowry but that nonetheless he would not force me out of the house, which was mine to live in for all my years.

I could not, however, keep the child. To ensure this and to protect the good name of our family, he would contact his friend, Charles Loring Brace, the American who runs the Children's Aid Society, who he said knew how to deal with such situations. One week later, at Mr Brace's suggestion, before my condition became visible, I was sent here to Zurich, where I have remained these eight months.

She was a baby girl. I barely had sufficient time to discover that. They let me hold her only for the few minutes it took to cut the cord and for the doctor to examine her. Then she was taken away. I am told she will remain here in Zurich for a while until she is old enough to travel and then will be placed with a good family.

I sometimes believe I can still feel her, now ten days after she has gone, and I recollect the feel of her in my arms. Her face was pink and wrinkled, her skin covered with a soft birth substance, and she had a full head of black hair. The doctor said she was a fine and healthy baby girl.

I am leaving here tomorrow and will return home. By then Papa will have received the letter I wrote last week in which I told him that I was sorry for what I had done but observed that we all have committed grievous errors in our lives. I said it ill behooved him to lecture me on morality. I added further that I knew he was not such an upstanding man because I had discovered what he had done thirty years ago on his trip to South America.

Here on the sun-porch, where I sit every day for hours on end, with nothing to distract me but my own dark thoughts, they bring me lemonade, as if my problem were nothing more than a parched throat.

I prithee, my sweet Mary Ann, think of me not too harshly and pray that I may find peace.

Yours in grateful remembrance,
Bessie

20 April 1872

My dear Mary Ann,

    I received your letter only moments before I left Zurich. I thank you for it, deeply. Without your support and your comforting words, I do not know how I would survive.

    You asked me to tell you about my home-coming. It was not as dreadful as I had feared. Parslow himself met me at Orpington and filled me in on the family news. He said that it was a pity that I had not attended Etty's wedding and his tone was so unaffected that I deemed it unlikely he had any inkling of why I had been absent. I pleaded ill-health and said that was the reason I had gone to rest in the Swiss mountains. He said that Papa too had not been well and had barely been able to give her away at the church. It was a short ceremony with scarcely any festivities, though Parslow was much surprised at the presence of a group of men who were unknown to him—it turned out that they were friends of Richard's from the Working Men's College.

    Papa was upstairs in his bedroom when I arrived and he did not come downstairs to greet me. He stayed there all the afternoon, only descending for dinner. When he saw me, he nodded, nothing else. The meal would have passed largely in silence except that Horace was home from Trinity and he at least was garrulous. I enquired after Etty (which caused Mamma to shoot me a dark look) and Horace said that the newly-weds had both fallen sick on their honeymoon in Europe. 'Tell Bessie what Etty wrote from Cannes,' he said, turning to Mamma. Most reluctantly, she recited a passage from a letter in which Etty wrote that the two of them felt very married, each lying in a sickbed as if they'd been together thirty years, just like Mamma and Papa. It made my ears burn to hear of it.

    Two days have passed now since my return and Papa has not referred to the letter I wrote him from Zurich. I decided to give Papa an opportunity to raise the subject if he so desired. Consequently, this afternoon when he readied himself to take his constitutional along the Sandwalk, I asked if I could accompany him.

    He appeared surprised but agreed and we set out. After discussing the weather and other such topics of little consequence, we fell silent. I realised that Papa had no desire to broach the subject that was on both of our minds— nor did he want me to do so. As for myself, I was content, as the saying goes, to let sleeping dogs lie.

The longer I live here with my parents, the more I find myself sinking into a familiar lassitude. I am at their beck and call. It makes me feel that I am losing my shape, my footing in the world, and becoming insubstantial, like the morning fog on the garden. My condition reminds me of a passage in Middlemarch, *in which you described a woman very much like me and wrote that she was 'nipped and subdued as single women are apt to be who spend their lives in uninterrupted subjection to their elders'.*

I do miss you so much, Mary Ann, and long to see you. No one else understands the depth of the misery that has befallen me.

Yours in eternal friendship,
Bessie

1 *January* 1873

My dear Mary Ann,

It is the New Year and I have seized upon the day to write you and bring you abreast of my doings, such as they are. It is hard to believe that more than half a year has passed since my misfortune. I have vowed to throw myself into my life as a dutiful daughter and spinster, much as I detest the word. We have settled into a quiet existence at Down House. All of the other children are gone now—William to banking in Southampton, George to law, Francis to study medicine and his beloved plants, Leonard to the Royal Engineers and Horace back to University. Mamma and Papa and I live as a threesome, with little to disturb the daily routine.

Papa no longer plays billiards with Parslow but still has a go at Backgammon with Mamma every night after dinner. He keeps a record of their respective wins and losses over the years and each time he is forced to increase her tally, he thunders, 'Bang your bones!' or 'Confound you, woman!' Afterwards she reads novels to him while he reclines upon the sofa.

As you know, he has finally finished his book on human and animal expressions—at last, we no longer live with those horrid photographs of people grimacing and animals snarling! Now he putters around the greenhouse doing God knows what with orchids and pea-plants and those insect-catching sundews. He has been talking lately about writing his autobiography, largely, he says, to provide amusement to his grandchildren and perhaps instruction to others.

I try not to think of my baby girl and am able, through sheer force of will, to banish the memory from my mind for days on end. When the barest thought of her begins to intrude, I consciously push it away by quickly seeking out someone for conversation or by finding something to read. This strategem, however, does not always succeed, especially if I am out walking and see a young child who would be about her age. Then the floodgate opens. On those occasions I cannot help but ask myself scores of questions: How big is she now? What colour hair does she have? In looks does she take after her father or me? Is she quick of mind like me or slow like Horace? After torturing myself with such questions, I fall into a black melancholy that lasts for weeks.

Yours always,
Bessie

6 July 1873

My dear Mary Ann,
Today I am content and I would like to share that sentiment with you. It being a summer Sunday, we had a host of visitors. About seventy men and women came from the Working Men's College. Their number was augmented by the Huxleys and their children and all manner of local people. The weather was glorious, with the sun shining and the roses in full bloom. In the garden we had set up long tables for tea and strawberries. People danced on the lawn and relaxed in the shade of the new verandah. The children rolled in the newly mown hay and played at Red Indians along the Sandwalk, using javelins of hazel from the gardener's shed.
I am accustomed to finding Richard's visits most upsetting. In anticipation, I would feel my heart beating against my ribs and my breath so shallow that I feared I would faint. The very first time I saw them as a married couple, Richard ignored me, as if I were of as little consequence as a piece of furniture. Etty gave me a big hug and took me by the hand for a walk in the garden, which calmed me considerably—for I had been afraid that during their honeymoon he had felt a compulsion to confess our transgression. So little did I know of his nature! And yet from time to time I caught a hint of jealousy on her part. She would appraise me during unguarded moments, as if she were trying to burrow into my secret. Once, by accident I sat close to Richard in the drawing-room, and as he quickly stood up to change his seat,

I saw her observe him and a chill passed over her features as distinct as a cloud.

But today was different. Everyone seemed to enjoy the outing. As the men gathered under the lime-trees for a sing-along, Richard brought out his concertina. At one point I heard his deep bass rising above the others and I looked at him closely, able to scrutinise him fully while being myself unobserved. My Mr X. He has gained a bit of weight. I thought back to the time when he and I would take the men on countryside excursions on the train. They were the happiest days of my life. And yet, as I recalled them, I felt not simply an ache of regret that they were forever gone but a quiet joy that they had happened at all. I walked under the shade of a lime-tree and stood to one side, looking at Richard as he tilted his head back to sing, and I realised that I no longer felt the same about him, that my passion had ebbed or turned into something else, something more tranquil and not at all hurtful. Perhaps it has become a memory of itself.

Today it is, I think, that I begin my journey to recovery.
Yours always,
Bessie

10 January 1874

My dear Mary Ann,
You asked me to describe the séance we attended at Uncle Ras' house the other night from my point of view, so that we might compare our experiences. As you perhaps do not know, Papa attended only at the urging of my cousin Hensleigh; customarily he disdains such events that turn on mysticism and spiritualism.

As you remarked at the outset, mesmerism, mediums, spirit-guides, table-rappers and spirit-photographs are all the fad in London these days. In a thousand darkened parlours people gather around tables to commune with the dead or find divertissement in the prospect. Papa pours scorn on the whole idea and in this he is joined by the ever faithful Mr Huxley.

The 'manifestation' was arranged by George. It was he who chose Charles Williams as the medium. In addition to Mamma and Papa, I was surprised to see that all manner of people joined us for the session, including Etty and Richard, Hensleigh and Fanny and Francis Galton. I was most happy to see

you and Mr Lewes there, since I always find your presence reassuring. I won-
der if you spotted the man who slipped in at the last moment. I am convinced
it was Huxley himself, dressed incognito, undoubtedly to heighten the drama
of his attendance.

I thought the setting-up was great fun. I giggled when the doors were shut,
the curtains drawn and George and Hensleigh tied Mr Williams' hands and
feet and we all sat there in the dark waiting for the show to begin. It soon got
horribly stuffy and since the room was pitch-black even I began to imagine
various shapes and forms. It was all quite spookish, since one heard breathing
and all kinds of sounds—and it was impossible to tell who was making them.
By this time the heat was almost insufferable. Then the show began with the
ringing of a bell and we heard the sound of wind rushing through the room.
Someone exclaimed and stood up—I heard a chair scraping against the floor.
The chair fell over and I heard a gasp, the sound of someone in distress. The
lights were put on. Imagine my surprise when it turned out that Papa, as you
must have noticed, seemed unable to breathe. He insisted on lying down and
was taken upstairs and put to bed. Afterwards, the session resumed with
more sounds and sparks flashing and the table rising up above our heads.

When it was over, most of those present appeared giddy from the excite-
ment. Papa recovered and later pronounced it all 'rubbish', though I must say
that he appeared genuinely distraught. George, who is a believer in the spiri-
tual world, saw the look upon his face as he came down the staircase, and
whispered to me: 'If I did not know better, I would have said: here is a man
who is loath to have a reckoning with someone in the afterworld.'

Later, I was moved when you took my hands in yours and squeezed them
and referred to what you called my 'travails'. You said: 'My dear, it is we
women who bear the suffering of the world. It has always been so and will
always be. The consolation is that while men may wash themselves in our
tears, it is we who drink deeply at life's source.' As you said this, I spied a
single tear running down your face. When you leaned over to kiss me good-
bye, I felt it upon my cheek, which made me think, years ago, of the sister in
Goblin Market *and the juice that dripped over her face and lodged in the*
dimples of her chin.

I shall never forget the support you have provided for me during my time
of tribulation.

Yours always,
Bessie

18 November 1877

My dear Mary Ann,

To think I have not seen you in almost four years. So much has happened, and yet so little. As you know, we have taken Francis' son Bernard into our house following the death of poor Amy in childbirth. Although I dearly wish it had never happened, I will admit that the presence of a one-year-old has enlivened the old place; his cry seems to shake the dust from the rafters and rattle the mulberry-tree outside the nursery. I suspect that in no time the old toys will be broken out, including the sliding-board on the stairs. Mamma says Bernard is as solemn as a Grand Lama. I, of course, have found it wonderfully bittersweet to hold a baby in my arms once again. Sometimes my eyes fill up with tears, and whether it is from joy or sorrow, I cannot tell.

Papa has become interested in earthworms, which, Mr Huxley noted, is appropriate for someone 'whose mind is casting ahead to the grave'. He has placed a mill-stone in the garden, attached to a device that can measure how much it sinks, to measure their underground activity. He is convinced they are intelligent and has Mamma playing the Broadwood and Francis playing the bassoon to test their reactions, despite the fact that, as Mamma points out, they have no ears.

Parslow retired two years ago; he lives in the cottage on the property and has become a superb gardener, winning first prize for potatoes in the village show two years running.

As you are no doubt aware, Papa's fame continues to grow. Yesterday he received an honorary degree of Doctor of Laws from Cambridge. Mamma worried that he would not be able to last the ceremony, but he did; it was not without its lighter moments. The Senate House was packed to overflowing, with rowdy undergraduates standing in the windows and sitting on statues. Moments before Papa appeared in his bright red robe, a stuffed monkey in gown and mortar-board was suspended from the gallery. A proctor confiscated it, much to the crowd's disappointment, but the boys rallied when an object said to represent 'the missing link' was lowered from above and remained hovering just over Papa's head. He did not appear to notice it. The crowd both cheered and jeered him but it was clear that it was all in good spirits. The Latin was largely incomprehensible, save for the Orator's final declaration that men and apes are morally different.

I could not help but feel proud. There are many things which I have told no-one, not even you. Perhaps at the end of the day, despite the fact that his studies and writings flow from an event that is singularly reprehensible, of which only I and a few others have knowledge, he does possess some attributes of greatness. For he is at least the messenger of a great idea. I take solace in thinking of him as the Angel Gabriel of natural science.

Now that I know the worst about the man, forgiveness can begin.

Yours always,
Bessie

CHAPTER 21

Hugh leaned against the railing on the South Bank near the entrance to the National Theatre and checked his watch. Neville was forty minutes late—forty-two, to be exact. Hugh worried that he wouldn't come. God knows, he hadn't been all that eager to meet, but still—he wouldn't have set a time and place with no intention of showing up, would he?

Hugh paced along the Embankment, each time lengthening his path. Then, when he reached a point about one hundred yards from the theatre entrance, he spotted Neville sitting on a bench, reading the *Financial Times*. When Hugh walked over, Neville did a slight double take, fumbling with the paper and standing up and sticking out his hand almost as if it were a coincidence that they met.

"Afraid I'd missed you," he said.

"I was waiting over there." Hugh pointed to the entrance.

"I see. There's another one, you know, just around the corner here. My mistake, I'm sure."

"It doesn't matter. The main thing is we found each other."

They started walking slowly along the Embankment. Neville, still wearing the bulky sweater of the other day, looked at the ground. Hugh could tell his companion was nervous; for that matter, so was he.

"Shall we take a ride? I've always wanted to." Hugh motioned toward the London Eye, rising high in the sky.

To his surprise, Neville agreed. Hugh bought their tickets for the slow-motion Ferris wheel and within minutes the two were ushered into a cabin that began to move slowly upward, rocking slightly.

They were silent for a few moments, then Hugh took a breath and began: "Look, I know this is difficult for you—"

"That it most definitely is."

"But I hope you'll be able to tell me *something*. Everyone's acting so mysterious. Bridget keeps implying that a lot of things happened that I didn't know about. That Cal was disturbed about something. And you—I don't know—you seem so secretive. As if you know something important but don't want to tell me."

"I see. That's what you took away from our conversation?"

"Yes. You said his death was upsetting—"

"It certainly was. Nothing mysterious about that."

"No, but you implied that something had happened. You talked about going back over old ground and reassessing things. What did you mean?"

The wheel was moving steadily upward now. They could see the bridges up and down the Thames and the two towers of Westminster Abbey.

Neville didn't answer. Hugh thought he would ease the man's discomfort by taking a less direct tack.

"What did you do in the lab, anyway? I mean, what was the work?"

"Ah," said Neville, falling silent. He peered out the window, rubbing it with his sweater sleeve to see more clearly. But when he turned back, he looked at Hugh directly for the first time. "I might as well tell you what I know. Please treat what I'm about to say as confidential."

"I will. I promise."

He gave Hugh a penetrating look. "You've heard of bovine spongiform encephalopathy?"

"Isn't that mad cow disease?"

"Yes."

"We had some in the States—a cow from Canada, if I remember."

"Exactly. It's been linked to a strain of Creutzfeldt-Jakob disease in humans. Aberrant proteins eat away at your brain, turn it into Swiss cheese. You go crazy, you're wracked with pain, then you die a horrible death. Altogether, a nasty business."

"And your lab investigated it?"

"We were in the forefront of the research. The big question was whether the disease could leap the species barrier. We figured it already had—that it began with scrapie in sheep and because sheep offal was fed to cows, they came down with it. It's widely known that slaughterhouses don't abide by regulations, so bits of cow brains and spinal cords were getting into the beef we eat.

"I don't know if you remember, but back in 1996, when the link was established, there was a sort of hysteria over here. The European Union boycotted British beef. Wimpy's, Burger King, and McDonald's took it off the market; even British Airways. It was a crisis for John Major. The Tory government had been on a PR offensive for years—I still remember a cabinet minister going on the telly to feed a hamburger to his four-year-old daughter. Her name was Cordelia. You don't forget something like that."

"I guess not. But why are you telling me all this?"

"To give you some idea of the pressures we were under. They were culling herds right and left. Beef is a ten-billion-pound industry and it was in free fall. The ranchers were screaming and there were demonstrations. It was quite a circus—simply unbelievable."

"So your lab was under pressure to . . . what? Come up with a cure?"

"No, we were nowhere near a cure. We were just trying to answer the basic question, could diseased cow meat contaminate the human food chain? Believe me, it was a loaded question politically."

"But you were able to prove it. Right?"

"Well, yes. But these scientific questions are never clear-cut. They're never black and white. They're subject to interpretations, statistical analysis, all sorts of variables. There's room for maneuver."

The wheel paused. They were at the summit. All of London was spread out before them; the parks were oddly shaped patches of green. Hugh turned back to Neville.

"You're trying to tell me my brother did something unethical, aren't you?"

Neville frowned by way of confirmation.

"What did he do? Give in to government pressure?"

"No, no, not at all. Quite the opposite. You knew him better than any of us. You know he wouldn't do that. He'd go the other way—a natural iconoclast, against the multinationals and big business. And that's just what he did. He let his views interfere with his work."

"How? Tell me."

"He was working on a study with mice. They were genetically altered to mimic human reaction when exposed to the cow disease. His results—they were very strong. They clearly showed humans were susceptible."

"And?"

"They were a bit too strong. No one else could replicate them. The head of the lab was suspicious—he's a real shit, by the way—and he demanded replication before publication. That's when it became obvious that some of Calvin's data sheets had been changed."

Neville took a deep breath, then spat out: "Basically, your brother falsified his outcome."

Hugh couldn't believe it. Before he could react, Neville resumed.

"I've been trying to understand why he did it and I almost can. We all believed the danger was very real for humans. The damned disease took over ten years to incubate. Who knew how many people were walking around with it? Thousands, hundreds of thousands? It could have been disaster on a massive scale. And the government was paralyzed in a position of quasi-denial—'stonewalling,' your brother called it. The politicians were playing with people's lives by underestimating the dangers, at least that's the way he saw it. He felt he couldn't sit back and simply let it happen."

"But still, *falsifying* . . . how can you be sure?"

"It's incontestable. The changes on the sheets were obvious. It wasn't very well done. Besides, he admitted it. We were just lucky we hadn't gone to publication—it was only weeks away."

Hugh shook his head. The wheel was descending slowly now.

"So," Neville continued, "there was nothing for it but to let him go."

"Let him go! He was *fired*?"

"Not to put too fine a point on it—yes, he was fired. It's an extremely serious breach of ethics for any lab. Motive can't be considered. . . ."

Neville talked on, about the inviolability of scientific research, but Hugh tuned out. He was thinking of Cal and how hard he would have taken it, he who had always taken such pride in his work, in getting ahead.

"When did all this happen?" he asked.

"About two months before he returned to the States. Maybe three."

They had completed the ride and the door flew open. They stepped out and walked in silence back to the bench. Hugh shook hands with him.

"Well, I'm glad you told me all this—I suppose."

"Don't be too hard on him. Believe me, you don't know what pressure is until you've had to stand up to a cabinet minister whose job is on the line." Neville smiled weakly. "And please. I don't mean to go on like a broken record—"

"I know, don't worry. I'll treat everything as confidential."

Hugh felt he should be grateful to Neville but he couldn't bring himself to thank him. In fact, he had irrationally begun to dislike the man. Now *he* was the one who wanted to get away. But Neville kept talking.

"You know, a situation like this, an untimely death—sometimes you get some new information and you view it differently. It's like anything in life: step back and take the broader view and you might see things differently."

To be polite, Hugh nodded.

"Like your man Darwin. That was his specialty, the broad view."

"I really must be off," said Hugh, moving away.

At that moment, Hugh couldn't care less about Darwin or about Lizzie or about their effort to uncover the mystery of the *Beagle*'s voyage. He was thinking only of the anguish Cal must have experienced—and that he had experienced it alone.

Later, riding back to Cambridge on the train, he saw things more clearly. Neville had been trying to help him, after all; he had undergone a risk, in his own mind at least, in revealing the secrets of the lab. So was Bridget, for that matter, though she had little but her own instincts to go on. They were *all* trying to help him. Now he needed to reach Simon, Cal's roommate, to see what other secrets might remain.

He thought of Beth, how she was his guide through all of this, in dealing with the revelations both about Cal and about Darwin. In his mind, the two searches were coming together, weaving into a single strand. He smiled as he recalled how excited she had been when she returned from Nuneaton with copies of George Eliot's letters. She had prepared a picnic in Parker's Piece and there read them to him with dramatic inflection, between sips of wine, from time to time combing her hair with her fingers. The final letter, she said, was unspeakably sad, and she had given it to him to take home and read later.

Back in his room, Hugh again felt a rush of admiration for Darwin, the admiration that had sustained him during those horrible months in the Galápagos, before he had read Lizzie's diary. Neville was right. Darwin's gift—his genius—was more than doggedness; it was that uncanny ability to step back, take the broadest possible view, and make connections that others could not, so that a *pattern* appeared. He *deduced* things: how mountains formed, how creatures evolved, how the world as he knew it came into being over immeasurable eons. He was able to immerse himself in deep time. How did that pattern spring into place, appearing before him like some fully formed retinal image, the connections suddenly made? How had he done it?

Perhaps the genius lay elsewhere; perhaps it emanated from the work itself, the obsession with detail. How else could a man be riveted by barnacles for eight years when a world-shaking theory was bubbling up within him? And the work told him something. Roland had been right: the barnacles Darwin examined so assiduously had been hermaphroditic; the very first had two little orange penises. Darwin, intrigued—and perhaps horrified—realized that sexual identity had evolved slowly and was not fixed, as the Church would have us believe. Would God work from such a plan? The microcosm and the macrocosm. That's how the pattern is formed. Not just by connecting the dots, as the saying has it, but by being able to *see* the dots.

Hugh opened a desk drawer and pulled out some sketches from the *Beagle* that he had printed off the Internet. There were drawings of the crew, people he had come to know: Captain FitzRoy, brave and haunted; Lieutenant Wickham, jaunty in a naval cap; Philip Gidley King, striking a Byronic pose; Jemmy Button, round-faced and inscrutable; the teenage missionary Matthews, with a moonlike face and long stringy hair.

He stared at a pair of watercolors of the ship by Conrad Martens. One showed the *Beagle* anchored at Papeete in Tahiti, a tiny gash of brown in a peaceful harbor surrounded by palms. The other was of a cluster of ships at rest in Dawes Point, Sydney, some with their sails unfurled, ready to catch the wind.

And then it struck him. He thought back to the sketch of Darwin and McCormick standing on either side of the tree. In an instant he understood its significance. Of course! That was its secret. That was what Lizzie had grasped right away. *How stupid not to have thought of it.*

He reached into the drawer and pulled out the drawing. The key wasn't *where* the sketch had been made; it was *who* had made it. The artist was Conrad Martens, not Augustus Earle, and Martens had joined the voyage only halfway through, in Montevideo.

So there it was! Proof positive that McCormick didn't abandon ship in Rio, after all. He had remained on board, Darwin's rival to the end—jealous, ambitious, unscrupulous. And Darwin had lied about it. Lizzie was right: her father, for some unknown reason, had engaged in a monstrous deception. But why?

CHAPTER 22

The last day in the Galápagos was to prove, for Charles and FitzRoy, the tragic centerpiece of the *Beagle*'s entire voyage. But no one among the crew was to know what really transpired, or could have guessed how crucial the day would become to the futures of those concerned.

That morning Charles, FitzRoy, and McCormick took a boat to Albemarle, the largest island, to explore volcanoes. They had been watching them from a distance, fascinated by the line of smoke trailing high into the sky and the intermittent belches of fire.

Albemarle had five volcanoes, and the largest of them—Wolf—was active. For days it had been rumbling and trembling. That morning they had looked on in fascination as it sent up a roiling white cloud that rose to a height of some ten thousand yards and then spread across the sky like a vast collapsing tent. A breeze brought a dust of fine ash that settled over the *Beagle,* turning her white.

Charles was eager to get as close as possible to a crater to bring back rock samples more intriguing than the common tuff that littered the base of the cones. FitzRoy, still shaky after his nervous collapse, was keen for an exploit that would prove his mettle; and for his part, McCormick was not about to let Charles attain any glory without him.

Four crewmen rowed them to the island and beached the boat. They were under orders to remain there until the three returned, but it was clear they were anxious to leave. The fact that the bay's surface was marked by thousands of ripples, as if the water itself were about to break into a boil, did little to soothe their nerves.

The moment Charles crossed the beach, he realized that something was odd, but it was not until he reached the treeline and turned to look back that he could pinpoint what it was: there were no sea lions on the sand—in fact, no sign of any animal life of any sort, not even birds. It was dead quiet except for the intermittent rumbling from deep within the volcano.

They searched for a path up the slope and finally decided to follow a dry riverbed. The jumble of rocks made it difficult to find footing, but at least there were no branches and vines to impede them. After an hour or so, the trail was covered with ferns and small bushes of lantana, whose white flowers had been seared brown by heat.

FitzRoy led the way, setting a vigorous pace. Charles came next, carrying his usual assortment of implements: a pocket microscope, a compass, a geological hammer, and his cosh, tucked inside his belt. McCormick brought up the rear, carrying the lunch and breathing heavily.

Finally, they came to a clearing on the slope. Far below they could see a lagoon enclosed at the far end by black lava flow. Beyond that was the sea, and off in the distance, looking tiny, the *Beagle*. Charles claimed that the lagoon was itself once the cone of a volcano.

"I say," he added. "Look at this." He had extracted his compass and placed it on a rock. They could see the needle moving wildly, not turning to register true north, but trembling and spinning in all directions.

"The volcano is disturbing the magnetic field," he said.

"Do you feel the vibrations?" asked McCormick, who was seated, his hands palms down on the ground. He sounded nervous.

Charles sat and instantly felt the tremors, though he soon realized they were not just coming from deep within the earth but seemed to exist in the very air around them. Atmospheric disturbance of this sort, he had once read, was a sign of volcanic eruption.

From McCormick's bag FitzRoy pulled out a thick slab of salted beef, cut it into slices with his hunting knife, and passed them around, followed by a loaf of bread from which they tore off pieces.

"We may well require Dutch courage," he added with a laugh, pouring generous glasses of red wine.

Tired, they were reluctant to resume the trek right away. FitzRoy kept pouring more wine until they had finished two bottles. Then he reclined, his head upon a log, his hat pulled down over his face.

After some time, Charles opened his eyes. FitzRoy and McCormick lay motionless, sleeping. He believed the tremors had grown stronger. He noticed a smell of burning sulfur in the air. On the slope behind, he spotted a hardened flow of lava. He scrambled up, struck the lava with his hammer, and uncovered a vein of smooth, dark obsidian. He chipped off a piece and slipped it into his pocket.

Clambering back down, he saw that McCormick was awake. The two exchanged looks. With a nod of his head, Charles gestured to the summit. Without a word, McCormick stood and nodded yes. They traipsed off together, leaving FitzRoy asleep. All around them, the tremors increased.

After an hour, they reached the top of the crater. The heat rose in vibrating waves that reddened their faces and forced them to take short breaths. They peered down in amazement, past an outpouring of sulfurous smoke and ash, into the deep, dish-shaped basin. A shiny black crust undulated around the edge. In the center a miasmic lake of molten red and yellow lava bubbled, emitting a column of smoke and periodically a loud booming noise.

There was a ledge twenty feet below that contained rocks unlike any Charles had ever seen—deep, black andesite, the sort of rock the ancients must have found in Vesuvius. He saw it was possible to reach them. The inside of the crater wall was not sheer. One could walk down partway and below that were ample footholds. It could be done.

What explorer had ever dared to attempt such an adventure?

The sailors on the beach had lost their fright some time back, growing bored instead. They wandered up and down the beach, careful not to venture too far from the boat, then devised various games to pass the time, including a javelin throw with long pieces of driftwood. Finally, they just lay down in the shade and waited.

The first crack brought them up short. It sounded like a cannonball, only louder and closer. Nervously, they turned to search the horizon for the *Beagle*. She remained where she had been all along, anchored at the outer reaches of the bay.

They next felt the vibrations, an unsettling sense of the earth not quite solid underfoot. Then another resounding crack came from above, accompanied by a burst of smoke. The volcano sent a shower of pumice that landed on the beach like hailstones, followed by clouds of ash, floating down like snow.

The crew members debated what to do. They could hardly abandon the Captain, but they readied the boat for departure, pushing it out into the water. Three sailors sat inside it and the fourth remained on land, holding the rope. They waited there in that position for quite a while, not knowing what else to do.

At last they saw two figures careening down the slope, reaching the beach, running across the sand—the Captain and Philos. The sailors stared. There was no third.

The two made it to the boat just as another crack resounded in the sky, foreshadowing the next eruption. As they fell inside the craft, much agitated and out of breath, the Captain barked out an order: "Depart! Depart at once!"

They were halfway to the *Beagle* when one of the sailors dared to ask, "But what of Mr. McCormick?" The others leaned forward to hear Charles's answer, which was soft under any circumstances but especially so with the volcano rumbling above.

"Perished."

That evening, when Charles and FitzRoy dined alone in the Captain's cabin, both men were silent throughout most of the meal. Finally, Charles, who was still too agitated to eat, threw his napkin upon the table and spoke in a voice that was unconvincingly calm.

"I am not sure it would serve anyone's purpose to recount what transpired here today. The man had a horrid death and his family would be most upset to read about it in detail—that is to say, when it comes time for us to write up the narratives of our voyage. Do you not agree?"

FitzRoy looked at him, carefully reading his face.

"In the general scheme of things, it is scarcely more than a footnote," continued Charles. "As far as the Admiralty is concerned, you must of course inform them. But you could always do so . . . judiciously."

FitzRoy remained silent. He had detected a new authority in his messmate.

"I presume you've told them he invalided back in Rio."

"I did."

"And that the order was countermanded."

"Yes."

"Well, it was a ghastly way to end one's life. I'm afraid I cannot help but feel responsible."

"No, you must not blame yourself," replied the Captain. "I am sure you did everything you were capable of."

The *Beagle* set sail early the next morning, heading west at a speedy clip of 150 miles a day. The remainder of her circumnavigational voyage around the world was uneventful.

At long last, on a rainy Sunday, the ship sailed up the English Channel to Falmouth. FitzRoy ordered a final service on board to render thanks to God for a safe homecoming. He had to hold it belowdecks because of the inclement weather. The rain pounded down on the boards inches above the crew's heads as the Captain read passages from Genesis, including one on Adam and Eve and God's wrath when he discovered their sin: *What is this that thou hast done?*

The date was 2 October 1836.

CHAPTER 23

30 May 1878

My dear Mary Ann,

I have not written in the longest time, for which I apologise. I have no excuse—certainly not that my life has been too busy. Far from it, I have little to occupy my days. I have stopped giving my readings to the women at High-gate and stay close to Down House. Mamma, Papa and I have fallen into a rhythm that never varies and that has the contradictory effect of both slowing time down and speeding it up. We rise at seven in the morning and dine at noon. At ten-thirty every night, after two games of Backgammon and a pinch of snuff, Papa blows his nose—one could set one's watch by it—then he slowly mounts the stairs and we all retire. I find pleasure in little things and lose myself for hours on end in my musings. I will provide you with an example.

Today at noon I accompanied Papa along the Sandwalk. It had been a while since we took this tour together. As always, we walked through the garden to the back of our property, turned left through the wooden door in the high hedge and then began to traverse the path. For some reason I was in a most nostalgic mood and began thinking back upon the distant past. Perhaps there was something in the play of sunlight that prompted my thoughts.

The path was just as I remembered from my childhood. The first part traced the edge of the wood in sunlight, overlooking the valley. The meadow was already astir for the season, alive with a host of bluebells and ox-eye daisies. At the far end we came to the lonely summer-house where we used to play for hours on end, an imaginary kingdom where we were transformed into valiant princes and beautiful damsels. I could just make out our faint chalk drawings of dragoons. Then Papa and I turned and followed the loop back, only now we were walking under the thick canopy of trees, dark as a tunnel, which used to frighten us so. I remembered being here sometimes in the late evening when pending nightfall changed the familiar shapes of trees into monsters—the Hollow Ash turning into an ogre, the Elephant-Tree with its gnarled growth in the trunk becoming a grotesque giant. I used to run past it, my heart pounding in my chest, giving it a wide berth so that its branches could not reach out to grab my hair.

Papa and I completed the loop and decided to do a second. My memories carried on in a parade of their own choosing. I remembered the mewling of the new-born lambs in the spring and the sound of the scythes being whetted for the mowing in August. I recalled carrying cherry-boughs from house to house to collect pennies for the May Pole and hiding in the hay-carts during the harvest. I remembered the hollow thwack of croquet balls colliding on the lawn and the sizzle of potatoes roasting in the embers of an open Gypsy fire. One time Papa took me to an exhibition hall on Regent Street, where I observed a diving-bell and obtained my weight in a new machine. I watched a man blowing glass. He gave me a perfect crystalline horse, and when it broke its leg during the carriage-ride home, I burst out crying. Papa took me in his arms and tried, unsuccessfully, to console me. I recalled going with Papa to the Daguerreotype studio, outfitted in a white dress with a lace collar and a black velvet hair-band that pinched my head, and being taken to the roof and trying so hard not to make the slightest movement during the time it took to compose a sun-picture. I recalled Mamma reading to us from John Bunyan, how we would gather around the spreading folds of her skirt to hear about Christians fleeing the City of Destruction and reaching the Celestial City where the streets were paved in gold and crowned men strummed golden harps to sing the praises of God.

I remembered playing roundabouts, when I was always the last to be found. And hiding near the billiard-table to eavesdrop on adult conversation. And walking into little Horace's room and finding him and Camilla, our German governess, under the blankets, and how she sat up, flustered, and made me promise not to tell anybody. And I remembered kissing the Lubbock boy in the hollow of the walnut-tree. And being sick in bed with Mamma bending over me, the sweet smell of her, and Papa at the foot of the bed, his brow wrinkled in worry.

As we walked I looked over at Papa, who appeared lost in his own thoughts. We passed a tiny mound of flints and I recalled how in earlier *times, when he was working on his theory, he used to knock them off with his cane, one for each circuit, to keep track of his progress. But now he has dropped this engaging habit. And as he moved unsteadily along the familiar route through the copse, he suddenly appeared uncommonly old and sad to me, hunched over in such a way that his white beard touched his chest, and his cloak sagged around his shoulders. The clicking of his cane upon the path seemed to me the sound of time itself passing, like the ticking of the grandfather-clock in the hall, counting the days remaining before Death's harvest.*

When we were young, he used to send us searching for beetles. We fanned out across the meadows and the mudbanks whooping like Indian scouts. We ripped up stones and old rotted tree-trunks for insects, and I was always the one who could bring him the greatest treasure. Then he would call me Diana, fleet of foot, lovely of mien, his own special Huntress.

I blush to be telling you this and speaking of myself at such length.

Yours always,
Bessie

Beth finally penetrated the outer defenses of the law firm of Spenser, Jenkins & Hutchinson and reached the inner sanctum: the wood-paneled office of old Alfred P. Jenkins himself. There, having duly produced reams of documents proving her identity, she was at last presented with the package from Lizzie that had remained in the company vault since 1882. It was handed over on two uplifted palms, as if it were a royal treasure.

Now she wanted to share the prize with Hugh—"the final piece of the puzzle," she told him breathlessly on the phone. "Meet me in one hour at Christ's College," she commanded. When he asked why, she chuckled and said: "Every good treasure hunt has to have a good finish line."

Hugh walked down Hobson Street and turned into the tunneled archway under the pentagonal towers. The green of the circular lawn in the central courtyard was so bright it almost hurt his eyes. A walkway of smooth rocks surrounded it. The ancient walls of the college rose up three stories high on all sides. Each wall had four separate entryways and perfectly proportioned rectangular windows cut into the stone, some with flower boxes cascading with pink and white blossoms.

On one wall was a coat of arms and the epigram *Souvent Me Souvient*. He translated it almost without thinking: "Remember Me Often." Under it, appropriately enough, was Beth. She carried a basket. When she saw him, she smiled wickedly and walked over to put her arm on his. "Come with me."

She led him to the far wall and an entryway marked "G." The stairwell inside was painted blue. They walked up to the first floor and she pulled out a key, opened a door on the right, and stepped aside to let him enter first.

"Recognize it?" she asked.

"Recognize it? How could I? I've never been here."

"And here I thought you were the Darwin expert."

"I get it," he said. "His old rooms."

He looked around. The place was shabbily elegant, like most of Cambridge's student accommodations. There was a brick fireplace with a marble mantel, a worn window seat, and mahogany wainscoting nicked with scars. A small teardrop glass chandelier hung between two beams embedded deep in the plaster. The floors were ancient oak, tough as iron. It was odd how the knowledge that Darwin had spent so much time there as a young man transformed the place in Hugh's eyes.

"Nobody's here?"

"It's between terms."

"How'd you get the key?"

"The porter. He's been asked so many times he just hands it over. The tip's come down, too—now it's only five quid."

They sat side by side on a soiled, lumpy couch. She reached into her basket and lifted out a heavy green bottle with a label in the shape of a shield—*Dom Pérignon*—and two flutes. "That's for later," she said. Then she pulled out a small briefcase, unzipped it, and held up a package, which was wrapped in faded brown paper and tied tightly with twine.

"Don't tell me you haven't read it?" he said. "You who goes around reading other people's journals."

"No, I haven't. I thought we'd do that together. I just read the letter that was attached to it."

And with that, she opened a plastic folder and pulled out several pieces of stationery, delicate as moths' wings. "It's from Lizzie to her daughter. Now sit back, be quiet, and listen." She began in slightly theatrical tones but soon turned serious—almost, Hugh thought, as if traces of Lizzie's imagined voice were melding into her own.

26 April 1882
Down House
Downe, Kent
England

My darling Emma,

I am writing to you as the one who brought you into this world and the one who, were it not for a calamitous chain of events too sorrowful to recount, would have remained more precious to you than anyone else alive. You were taken from my arms when you were a babe, not yet a full day old, owing to the fact that you were conceived in the recklessness of a passion that would not be denied and born out of wedlock, a circumstance for which I have only myself to blame. For this unhappy state of affairs, and for every consequence that has sprung from it, I beg your forgiveness. I can only pray that, as you are bound to retain in your temperament some trace of my own, you will temper your judgment of my shameful deed with compassion, and that in the fullness of time you will, if not comprehend my actions, at least find it in your heart not to look upon me with abhorrence.

I have no assurance that this letter will reach you. I am sending it through the offices of the Children's Aid Society, the agency that arranged for your placement. Although I am told that their policy is to not permit contact between children and the mothers who relinquish rights over them—a necessity, it is said, to allow the children to embark upon their new lives unfettered by chains from the past—I entertain the hope that because Mr Charles Loring Brace is an acquaintance of my father's, an exception may be made in this instance and that my letter will eventually find its way into your hands. Should the Society decide not to forward it to you, it will remain in the possession of their solicitors, who, I am informed, will then determine what to do with it.

My purpose is to tell you something of your distinguished lineage and to bequeath to you an extraordinary document. You will readily understand its significance when I tell you who wrote it and under what circumstance. I have been unable to decide what to do with it and have alternated between two opposite courses—making it public or destroying it outright, seeing advantages and disadvantages to each. My charge to you, should it reach you, is that you guard it for an extended period. Then, when time has dimmed passions and eroded remembrance of the people concerned, and per-

haps with the distance of a young continent and a new age lending wisdom to your deliberation, you may reach a proper decision as to its fate. I am, in short, providing you with both a gift and a heavily laden responsibility.

You come from a distinguished line through my parents, your grandmother and your grandfather, who were first cousins. The Darwins have been doctors and scholars for generations and the Wedgwoods have been prominent manufacturers of china pottery. Your grandfather's grandfather was Erasmus Darwin, a poet and a philosopher; he was one of the first scholars to embrace the theory of what is today called evolution, though he did so without any understanding of the mechanism by which it may be said to occur. Supplying that critical element fell to your very own grandfather, Charles Darwin, the famed naturalist. As you undoubtedly know, he is credited with the proposition that Nature itself, confronted with a variety of creatures, often bearing infinitesimal differences, works to select those best suited for survival and in so doing shapes the transformation of new species. This idea gained him considerable notoriety, since it contravened the Biblical story of God's creation of each and every species, which then remain fixed and immutable throughout all eternity. Gradually, as his theory gained in acceptance, due in part to the efforts of a handful of articulate proponents, he assumed a position of worthy respect in English society.

This very day Papa (as I have called him for most of my thirty-four years) was laid to rest in Westminster Abbey, which explains my need to write to you. Interment there is no small honour, especially for a free-thinker. (Indeed, a dear friend of mine, Mary Ann Evans, was denied such a privilege only two years ago.) Papa wanted to be buried at St Mary's, in the village of Downe in Kent, where we live. But his wish was overruled posthumously by a coterie of admirers, including his old champion, Thomas Henry Huxley, who believed that burial in the Abbey was his due and that, not incidentally, it would elevate the status of science. They conducted a campaign in which powerful figures interceded with the Church, and their petition was approved in the Houses of Parliament.

Let me describe today's ceremony. I hope that your reading of it may lay a foundation of respect for your grandfather that any subsequent revelations will not altogether destroy. You should know that he was widely venerated. All day yesterday, through a horrible drizzle, four horses drew the hearse from Downe to Westminster, and along the route gentlemen paid their respects by doffing their hats. The coffin was held overnight under an honours guard in the dimly lit Chapel of St Faith and this morning people streamed into the Abbey from all parts. The Queen did not come, nor did Mr Gladstone, but many other notables filled the transepts—judges in their mourning dress, members of Parliament, ambassadors from numerous countries, officials from learned societies and many more. The family was there, all save Mamma, who remained at home, too deep in mourning to attend. I was pleased to see a crowd of common folk, including Parslow, our butler, who packed both sides of the nave and spilled onto the steps outside. At midday, as the bell tolled, the dignitaries passed by the coffin, which was draped in black velvet decorated with a sprig of white blossoms. The choir sang a hymn taken from the Book of Proverbs, which began 'Happy is the man that findeth wisdom and getteth understanding.' The service was brief and not overly religious, which Papa would have found befitting. Afterwards the pall-bearers, including Alfred Russel Wallace, the man cited as the co-discoverer of the theory (whom Mr Huxley forgot to invite until the very last moment), carried the coffin to the north-east corner of the nave, where it was buried beneath the monument to Sir Isaac Newton.

I would like to recount the circumstances of your grandfather's passing, and I beg your indulgence in so doing. It may help you to understand him by creating a fuller portrait. Your grandfather—my papa—had been in decline for some years. Indeed, it is fair to say that his health has been poor for all of his life, ever since he returned from the Beagle, a truth attested to by the voluminous, almost daily records that he kept. His final years passed in the comfort of a daily routine that hardly varied in any detail, though they were not, as you shall learn, free from inner turmoil.

He was dealt a blow eight months ago when his beloved elder brother, Erasmus, passed away. Your grandfather fell into the slough of despond, convinced that he himself was terminally ill. Last month, on 7th March to be exact, he had an attack while walking alone on a favourite path on the outskirts of our property. He barely managed to return to the house and for days he lay upon a sofa. However, a young doctor persuaded him that his heart had not given out and eventually he rallied and even took the air in the spring garden. Your aunt, Henrietta, came and left after a visit of several weeks, and various doctors—four in all—traipsed in and out at various times, each recommending different remedies and providing conflicting prognostications.

On Tuesday last, 18th April, Papa began failing. Just before midnight he was gripped by a pain that seized his heart. He awoke Mamma, who came *running from her bedroom to his. She quickly went to fetch the amyl but in a panic became confused and called me for assistance. By the time we found the medicine in his study and returned to his room, he was slumped across the bed, looking close to death. Mamma screamed, which brought the servants. We managed to give him the capsules and then tried to make him swallow some brandy. Much of it spilled through his beard and trickled down his night-dress but it revived him. His eyes suddenly opened, he retched into a basin, and though trembling violently was finally able to speak. Then he did something I never would have expected from such a confirmed atheist—he pulled Mamma close to him and whispered urgently in her ear, begging her to send for a priest. She leapt up with a willingness that almost rent my heart. For it turned out that Papa's plea was in the nature of a ruse, though not a vicious one; he simply wanted to be alone with me for a few moments. He had some important information that he could give to me only.*

I should now move my narrative backward and tell you that Papa and I have had a stormy relationship for a long time—indeed, ever since I was a child. This may have come about from differences in our personalities (which there is little point in exploring here) but also from various facts that I was able to establish with regard to Papa's work. I uncovered clues that something untoward had happened in the course of the Beagle's *five-year voyage. I will not go into them all here; suffice it to say that not long before you were born I came upon proof that he was not, in fact, an estimable thinker of scope and depth, but rather someone of a different moral order. I confronted my father with the evidence in a letter from the very clinic in Zurich where I was forced to abandon you.*

My father and I never discussed the matter in all the intervening years, not until the night of his death. Then, once Mamma had been dispatched on her errand and once the servants were sent from the room, he pulled me to him, much as he had her, and in a raspy voice said that although he was not at all a religious man, and not a believer in God, he did have an overbearing need to confess a wrong. There was no-one other than myself to whom he could unburden himself, for I was the only one who knew his secret. But—and at this my blood froze—there was more to be said. He reached up and clutched the edge of my night-dress with a strength that I could scarcely believe.

'You are aware that for some years now I have been engaged in writing a biography of myself.' To this I nodded assent, and seeing that he still looked up at me questioningly, I replied loudly, so that he would be sure to hear. 'Yes, Papa. I know.'

At that, he released me, fell back upon the pillow and said, now in an exhausted voice, 'But you do not know that I have omitted one chapter—rather, I have written it but have hidden it away so that no-one may see it. I thought the writing of it would ease my conscience, but this was not to be.' I stared at him, not knowing what to say. He lay silent for several minutes, looking up at the ceiling, as if he were still undetermined as to what to do. Then, with a sigh, he directed me to fetch something from his study. To my surprise, he asked me to find his cosh.

I did so, and when I returned and held it out to him, he grabbed it from me and clasped it tightly in one hand. Then, with almost a sob, he said that after he died, not before, I should open the chest that he kept locked beneath his desk. He told me that I would find the key to it in the top drawer of his bureau and he watched while I walked across the room, opened the drawer and took out a strong-box key. Confused, I returned to him. He was still clutching the cosh, which I would fain have taken away. Then he said something that I shall always remember. He said: 'Of them all, only you know me for what I am.' At that, he closed his eyes and fell into a weakness that again drained his system and turned him pale.

In some time, Mamma returned with a priest, of whom I said Papa had little need. She ignored me and was surprised to find the cosh there, still in Papa's hand, but I did not feel the need to explain and left the room without a backward glance. The doctor came at two in the morning and applied mustard-plasters to Papa's chest, which made him vomit. He was heard to remark 'If I could but die,' and began spitting blood. His skin turned grey. He was fed spoonfuls of whiskey and alternated between drowsiness and pain throughout the night and the next morning. Then, in the afternoon, he lost consciousness and fell into raspy breathing, finally dying at four o'clock in the afternoon of Wednesday, 19 April 1882.

I honoured my promise to Papa—I did not open the chest until after his death, not until today, upon returning from the Abbey. Inside, I found a sealed parcel filled with paper. On the outer wrapping in Papa's hand was a quotation from a book that he used to read many years ago, Milton's Para-dise Lost. *I decided not to open the package—for I have for some time known my father's secret—and instead am passing the missing chapter of his life on to you with this communication. Do with it what you will; I am confident that you will know how best to dispose of it in years hence.*

You should know, Emma, that not a day passes but that I punish myself for losing you and think of how, had I been wiser or more righteous, my life and yours would have turned out differently. Then I would have been able to gather you in my arms, not just for that one passing moment but whenever the wish overtook me. Scarcely a day passes that I do not try to summon up in my imagination an image of what you must be like, in your habits and your looks and your spirit. You are ten now—only this month having passed that milestone birthday. In my mind's eye I see you as robust and healthy, as I was, but infinitely more beautiful.

I know nothing of your situation—only that you are being raised by a 'fine family' somewhere in the American Midwest, a land that I have seen in picture-books and that calls to mind, for me at least, wild Indians on the rampage. This naturally makes me concerned for your safety, but I believe my worry on this score is misplaced. I have developed an insatiable appetite for all manner of information about America. I have even imagined visiting that land someday, but for the idea that I would be consumed with the thought of you and preoccupied in looking for you everywhere, even knowing that such a search was destined to fail.

You will be mine always in my mind.
Your loving mother,
Lizzie

When Beth finished the letter she put it carefully back inside the plastic envelope, which she sealed for safekeeping, and looked over at Hugh.

"Well," she said, raising her eyebrows, "that's proof—if ever any was needed—of just how cruel the Victorians could be. They wielded that old sanctimonious Puritan sword with a vengeance, didn't they?"

"Yes. These are the people who brought you skirts around piano legs. But tell me—the letter, it stayed in some lawyer's file all these years? Emma never got it?"

"No, she never got it. And of course her name wasn't Emma. Her new family named her Filipa. I've got the lineage straight now. She was my great-grandmother—a pretty strong woman by all accounts."

"Any men along the line?"

"One. Her son. He was named Benjamin. His daughter was my mother. As you know, she was the first to be told of the Darwin connection."

"Which is why she named you Elizabeth?"

"No, that was pure coincidence. I was born before she got the notification from the lawyers. You want to see something heartbreaking? Look at this."

She handed the folder to Hugh.

"Look how she signed it," she said.

"Lizzie. But she had been calling herself Bessie for—how long?—almost two decades. What's that all about?"

"I don't know. I'd say she was definitely carrying some heavy psychological baggage. Which is not surprising given her family—a famous father who's a sham, a mother who dotes only on him, a goody-two-shoes sister who's the apple of everybody's eye."

"A brother-in-law who seduces her and leaves her in the lurch."

"Exactly."

Hugh's eyes fell upon the package. He picked it up and read the quotation, in Darwin's script, written so long ago that the black ink was flaking. It read:

> *Accuse not Nature, she hath done her part;*
> *Do thou but thine.*

He weighed it in one palm, his hand moving up and down like a scale. It wasn't heavy.

"What do you say?" he asked. "Shall we open it?"

CHAPTER 25

Down House

I have been much affected by the death this month of my elder brother, *Erasmus*. When I was a youth I looked up to him and made him the model of my behaviour, a course I dearly wish I had continued to pursue, for he was a good man and remained so until the end of his days. He neither married nor raised a family nor achieved recognition from the world commensurate with his abilities and native talents, but he could look back at his life at its close and say that he had lived it honourably. I cannot do the same, alas. For over fifty years I have not been able to travel, to sleep through the night, to spend one week in full health. For the truth of the matter is that the greater part of my life has rested on the twin pillars of cowardice and deceit. They are the Scylla and Charybdis through which I have sailed these many years on a voyage of fame and fortune. I have gained all this and more—I am consulted by wise men the world over who take my word as gospel—but I have not achieved peace of mind. For despite the world's opinion, and despite the honours that have accrued to me, all has been undeserved. I am a rogue and blackguard and worse. My life has turned to dross. Were I a believer in Heaven and Hell, I know that, like Lucifer, I would spend my eternity in the darker place.

I do not wish to dwell on the particulars of my shame and so I will make my narrative short. Among my shipmates on the **Beagle** was a certain Robert McCormick, the ship's surgeon, who from the commencement of the voyage had been vying with me over the collection of specimens. At one point we struck upon the theory of natural selection and transmutation of species. In one magnificent stroke, the theory made sense of the natural world in all its splendid variety and explained the existence of disparate species without recourse to a belief in a Supreme Being. I realised that Mr McCormick had grasped the essentials of the theory and I knew that whoever first presented that theory to the civilised world would achieve lasting scientific renown.

I suppressed my feelings about Mr McCormick, however, and did not intend to harm him, this despite several indications that he was not above placing my life in jeopardy. To cite but one episode, in the Galápagos he enticed me into swimming with sharks. Luckily, the beasts on those isolated islands are so unacquainted with men that they have not developed an instinct to kill us. I soon came to the realisation that if I did not take care to defend myself, Mr McCormick might well succeed in disposing of me.

Fate played us both for fools. I found myself on an outing with the man, along with Captain FitzRoy. Our goal was to investigate a volcano which even then was showing signs of activity. After a laborious climb we stopped to dine and consumed two bottles of wine, which made us fall asleep. A short while later I awoke, as did Mr McCormick, though Captain FitzRoy continued deep in slumber. The two of us then resolved to carry on. When we achieved the summit, I proposed entering the volcano's cone. This we did without too much difficulty, lowering ourselves down with a rope that we attached to a rock above. The heat was suffocating, the smell of sulfurous gases overpowering and the sound of bubbling lava unnerving, but we were both exhilarated at the prospect of exploring a natural phenomenon unknown to anyone else. We went down to a depth of about ten feet below the volcano's lip. There was a ledge that served as a convenient work-space. After some minutes I was bending over to chip away at some rock with my back turned to Mr McCormick when I heard him cry out. I turned around and saw him motioning towards the centre of the basin. It was belching smoke, and searing hot magma was bubbling up like an angry red and yellow sea. The whole was beginning to shake so violently that we realised it was about to erupt. We raced to the rope but found to our dismay that it had disintegrated in the intense heat.

McCormick yelled above the roar that we must find a way to save ourselves from that infernal place. A plume of smoke and fire rose up before us and out of fear we grabbed each other for comfort. Just then, I spotted a ledge over our heads, about thirty feet away. By hugging the walls with our backs we carefully manoeuvred our way to it. Once there we were closer to our goal, but not home free. The ledge was about eight feet above. I shouted for Mr McCormick to give me a boost, since he was considerably shorter than I. Without a moment's hesitation, he placed the fingers of his hands together in a cup that I used as a stirrup. Swinging my full weight upwards and steadying myself with one hand on his shoulder, I thrust myself high and managed with my other hand to catch hold of a protuberance of rock. Using this, and aided no doubt by the fear of death, I pulled myself up with a strength I did not know I possessed. I landed on the upper ledge, gasping for breath but alive.

It was then my turn to help Mr McCormick. I could hear him shouting, encouraging me in no uncertain terms to waste no time. I ran to find the remaining piece of rope but found the remnant too small to be of use. I returned to the spot, lay down on my stomach, spread my legs upon the ledge for leverage and leaned over the edge. When he saw me reappear, Mr McCormick's face turned hopeful. The trembling was increasing now and I could see the lava begin to rise below like a boiling cauldron. I took my cosh from my belt and reached down, holding it as low as I could with one hand while I braced myself against the edge with the other. By jumping, he could just reach it. He grabbed it. But his body, short as it was, was fully extended so that he could not pull himself up. I realised I would have to lower it another five or six inches, even though doing so would make my own position more precarious.

I looked down at Mr McCormick and saw him staring back at me with an appraising look. His face was contorted and he was sweating profusely. He had grabbed the cosh with both hands and was holding on for dear life. I lowered it an inch or two and he began to try to scramble up, kicking desperately at the wall with the soles of his shoes but making little headway. At some point I heard a sound behind me and became aware of Captain Fitz-Roy's presence. He was not yet close enough to help and could scarcely see what was happening, though he could plainly hear us. I do not know what occurred next. A giant plume of smoke rose from the belly of the volcano. I pulled the cosh. McCormick was still holding on. Perhaps I should lower it a little more, I thought. There was room, though perhaps not. I hesitated, uncertain. The more I extended it, the more tenuous was my own position, as my balance was giving way. When I concentrated again on the figure below me, I saw that his hands were slipping a bit from sweat and he was looking deep into my eyes with a hard glower. I heard his voice rise up, thin but distinct, and he spoke the words I shall never forget: 'So that's how it is, eh,

Mr Darwin? Survival of the fittest!' And with that he let go, or I lurched upwards so violently that it broke his grip. In any case I saw him tumble backwards, turning in mid-air slowly as he plunged into the bubbling lava. He screamed on the way down.

I do not remember how I got out of there, though I expect that Captain FitzRoy helped me. The two of us ran down the mountain-side to the crewmen waiting at the boat. They quickly rowed us out to the ship and we set sail.

I have often thought that that afternoon was the determining event of my life. Having taken one course, or having that course thrust upon me, everything that followed was inevitable. I became a conniver, and much of what I did makes me blush to the roots with shame, not just that I did it but that I was so adept in the doing of it. Nothing was too large or small to escape my notice in fashioning my deception. Thus, I put it out that Mr McCormick had left the Beagle earlier in the voyage, and I even throttled his parrot, adding it to my specimens. Sailing away from the Galápagos, I intentionally mixed together all the finches I had gathered from the separate islands, so that I could maintain the fiction that I derived the theory of natural selection on my own at a subsequent time. I went through my notebooks, changing and censoring various entries to make the narrative conform to my story. As a ruse to explain my many illnesses, which somehow came in retribution for that horrible episode, I fabricated an incident in which I was bitten by a benchuca insect. I paid blackmail to Captain FitzRoy, the poor soul, who until the very last remained suspicious of my actions in attempting to save McCormick. Without definitive proof, he embraced religion with fanatical zeal—I believe as a result of the events that transpired that fateful day.

A few men may have guessed that the burden I carried was one of guilt, but only one person came upon my secret, and that is my daughter Elizabeth, who inherited my cunning. We have never discussed it. I have not done right by her but my actions in that regard pale in comparison with my other deeds. Many a time have I thought over the events of that day on the volcano and wondered if I could have done more to save the poor man. Although he is dead, I still fear him. One time I even fled from a séance, so apprehensive was I over the prospect of a spectral encounter.

Occasionally, when I tread the Sandwalk with Elizabeth, I think upon the path itself and how it resembles my life. It begins in open air and sunshine, full of promise and hope, but then takes a turn into darkness and despair.

The vehicle that carried me around that fatal turn was the **Beagle**. *All I ever wanted to do was to succeed at something and please my father. Now all is lost. Like Faust, I have made my pact with the Devil and there is nothing more to be done but wait in the twilight of my life for him to claim his due.*

Charles Darwin
Set in his own hand, this day
30 August 1881

CHAPTER 26

The champagne began to lose its fizz.

At first they drank with abandon, already high from their incredible find.

"This is an invaluable piece of history," Beth remarked, suddenly serious. "Think of it. A confession coming to light after all these years—Darwin and McCormick, bitter rivals, struggling on a volcano, Darwin trying to save him—"

"Or maybe not trying all that hard. You could read it that way. Why else did Darwin feel guilty for the rest of his life?"

"Because despite his best efforts, he failed to rescue him. Because at heart he was a good man. And because even though he was an atheist, he continued to uphold Christian morality. McCormick's death was an accident."

"You're probably right."

"The whole thing is so unbelievable—except that it's written in Darwin's own hand. Thank God for that."

"And he admits that McCormick had grasped the theory of evolution, that's the significant thing. For all anybody knows, McCormick could have gone down in history as the co-discoverer. And here he is today, a complete unknown."

They raised their glasses to the past and to the whole lot of them: Darwin, FitzRoy, McCormick, Jemmy Button, and, of course, poor Lizzie.

"But in the end she was vindicated," Hugh said. "Her father gave her credit—she was the only one who was able to ferret out his secret."

"Small consolation," Beth shot back. "The way I look at it, her whole life was kind of a waste."

"I wonder why she didn't read his missing chapter. She's supposed to be curious. Maybe she was scared of what she might find."

"Could be. But she already knew the secret. So she assumed, rightly, that her father was spilling the beans about his role in McCormick's death. She didn't need to read it. She couldn't bring herself to actually destroy it—after all, her Papa was already world-famous—and yet she didn't want to be the one to make it public. So she sent it off to her daughter in the New World, basically passing the buck—or leaving things up to fate."

"I guess," he replied.

"You don't sound so sure."

"No. I don't know."

She put an arm around Hugh and gave him a hug. That was when the fizz began to fade.

"Something else bothers me," he said. "Did you notice the language Darwin used? At one point he says, 'My life has turned to dross.' At another he's talking about his fame and fortune and says, 'All has been undeserved.' That's a bit strong, don't you think? I mean, if McCormick's death was totally accidental. Because Darwin *did* deserve *something*—he came up with the theory."

"Again, guilt. A good man takes his sins harder than a bad man. And maybe if he was honest, he knew that he really had wanted McCormick to die. Don't forget—the guy was trying to kill him."

"A minute ago you were saying Darwin was trying his hardest to save him."

"Maybe it's not so clear-cut. At least in Darwin's mind. Maybe he fears on some level he allowed the death to happen—a sin of omission rather than commission."

Hugh refilled their glasses. He remembered someone observing that Darwin had shied away from investigating the human mind. Why did he have the feeling that they hadn't fully plumbed Darwin's secrets?

"And he never actually says when the theory comes to him," he continued. "He makes it sound as if he and McCormick just stumbled on it somewhere."

"That's nothing new. He struck that tone in everything he wrote. He was never precise about it. This just shows he formulated the theory a bit earlier than anybody knew."

"But covering up exactly when it struck him? Messing up his finch specimens? Making up that whole episode about an insect bite? What was the point?"

"I grant you, that's a bit strange."

"I'll say. And another thing—all these people trying to blackmail him. Don't forget that. And why would Huxley and all the others need to protect him?"

"They're not really protecting *him*. They're protecting the theory. They know it's too important to let one man's reputation drag it down."

"But how did they know what Darwin did? Where did they hear of McCormick's death?"

"From FitzRoy."

"But FitzRoy didn't actually see what happened on the volcano. All he came away with was suspicions."

"Maybe Darwin confessed it to them."

"But he says Lizzie was the only one who knew his secret."

"The only one who *discovered* it," answered Beth, but without conviction. She was beginning to feel stymied.

"And Wallace—he was on the other side of the earth," said Hugh. "Don't tell me Darwin confessed to *him*."

"He eventually returned to London. Maybe he heard about it from someone in the inner circle then."

"But Wallace had already come up with the theory on his own. Wouldn't he want to assert his ownership if he thought Darwin was possibly a murderer?"

"Could be he needed the money."

"It could be. But if he exposed Darwin, he would have been credited with the theory and gotten fame and money into the bargain. Besides, if you include Wallace as one of the conspirators—if that's the word for it— the circle gets wider and wider."

She withdrew her arm.

"Face it, Beth. It just doesn't add up. Too many loose ends."

"I admit you're raising questions that are hard to answer."

He suddenly stood up. "I just thought of something," he said. "How could we have missed it?" He put his glass down on a table. "There's one question that's even harder."

"What?"

"Assume for a moment that you're correct: Lizzie turned against her father because of what happened on the volcano."

"Right."

"And she learned about it from reading the letter McCormick wrote to his relatives."

"Right."

"How could he have written it? He was dead."

"Shit."

"Let me ask you something," Hugh said to Roland, after the three of them left the library for the evening, the doors locking behind them, and strolled along Burrell's Walk toward Garret Hostel Lane. "You're a fount of knowledge."

"Thank you," replied Roland. "Flattery will get you everywhere."

"Does the expression *nuit de feu* mean anything to you?"

"It brings to mind several things. But I'm not sure I should discuss them in mixed company."

"No, seriously."

"May I ask what lies behind this rather odd query?"

"It concerns our Darwin research," put in Beth. "We're at something of a dead end."

"I don't suppose you'll tell me what you're up to. I'm distinctly out of the loop, as you Americans say."

"We'd tell you but we don't know what we've got," said Hugh. "So far we've just exchanged one mystery for another one. And the second is even more mysterious than the first."

"It's like what Churchill said about Russia," added Beth. "A mystery inside an enigma wrapped in a riddle."

Roland grimaced. "You mean, a riddle wrapped in a mystery inside an enigma."

"Whatever. It means the same thing."

"No, it doesn't. You can't wrap something inside a riddle."

"And I suppose you can wrap it inside an enigma?"

"Not to put too fine a point on it, but the *wrapping* was done to the riddle by the mystery. Then the whole thing went into the enigma."

"Will you two stop it!" cried Hugh. They crossed the bridge over the Cam. The swans had turned in for the night behind the willow boughs. He explained: "Darwin used the expression *'nuit de feu'* and we're trying to figure out what it means."

Roland stopped short. "I don't remember that," he said.

"It's in Lizzie's journal."

"I see. The book you found when I smuggled you into the stacks."

"Right," said Beth. "And we thought we knew what he meant by *nuit de feu,* but it doesn't exactly fit."

"For one thing," said Hugh, "the event we're thinking of didn't happen at night."

"Though it did involve an awful lot of fire," added Beth.

They came to the narrow lane behind Trinity College.

"There is one person who comes to mind when I hear that expression," Roland said. "He used the same words—and in French. But it was two centuries earlier."

"Go on," urged Hugh.

"Blaise Pascal, the French mathematician and philosopher. He used it to describe an incredible night in which he had a deep religious conversion. He believed he actually saw God. And afterward he entered a Jansenist convent and never again published under his own name."

"And Darwin would have heard of this?" asked Hugh.

"Of course."

Now Beth was skeptical. "But that doesn't really fit. You're not going to tell me Darwin became a believer?"

"No," replied Roland. "And without the context, I obviously have no idea what he was talking about. But it's possible he was using it generically. The expression suggests some kind of conversion, like St. Paul on the road to Damascus or Archimedes in the bath. Some flash of revelation like a lightning bolt—a moment when everything becomes clear."

"I see," said Hugh.

They came to Market Hill. The shops were full and the sidewalks crowded for the evening rush hour. They threaded their way around dons on bicycles, red-faced tourists piling back into their buses, and groups of students heading for the pubs.

Roland stopped and entered a bookstore. "I'll be back straightaway."

Hugh turned to Beth. "Revelation is one thing. Murder's another. If you killed someone—or thought you'd killed someone—you'd hardly describe it as a *nuit de feu*."

They waited by the entrance. A teenager came out carrying a pile of books under one arm. With his fresh face and long silky blond hair, he seemed young to be a student. Hugh, deep in thought, watched him walk away.

"What's wrong?" asked Beth.

"Nothing's wrong. He reminds me of someone—someone I saw in a sketch." He stopped suddenly, becoming motionless. "Beth, my God. That's it!"

"What?"

"We had the wrong R.M. It wasn't Robert McCormick. It was the teenage missionary: Richard Matthews."

CHAPTER 27

The call came to Hugh's rooming house two hours later. When he hung up the phone and returned to his room, where Beth was lying on the bed, he told her he had to answer the summons. He would go to Oxford the next day and she would go to the library and try to track down the Matthews relatives on her own.

The following morning he rose early, went to London, and caught the train to the place he had dreaded. London was one thing—it held only a scattering of memories. Cambridge was another—it was safe ground. But Oxford . . . here the ghosts were on their home turf. And sure enough, as he walked through the old university town and past the Gothic colleges with their spires and crenulated walls, they did not disappoint.

He passed the bend on the Isis where he and Cal had gone punting together. There was the boathouse, still painted white, and the floating dock. (Hugh's pole had stuck in the muck and he had clung to it, stranded above the water, until his strength ebbed and he plunged in. Cal had laughed his head off.) On the High Street, he passed the pub where Cal had confessed to making a pass at one of Hugh's girlfriends—successful, it turned out—and for days afterward Hugh had pretended to sulk. And there, down the street, was the movie theater where they had seen *La Dolce Vita* on a rainy Sunday afternoon. That was the trouble with England: the boathouse, the pub, the theater—landmarks didn't change.

He passed All Souls, the college where he and Cal sometimes dined at the invitation of a friend, a historian who bragged that the wine cellar was second only to the Queen's. He remembered the dinners, in which the fellows moved from dining hall to common room to consume various courses, donning and doffing academic gowns according to some ancient prescript that Hugh never could grasp. In an alcoholic blur Hugh had thought the conversations profound and enlightening but could never recall them the next morning.

Hugh was on his way to see Simon, who, like Neville, had agreed to the meeting with a reluctance that he took no pains to conceal.

"I'm not really sure what point would be served in getting together," Simon had said over the phone in a thin, high voice.

But Hugh insisted. "You were Cal's roommate. I think it might be useful to me to talk to you. So does Bridget—in fact, she suggested it."

"And the purpose?"

"I'm trying to sort some things out." Hugh worried that his response sounded like psychobabble, anathema to the British.

But the reply was positive: "Well—perhaps. Yes."

They agreed to meet in the cloisters of New College at one o'clock. Simon was leaving for France early the following morning.

Before hanging up, Simon had said: "Incidentally, I hope you don't mind my saying this but your voice sounds much the same as your brother's, almost identical, in fact."

New College was at the epicenter of the town and a stone's throw from the bustling High Street, but it was a world away. Hugh turned at Queens Lane, a narrow cobblestone street no wider than an oxcart. It zigzagged, following the ancient stone walls until it passed the college gate. Beyond the porter's lodge, he came to a medieval courtyard, and to his left he saw the cloisters. At each turn the sounds from the town had grown fainter. Now, as he stepped inside, it was utterly still. The shadows that fell across the central quadrangle of grass remained unchanged from the fourteenth century.

Hugh passed by the entrance to the chapel. The arcade was roofed with boards fitted together in a pattern like a ship's hull. Memorial plaques lined the walkways and the pillared windows facing the garth were decorated in Gothic tracery.

Simon was the only other person there, pacing nervously, carrying a briefcase. Seeing Hugh, he gave an awkward wave and marched toward him, his hand extended. He was thin and bony, with an angular face and wire-rimmed glasses. Despite the warm weather, he was wearing a heavy tweed jacket; his tie was tightly knotted and askew.

"Glad you could come," said Hugh, adopting a British speech pattern to put the man at ease. "A bit short notice, I realize."

"No, it's fine. The least I could do."

He made it sound as if he had acquiesced readily.

"Shall we walk?" said Hugh. In fact, they were already following the walkway. Simon moved like a bird, taking tiny steps, his head bobbing slightly.

"I hope I haven't inconvenienced you," Hugh continued. "I'm over here doing research, and . . . I wanted to meet you."

"Yes, you're investigating something about Darwin—isn't it?"

"That's right. How did you know?"

"Bridget. She phoned me shortly after you did—that is, after the first time you called."

Hugh was tempted to ask why, in that case, he hadn't returned his calls sooner, or, for that matter, why he had pretended ignorance of his motive, but he let it ride.

"What do you do?" he asked.

"Ah, the American question."

Hugh was annoyed. "You don't have to answer it. I'm simply making small talk."

"I appreciate that. No, quite all right." He was an agronomist, specializing in crops and the transfer of land to poor farmers in the Third World, specifically in South Africa. That made sense, thought Hugh; a profession with a social conscience was the kind of thing Cal would look for in a friend.

They came to a corner in the cloisters and turned left, into the shadows.

"How did you meet Cal?"

Simon looked at him before answering.

"At a party, when Cal was finishing up his degree. It was here at New College. Something of a bash, actually—we got drunk as lords. We liked each other from the start. It happened that we had a vacancy in my rooms, so I offered it to him and he took me up on it straightaway. And he moved in."

He paused, uncertain about what to say next.

"Look," he said abruptly. "This is difficult. I don't know where to begin. But Bridget—by God, she's a force of nature, isn't she? She thought it would be a good idea if I told you some things about Cal."

It bothered Hugh, the idea that they were talking behind his back, measuring out what to tell him.

"Exactly what is it that she thinks you should tell me?"

"Hard to say, in so many words. I don't want to be presumptuous. There are some things even she does not know."

"I want to know everything. That's why I asked you to meet me."

"Well, let's see. We were very close, the two of us. Intimate discussions. He talked a lot about you, incidentally."

"We were close too." Hugh thought: a lot closer than the two of you.

"I'm sure you were. In any case, seeing so much of each other, we got to know one another well. We took our meals together. Went for a pint from time to time. In some ways he was closer to me than anyone else—excluding family, of course. And early childhood friends; one never quite replicates those."

He paused again, uncertain.

"Why don't you just say what you want to say?"

"Hmm, yes. I expect I needn't fill you in on everything; it was some time ago, after all. And I suppose you don't need to hear about our life here, except that we got along fine. That's important. We became—I think we would have been—lifelong friends. I'm telling you all this because I want you to realize that we loved Cal and we, um, tried to help him."

"Help him? How?"

"Um, I gather Neville has talked to you about that business in the lab."

Hugh nodded. So they all had been in touch with one another. It felt like a God-damned conspiracy.

"That was serious, extremely so. At first I didn't realize just how serious, but these are scientists, you know, working on government projects. They simply do not tolerate deviations from accepted practice."

"I can imagine," said Hugh. His irritation was growing.

"Even Bridget doesn't know he was fired. To this day I believe she thinks he was on some kind of leave."

"I see."

"So, as you might expect, Cal fell into a depression. A deep depression." Simon looked over at Hugh, judging his reaction, then pressed ahead. "In fact, for days he didn't want to get out of bed. He didn't want to eat, he didn't want to do anything. Finally—there's no other way to say this—he simply didn't want to go on."

"To go on?"

"Go on living."

"What are you saying?"

"That, uh, I believe he tried to take his life—twice, in fact. Once with pills and once in a car crash. The first time I walked in and found him unconscious on the floor and rushed him to hospital. They pumped his stomach. The second time—that's not so clear. He was found near the Ring Road, the car smashed to smithereens. No other vehicles involved. The police couldn't say for certain but they hypothesized that he rammed a tree, intentionally. Given the first time, we thought perhaps they were right."

"Why did they think it was intentional?"

"Well, there were some indications—he wasn't wearing his seat belt, which he usually did. He had been drinking. There were no skid marks. Things like that."

"So what did you do?"

"Did we do enough, you mean. I hope so. I think so. We supported him in every way as best we could. We got him professional help. He went three, four times a week. The diagnosis was clinical depression and he was given pills. By the way, he said this had happened to him before, when he was young."

Hugh did not know what to say. Perhaps those times long, long ago when Cal stayed alone in his room all the time. His father had never mentioned it and of course they never discussed it.

"I don't know," he said.

"Anyway," Simon continued, "he seemed to be getting a bit better, with some ups and downs along the way, of course. And then he decided to go back to Connecticut, and we all thought that was a good idea, given that Oxford held such painful memories. Best to just start over and all that. So he left."

They had taken several complete circuits of the walkway.

"Did you ever talk to him?" asked Hugh. "Ask him what was wrong, if you were so close to him?"

"Not in so many words. And we knew what was wrong, or at least what had kicked it off—that business at the lab."

"Why are you telling me this now? Why didn't anyone say anything before?"

"Well, as I said, we've taken our cues from Bridget. She doesn't know the half of it, mind you. She never learned about the pills, but I believe she always suspected something was wrong. Still, the first thing many of us thought when we heard Cal had died was that, you know, he had taken his own life. When we heard the circumstances, we were fairly sure."

"Why?"

"Well, it was odd in that . . . I mean, he was on that ledge and he plummeted to the one spot he knew would be certain death. What are the odds of that happening? I guess it could have been either—he could have fallen—but I think it's equally possible that it wasn't an accident, that he jumped."

Hugh was too shocked to speak.

"I gather you were ahead of him on the path. You didn't actually see him lose his footing or anything, did you?"

"No."

Hugh replayed the memory loop: the rocks, the waterfall, the falling body, the deadly pool of bubbles.

"That's what Bridget told us. By the way, you should know—she loves you, no doubt about that. That's the reason she's insisting we all talk to you. She thinks you've been blaming yourself for Cal's death, and this new information might help."

Hugh grunted. He didn't know what to say. He felt as he had in that first meeting with Bridget—he just wanted to run away. Simon was trying to help him, but all he felt was an intense dislike for the man. He stopped walking and turned toward him.

"I want to thank you."

"Please, it's nothing," said Simon. "Rather, I mean it's important, very important, and I only wish you could have known it sooner."

He opened his briefcase and fished inside. "Here. I have a letter for you to read. But I'll have to ask you to return it."

Simon handed Hugh a sheet of stationery and waited, fidgeting. It was from Cal, written from Connecticut. The note was brief; it said he was feeling better, not doing much of anything, trying to relax. He thanked Simon for all he had done. Hugh was relieved that it did not mention him.

He returned it. The two shook hands and Simon hurried off into the central courtyard, carrying the battered briefcase, his birdlike gait accentuated by speed.

Hugh wandered along the High Street. Was it possible? Looked at in a different way, could Cal's death have been not entirely accidental? He tried to think back. Cal had been acting oddly those last few weeks. In the car driving to Devil's Den, he had blurted out a series of apologies—he was sorry that when they were younger, he and his friends didn't include Hugh in all their games. He was sorry for the times he had hurt him and for turning his back and leaving for Europe when times were still tough at home with the old man.

It was true, he seemed to want to talk; once or twice they almost did, but Hugh had been confused. This was not what their relationship was about. Cal was the older brother who gave all the advice and cleared the way. He was the anchor; Hugh was the one adrift. It felt odd, this turning of the tables.

"Wanna grab a beer?" Cal had his coat on, ready to go out.

A twinge of guilt. "Man, I'd love to. But I'm running late. I got so much to do. Maybe later . . . tomorrow."

Slowly Cal began to unbutton his coat. "Sure. That's cool."

On the path, Hugh had repeated the warning about the pool beneath the waterfall. Cal had just laughed.

"You think I could forget poor Billy Crowther? He was the first dead body I ever saw, his mom bawling her eyes out at the funeral home. Remember how we used to drop sticks and logs into the water and watch them get sucked down? That time we threw in Jimmy Stern's sneakers—he cried all the way back. This place used to loom large in our adolescent fantasy life. Good old Devil's Den."

He tried to remember everything about that afternoon. He was ahead on the path, anxious to reach the swimming hole. Why was Cal taking so long? He turned to look—did he see him? Did he see him lose his footing? Or did he see him leap? And did Cal really cry out? Or did he remain silent as he fell straight down into the middle of the churning pool?

Then came the hard part: Should he jump in after him or shouldn't he? Wouldn't he die, too? As he tried to decide, time passed. Then more time.

Your memory can play tricks on you, he thought. Each time he replayed the loop now, he saw it differently, more clearly. At least it seemed to be more clear. An accident! It was no accident. Or was it?

And then he began to feel a whole new raft of feelings. He was angry at Cal—for fabricating the lab results and messing up his life and then dying and leaving Hugh to drown in guilt. Then the anger turned to sorrow; it was sad that Cal had felt so desperate and alone and that none of them had known enough to help him. But the more he thought about it, the more he began to feel he was looking down on everything that had happened from a great distance.

The sadness was followed by a spreading sense of calm. And then, unaccountably, Hugh felt a sudden lightness—there was no other way to describe it. He walked down the street with a lighter step, looking at the people and the shops and the cars with a new intensity.

It was a pleasant afternoon, getting cool. The sidewalk was crowded. He would take the bus to the train station. Then in London he would switch trains and go to Cambridge. He would meet Beth and they would have a quiet dinner somewhere and he would tell her what he had learned. First, he would call Bridget.

He spotted a phone box and felt in his pocket for a phone card. She answered right away, almost as if she had been waiting for the call. He told her what he had learned: that Cal had probably taken his own life. She did not seem surprised and was quiet for a moment, then just told him that she loved him before quickly hanging up.

He had plenty more time left on the card. Why not? He lifted the receiver and dialed the number he knew by heart. It was odd, how much he suddenly wanted to hear his father's voice.

CHAPTER 28

During dinner at a small French restaurant—they had decided to splurge—Beth listened carefully as Hugh described his meeting with Simon and what he had learned about Cal's death.

"For the first time I think I'm remembering that afternoon clearly." He told her everything, slowly and quietly, including the odd sense of calm that had come upon him after he left the New College cloister.

"I think that's natural," she said. "You're finally dealing with what actually happened and what you really felt. You're putting it to rest."

He told her that he had called his father and that they had talked for a long time, the words coming easily, for the first time in years.

They ordered a second bottle of wine and relaxed. She was proud that she had succeeded in tracking down Matthews's relatives, in the northern city of Blackburn. She had arranged to rent a car to go there the following day and planned an excursion afterward to the Lake District—that is, if they had cause to celebrate.

"How'd you find his relatives?" he asked.

"It wasn't so hard, once you realized that Lizzie's R.M. was Richard Matthews. That explained everything. The person Matthews was writing to wasn't his wife—remember, he was only a teenager. It was his mother. She had one other son, Richard's older brother, and neither ever returned to England. So when she died, her place went to some cousins, which is what Lizzie wrote in her journal.

"I reread the part where she describes her trip to visit R.M.'s relative. She wrote that she traveled southeast, changed trains at Kendal, and that the trip lasted some two hours. That gave an approximate area for her destination. Then I checked her expenses—don't forget, the journal doubles as an account book—and I found she had spent one pound one shilling on the day in question. I called up the British Rail Museum and it turns out they've preserved old timetables and rate cards. A friendly guy there helped me and we figured that one pound one shilling would get her to Blackburn. The travel time matched, about two hours.

"So I concentrated on Blackburn. And sure enough, there are still some Matthewses there, spelled with two *t*'s. I called and eliminated five families until I found the right ones, descendants of Richard's cousins. On the phone they were friendly and sounded more than happy to cooperate."

An hour later, Hugh walked her home. The house was dark but Alice had left the outdoor light on. Beth took his hand and pulled him inside and they mounted the stairs quietly. In her room, as he began to undress her, she kissed him, then drew back. He looked at her quizzically. She gave him that wicked smile, pulled him close, and whispered: "Come buy my fruits, come buy, come buy."

The next morning, still groggy, they drove straight to Blackburn. Eventually they found the house, shabby on the outside but warm and comfortable on the inside—heavy in chintz, flowered draperies, and tables cluttered with family photographs.

The owners, a chipper couple in their seventies, were delighted to hear of the visitors' interest in their old letters in the attic. They were happy to turn the whole packet over—"Read through them, take what you want, make copies, and return them at your leisure"—but first insisted that their guests have a pot of tea and hear about the family tree, down to and including the youngsters off in different parts of the globe. Beth and Hugh were happy to oblige.

They decided not to open the packet right away. Instead, they set out, stopping off for sandwiches on the outskirts of Blackburn, then driving north to the Lake District.

It was after 10 p.m. by the time they arrived at the bed-and-breakfast in Ambleside, but they were too excited to sleep. Beth opened the French windows and stepped out onto the tiny balcony. Below, as far as she could see, stretched a lake bordered on all sides by woods and meadows. The full moon laid down a path of shimmering gold on the calm water. The air was cool and fresh. She went back inside.

They had called ahead to say they'd be late, and the owner of Ambleside Lake Cottage, before going off to bed, had left the front door unlocked and two ham sandwiches and two bottles of warm beer in their room. They ate ravenously. It had been a long day's drive.

Hugh pulled the packet out of his backpack. It was still tied up with an old blue ribbon, perhaps the very one Lizzie had noted in her journal. He spread the letters on the bed and they sorted them by date, reading them in chronological order.

After forty-five minutes Hugh picked one up, read the opening, and said: "Pay dirt."

He handed Beth the letter. She squinted—the handwriting was poor and tumbled out in lines that slanted increasingly downward at each row's end. But she could make out the words.

It was written from Bay of Islands, New Zealand, and dated Christmas Day, 1835. The writer began by saying how much he missed his home on this particular holiday and how much he longed to see his mother. He said he was "feeling much improved in outlook" now that he had left the *Beagle* and was soon to live with his elder brother, doing God's work among the Maori on the south coast. He did not describe the horrors of being left alone with the Indians in Tierra del Fuego, leading Beth to conclude that he must have provided a full account of that in a previous letter.

But he did say that he was going to relate an incredible night that he had spent at the home village of Jemmy Button, which he said "seemed to have made an indelible mark upon everyone present and even changed them in some manner difficult to ascertain or even to describe."

"You're right," said Beth. "This is it. I'll read it aloud."

We started out under threatening skies. We were going almost due north, following a well-worn trail, and the terrain changed after a few hours from the desolation to which we had become accustomed to a surprising lushness. All about were giant ferns and long grass and eventually bushes and even trees. From the fact that we had to stop from time to time to rest, I took it that we were gaining in altitude, which meant we were moving closer to the sun, thus accounting for a warmer climate. In any case, the greenness all around was a pleasure to the eye.

There were four of us—myself, Mr Darwin (or Philos, as we called him), Mr McCormick, the ship's surgeon, and of course Jemmy Button, of whom I wrote you before. Mr Darwin you will also recall from my earlier letters. He's a gent and he talks with a high accent but he managed to gain the respect of my shipmates because he took hardship well and was willing to embark upon any adventure. It was no secret that there was bad blood between him and Mr McCormick, who seemed to carry a grudge (in that respect he is like many short men I know). The two were continually vying for the favour of Captain FitzRoy, and as Philos took his meals with the Captain, he inevitably had the upper hand. I'm glad the Captain was not among our party, which would have soon fallen to feuding—that plus the fact that he has been so changeable lately that you never know when he is going to smile and when he is going to scald you with his hot temper.

As we walked, I kept a close eye on our guide, Jemmy, who was all puffed up with himself and acting as if he were some sort of Royal Scout on King William's hunting party. Indeed, he behaved in a most peculiar manner. He jumped about like a Jack-in-the-box, running up ahead on the path and then darting back to join us, cantering about like a small boy and repeating over and over: 'My contree, my contree.' From what I had heard earlier from Mr Darwin, he was in such high spirits because at long last he was going to be able to show his village to us and introduce us to the tribal elders. I mentioned before what a natty dresser he is; for this occasion he was done up even more than usual, in long dress-coat and such, which made him perspire dreadfully and looked ridiculous in the bush.

After some three hours of hard going we stopped alongside a stream for a quick supper. It was a most picturesque setting, with the water flowing past rounded banks of earth. But at the very moment we finished eating, the skies broke open and poured out a flood of rain such as I have rarely seen. There was much lightning and crashing of thunder, which seemed to shake the very ground. We huddled for shelter under the leaves but soon enough we were soaked through and there was nothing for it but to stand there getting wetter and wetter. This did nothing to lighten our moods. It also aggravated the ill-will between Philos and Mr McCormick, since they had been arguing over where best to wait out the storm and whether it was advisable to hide from *lightning by standing under a tree or altogether clear of it. Jemmy was much distressed at the delay. Eventually, the rain halted and bless my bones if the sun didn't immediately show itself—that's how fickle the weather is in this part of the world.*

When we resumed, we headed straight up a mountain. Jemmy scampered ahead like a monkey, bounding over boulders and climbing up crevasses; we were hard put to keep up with him, and whenever we fell far behind, he would glare down at us as if willing us to move faster. After an hour or so, when the rocks dried in the sun, the climb was easier. I began to notice that the ledges contained paths, though whether they had been made by men or animals I could not say. I had the feeling that we were entering upon an inhabited area, and soon enough I was confirmed in my feeling. We came to a small hut, conical in shape and built entirely of stones piled one upon the other. Jemmy said it was for 'food'. There was a wooden door no taller than three feet, carved with figures of people. Philos opened it and, poking his head inside, observed that it was filled with grain. 'By the lord Harry,' he said, 'this tribe is more advanced than any we've seen. They engage in agriculture and store the produce.' Hearing him, Jemmy beamed and said 'like Inglan' (his pronunciation of our country confused me at first). We then resumed our trek upwards and soon passed by small terraces set round with rocks and used for growing green shoots of some sort, which I took to be vegetables.

At this point we began to see people. A small boy appeared out of nowhere, looked at us boldly, then spun around and ran back up the mountain. Soon, he returned with a handful of older folk, who regarded us with curiosity but not, insofar as I could tell, with fear. They were dressed better than the Indians to the south, with cloaks around their shoulders, loin-cloths and rudimentary sandals. Jemmy was unable to contain himself, leaping up and down and speaking a language that sounded different from that used by the savages we had encountered thus far. He greeted friends by grabbing both their forearms in his hands and squeezing; they soon responded in kind. By this time, seeming to know who he was, they became animated, looking at him and touching his fancy clothes and talking excitedly among themselves. They grabbed him and virtually dragged him up the mountain, leaving us to follow while more children came to stand along our route, looking at us with large round eyes.

After some minutes we came to the summit of the mountain. Here was the village. It was set inside an encircling wall of rock; we were admitted through a narrow crevice and, once inside, I realised that the formation acted as a natural fortress. The houses, of which there were dozens, were more elaborate than the huts we had seen elsewhere; they were made of strong material, a combination of grass packed with mud and wood, and even had windows. Many were two storeys high, with ladders to reach the upper levels, which used the roofs below as balconies. All in all, it was a remarkable place, splendidly designed for communal habitation and, as I said, for defence.

By now the entire populace had turned out. We were led to the centre of the village, which was set around a circle of ashes and scorched rocks. Nearby were half a dozen even larger houses, which I took to be for the tribal elders, and one that was the largest of all. Off to one side was an immense tree with a trunk as wide as a steam-engine and branches that rose up high in the air.

The elders came out to meet us. I could tell they were set apart from the rest, not only because they wore cloaks that were different, dyed a deep red, but also because their bearing was distinguished; most had fine white hair and, unlike the other savages in this part of the world, they did not eschew beards.

Jemmy repeated a word several times that I did not understand. Mr McCormick explained to me that he was calling for the head wise man of the village, someone named Okanicutt, or something close to that. He apparently was what they call a medicine man, meaning he dabbles in various kinds of black arts and other foolishness. This man, the Chief, did not put in an appearance straightaway. I noticed that Mr McCormick had a nervous look upon his face. He said that he had had an unnerving experience: on our way here, not twenty feet from this very spot, he had chanced to look into a hut and saw the floor entirely covered with bones. 'I shudder to think from whence they came,' he whispered.

In short order all kinds of food was brought out and wood was stacked up for a fire. Philos reached into his pocket and pulled out a packet of Promethians, meaning to start the fire (a feat he had been performing in other places on our voyage), but much to his disappointment they were soaked and did not ignite. A young girl produced some burning embers to get the blaze going. Meanwhile Jemmy was mixing with his people, especially with an old woman, whom I presumed to be his mother, and several younger men, undoubtedly his brothers. They were having a rousing old time, given over to a great deal of babbling, back-slapping and forearm-squeezing. Then the moment arrived. As if on signal the savages fell silent and sat down around the fire. The door to the largest house opened and out walked an old man whom I took to be the great Chief himself, Okanicutt.

At that very instant—and I know this sounds uncanny—a rumbling of thunder sounded, which added to the strangeness of the apparition. I don't mind admitting, Mother, that the Chief was an impressive sight. He was tall and straight despite his age, decked all in red robes, and had a snowy beard that came down to his chest. He gave what appeared to be a fond greeting to Jemmy and then came up to meet each of us; he appeared to treat Philos with what I might call, in our civilised world, deference, clasping his forearm for quite a while and holding his head low. When it came my turn, I looked into his eyes and saw such fiery intelligence burning there that I had to remind myself that he was an Indian. But he was clearly not above the primitive superstitions common to such people—in fact, he was the main purveyor of them, as indicated by the staff that he carried, a long pole with various markings and animal skins upon it.

You then can well imagine my shock when he addressed us in English. He explained that as a young boy he had been taken up by pirates and sailed with them for several years. He tried what sounded like bits of Spanish and Portuguese, which none of us could understand. Resuming in our language, he told us the story of his tribe, which had once lived far to the north but was driven south through the wilds of Patagonia until it reached this inhospitable country. I assumed he meant that hostile tribes had evicted them from their native area, but Philos whispered that perhaps General Rosas' brigands had done it.

There followed a feast. For dishes we were provided with gourds cut into bowls. We were served all manner of edibles, most of which I could not identify; some were surprisingly good, others I put aside untouched after smelling them. The food was washed down with a brew liberally dispensed; the taste, at first bitter, seemed to improve with consumption and I found that it carried a slight inebriating effect.

The gathering was indeed unlike any other on this earth. Chief Okanicutt sat there on a tall rock that looked something like a throne, his robes billowing down, and spread around him were Englishmen and aborigines, communicating as best they could through signs and gestures, all of it thrown into ghostly relief by the reflection of the fire and the intermittent rumble of thunder.

I was sitting far from the Chief and so could not hear him but I was close by Jemmy. At one point he leaned over and confided in me. Pointing to Okanicutt, he said, 'He my father.' His own real name, he said, was Orundellico (though I'm only guessing at the spelling), and he recounted a long tale that I could not grasp in all its particulars but that in general outline was this: The tribe was in desperate straits, its numbers were falling and it was faced with extinction. After Jemmy's adventures in the white man's land he hoped that we Westerners could impart some wisdom that might help them out of their predicament. 'You mean you want us to rescue your tribe?' I asked. Jemmy smiled a big smile and nodded yes most vigorously.

After the meal, the women cleared away the gourds. The fire was built into a roaring blaze for our benefit, since with nightfall we Englishmen had begun to feel the chill in the air. We moved closer to the fire and the Indians, perspiring, moved away. Chief Okanicutt produced some sort of primitive cigars, which were passed around among the men, since the women had left (this prompted Mr McCormick to remark that it was no different from an English drawing-room). The smoke, however, seemed to exert a strange effect upon us; we felt a numbness and became at first giddy and then seemingly overly serious. The thunder sounded magnificent.

Finally, Okanicutt motioned Jemmy to sit at his feet. This appeared to be a signal for the business at hand—namely, an exchange of views on important issues. I am afraid I cannot recall the early part of the ensuing dialogue—the strange food and smoke had gone to my head—but I am able to conjure up a memory of the Chief opening his arms as if to encircle us and appealing for an explanation of the principles that underlay our civilisation, although of course he did not put it that way. Indeed, I wish I could recollect his exact words, for they seemed impassioned and powerful.

The request, which touched us by its simple nature, prodded Philos to action. He immediately launched into an explanation of Christianity. He began with the Old Testament and spoke of how God created the earth and the heavens in six days, resting on Sunday. He then talked eloquently about the creation of Adam and how Eve was made from his rib (there was some confusion over this part of the anatomy; finally Philos reached over to touch the Chief's abdomen, which startled him). He then talked of the Garden of Eden and how the evil serpent tempted Eve, who succumbed and turned her wiles upon Adam, leading to God's anger and His expulsion of them. Seeing that the Chief was amazed, he backed up and explained that the serpent had been enlisted by the Devil. This led to the recounting of the tale of Lucifer *and other angels being thrown out of Heaven. To lend it more power and colour, Philos sowed the narrative with quotes from Milton's great epic, though how much of this got through I cannot say.*

He then recounted other teachings from the Bible. He spoke of Cain who slew his brother Abel, of Job and his many tribulations, and of Abraham who was commanded by God to kill his beloved son Isaac. (At this point I saw the Chief place an arm around Jemmy.) Philos was most eloquent in speaking of Noah and the Flood and of Moses parting the waters to lead the chosen people out of Egypt—an historical event I imagined the Chief would take to heart, given his own tribe's history.

It was hard to say how all this was affecting the Chief, whose eyes seemed to grow larger as the night wore on. At various times he asked questions—such as how did the animals survive on the Ark without killing each other—that suggested a certain literal naïveté. Seeing this, Mr McCormick joined in to continue the instruction, and he drew his teachings from the New Testament. He said that God had had a son named Jesus and that this son was called the Lamb. He arrived on earth through a woman named Mary who got pregnant without a man. This entailed more confusion and much discussion and I am not certain that we ever succeeded in getting the idea of the virgin birth across. Eventually Mr McCormick resumed the story. He said that Mary knew she was bearing God's child because the Angel Gabriel had flown down to tell her. He then had to explain all about angels and their benign role in looking after men. The Chief was confused because he recalled that earlier Philos had called Lucifer an angel.

Eventually Mr McCormick returned to the main thread of the narrative. He told how a star appeared in the sky and three spice merchants followed it and it led them to Bethlehem, where the baby was sleeping in a stable because all the rooms were occupied. He recounted some of Christ's spectacular doings, like walking across a lake without sinking in, touching a glass of water and turning it into enough wine for a whole crowd of people and making a dead man come alive. The story built up finally to the Last Supper and the Crucifixion. A lot of it seemed to go over the Chief's head, but I have to give him credit—he seemed genuinely horrified at the description of the Lamb being nailed to the Cross.

When Mr McCormick said that Christ hadn't really died—or that he had died but that he rose again after spending several days locked in a tomb—you should have seen the Chief's expression. He wanted to know what was meant by that—did Christ walk around and talk and so forth? So Mr McCormick, exhibiting no small patience, explained that, no, He had gone up to Heaven to sit at the right hand of God. He began to expound on the Book of Revelation and the Seven Seals and the coming battle between Christ and Satan leading to one thousand years of peace, but the Chief looked so puzzled that he abandoned this tack. Instead, he simply observed that Christ's death was in reality a good thing because it proved that God loved us all so much that He was willing to sacrifice his only son to redeem us from the sin that had been committed long ago. The Chief asked: what sin was that? Philos jumped back in, saying the sin was from the apple that Adam had eaten. This confused the Chief even more, since it turned out that Philos had neglected to mention that the original transgression involved eating that particular fruit. But it brought the story around full circle.

At this point Chief Okanicutt's interest appeared to flag and he fell silent. Then out of nowhere he asked: 'What does this god look like?' Philos explained that no one really knew because no one had ever seen him, adding that little children liked to think of him as a wise old man with a white beard. When this was said, the Chief looked down at his own beard and gave a big belly laugh. From then on he seemed to stop listening.

I was still dizzy from the effects of the drink and smoke and more than ready to sleep when the natives passed around more of those intriguing cigars.

"Do you believe it?" said Beth, momentarily lowering the letter. "This is the most amazing thing I've ever read."

"Keep going," urged Hugh.

CHAPTER 29

The smoke made me feel drowsy. Indeed, I closed my eyes but I rested only for a short spell, as I was awakened by a sudden clap of thunder so loud I almost fell off my blessed rock.

I looked over at Chief Okanicutt. He seemed in low spirits—difficult as that might be to spot in an aborigine like him—judging by the fact that he was slumped in his seat, resting his head on one arm and staring off into the distance. I suppose it's hard to be a ruler, even of a meagre group of tribesmen in a brutish place such as this.

Mr McCormick, too, seemed to notice the change in our host's disposition, and he was glum, too. He was probably disappointed in the Chief's reaction to his exposition on Christianity, which, for all its eloquence, had fallen on deaf ears, as they say. But he valiantly tried to keep the conversation going.

'Chief,' I heard him say, pronouncing the words loudly so that they might more easily be understood, 'please be so kind as to share with us some of the beliefs of your tribe. Do you—for instance—have any interesting myths? Do you believe in a fire god and a rain god and so on? Ancestor-worship—that sort of thing?'

The Chief motioned for the cigar to be passed. He inhaled a goodly draught of smoke, held it in his chest for a while, then expelled it, looking around the fire at the three of us. He appeared to be pondering whether to oblige Mr McCormick with an answer or not. I could well understand his reluctance, after hearing the intricacies and glories of the Anglican Church extolled so persuasively; but he cleared his throat and sat up straight upon his rock.

'We do not believe in such a powerful god as you do,' he said slowly, seeming to measure his words. 'Our beliefs are simple. They come from our experience. As I said before, our tribe has been pushed out of our land. There we had large fields to plant, and sunshine. Here it is cold and wet, and we can hardly live. We must fight every day to stay alive.'

Here he hesitated and gave us a curious look. He may have been wondering, as I was, how it came to be that three Englishmen had turned up in this dark hole at the bottom of this vast continent to hear his tale.

'Still,' he continued, 'we have the memory of better days, when food was plentiful and we could sit in the sun. So what we believe fits what we know—that life can be good and our numbers can grow, but it can also be hard and our numbers will shrink.'

'Yes, plentiful on the one hand and cruel on the other!' cried out Philos. 'A bounteous past—just as in the Christian faith. By Jove, that's Eden, and today we live in a world of corruption because man has been expelled from it; we are on the same page in our different hymnals. Don't you see?'

'Perhaps,' replied the Chief. 'But we were not expelled from our garden by a god. It was done by other people.'

'Don't you see? That was God's plan,' said Mr McCormick. 'Your enemies were acting out God's will.'

'Why choose an explanation that you cannot see when there is one that you can see?' replied the Chief. 'If a man throws a spear at me, I say that the spear was thrown by a man.' He paused a moment, then added: 'We do not believe in such a one as this God you speak of. We do not believe the world was created in six days. That is a short time to do so much work. We believe that the world came into being a very long time ago.'

'But how without a god?' put in Philos. 'How was it created?'

'This we do not know, and since we do not know we do not ask the question.' The Chief bore the interruption with little patience and frowned at Philos as if to silence him.

'It happened, that is all that matters. Very long ago. So long it is impossible to imagine. Over time many things can happen. Seas happened. Mountains happened. Islands happened. Even this horrible place, which we call the end of the earth, happened. Over time many grains of sand make a beach.'

At that precise moment, Mother, there was a bolt of lightning and a clap of thunder so close to the mountain-top that, I don't mind telling you, I *almost jumped out of my skin. Part of me wondered if God was taking umbrage at hearing such heresy. But the old Chief—he just sat there as calm as could be.*

'We do not believe that a god made the plants and the animals. Or that he made man and'—here he touched his rib—'woman. In our belief, everything began very simply. There was one single small thing and everything grew out of it. It happened over a long time and with many changes. When time is so long, many little changes can occur, and put together they add up to a big change.'

I heard Mr McCormick mutter something puzzling under his breath—'Erasmus Darwin.' The Chief did not seem to hear him and went on.

'So the simple thing became many complicated things. And those things changed and became more complicated and so on. Life is like that. At first there were small animals such as you see in a pond. Then came bigger ones such as you see on land. Legs happened. Eyes happened. That is why so many animals look like so many other animals. They are all the same. We are all the same. We all come from the same small thing.'

'But how?' This time it was Mr McCormick who interrupted. 'How could that possibly happen without God?'

The Chief turned to him and then to Philos, whose eyelids were beginning to droop with fatigue, as if he were deciding whether or not to proceed.

'Temaukl,' he replied.

'What?'

As you might imagine, the answer mystified us. There was a lot of back and forth, as Jemmy tried to find words in English to express the conception and we fired questions to pin it down. Maybe the Chief believed in some kind of Supreme Being after all, I thought, but a deity that was more elementary. The more he talked, the more it sounded like a will-o'-the-wisp.

Finally, the Chief made a sweep of his arm that took in the village, the mountain, the threatening clouds in the night sky, and said: 'Temaukl is all of this. It is everything you see around you and even what you cannot see. It is the bird and the worm that the bird eats and the nest that the bird makes and the branch that the nest sits upon.'

That stumped us for a while—we all began guessing. I was beginning to enjoy this—it was something like the parlour games we used to play back home—until Mr McCormick, almost jumping out of his seat, yelled: 'Nature! That's what he's talking about. Nature!'

Having found a way to translate the idea, we all felt much better, as if we had a clearer idea of what he was struggling to say. Seeing that the Chief no longer seemed to mind interruptions Mr McCormick persisted, saying, 'Yes, but tell me this: how does what-do-you-call-it, tee-mack-kill, work?'

'It does not work. It is what happens. Many things are born but many of them die. Temaukl allows the ones that are the best to live and the ones that are not the best to die. The ones that live have children who in turn will also be best. It goes on and on like that over a long time.'

Looking through the darkness and the smoke, I noticed that Mr McCormick had dropped his eyes from the Chief and was staring instead at Philos as if to read his reaction, but dear old Mr Darwin, as far as I could tell, was all but asleep. From time to time his chin would fall to his chest, and whenever this happened, he would raise his head with a start and look around as if in surprise to find himself in such strange surroundings. I expect he was feeling the effects of those powerful cigars. I looked again at Mr McCormick. Rarely have I seen a visage so fraught with emotion. I imagine that, like me, he was more than a little shocked to hear such ramblings that sprang from heresy.

In the distance more lightning struck and more thunder cracked.

'Have you not heard,' said the Chief, 'that the sea turtle lays its eggs upon the shore? And when the eggs hatch, hundreds of baby turtles run for the water. Many are killed by the birds. Only the strongest make it to safety. They are the ones who will carry on and make more turtles. That is Temaukl.

'Have you not heard of the giraffe whose long neck allows him to eat from the tall tree? Or the tortoise who carries his house around with him for protection? Or the skunk whose odour keeps away other animals? That is Temaukl.'

'If you are correct,' said Mr McCormick, 'then every living thing has grown from an earlier but lesser version of itself. And everything is related. The zebra is related to the horse. The wolf is related to the dog. And men— we're related to—'

'Apes!' I interjected, for at this point I could keep my silence no longer. 'Look here', I added, 'that's a bit much.'

Having spoken from feeling, without having planned out what I was to say, I looked around and my eyes happened upon a ladder leaning against a nearby house. I pointed to it and said: 'See that. That represents the world as God made it. There are higher and lower species and they are forever fixed. We are at the top. Monkeys are on a lower rung and your skunks and your turtles and your what-nots, they're on still lower rungs.'

The Chief smiled and I must say, I did not like the smirk upon his face. I had already taken note of the fact that he had not directed much of his speech towards me.

'That ladder was made by man,' he said. Then he pointed to the large tree. 'That is the world as we see it. Each leaf is an animal, each branch a group of animals. You see how they grow one from another and how they all come from the main trunk?'

I held my ground, insisting that each and every species had been made by the hand of God and that they remained fixed and immutable through all eternity. I said I did not believe that accidents could simply happen, such that an offspring would be so very different from its parents.

Without replying directly, the Chief rose and motioned for us to follow. Philos was roused. The ground was slippery but the Chief moved with more agility than I expected. His staff, I observed, was nothing more than a walking stick, with animal skin to facilitate the grip.

The Chief led us to a hut—the very one whose contents had shocked Mr McCormick on the way into the village. He held up a flaming torch, which a boy had handed him, so that we could see what was inside. There was a pile of bones, a whole sea of them, old and bleached and laid out in patterns I could not fathom.

Holding up one that looked like a large femur, the Chief said that the animal it belonged to was no more. I replied that that was obvious. But he said, no, I did not understand him—it had belonged to a creature that once walked the earth but was gone out of existence. All of the bones, he said, were of animals that had lived long ago and disappeared.

How, he asked, could that be if, as we had maintained, all the species were created by God and never varied?

I must say that was a difficult question to answer. My mind was still addled by the cigar I had inhaled and I found the distant thunder and lightning very unsettling. I was beginning to regret that we had ever come to this place.

Then the Chief did something I shall never forget all my days. He led us to a house nearby where several women were tending babies. I imagine it was a sort of communal nursery. We walked through to an adjoining room where we saw a single mother and baby, nesting upon a mat. We crowded in and all managed to just fit inside the room.

The baby was red-faced and holding his fists tightly as if to keep from crying. The Chief asked the mother to perform some task, which she was clearly reluctant to do. Jemmy said he wanted her to unwrap him from the swaddling-clothes. Still she did not move, until the Chief barked out something in a harsh tone, which I took to be a command.

Outside, we could hear the rain starting up again, pounding down upon the roof.

As the baby's clothes fell to one side, we looked at the infant. So help me, at that very moment a brilliant flash of lightning lit up the room so that we got a full and clear view of the horror before us. Philos gasped and Mr McCormick turned away in disgust. I could not believe my eyes, for I had never even dreamt that such a thing could exist. We saw that its genitals were deformed: it bore organs both male and female.

'Temaukl works in ways that none of us understand,' said the Chief, as we all quietly left.

That night, after all that had passed and with the storm still raging, we did not sleep well. The next morning we departed early, without saying good-bye to the Chief, who remained inside his house. Perhaps he was sleeping late. Jemmy guided us back to the ship, as the route was hard to follow. The trip seemed shorter this time but it passed mostly in silence; neither Philos nor Mr McCormick uttered a single word the entire way. When we came to the harbour and saw the dear old Beagle *anchored there, I don't mind telling you, I breathed a sigh of relief.*

But Jemmy had fallen into a sulk the likes of which I have never seen. His mood seemed to build so that by the time we reached the bay, his temper exploded into a full-out tantrum. He ripped off his dress-clothes, throwing them on the ground, and said he no longer wanted to be called Jemmy Button. From now on he was Orundellico and he wanted nothing more to do with us.

What do you make of that? After all we had done for him! I for one believe I will never understand the minds of these primitive people.

There is one more thing worth mentioning. That evening when we were all safely aboard the Beagle, *I chanced to overhear Mr McCormick and Philos talking about the encounter. Mr McCormick was most animated. As far as I could tell, he was recounting everything the Chief had said, explaining that business about how all creatures came from a single form of life and even describing the 'tree of life', as he called it. 'Yes,' Philos replied. 'But what is the mechanism? The question is not what happens but how it happens. How can an entirely new species come into being?'*

And here Mr McCormick grew even more excited, saying that he had been thinking of little else all evening and had come upon the answer (which I wrote down, wanting to be able to reproduce it), namely, that 'given the intense struggle for existence, Nature favours those whose variations, no matter how small, give them an advantage.' And on top of that, he said, 'animals change in such a way as to occupy their own little place in the general scheme of things. They evolve or otherwise run the risk of losing out and turning into fossils such as those exhibited by the Chief.' Furthermore, he continued, 'Nature sometimes throws up an obstacle, such as a desert or an ocean, with the result that animals that were once alike are separated and grow up to be different.' As an example, he cited the two varieties of ostriches in South America, the larger species in the north and the smaller one in the south, the very one whose bones Philos had collected as specimens.

I must say that even though I could catch only the barest drift, what he was saying struck me as nothing short of ridiculous. To take but one example, I have, as you well know, been separated from my brother by half the world; I have been growing all that time, and yet I am confident that when we finally meet he will see that I have not changed all that much.

But Philos seemed to accept what Mr McCormick had to say and he too became excited, rubbing his hands together and pacing around the deck. 'By Jove, do you realise the implications of this?' he demanded, very solemn.

'I do,' replied Mr McCormick, his equal in sober demeanour. 'I have just struck down the basic tenets of the Church.' To which Philos declared: 'You have aimed higher than that. You have struck a blow at the Creator Himself!'

'Blasphemer!' a voice suddenly thundered. 'You have nailed Our Lord to the Cross once more! You shall pay dearly for this!' Captain FitzRoy stepped forward. He had apparently been standing in the shadows, listening to everything. He ordered the two men below and they complied like children guilty of raiding the pantry.

I must say, I was glad the Captain intervened. For though I could not fully capture the gist of the conversation that night, I did not like the smell of it. Nothing good comes from mixing with savages, I have often thought.

And that, Mother, is what occurred during that extraordinary visit to Jemmy Button's village. Sometimes, thinking back upon it, it seems to me as if it all transpired in a dream. Perhaps that sensation comes from those strange cigars.

Your loving son,
Richard

CHAPTER 30

Hugh and Beth slept late, then descended to an outdoor terrace over-looking the lake, where they treated themselves to an old-fashioned English breakfast: eggs, sausage, bacon, tomatoes, and baked beans. Beth smiled, stretching in the sunlight—like a contented cat, thought Hugh. He had also slept well. He could not remember the last time he had felt as good as he did now, both completely alive and completely relaxed.

They decided to spend the rest of the morning touring the Lake District and set out in the car. The road rose and fell before them, curving along hedgerows, leading them into wooded valleys one minute and the next shooting them up hills where they could look down on green pastureland dotted with tiny villages. White clouds rolled across the blue sky.

They had recovered from the shock of Matthews's letter, but in the cold light of day, they realized they had certainly uncovered more than they had bargained for.

"Think anyone will believe us?" Hugh asked.

"I don't see why not," Beth had replied. "We've got proof. Though I grant you it's a lot to swallow all at once."

They discussed their evidence: Lizzie's journal, the missing chapter from Darwin's autobiography, Matthews's letter. Each told a different part of the story and each reinforced the other two.

They stopped for lunch at a roadside pub in the town of Hawkshead, sitting at a table outside, barely an arm's length from the winding cobblestone road that cut through town.

They ordered the ploughman's lunch—bread and cheese—and split a shepherd's pie. When Hugh returned with a second round of beers, Beth was staring off into the distance and he asked her what she was thinking.

"About Lizzie. Poor Lizzie. Her father was even worse than she knew."

"You could say that. He not only managed to dispose of his rival, intentionally or otherwise, and wipe him clean out of the history books, but it now turns out he stole his famous theory from him."

"Isn't it curious that he never owned up to that part of it, even in his missing chapter? Do you think that was because he was so ashamed of the theft or because he didn't view it as all that serious compared with McCormick's death?"

"He probably thought McCormick was well within his rights in expropriating it from the Indians," Hugh replied. "Don't forget, the Victorians were nothing if not entitled. They were the advanced British, the superior white race. The same way Lord Elgin could take statues from the Parthenon without a second thought and Rhodes could cart boxcars of diamonds from southern Africa, McCormick could help himself to a little bit of theoretical talk over a campfire.

"But McCormick didn't really plunder the theory wholesale from the shaman. What the shaman said about evolution—that one species is derived from another—had been said before by a number of Westerners. Darwin's own grandfather, Erasmus, said it. The new element, the crucial one supplied by McCormick, was how it happened—by natural selection. That was the touch of genius. So Darwin stole it all right, but basically he stole it from a white man, a fellow Brit."

Beth sighed. "And once they had it, they realized that whoever could hotfoot it back to England first and publish it would get all the credit. A world of wealth and fame. No wonder the *Beagle* was too small for the two of them. And no wonder Darwin was wracked with guilt over McCormick's death. On some level he wanted him to plunge into that inferno. He ends up with the glory, but as a consequence he spends the rest of his life sick and paranoid. It almost makes you feel sorry for him."

"McCormick's last words must have haunted him. Darwin may not have believed in God, but I bet he came to believe in the Devil."

Beth nodded. "You know, the one I feel sorry for is Jemmy Button."

"He lived in two worlds and got the worst of both."

"And how about the Chief? He was hoping for enlightenment and all he got was feckless Brits spouting mumbo-jumbo. How disillusioning was that?"

"Well, it explains a note I found up in Scotland. I forgot to tell you about it. Jemmy wrote it to Darwin a long time after the voyage. It said: *'Yet you Inglish know life less as we poor Yamana.'* "

"That's certainly true. They did know less about life—literally. Do you think Jemmy engineered that massacre?"

"I do."

"What do you think filled him with such rage?"

"I don't think he was angry just because the all-powerful English weren't able to help save his tribe. I think it was because he realized that his Chief had a deeper understanding of the world but the English were too arrogant to recognize that—aside, of course, from McCormick and then, when it was explained to him, Darwin. But Jemmy didn't know that."

"Whatever happened to the tribe?"

"Wiped out. Every last one of them."

They drank deeply.

"One more thing," Beth said. "As I see it, all this means that Alfred Russel Wallace came up with the theory. Darwin himself conceded as much—so Wallace should end up getting some of the credit, right?"

"Wrong."

"Explain. And while you're at it, what was all that business about Huxley and the others paying him off? What could he have been black-mailing them about?"

Hugh reached into his pocket and pulled out a piece of paper. "Here's another letter written by Matthews. This one is to his cousins. He wrote it sometime in early 1858, long after his mother's death."

"What does he say?"

"He tells of his subsequent travels. He bummed around for quite a while and, incidentally, gave up his religious beliefs, and—I'm reading between the lines here—he went native, or whatever passed for going native in those days. He washed up on the shores of Sarawak."

"Where's that?"

"A tiny kingdom on the north coast of Borneo. Back then it was run by an eccentric Englishman named James Brooke. He had a wide circle of friends, including the Dyaks, the notorious headhunters."

"Go on. Get to the point."

"Well, Brooke was a generous man. He let just about anyone put up for free—provided of course that you were white. So Matthews turns up and stays a while. And guess who else is a houseguest?"

"No! Wallace?"

"Yes. Collecting beetles and having a grand old time. One night the two of them get drunk, start telling war stories, and Matthews pours out this interesting tale of what happened in the mountains of Tierra del Fuego."

"I don't believe it!"

"Matthews, clueless to the end, thinks it's just an interesting yarn. He has no idea that he's just passed along one of the great theoretical insights of all time. Wallace is as good a liar as the rest of them. He makes up this story about the theory coming to him in a malarial fever; he writes to Darwin—who, he knows, has the same information but for whatever reason can't seem to set it down on paper. Then he finds out that Darwin has basically put forth the theory as his own. So he decides he might as well make a little money and he threatens to reveal every-thing unless the X Club pays him. They also had to pay off FitzRoy, who overheard enough to cause trouble. And the rest, as they say, is history."

"So the true discoverer is a little Scotsman we've barely heard of. And he was inspired by an ignominious shaman whose bones are buried somewhere at the ends of the earth."

"That's right."

Beth was quiet for a few seconds.

"Think they'll believe us?"

"Don't forget, as you say, we've got proof."

They left the table and walked through Hawkshead until they came to an old building, whitewashed stucco with wooden trim. Over the door hung a sundial and a tablet dedicated to its founder, the Arch-bishop of York. A plaque proclaimed it the Hawkshead Grammar School, which closed in 1909.

"I'll be damned," said Hugh. "Let's go in."

The ground-floor classroom seemed undisturbed from generations back. Wooden desks were bolted to the floor, blackboards lined the walls, the plaster was yellowing and bulging here and there. Hugh quickly found what he was looking for: a long desk to the right of the entrance. On the near end a small piece of glass was affixed to the surface. Underneath it, gouged into the wood, expertly carved in large letters, was the name *W Wordsworth*.

A sign noted that the poet attended the school from 1778 to 1787 and quoted a few words from "Lines Composed a Few Miles Above Tintern Abbey":

> *. . . nature never did betray*
> *The heart that loved her*

Hugh smiled at the sentiment and put his arm around Beth as they walked back out onto the street.

"I'm not sure he got that right," he said.

They walked back through the town, got in the car, and headed back toward the bed and breakfast. Hugh turned on the radio and found a good station, playing the Beatles. He drove with the windows open and the wind streaming in so fast his eyes teared. Beth looked over at him and smiled. Tomorrow would be time enough for them to start writing.

Afterword

Thomas Carlyle, Darwin's contemporary, called history "the distillation of rumor." This book was undertaken in that spirit. It is a work of fiction. The historical characters are all real—in the sense that they actually existed—and almost all their actions here correspond with what the historical record tells us about them.

I have, however, taken significant liberties in several areas. One is the end that befell Robert McCormick, Darwin's jealous rival on the *Beagle*. Another is the portrayal of Elizabeth Darwin, about whom little is known. I have seized upon this blank canvas to construct a portrait and an imaginary lineage that suits my alternative narrative.

The modern-day characters are entirely fictitious. There is a well-known longitudinal study of evolutionary changes among finches in the Galápagos, documented in the Pulitzer Prize–winning book *The Beak of the Finch,* which provided material for scene-setting details and information on natural selection, but any resemblance to real persons is unintentional and purely coincidental.

Acknowledgments

Darwin scholars and institutions housing and promoting his work turn out to be extremely generous when it comes to helping a writer, even one who admits to crossing the boundary from scholarship into fiction. Among them, I would like to especially thank Frederick Burkhardt and his colleagues, engaged in the long-term research project *The Correspondence of Charles Darwin,* for their guidance, and Adam Perkins of the Cambridge University Library, for making available material from the Darwin archives. I am also indebted to John Murray, Darwin's publisher; the Linnean Society of London; the Darwin Centre at the Natural History Museum in London; and Down House in County Kent, all of which provided extensive tours and explanations about his life, research, and publications. I also thank the Field Museum and its president and CEO, John W. McCarter, Jr., and Donald Stewart, for sponsoring an essential and unforgettable voyage to the Galápagos in July 2002.

Books on Darwin are so numerous that they could stock an entire library wing. Among them are some I found especially useful. Janet Browne's two-volume biography—*Voyaging* and *The Power of Place*—were indispensable. I also borrowed liberally from Alan Moorehead's highly readable *Darwin and the Beagle.* I culled details on life at Down House from *Annie's Box* and *Period Piece;* on Darwin's supporters and enemies from *Apes, Angles and Victorians;* on the voyage around the world from *HMS* Beagle; and on Captain FitzRoy's tragic story from *Evolution's Captain.* Jonathan Weiner's *The Beak of the Finch,* which describes the groundbreaking evolutionary study on the island of Daphne Major in the Galápagos, provided essential information (down to the nickname of the "welcome mat" for the docking site) that I used for my fictional counterpart on Sin Nombre.

On a personal note, I thank Phyllis Grann, my editor, for shaping and shepherding the manuscript; Sonny Mehta, my publisher, for his suggested revisions; and Kathy Robbins, my agent, for her ideas and enthusiasm. I thank Bill Keller, executive editor of *The New York Times,* for granting me three months' leave and Marion Underhill of the *Times'* London bureau for tracking down information. And finally, I thank my family—my brother, Bob, and my children, Kyra, Liza, and James—for vetting the manuscript. Above all, I thank my wife, Nina, for reading every word, discussing every idea, helping create every character, and never once saying she was sick and tired of the whole damn thing.

Bibliography

Barrett, Andrea. *Ship Fever*. New York: W. W. Norton, 1996.

Bowlby, John. *Charles Darwin, A New Life*. New York: W. W. Norton 1991.

Browne, Janet. *Charles Darwin, Voyaging*. New York: Knopf, 1995.

——. Charles Darwin, *The Power of Place*. New York: Knopf, 2002.

Darwin, Charles R. *The Voyage of the* Beagle. New York: Penguin Books, 1989. First published in 1839 by Henry Colburn.

——. *Charles Darwin's Letters: A Selection, 1825–1859*. Edited by Frederick Burkhardt. Cambridge: Cambridge University Press, 1996.

——. *Charles Darwin's* Beagle *Diary*. Edited by R. D. Keynes. Cambridge: Cambridge University Press, 1988.

——. *The Origin of Species*. New York: Penguin Classics, 1985. First published in 1859 by John Murray.

Desmond, Adrian, and Moore, James. *Darwin*. London: Michael Joseph, 1991.

Ferguson, Niall. *Empire*. New York: Basic Books, 2003.

Harlan, John. *Seamanship in the Age of Sail*. Annapolis: Naval Institute Press, 1984.

Hart-Davis, Adam. *What the Victorians Did for Us*. London: Headline, 2002.

Hazlewood, Nick. *Savage: The Life and Times of Jemmy Button*. New York: St. Martin's Press, 2001.

Irvine, William. *Apes, Angels and Victorians*. New York: Time-Life Books, 1963.

Jackson, Michael H. *Galápagos, A Natural History Guide*. Alberta, Canada: University of Calgary Press, 1985.

Keynes, Randal. *Annie's Box: Charles Darwin, His Daughter, and Human Evolution*. London: Fourth Estate, 2001.

Marks, Richard Lee. *Three Men of the* Beagle. New York: Knopf, 1991.

McDonald, Roger. *Mr. Darwin's Shooter*. New York: Atlantic Monthly Press, 1998.

Moorehead, Alan. *Darwin and the* Beagle. London: Hamilton, 1969.

Morgan, Kenneth O. *The Oxford Illustrated History of Britain*. Oxford: Oxford University Press, 1984.

Nichols, Peter. *Evolution's Captain*. New York: HarperCollins, 2003.

O'Connor, Stephen. *Orphan Trains*. Boston: Houghton Mifflin, 2001.

Perkin, Joan. *Victorian Women*. New York: New York University Press, 1995.

Raverat, Gwen. *Period Piece: A Cambridge Childhood*. London: Faber and Faber, 1952.

St. George, E. A. W. *The Descent of Manners: Etiquette, Rules, and the Victorians*. London: Chatto & Windus, 1993.

Thomson, Keith Stewart. *HMS* Beagle: *The Story of Darwin's Ship*. New York: W. W. Norton, 1995.

Tort, Patrick. *Charles Darwin: The Scholar Who Changed Human History*. London: Thames & Hudson, 2001.

Weiner, Jonathan. *The Beak of the Finch*. New York: Knopf, 1994.

White, Michael, and Gribbin, John. *Darwin: A Life in Science*. New York: Dutton, 1995.

Wilson, A. N. *The Victorians*. London: Hutchinson, 2002.

Winchester, Simon. *Krakatoa*. New York: HarperCollins, 2003.